THE
DETECTIVE

ALSO BY AJAY CHOWDHURY

The Waiter

The Cook

THE
DETECTIVE

AJAY CHOWDHURY

Harvill
Secker

1 3 5 7 9 10 8 6 4 2

Harvill Secker, an imprint of Vintage, is part of the
Penguin Random House group of companies whose addresses
can be found at global.penguinrandomhouse.com

Penguin
Random House
UK

First published by Harvill Secker in 2023

A CIP catalogue record for this book is available from the British Library

penguin.co.uk/vintage

HB ISBN 9781787303164
TPB ISBN 9781787303171

Typeset in 10.75/15.75pt Scala by Jouve (UK), Milton Keynes
Printed and bound in Great Britain by Clays Ltd, Elcograf S.p.A.

The authorised representative in the EEA is Penguin Random House
Ireland, Morrison Chambers, 32 Nassau Street, Dublin D02 YH68

Penguin Random House is committed to a sustainable future
for our business, our readers and our planet. This book is made
from Forest Stewardship Council® certified paper.

MIX
Paper from
responsible sources
FSC® C018179

For Layla, Eva and Tia

जाने कहाँ गए वो दिन

Where did those days go?

Prologue

East End of London.
Wednesday, 31 December 1913.
Eve of the Great War.

'HE DIED FOR YOUR SINS!'
Determined to be heard above the hubbub in St Katharine Docks, the preacher tilted his head back and his voice rose above the racket. 'God will damn you all to hell unless you embrace our Lord and Saviour Jesus Christ. This is your last warning.'

'What is he saying, Papa?' Leah's sticky hand wormed its way into her father's as she skipped along to keep up.

Avram pulled down his fur hat against the late-night fog creeping in from the Thames. The cold in London was nothing compared to what he had experienced growing up in Pinsk. It was the damp he couldn't stand. It crept over you like a malaise till you felt you would never be warm again. Kneeling to button up the coat his daughter had kept open to show off her new white pinafore with its pink sash, he muttered, 'A meshuggenah, Leah.'

She looked at him, little face questioning. Avram smiled and switched to halting English, the language with which he wanted her to grow up. 'Come, quick, or we will miss the bells.'

Over his shoulder he saw Malka pushing the perambulator, baby swaddled and asleep, oblivious to the surrounding tumult.

I

He raised an eyebrow, and she nodded she was fine, tucking a stray lock of hair back under her headscarf.

They made their way through the hordes, avoiding the entreaties of the gutter merchants selling stripy hooters and the hawkers with their sweetmeats. The fog seemed to thicken, and they found themselves near the oil-black Thames where a young girl's voice sang a plaintive air above the crowd's excited chatter, until a stentorian 'Chestnuts, get yer hot chestnuts!' drowned her out.

'Papa?' Leah's enormous eyes did the trick, and Avram handed her a farthing. She dashed off, returning with a bag that she tossed from hand to tiny hand, squealing, 'Hot! Hot!'

As if a switch had been pulled, the pack went mute, the old year seeming to exhale its last breath. Then the first bell chimed from St Paul's and a murmur began. The buzz of the throng grew in intensity as people started counting down with a single voice, Leah joining in. Seven. Six. Five. Four. After the final 'One', the crowd erupted with fireworks, blaring trumpets and clanging pans, welcoming in 1914, kissing anyone who might be in their vicinity.

The little girl took it all in, four-year-old face rapt as she munched on a chestnut. Glancing at the pram, she stood on her toes and, almost toppling into the buggy, kissed the baby, saying, 'Happy New Year, Miriam!'

'Leave her, Leah,' said her mother in Yiddish. 'Let her sleep.'

Avram's love for Leah rose as a warm sea inside him as he saw her excitement. 'May HaShem make you as Sarah, Rebecca and Rachel.'

As the crowds pushed, threatening to pitch them into the trembling water, he gazed downriver, stung by the memory of the stinking boat that had brought him and Malka from the Pale of Settlement eight years ago, their small suitcase of belongings in hand. Those days were over, the pogroms but an echo haunting their dreams; but even now, Malka would toss and turn at night, sweating, whimpering; Avram holding her till she quietened. He saw Leah's eyes shining in the dark; her children would not experience that suffering. He had done well by his offspring – Baruch HaShem.

He called in Yiddish over the singing, 'Maybe next year we will go upriver, with the rich people on Westminster Bridge, not here with . . .' He waved an arm at the assembled pedlars, tanners and beggars.

'They will never let a Jew there,' Malka shouted back as a group of revellers wearing colourful hats and playing tin whistles marched down the street, the throng parting for them as the Red Sea had done for Moses. The music faded as she added, 'Be happy with what we have, Avram.'

'We shall see. Anything is possible. We must believe things will be better for the Jews. They cannot get any worse.'

'Everything can always get worse,' she grumbled. 'You should realise that by now. Be content.'

'Be optimistic. Come, let us go home. It is raining. Leah should be asleep.'

An organ grinder whipped up a tune, and merrymakers sang along as the family weaved on, dodging the horse dung that littered the cobbled streets. As they walked up Christian Street, the crowds thinned and Leah, chestnuts tight in hand, ran ahead, the bottom of her swaying dress a sliver of white in the darkness. The perambulator rattled over the slippery cobbles, the infant immune to the bumps, jerks and the bangs of the fireworks in the adjoining roads.

A voice.

'Pinsky?'

A figure emerged from the fog in top hat and tails, silhouetted against the light from the gas lamps.

Malka stiffened as Avram shot her a warning glance and said, 'Mr Pennyfeather.'

3

The man swayed towards them, hairy hand clutching a bottle of Krug. 'How are you, Pinsky? This is your family?' Pennyfeather's upper-class accent contrasted with Avram's rough Slavic tone.

Avram gave a curt nod and walked away as Pennyfeather called after him, 'Liking our English New Year's Eve celebrations?'

Avram's inbuilt politeness forced him to stop and wait for Pennyfeather to catch up. 'Very much. And are the festivities to your satisfaction?'

'They are, they are indeed.' Ruffling Leah's hair as she shrank into her father's side, Pennyfeather peered into the pram and said, 'Ah, the new child. I heard. What is her name?'

'Miriam,' said Malka reluctantly.

'A beautiful name for a beautiful girl. Congratulations, madam.' He tipped his hat to Malka. Tickling the baby's head, he turned to Avram, who flinched at the stench of alcohol assaulting his nostrils.

'So? Have you reconsidered, Pinsky?'

'Mr Pennyfeather, I have already told you many times. My business is not for sale. I must go now. My children are tired.'

'Of course it is. Everything is for sale with you people. I am a patient man, Pinsky, but I need an answer.'

Not responding, Avram picked up his pace, pulling Leah along with him as Pennyfeather trailed behind them up Field-gate, passing the Great Synagogue that was shrouded in darkness. The lamps were out again, and the small side street was ill-lit and empty, save for the smell of the leather factories and raw soot. A hansom cab swept by, horseshoes clopping on the cobblestones in syncopation with the ever-present fireworks. The driver kept to one end to avoid the black hole of the construction site where Pennyfeather was expanding his department store. The carriage turned the corner onto Whitechapel Road and Pennyfeather said, 'Well, Pinsky?'

Avram's name sounded like a curse, emerging from Penny-feather's fat red lips. They were outside their small house now, the windows dark. Avram said, 'You have my answer. I am sorry. Malka, go upstairs.'

Pennyfeather's eyes glittered. Draining his bottle, he dropped it together with any pretence of civility. As it smashed on the street, he grabbed Avram by the throat and slammed him against his front door. Avram's hat fell off and rolled into the sewer, and Pennyfeather hissed, his face an inch from Avram's, 'Listen to me, Yid. Sign those papers tomorrow or I will make sure they throw you and your family back to whatever shitting country you came from.'

Leah screamed at the sudden violence and Miriam wailed as Avram struggled, trying to prise away the excruciating grip from his neck. Malka grabbed Pennyfeather's arm and sank her teeth into his hand, drawing blood. Pennyfeather shouted, 'Hellcat bitch!' released Avram and spun around. He punched Malka on the side of her face. She fell back. Her head cracked against the pavement's edge with a sickening thud. Blood gushed from under her sheitel.

'Mame!' Leah screamed and ran to her mother as the baby screwed up her tiny face, her cries filling the street.

Avram dropped, knelt beside his wife, and shook her. 'Malka? Malka?' But there was no response. Her eyes were open. Unsee-ing. Avram unwrapped her scarf and lifted the edge of her wig to see a crack in her skull weeping gore. Looking up in horror at Pennyfeather, he said, 'What . . . what is this you have done? *Hilf!* Someone. *Hilf!* Help!'

Pennyfeather stared at Malka's dead body, then at Avram and Leah, panic on his face. He turned to run, then paused and glanced around the darkness of the empty street. Swivelling, he pulled a derringer from his pocket and pointed it at Avram with a quivering hand. Avram looked up at him, uncomprehending.

Pennyfeather muttered, 'I'm sorry, I can't let you—' and fired, hitting Avram point blank in the head, the gunshot causing the baby to stop crying.

The sudden rain-drenched silence of the street was broken when Leah whimpered and hid her face behind her hands. Fist shaking, Pennyfeather turned the gun on her and, shutting his eyes, squeezed the trigger once more, the shot lost in the rat-a-tat of firecrackers in the distance. Her moan was cut off. Seeing her lying dead on the road, he fell to his knees and vomited.

He stayed kneeling for a minute, then stood. He passed his arm over his mouth and dragged Avram across the street to the rim of the construction cavity. With his foot poised on Avram's hip for purchase, he tipped him over the edge, the corpse falling twenty feet, swallowed by darkness. Another concerted effort, and the bodies of Malka and Leah followed their patriarch into the pit.

Breathing hard, he walked over to the pram and stared at Miriam. She gazed back up at him with huge dark eyes, silent, as if she realised something momentous had taken place.

Pennyfeather hesitated, saw he was out of bullets, and put away his gun. He snatched Miriam under one arm and rolled the perambulator into the hole. A final brief look around, and he vanished into the night with the baby.

The rain washed away the blood and vomit and soon there was nothing to show that anything of note had happened, except for a sodden fur hat in the gutter, a smashed champagne bottle and a scattering of chestnuts on the cobbles.

PART I
The First Week

There was of course no way of knowing whether you were being watched at any given moment. How often, or on what system . . . It was even conceivable that they watched everybody all the time.

George Orwell, 1984

Chapter 1

London.
Today. July. Monday night.

I t sounds like the start of a joke.

An imam, a restaurateur, a constable and an inspector are having a curry. The imam says to the constable, 'Congratulations on your life coming full circle, Kamil. With two Muslims in the police, we can finally establish the Brick Lane Caliphate.'

The three of us guffawed. 'Great idea, Sheikh,' said Tahir. 'Then Anjoli will have to exchange her personalised T-shirts for a burqa and always obey Kamil.'

Anjoli mopped up the last of her Iberian pork belly in a chilli sauce with a corner of naan and looked down at her T-shirt that read *Distant Socialising Goddess*. 'I'll fight tooth and veil to keep my T-shirts. I'll have you know Kamil does *my* bidding. I'm his boss, remember?'

'*Used* to be my boss.' I emptied my glass, relishing the last drops of the cold Cobra. 'Anjoli imposes *She*-ria Law!'

Another round of laughter.

'Very funny. To Detective Constable Kamil Rahman!' She raised a glass and waved my shiny new Met Police badge in the air. 'He'd like to thank me for everything I did to get him here. He couldn't have done it without me.'

'What is it they say?' said Tahir. 'Behind every great man there is a . . .'

'Woman cleaning up his crap. Sorry, Sheikh!' Anjoli grinned and clinked her glass with Tahir's.

My celebratory dinner was turning into a roast.

'I also know a joke like that,' said the imam, a smile escaping his full beard. He took a sip of his nimbu pani and said, 'Why do women walk five paces behind the Taliban in Afghanistan?'

'Why?'

'Landmines!'

He roared with laughter, the topi on his head bobbing up and down.

'Lol, Sheikh!' Anjoli fanned herself with a menu. 'Waiter! My glass is empty.' She waggled it at me, and I went to the bar to top her up in a final tip of the hat to my old job.

The imam was right about one thing – I *had* come full circle. A cop in Kolkata five years ago, then a waiter and cook in Brick Lane and now a detective again. In *England*. The spark of pride that flamed inside me was at once doused by contrition. Why was my recruitment into the Met a greater glory than getting into the Indian Police Service? Was it because I had dragged myself back up after hitting bottom? That I'd erased the disgrace of being fired from the Kolkata force? Or was it just that Indians have always had daddy issues about England?

Either way, here I was in Tandoori Knights, the restaurant I knew better than my parents' kitchen, being feted by the three people dearest to me – Imam Masroor, my spiritual guide; Anjoli, my landlady; and Tahir, my closest friend and now, boss – in the hottest week London had experienced for a decade.

And the last few years had felt like dog years. The twenties had a dismal beginning, as we tried to take the panic out of the pandemic. When Saibal and Maya, Anjoli's parents, died of the virus while they were in India, Anjoli was inconsolable. We couldn't attend their funeral in person, so we watched the livestream of their bodies on the cremation pyre – it was heart-breaking. I swallowed my grief to support her – holding her up as she sobbed herself into oblivion. That these were just two of the millions of unnecessary deaths that had occurred around the planet and fires like these were burning twenty-four hours a day didn't matter – this was *our* family – not points on a graph.

And poor orphaned Anjoli. Her pain wrapped around her like a shawl, she slogged hard, so hard, to keep the restaurant afloat. The terror of losing the business built by her parents, which was not only their legacy but also our livelihood, kept us going; and we just about survived. After the abrupt ending of my last relationship, Anjoli was my support and a genuine friend. I realised how well we fit together. It felt right, the two of us in our tiny bubble. We slipped from sharing meals on the kitchen table to sharing cuddles on the sofa, to . . . nothing. Every night ended with a closed door between us. I tried to talk to her about why I was perennially in the companion zone, but she would always bat it away with 'It would be too much, Kamil – working together and living together and sleeping together. You know how I feel about you, but I need some space.'

The problem was, I *didn't* know how she felt about me or how to give her the space that she said she wanted. So, we remained flat mates and best mates, drifting like two goldfish in our bowl, always circling and never quite meeting, with me waiting for us to connect and Anjoli waiting for . . . something.

On sleepless nights, hearing her bed creaking just metres away from mine through the wall as she struggled through her dreams, I'd think of what might have been. What was Maliha, the love I'd left behind, doing in Kolkata at this moment? And Naila . . . the other woman I'd fallen for in London four years ago? No. I still couldn't think of her green eyes drilling into mine without being overwhelmed by feelings of shame.

I had to move on.

Then the lockdowns lifted, the restaurant hummed, and business boomed. Anjoli gave up her side hustle selling T-shirts on Etsy, hired Chanson, a new Indian chef who had trained in molecular gastronomy (pretentious name, pretentious shaved head and even more pretentious food), revamped the menu, and left little for me to do as a cook. On Tahir's urging, and with Anjoli's encouragement, I'd applied to the Met and spent my two pandemic years at the University of East London's Detective Degree Holder Entry Programme, still paying my way by cooking part time, chafing under Chanson's charlatanry.

But my days of chopping onions, grinding peppercorns and peeling garlic were behind me. As of today, I was Detective Constable 20097 in the CID division, on the princely salary of £33,500 per year. And it *was* princely. Four times what I'd made as a sub-inspector in Kolkata and higher than the £27,500 (prebribes) that my father had reached as a top rank commissioner in the IPS. This hike in my earnings also saw the return of my self-respect – no longer was I dependent on Anjoli's largesse – and it felt like another new beginning.

I gave Anjoli and Tahir their drinks and sat down as he said, 'So, top of your year, eh? You Kolkata cops have sharp elbows. I'm going to have to watch my back!'

'You'll soon be reporting to me.' I winked. 'I come, I see, I conquer!'

Anjoli snorted. 'Veni, vidi, vindaloo, more like. You came, you saw, you cooked!'

Tahir guffawed. 'Good one! Do you know how many strings I had to pull to get them to assign you to my unit?'

'Yeah, yeah.' I polished the crown on top of my badge with my napkin. 'What you fail to mention is that you only got your promotion to inspector because I handed you a murderer on a plate four years ago and you took all the credit.'

'Hey,' Anjoli elbowed me hard. '*We* handed him the killer. No way you could have done it without me.'

'Sorry. Of course, you were an integral part of the team. Any tips for my first day, boss?'

Tahir considered this.

'Focus on the work. Don't feel you have to be a nice guy. The cops in CID are a good lot, but remember you're not looking for new mates, you just want their respect. And, as the sheikh said, you and I will be the only brown faces.'

'How do the goras regard you, Tahir?' asked the imam.

Tahir grimaced. 'Well, I was the first brown guy to make DI in Bethnal Green nick. When I got promoted, some started calling me Diversity and Inclusion Ismail behind my back. So, yes, Sheikh, institutional racism is a thing, but it's improving. When I joined, it was much worse. The coppers would joke about me being a terrorist, shout "Allahu Akbar" and pretend to duck when I entered the squad room – now it's more subtle and you have to brush it off. But you still must be way better than your white colleagues to make it up the ladder.'

'You'll have to teach him, Tahir,' Anjoli said. 'Kamil doesn't recognise racism. He floats along in his own little world.'

'Oh, believe me, I experienced discrimination in Kolkata, being a Muslim,' I said, nettled. '*And* had to deal with accusations of nepotism.'

'Well, you may face the same here, since I wangled you in as my partner,' said Tahir. 'I *should* have a sergeant reporting to me, instead of slumming it with a newly minted DC.'

'How are the others going to take that?' I asked.

'It'll put a few noses out of joint. But I've cleared it with Superintendent Rogers – told him that given we are in a Bangladeshi area, we can interact better with the locals as a team. And I'm not sorry you're replacing Protheroe. He's a fucking bongo. Sorry, Sheikh.'

'What's a bongo?' said Anjoli as the imam gave Tahir a vague smile. She giggled and said, 'Bingo Bango Bongo. Kamil you're a Bong Bongo.'

'She's out of it, isn't she?' laughed Tahir. 'Yeah, Protheroe just books on, never goes out. He's more interested in making himself look good than doing the hard graft. I've had to redo his work half a dozen times – he's missing in inaction. You provided an excellent opportunity for me to get shot of him.'

I wasn't sure how to take that; I'd rather Tahir had picked me for my skills than someone else's incompetence; but to hell with high-minded principles. If I had to show I was twice as good as the others to make it, well, that's what I would do.

The imam popped a last saffron-infused gulab jamun into his mouth and said, 'I must go now. Congratulations again, Kamil; I am very proud of you. You are a true inspiration to our people.'

'Thank you, Sheikh. Your guidance helped me get through the hard times.'

He patted my shoulder, and wheezing, raised himself from the table. Tahir followed suit, giving Anjoli a peck on the cheek and winking. 'Well you don't have to hear Kamil diss you anymore, Anj. He's my problem now.'

She started to clear the dinner table. 'Who knows, I may miss his dissing.'

'Not a chance. Anyway, nice new haircut.'

Anjoli blew her fringe out of her eyes. 'Good of you to notice, unlike Bingo Bango here.'

I protested, then realised I *hadn't* noticed. 'You always look so lovely . . .' I began as Tahir interrupted: 'I'll expect you at the shop nice and early tomorrow, Constable Bingo. You need to learn how to do *all* my paperwork.'

'I know, I know, Inspector. You're the lead singer; I just stand at the side of the stage, banging my bongos.'

The imam embraced me, and the scent of his rose attar

followed him to the door, the bell tinkling behind him and Tahir as they left the restaurant. Anjoli locked it, took my hand, ran the tip of her tongue over her lips and whispered, 'Come. Now that you don't work for me, let me show you another "ing" we can do besides dissing.'

My heart leapt. 'What did you have in mind?'

'*Rinsing* – bring the plates and glasses.'

Rolling my eyes, I followed her uproarious laughter into the kitchen. This policeman's lot was not a happy one.

Chapter 2

Tuesday morning.

Anjoli was staring out of the window at a still waking Brick Lane, a mug pressed against her temple, when I entered the kitchen, resplendent in the £79 M&S suit she had bought me for my first day.

'Sleep well?' I said.

She started, spilling some coffee on her *A Clown With a Crown is Not a King* T-shirt, then massaged her head. 'Don't.'

'Been bitten by too many Cobras?'

The lines around her eyes and mouth deepened. 'My skull feels like a donkey's dancing on it.'

'Nurofen?'

'Took two.'

'*I* slept like a corpse.'

'*You* snored like a walrus. I could hear you through the wall,' she grimaced. Anjoli couldn't hold her drink. This was her third hangover in a month, and she had a full day and night of restauranting in front of her. We *had* to cut back – I was feeling a little delicate too and needed to be alert today.

My phone pinged as my cornflakes rustled into the bowl.

'Huh.' I poured milk onto the cereal.

'What?'

'It's a text.'

'Duh! Who's it from?'

I ate a spoonful. 'Maliha.'

Anjoli wrinkled her forehead. 'Maliha, your fiancée?'

'Ex. Weird. I was just thinking about her yesterday. I haven't heard from her in five years and . . .'

'What does she say?'

'Erm . . . she's in London. Wants to meet.'

My heart was hammering. Must be the hangover.

She paused for a moment, then said, 'That's nice. You should,' and looked away from me.

'Maybe.'

I glanced at the text again, trying to parse the words, then put my phone away and emptied the bowl. 'I need to run. Can't be late on my first day. Hope you feel better.'

I leaned over to kiss her cheek, but she waved me away. 'My breath smells like four-day-old dhansak. Good luck.'

I could sense my armpits getting damp under my suit as I walked up Brick Lane towards the police station, thinking about Maliha and how to reply. The heatwave looked set to continue this week, and it felt like the air itself was sweating. With a little luck, the office would be cooler, and I could keep my jacket on; sweat patches would not be a good look on my first day.

Why was I finding it difficult to respond to Maliha's text? I'd like to see her again, so why this nervousness? She always used to sign off her texts to me with a *Mxxx*. This time, there was just a simple *Maliha*. Well, of course, that's all she would write. I was being ridiculous. I had to focus. To quell the butterflies that had taken up residence in my stomach to dance the day away. Maybe this was a sign. New job. New relationship. Well, rekindled old relationship, but still.

I passed the graffitied metal shutters on Bethnal Green Road.

A lot of the small shops that had closed during lockdown hadn't reopened and I missed the street's pre-pandemic vibrancy; maybe with time, the bustle would return.

The CID office was empty except for the bongo.

'It's the hotshot, Camel Rammin'.' Protheroe put down his copy of the *Sun* as I entered. 'First in your class, I heard. Swot. Well, you'll learn soon enough that book learning is very different from what happens on the street.'

He gave me a smile, showing crooked teeth that were a little too large for his mouth. I didn't bother to correct his obscene pronunciation of my name or ask when *he'd* last been on the street, just gave him my biggest grin and said, 'I look forward to learning from you, Sergeant.' He grunted and went back to his newspaper as I sat down at the desk I'd been assigned.

Half an hour later, the room filled with officers, but there was no sign of Tahir; my first day at work was turning out to be a bit of a damp squib. As was I, given the air conditioning wasn't working and my shirt was soaked under my jacket, which I didn't want to remove because I looked like a wet rag.

While I hadn't expected balloons and bunting with a '*Welcome to the Central East Basic Command Unit, Kamil*' banner, I'd hoped for a little more than equal opportunities forms and email reminders of onboarding programmes I needed to take. I dabbed the sweat from my forehead and wrote in the details of my address (above Tandoori Knights Restaurant), ethnicity (Indian) and emergency contact (Anjoli), when a cop put his head around the door:

'Superintendent Rogers wants you, DC Rahman.'

I stood and brushed down my suit, Protheroe looking at me out of the corner of his eye. I'd first met Rogers four years ago when he'd been an inspector and I had irritated him by 'interfering' in the Salma Ali murder. But Tahir had convinced him they would not have found the killer without me, and he warmed to me, sponsoring me for the two-year post-grad course at UEL. My gratitude had increased when he took me under his wing during my rotation through the station. Protheroe and others had noticed. Another black mark against me.

'You made it then, Kamil,' said the Superintendent as I entered his air-conditioned office, getting some blessed relief from the sauna behind the door.

'Yes, sir,' I stopped myself from saluting. Superior officers here were far less formal than in Kolkata.

Rogers was a big man, sleeves rolled up, shirt tight across his chest, buttons threatening to pop – he'd put on even more weight during lockdown. Not that I was one to talk – I had to start working out again. My new suit was already feeling constricting.

He walked around the desk and shook my hand. 'Congratulations, I heard you did very well on the course.'

'I appreciate all you've done for me, sir.'

'Well deserved, young man. I saw your scores. Very impressive. Your instructor said you had a very logical mind – a useful asset in a detective. But remember, to be exceptional, logic isn't enough. You need imagination as well.'

He'd said the same thing using the same inflection when he had spoken to the troops at my college. 'I will. Thank you, sir.'

'Just remember your ABC's and you'll be fine.'

'Yes, sir. Assume nothing. Believe no one. Check everything,' I recited.

He clapped me on the back. 'Good lad. And Tahir is looking after you?'

'He is, sir. Thank you, sir,' I gave him a sir sandwich to show just how grateful I was. 'Thank you for putting your trust in me, sir. I will not let you down.'

'I know you won't. I don't need to tell you, Rahman, that proper community policing is what it's all about these days. This is a difficult time for the Met. The home secretary wants to cut our numbers, threatening to replace us with technology. We have never been held in lower esteem by the people. Barely a day goes by when someone doesn't spit at a policeman or incite us to do something while filming it. Be prepared for all this. Keep your eyes open and give us a strong clean-up rate – we're all being measured and have key performance indicators we must meet. Look, listen and learn. If you have any problems, come to me. I like to think of us as a family here. Diversity and inclusion are our watchwords, and I want to make sure my patch is welcoming to all. Tahir has done very well, and I am sure you will, too. Take—'

My mobile rang, interrupting his sermon. Shit, I'd forgotten to put it on silent.

I looked at the caller ID. 'I'm sorry, sir. It's DI Ismail.'

He smiled, 'Answer it.'

'Kamil. It's me. Meet me at 41 Fieldgate Street. We have a body.'

Chapter 3

Tuesday morning.

I grabbed a car from the pool and made it to Fieldgate Street in ten minutes, mulling over Rogers' words. Well, I would show people that the Met could rise above all the mud that was being thrown at us, admittedly some of it deserved.

It was a few minutes after nine when I sped past the parked police cars and arrived at a construction site surrounded by two-and-a-half-metre tall black hoardings with signs in primary colours highlighting site-worker safety procedures. A metal gate at the top of a wide earthen ramp leading down into the pit gaped open, and I spotted Tahir with a few officers twenty feet below street level on the side of the slope. Underneath me was a mess of cracked concrete, piles of rubble, exposed earth, metal pillars and tangled wires. Diggers, cranes and other construction equipment were all over the place, as though paused mid-job. A decrepit block of flats had stood here, another casualty of the creeping gentrification of the area.

The sun beat down overhead as, sauna sweating, I slipped on my paper coveralls, latex gloves, overshoes and hard hat and made my way down the ramp to Tahir. Ducking under the protective tape, I saw the body of an Asian man with the side of his head blown off, brains and blood staining the concrete. A vision of the first corpse I'd ever seen in Kolkata, also with his head bashed in, came to me and I felt my jaw clench with the effort of projecting the air of detachment that I knew was obligatory for the job. One of the forensic team snapped the scene from various angles as a pathologist examined the body, Tahir looking on.

'Welcome to your first official murder scene, Kamil. I got the call on my way in,' he said.

'Sorry I'm late. Superintendent Rogers was welcoming me on my first day.'

'Apologies for not being there to welcome you in person. I was at a party last night that overran.' He winked. 'How was the Super?'

'Fine. All good. Any idea who it is?' I bent down to look at the corpse. A male dressed in navy jeans, black polo neck, smart leather jacket and trainers, a trimmed goatee adorning what the killer had left of his face. My stomach knotted up, and I was relieved to turn my attention to the two plastic evidence bags Tahir was dangling in front of me, containing a business card and a driver's licence.

'We know exactly who. These were in his wallet along with a couple hundred quid. So probably not a robbery.'

SID RAM
CHIEF EXECUTIVE OFFICER
AISHTAR LTD
250 SHOREDITCH HIGH STREET
LONDON E1 6JJ
m: 07893073124
e: sid@aishtar.com

'Aishtar, weird name. That's not too far from here – must be, what, a twenty-minute walk?' I peered at the licence through the plastic. 'Forty-two years old and, oh, his home address is 81B Fieldgate Street. So, he lived somewhere up there.' I scanned the blocks of flats overlooking the construction site.

'Yes. Must run one of those Silicon Roundabout startups. They all have stupid names. Looks like a trendy techie dude.'

The tech scene around Shoreditch had exploded over the last two decades with smart restaurants, cafés and wine bars crowding out the old fabric, leather and clothing wholesalers in the area. Anjoli was dismissive of the influx of young new money but pleased enough when they spent it at her restaurant.

The pathologist stood up and brushed the dirt off her coveralls. 'As far as I can tell, he was shot at close range, then rolled into the pit. His clothes are covered in gravel. I'm Dr Grayson, by the way.'

'DC Kamil Rahman.' I looked up to see the sand and grit on the side of the ramp disturbed in a track leading to our body.

'Any idea of time of death?' asked Tahir.

'Hard to say. It's 9.13 now, so some time in the previous nine to twelve hours? Maybe between 9 p.m. and midnight last night? We'll narrow it down after the post-mortem.'

'And the type of gun?'

'Also difficult to tell. You could get lucky and find the bullet, although . . .' Grayson gestured at the mess that surrounded us.

'CSI are on their way,' said Tahir.

I glanced at the hoardings around the site. 'How would he have got in? Aren't these sites locked at night?'

Tahir nodded, 'Supposed to be.'

'*May* have been an attempted robbery if he fell in before the thief could get the wallet. I wouldn't want to climb down here at night.'

'A rucksack with an expensive laptop was on his back,' said Tahir.

'Who found him?'

'That digger driver there. Cracked the concrete, saw what he thought was a pile of rags, then discovered it was a body. Lucky he didn't crush the corpse.'

I looked around the site. Something caught my eye, and I squinted. 'What's that?'

'What?'

I pointed at a small white rectangle a quarter of the way up the slope, near the scuff marks caused by the body rolling down.

'Looks like a piece of paper,' said Tahir, scrunching his eyes together. 'Don't disturb the scene. Forensics need to have a go first.'

A long, thin rusted piece of metal lay a few yards from me, part of the detritus of the site. I grabbed it, went to the side of the ramp, and managed to get it under the paper. I flicked it in the air, and it floated down towards us.

'Remind me not to play tiddlywinks with you,' said Tahir as he picked it up in his gloved hands.

It was a blank envelope, unsealed. He opened it and extracted a folded sheet of typed A4, the pathologist watching with interest.

```
Today's humans idolise screens. Intelligent
software that operates heuristically often
neutralizes objective reality.
```

'What the hell does that mean?' I said, taking a picture.

'Some nutter?' said Tahir.

'It's not crazy,' said Grayson, peering at the note. 'I think it's trying to say that AI can create new realities and if we are addicted to screens, we lose touch with what is real. But I might be reading too much into it.'

'AI? Artificial Intelligence?' I said.

'Mm-hmm. Machine learning, that kind of thing,' she said.

'Is there such a thing as machine writing as well? The note reads as if a computer wrote it.'

We'd done modules on Information Technology on my course, as it was becoming a crucial part of policing, but it was an area I was weak in. I preferred physical objects I could see and touch to invisible operations going on behind a screen that I'd never understand.

'May have nothing to do with the body; could just be a random piece of rubbish. We'll see if forensics can get any prints from it,' said Tahir. 'Good work spotting it, though, Kamil.'

I gave a modest 'all in a day's work' nod. 'It was nothing, boss. Forensics would have found it anyway. But the paper looks new, not like it's been lying there for ages.'

'Could have fallen out of his pocket when he rolled down, maybe?'

'Or the murderer could have left it?'

'Hmm. Get all those construction workers off the site; this is a crime scene.'

I walked over to a man in yellow safety gear. 'Excuse me, are you in charge here?'

'I'm the site foreman. When can we get back to work?'

'Not yet, I'm afraid. Can I ask you to get your men to leave the site? The PC up top will take their details. You'll be contacted when we are done.'

'I can't afford to lose a day's work,' he said with a hint of aggression.

'We'll try to be as quick as we can. Is the site kept locked at night?'

His eyes scuttled away from mine. 'Of course it is, mate.'

Something didn't feel right here. I gave him a smile and held out my hand. 'I'm DC Kamil Rahman.'

He took my hand with some reluctance and said, 'Jim Sanderson.'

'Hi, Jim, good to meet you. Sorry for all this hassle. I'll try to persuade my guv'nor to get the site back to you as soon as possible. Any idea how the victim might have got in? Is there only one entrance?'

He thawed a little and pointed, 'Yes, that gate up there.'

'Who's responsible for locking it at the end of the shift?'

His eyes scurried away again. 'I am.'

I nodded. 'Thanks. Sorry for all these questions. It's my first day on the job and I need to impress my boss. And there's absolutely no other way in? Those hoardings look too high to climb over without a ladder.'

He shrugged.

'No worries,' I said. 'And just for the record, what time did you leave last night?'

'At six-fifteen.'

'Is that when the shift ends every day?'

'No, we normally finish at five-thirty. But we ran late yesterday. I had to wait for some goods to arrive.'

I gave him a sympathetic smile. 'Ah, that's a pain. I used to be a chef and nothing like finishing your shift and having to hang around. Did you have to rush off?'

He laughed. 'A chef to a copper? That's quite a jump. Yeah, as it happens, it was my daughter's birthday party and I had to dash.'

'Oh cool. How old is she?'

'Five.'

'Nice. And listen, just one more time, you definitely did lock the gate? It was locked when you arrived today?'

He looked down at his feet. 'No, actually, it wasn't. The chain was just looped through the gate, but the padlock wasn't engaged.'

'Oh really? So, someone must have had a key to open the padlock?'

He paused for a few seconds, then sighed. 'Okay, look. I *was* in a hurry yesterday and couldn't find the key. So I just left it. But don't tell my boss, okay?'

A bolt of triumph coursed through me. I *knew* it! I kept my face neutral and said, 'Thanks so much, Jim. That's really helpful.' I made a zipping motion on my lips. 'Mum's the word. But it was important we found out how he entered.'

He shrugged, went to a knot of workers and spoke to them, and I followed them up the ramp to the top of the site. I instructed the PC to take their details and, to my surprise, saw a familiar face peering down into the pit from behind the cordon the constables had set up.

'Imam Masroor? What are you doing here, Sheikh?' I said, wiping the sweat dripping off my brow with a sleeve as I pulled off my protective clothing.

'Salaam aleikum, Kamil,' said the imam. 'Your first day on the job and you are already busy. What is happening down there?'

'Aleikum salaam. We found a dead body,' I said, feeling a strange sense of pride, as if I was an explorer who'd discovered some long-forgotten pharaoh.

'A body? Ya Allah! That is a terrible thing. What happened?'

Guilt doused my flicker of pride – was I relishing a murder? What was wrong with me? 'I can't tell you, I'm afraid. Why are you here?'

'This is the mosque's land. We are building our extension here. Didn't you see the signs raising money for it for the last two years?'

I looked across the building site and realised we were behind the East London Mosque; I'd chipped in to help with the fund-raising that had kicked off before Covid but hadn't clocked that I was now in the newest part of the imam's fiefdom.

'Oh, yes, I see. We'll allow the workmen back as soon as we can.'

'A dead person on our property. Not a good omen.'

He left as the onlookers dispersed and two cars pulled up – the Scene of Crime Officers had arrived. I introduced myself, only to be ignored by the head of the unit, who looked down and said, 'Christ, this is going to be a nightmare. Come on, lads.' They took out their gear and went down to Tahir, where they set up their equipment and began a search of the area.

'They'll be a while,' said my boss, as he walked up to meet me at street level. 'Let's check out the vic's flat – his keys were in his pocket.'

'I spoke to the site foreman,' I said, and told him what I had found out.

'Good work,' he said and, pausing at the top of the ramp, looked down to take in a bird's-eye view of the site; the CSIs in their white coveralls looked like termites colonising a junk yard as they fanned out.

'This must be where the victim fell,' I said, looking at the disturbed gravel down the side of the incline. 'He was standing at the edge. Perp shoots him and he rolls down into the pit.'

Tahir looked over the edge and nodded.

'Maybe the killer then tossed the note I found after him?' I continued.

'Maybe. No CCTV on the street that I can see. Mr Ram may have been on his way home from work. Come on, his flat's just there. Let's find out some more about our victim.'

Time to start the painstaking work of detection. There were constabulary duties to be done.

Chapter 4

Tuesday morning.

Number 81 Fieldgate Street was an elegant steel and glass high-rise. Located right next to the construction site and opposite the oddly named Durdur Store, the building looked inappropriately plonked within its rundown surroundings. I wondered what the residents of this posh block thought, as they had their cornflakes, of the view of the identikit redbrick buildings with their grimy UPVC sills and infestation of satellite dishes. No doubt the properties would all be torn down and replaced over the coming years, to allow them to see something more in keeping with their self-image.

'What if he has a burglar alarm?' I asked, as Tahir let us into the entrance to the building.

'His key ring has a fob thing that deactivates it. First floor. Let's walk up.'

Two men, one fat, the other thin, dressed in black suits and dark glasses, nodded as they passed us on the stairs to Ram's flat.

Tahir stopped them, 'Excuse me, Met Police. Do you know who lives at Flat B?'

''fraid not,' said the bigger guy.

'And you live here?'

'Just visiting.'

I watched as they turned the corner, then followed Tahir. We put on our gloves, and he rang the bell. Getting no answer, he unlocked the door.

As we entered, he examined the keypad on the wall. 'The alarm's off.'

'So much for security.'

I was tense and hyper-alert as I strode into the living room. Sometimes the most innocuous thing was a clue, and I didn't want to miss it. 'Be a camera', my instructor at UEL had repeated ad nauseam. But there wasn't a lot for my inner Nikon to photograph. The flat was still and suffocating, more like a hotel room than a home, and I was immediately sweating like a horse that had won the Grand National. Decorated in muted greys, two comfortable-looking sofas, a 50-inch television on the wall, dining table – that was about it. I opened the doors to a balcony that overlooked the area where its resident had met his death. As I breathed in the morning air, I saw the men we'd passed on the stairs staring up at me. When they caught my eye, they turned and walked down the street.

'Boss?'

'Hmm.'

'Those guys we saw are hanging around outside. Bit strange.'

Tahir came to have a look, but they'd disappeared.

'Make a note of their descriptions in your rough book.'

The small kitchen table displayed an empty bowl and an open packet of Rice Krispies. I opened the fridge, the cool air a balm, to find it bare except for foil takeaway containers, an unopened bottle of champagne and a carton of milk. I wondered if the takeaways were from Tandoori Knights; we got a lot of custom from the startup crowd. The mantelpiece above the fireplace held various awards in glass and Perspex arrayed like modern religious relics – *Entrepreneur of the Year, Dealmaker of the Year, BAME Entrepreneur Under 30.*

Tahir started going through the drawers of the sideboard as I wandered into the only bedroom, which was as sparse as the living room. I looked in the cupboards and under the bed and found nothing unusual. There was a drawer in the bedside table which contained some ibuprofen and melatonin tablets, but nothing else. As I shut it, I felt it catch. I wiggled and pulled, and a document that had been stuck below it fell to the floor.

It was headed: *Share Purchase Agreement between Aishtar Limited and IntSoft LLC.* I riffled through pages of impenetrable legalese with gloved fingers, my eyes widening at one point. Pulling out my phone, I took a photo of two of the pages, then googled Aishtar but got a bland corporate one-page website which just said *We build world-class software for data analytics and decision making* with a nondescript picture of a computer screen with an email address and a phone number. Whoever they were, these guys liked to fly under the radar. There was no internet presence for IntSoft. Why had these papers been hidden? Or had they just fallen behind the drawer?

'Can't see anything unusual. Bank statements show he was well off, no odd payments at first glance. Medical report – healthy guy,' said Tahir, as I went back out after checking the bathroom. 'CSI can carry out a thorough examination and a specialist search team'll have a good look around afterwards. Arrange for uniform to do a house-to-house on the street. Someone must have heard the shot. Find anything?'

'It's pretty empty for a fellow in his forties. Lives alone – no one else's clothes in the wardrobe or extra stuff in the bathroom. I found this hidden under a drawer.'

I showed the document to Tahir. 'As far as I can tell, it looks like Mr Ram's company was being sold for . . . see here . . . four billion dollars!'

Tahir whistled. 'Interesting.' He flicked through it and said, 'All right. Leave it for CSI where you found it. Come on, let's go to Aishtar and see what we can find out about him – this place gives me the creeps. The guy was coming back after a long day at work, wanting a good night's sleep and – bam! He's chapli kabab. We'll take my car – get one of the DCs to take yours back to the station.'

I took one last look around the flat, hoping to see something Tahir had missed, but nothing sprung out at me, so I shut the door behind me and quickened my pace to catch up with him. As we were about to get into his car, there was a shout from the murder scene below. 'Inspector!'

Tahir looked down. 'Yo!'

'Can you come down please?' said one of the CSI guys. 'We've found something.'

'The bullet?'

'Just get down here.'

We walked down the ramp and the tech shone his torch into a large crack in the concrete, around twenty feet from where Sid Ram's body lay. I squinted into the hole to see a filthy, encrusted skull grinning up at me.

It didn't look like the imam would get his construction site back any time soon.

Chapter 5

Tuesday morning.

'Maybe a killer's been dumping bodies in that site over a period,' I said, weaving through the traffic on Commercial Street.

Tahir laughed. 'Hold your horses, Holmes – first day on the job and you've found a serial killer. Let's see what the techs find before you make any assumptions.'

He was right, but I couldn't help it if my pulse quickened at the thought of stalking another serial killer . . . Anjoli and I had done just that four years earlier. I'd been blind to something under my nose, and it took longer than it should have done to identify the culprit, but we'd got there in the end. I'd only had a chef's hat then – now I had a badge and a warrant card.

We arrived at Aishtar's offices, and I slowed down on Shoreditch High Street, which was chock-a-block, as usual, the fumes from the cars heavy in the oppressive heat.

'What are you doing?'

'Looking for parking.'

'You're a cop now, Kamil. Park on the double yellow in front of the building. I'll take the lead in the questioning, but let's rat-a-tat. Come in any time you think of something. I trust you.'

'Thanks, boss.'

I was lucky to be partnered with Tahir. We'd built a strong rapport, and I wasn't as constrained as I might be with an inspector

I didn't know. Who was I kidding? Without him, I'd be on grunt work for two years trying to earn my sergeant's stripes, not working a murder case. I owed him and had to show I was deserving of his confidence. He was a good copper, honest but prepared to take shortcuts if warranted, and he enjoyed showing me the ropes. He and Anjoli were friends from university – I suspected benefits had been exchanged, although neither ever confirmed it. He seemed to get a bit too much pleasure in exhibiting his Tinder dates at the restaurant in front of her. Anjoli had shown me his profile once, and we laughed as we swiped through pictures of him in uniform; with a cat; bare-chested on the beach. I'd taken screenshots, and she and I were waiting for the right moment to cause him maximum embarrassment. Although, knowing him, he'd bask in the attention. He was a handsome guy, but also smart and funny with it – the perfect package. If he *had* been with Anjoli, I hoped it was her who'd dumped him.

Aishtar HQ looked like an ordinary brick warehouse building from the outside. Just another dot com in premises that used to be a textile mill or furniture shop in a previous incarnation. But as we stepped inside, I saw it was more Tate Modern than modern office – a massive, cavernous space with exposed stone and pipes, interspersed with video screens and mirrors. Thankfully, it was air-conditioned, which brought me some relief. Through the glass wall behind the reception desk, I could see pool and foosball tables, bean bags and egg chairs, and, on one side, a low stage on which stood a Pearl drum kit, mic stand and guitars. There were about a hundred people, some tapping away at laptops on standing desks, others in conference rooms drawing on whiteboards and more milling around a canteen.

A barista next to reception asked if we'd like a latte, but Tahir shook his head and marched up to the desk, where the blonde receptionist looked at us expectantly. Her work surface appeared to be made from rough-hewn logs, at odds with the sleek laptop perched on it. If she got splinters as she worked, they probably had a medic on hand who'd come running with tweezers – it was that type of place. Etched into the glass above her was a woman with flowing hair, brandishing a sword while sitting on a lion with AISHTAR carved over her head in a stylised, curly script. Below this warrior were three clocks, showing the times in London, Jerusalem and San Francisco.

'Good afternoon, gentlemen. Are you here for a meeting?' she said.

We flashed our warrant cards. The last time I'd done that had been five years ago, in a different country with a different badge. It felt good, like coming home. Tahir gave her the smile he produced for every pretty woman he met, and said, 'Met Police. Can we please speak to whoever is in charge here?'

'I'm afraid our CEO isn't in yet. I'm Michelle Jennings, the office manager. Can I help?'

'Is there a deputy CEO or something?' I said.

'I can get Gaby? He's one of the founders?' Her voice had the upward inflexion that made everything a question. She jabbed at a button on her phone console. 'Gaby, I've got two policemen here at reception? They'd like to see you?'

'Quite a place,' said Tahir as we took a seat on some squishy, bright yellow sofas. 'I'd be willing to bet my badge they have an in-house Reiki therapist, a meditation room with piped whale song and – what the fuck!'

'Would – you – like – a – drink?'

A three-foot-high white robot holding a tray with labelled drinks in its hands flowed over to us.

'May – I – offer – you – a – drink?'

'Um – okay?' I said.

'Please – help – yourself.'

On the principle of avoiding drinking anything I couldn't

35

pronounce, I ignored the kombucha, kefir, ayran and şalgam and picked what looked least dangerous – a bottle of activated-charcoal water.

As I gingerly took my beverage off the tray, I said to the receptionist, 'What is this thing?'

'That's Robert slash A. They're non-binary.'

'It's a robot. It's *literally* binary, running on zeros and ones.' I noticed Robert/A's arm had five black bands on it. 'What are those things it's wearing?'

'Some of our coders put their activity trackers on Robert slash A to try to win the weekly step challenge.'

Tahir rolled his eyes, then grimaced as he tasted the ayran he had rashly taken from Robert/A. He put it on the table and said, 'That tastes like the underside of an . . .' as a tall guy in his late twenties with black close-cropped hair and dark stubble came through the glass doors.

'Morning. Gaby Fleishman, Chief Marketing Officer. Can I help?'

In faded jeans, muscles bulging under a Slipknot T-shirt, with a strong accent I couldn't place, he looked more like a bouncer at a nightclub than an executive.

We displayed our badges again. Would never get old.

'I'm Detective Inspector Ismail, and this is Detective Constable Rahman. Is there a room where we can talk in private, sir?'

'What is this about?'

'If we could find a room, please?'

He hesitated for a second as Michelle Jennings, who had been listening to us, agog, said, 'Turing is free, Gaby.'

He gave a sharp nod. 'You'll have to sign an NDA before you enter.'

'Why's that?' I said.

'We do a lot of confidential work.'

Jennings handed Tahir an iPad with a document on it. We

finger-signed it and had our photographs taken, after which she printed out our photo visitor's badges and Fleishman used his swipe card to let us in. What work did these people do? It felt like we were entering GCHQ.

We wound our way through a maze of desks to a glass-walled room at the back, curious eyes looking up from keyboards. As we approached the conference room, I saw an employee playing *Space Invaders* on a vintage arcade machine in the corner, the familiar zings and beeps returning me to my college days in Kolkata. Aishtar was a teenager's fantasy of a work environment.

'Would you like a beverage? Coffee? Tea? Juice?' Fleishman said, taking a seat at a glass table, bare except for a massive bowl of popcorn. On the walls surrounding us were whiteboards scribbled with abstruse equations. Next to a large, analogue clock hung a poster of a dark-haired man with a quote underneath: *Codes are a puzzle. A game, just like any other game* – Alan Turing.

'No thank you,' said Tahir. 'I'm afraid we have bad news.'

'Oh?'

'Sid Ram is your CEO?'

'Yes. He's not in.' Fleishman glanced at his phone. 'Strange. It's almost twelve. He should be here by now.'

'That's why we are here. We found a body and we think it may be Mr Ram.'

Fleishman went still. Face blank. The pings of the arcade game outside filled the room.

'Dead?'

'Yes, sir.'

His eyes drifted down to look at the table.

'How? Accident?'

'He was murdered.'

He looked up at us in disbelief. '*Mah?* I don't understand. What do you mean?'

37

'Someone shot him.'

'But I was with him last night.'

'What time was that, sir?' I said, feeling like I should make my presence felt.

'Murdered? Sid? No.' He shook his head. 'What did you ask? Yes. We went to the pub. At 8.45? Stayed for half an hour, then left.'

'Which pub was that?'

'The Blind Beggar. Whitechapel Road. Shot? Who would shoot Sid?'

'That's what we want to find out, sir,' said Tahir. 'Was anyone else from the company with you at the pub?'

'No. Just the two of us. We were supposed to meet someone, but he didn't show. So, we had a beer, shared a cold chicken pie and left.'

'Who did you go to meet?' said Tahir.

'A reporter from the *Guardian*. Miles Merrion. He left a message for Sid to meet him there, so I went along. I'm the Chief Marketing Officer. I deal with the press.'

'But Mr Merrion didn't turn up?'

'No.'

'Can you let me have his details?' I said.

'Of course. Sid dead? It makes no sense.'

'What did Mr Merrion want to discuss?' said Tahir.

I noted a brief pause before he said, 'I don't know. Like I said, he didn't show.'

I remembered the document I'd seen in Ram's flat and took a gamble. 'Was it about Aishtar being sold?'

Shock came over his face. 'How could you know that? It's not public information.'

'So, it *is* being sold?'

'I can't tell you that.'

'Mr Fleishman, we *know* it is, and it may be relevant to Mr Ram's murder.'

He remained silent as Tahir stared at him. Fleishman looked at me. I gazed back at him, watching him shift in his seat. I could hear the clock on the wall ticking. Finally, he nodded. 'Yes. I was afraid Merrion had found out and wanted to print it. We needed to stop him. Premature release could mess up the deal. And Merrion is not a fan of Aishtar. How did *you* find out? Has there been a leak?'

I had been trained in how to answer questions *and* how not to. 'What did you do when he didn't show?'

'Sid tried to call him a couple of times but got voicemail. We waited for a while, then left.'

'Where did you go?'

'I went home, and Sid said he was going home as well.'

'And where is home for you, sir?' said Tahir.

'Whitechapel. Where was Sid found?'

'What time did you get home?'

'I don't know – 9.20, 9.30?'

'Can anyone vouch for you?'

He paused, thinking. Then shook his head. 'I live alone. Did emails. Went to bed.'

'Are you sure?'

There was certainty now. '*Ken*. I mean, yes.'

'Out of curiosity, where are you from, sir?' I said, trying to place his accent.

'Tel Aviv. I'm Israeli.'

'And how long have you lived in the U K?'

'We came four years ago.'

'We?' said Tahir.

'Yes. Me and my two other founders. We set up Aishtar in Israel, then brought it here.'

'And Mr Ram was one of the founders?'

Something flickered in Fleishman's eyes. 'No. He joined last year. I was CEO, then he took over. My co-founders are Israeli. Oh my God, I have to tell them. They will be horrified. And the board, we must let the board know. Why, why, why . . . *eizeh balagan!*'

He got up to leave.

'Just a few more questions, sir,' said Tahir. 'Do you know anyone who might want to harm Mr Ram?'

He remained standing, face expressionless. There was another brief pause. 'No.'

'What does Aishtar do?' I asked.

'We help people find love.'

'Huh?'

He sat down again. 'We run a dating service.'

For some reason, I didn't expect this. Someone was buying a dating service for *four billion dollars*? Who were they setting up dates with? Beyoncé? Tom Cruise? Maybe I should use them.

Tahir wrinkled his brow. 'I've never heard of Aishtar dating?' Of course, he'd know! He was a veteran of all these apps and a platinum Tinder user.

'We work behind the scenes. We develop algorithms with billions of factors to analyse massive datasets, then license them to other dating sites. The results are quite impressive. We have helped millions of people find love.'

This was all geek to me. The note I had found on the murder scene had said something about intelligent software. Maybe that was connected to their billions blah blah blah. 'Your website doesn't say any of this,' I said.

'We don't court publicity. People who need our products know how to find us.'

Not a lot of work for a Chief Marketing Officer then. Was he given a non-job when Sid Ram took his CEO role?

'What does Aishtar mean?' said Tahir.

'That was my idea.' Fleishman's expression gave way to a slight smile. 'Ishtar is the Babylonian goddess of love. So, it made sense. With the AI in front.'

'Wasn't *Ishtar* also one of the most expensive movie flops of all time?' I knew there had to be a use for all the trivia I had amassed after playing board games with Anjoli during lockdown.

The smile disappeared as fast as it had arrived. 'That's what the VCs kept telling us. We've proved them wrong.'

'VCs,' repeated Tahir, without it sounding like a question. I made a note to use that in the future.

He looked at us as if we were idiots and said, 'Venture capitalists. Our financiers. We're backed by BCP – Bethlehem Capital Partners.'

'And now you're selling the company?' I asked.

'How *do* you know that?'

I put him out of his misery.

'We found this in Mr Ram's flat.' I showed him my picture of the document.

He grimaced. 'Sid shouldn't have left that lying around. This is very confidential. Please keep it to yourself.'

'And it's being sold for four billion dollars. To this IntSoft. Why would they pay so much for a dating site?'

He flinched. Then nodded. 'We are unique. Please, please, you cannot tell anyone! It could scupper the deal.'

Unique. That was putting it mildly. Who *were* these guys?

Tahir said, 'That would make your backers a lot of money.'

'Yes.'

'And how much would *you* get? Personally?' I asked.

Another hesitation. Then, 'The three founders own 15 per cent of the company. Sid owned another 5 per cent. Shit. I hope Sid's death doesn't derail the deal. I need this like a hole in the head.'

An unfortunate turn of phrase.

'So, you all would make . . .' I did the maths. '*$200 million* each?'

'Not quite,' said Fleishman. 'We have to repay the investment from the backers first. But yes, we all stand to earn nine figures.'

I couldn't imagine ever seeing that much money, let alone before I was thirty. That amount of cash wouldn't just be life-changing, it would be generational wealth – altering the lives of all descendants. My mind wandered to me and Anjoli, hand in hand with two toddlers walking along the beach on our private island in the Bahamas, my yacht moored in the distance.

'Don't mind me saying so, sir, but you don't seem very upset about Mr Ram's death,' said Tahir.

Fleishman got up from his chair and stood over us. 'What right have you to say that, Detective Ismail? I have been in the army and when you have seen your best friend blown up by a suicide bomber in front of a coffee shop in Tel Aviv . . .'

'What do you mean by that, sir?'

'Subconsciously, we are conditioned to the prospect of loved ones not returning home in the evening.'

Sad, if true. But something about this guy didn't feel right.

'Were you close to Mr Ram?' I asked.

'We were . . . colleagues.'

That didn't answer my question. I probed, 'Not friends?'

He looked uncomfortable. 'It wasn't that type of relationship.'

I glanced at Tahir as he said, 'Are your other founders in the office?'

'Yes, there they are.' Fleishman pointed at two men, around the same age as him, deep in conversation in the next room. 'We were in a meeting together.' He tapped on the glass and beckoned to them to join us.

They entered, one dressed in the standard tech uniform of skinny jeans, T-shirt and hoodie, the other in a sharp navy suit with no tie. Fleishman said, 'This is Ari Levy, our Chief Data Scientist and Saul Cohen, our Chief Financial Officer. These gentlemen are from the police. They've got some shocking news, guys.'

We shook hands. Ari Levy was a wiry guy, with a distinctive tattoo of a snake that came down his thumb and went up the index finger of his right hand. Saul Cohen was running to fat, with a sweaty and limp handshake.

Tahir said, 'We found a body this morning who we believe to be your CEO, Sid Ram.'

Cohen, the guy in the suit, gasped. 'What do you mean dead?' he said, scratching at his full black beard, brown eyes magnified under rimless glasses.

Levy stared at Tahir, eyes blank, sharp features giving nothing away. When we didn't reply, he said, voice soft, 'How?'

'Shot,' said Tahir.

'What?' Cohen's fingers were getting more agitated and moved to the nape of his neck.

'Where?' said Levy.

'We found his body at the bottom of a construction site on Fieldgate Street.'

They digested this, then Cohen said, 'But that's right next to his flat. What was it? A robbery gone wrong?'

'We're not ruling anything out,' said Tahir. 'Where were the two of you last night? After 9 p.m.?'

Without hesitation, Cohen said, 'I worked late here. Went home after midnight.'

'Can anyone vouch for that?'

'I was alone in the office till ten, then I joined a conference call.'

'We'll need the details of the call – what time it was, who was on it, and so on. And at home? Anyone see you there?'

'I live alone. On Rochelle Street.'

'Thank you, sir. And you, Mr . . .' Tahir looked at his notepad. 'Levy?'

43

Levy hesitated. 'I left work around eight. Went to a film in the West End.'

'With whom?'

'Alone.'

'What movie?'

He paused again. 'The new Marvel.'

'Which is called . . . ?'

Levy shook his head. 'I can't remember the name. It was the usual action crap. I was exhausted and needed to relax. I fell asleep in the film. Then went home at around ten-thirty.'

'And can anyone vouch for that?'

'My wife. She was up when I got in.'

He wouldn't meet our eyes.

I took over. 'How was Mr Ram over the last few weeks? Did you notice anything different about his behaviour? Was he worried about anything?'

The three of them looked at each other as Gaby Fleishman said something to the others in Hebrew.

'Not really,' said Fleishman.

The others nodded their agreement.

'What happens to his shares in the company now?' I said.

Another glance between them.

'They were allocated for the founders so it would come back to us,' said Cohen. 'Unless we hire a new CEO.'

'And you *used* to be CEO?' I said to Fleishman, who inclined his head.

'Why did you step down?'

'Sid was more experienced, a real hustler. He had exited a successful startup before. Wahid thought he would be a better front man for the sale. They know about the acquisition,' he informed his colleagues.

'Wahid?' said Tahir.

'Wahid Masri, our chairman. He's the boss of BCP.'

Wahid Masri. A Muslim name. And Aishtar was an Israeli company. I filed it away for future reference in the 'potentially interesting facts' locker in my brain next to 'useful trivia'.

'So, Mr Masri pushed you aside?' said Tahir.

Fleishman bristled. 'Nothing like that. I agreed to it.'

'But it was *your* company,' I said. 'The three of you founded it in Israel. Wasn't it galling?'

Cohen stepped in. 'No, we *all* believed it was the right thing to do. Sid was . . . an asset. He brought in the professionalism we were lacking.'

'You said you two weren't close,' said Tahir to Fleishman. 'Were *any* of you friends with him?'

'I didn't say I wasn't friendly,' said Fleishman. 'Just that we worked together. Are the two of you friends?'

'As it happens, yes. Were any of you more than colleagues with Mr Ram?'

They looked at each other, then Saul Cohen said, 'He wasn't a warm person but was very good at his job. We didn't *dislike* him.'

There was definitely an undercurrent we needed to get to the bottom of. I pulled out my phone and showed them a photo of the note I'd found. 'Does this mean anything to you?'

They passed it around, each frowning at it in turn, and shook their heads. Ari Levy returned it and said, 'There are a lot of crackpots around who believe AI is evil. It's only a technology. Neutral. Neither good nor bad. What is this, anyway?'

'Like guns are neutral – it's the person who points and pulls the trigger who is the problem?' I said.

'That's a stupid analogy,' Levy responded, an edge to his voice. 'AI has brought a massive amount of benefit to the world. Do you think they'd have found the vaccine so fast without it? Look at Alan Turing there on the wall – his data science helped win World War Two.'

'Where did the three of you meet?' said Tahir.

45

'Military service in Israel,' said Fleishman. 'Ari invented the core algorithms for Aishtar and when we left, we started the company.'

Military service, hah! I bet they were all in intelligence, given all this AI stuff. And how do you get from the army to dating? This was getting very murky.

'Why did you come to the UK?' I asked.

He shrugged. 'Europe's a bigger market. Even post-Brexit, London is still one of the best centres for tech talent. BCP is based here.'

I changed tack. 'Was Mr Ram married?'

'No,' said Cohen.

'Girlfriend? Boyfriend?'

'Not that I know of,' said Fleishman. 'He lived for his work. And the sale of the company, it is all-consuming. Takes a lot of time and attention.'

'Do any of you own a gun?' said Tahir.

Head shakes all around.

'But you know your way around weapons?'

'We are Israelis, man,' said Fleishman. 'We have all had combat training.'

There was a knock on the door and a young, olive-skinned woman in faded blue jeans and a red T-shirt with black, curly hair poked her head into the room. I noticed Levy shoot her a glance, then look down at his fingernails.

'Sorry to disturb you, Gaby, but the interview candidate is here,' she said.

'I'll be there in a minute.'

She nodded and left.

'Who was that?' I said.

'Yael Klein, our HR manager. She came with us from Israel.'

Cohen gave Levy a subtle look.

Levy said, 'Listen, we have to get Sid's phone and laptop back; do you have them?'

Tahir looked at him, 'I'm afraid that won't be possible. They are being retained as evidence. Once it's all over, then maybe.'

'You don't understand. They have ultra-sensitive information on them.'

'Why would dating information be ultra-sensitive?' I asked.

'It just is. We *must* have them back.'

'I'm sorry, but it's not happening,' said Tahir. 'But it would be helpful if you could give us the passcode to his phone and log-in for the computer.'

'We don't have them; only Sid would know,' said Levy.

'Really?' said Tahir sceptically. 'And what if he forgets?'

'We wipe them. It's a security precaution.'

'That's convenient. All right. If you could provide all your contact details to my colleague, as well as how to get in touch with Mr Wahid Masri. Also, a full list of your employees and the details of Mr Ram's next of kin – just email them to the address on my business card – we may need to interview them. And we'll have to get formal statements from you. Thank you for your cooperation.'

We left them staring at each other in their glass-walled fish tank as we walked out amongst the hunched figures tapping on their keyboards that sounded like mice skittering under floorboards.

Chapter 6

Tuesday afternoon.

It felt good to be back in the flow again – Tahir and I in sync with our questions, not giving suspects time to think before their answers. 'So, what do you reckon?' he said, as I clipped my seatbelt on.

'A lot to chew over. If they all stand to share Sid Ram's portion of the company, then that's another, what . . . just over sixty-five mil each?'

'Yeah,' he agreed. 'Not an insignificant motive there, I'd say. But for a *dating* site?'

'Yeah, I was wondering that. They didn't like the victim much, did they?'

'Seems not. We need to find out more about him. Get the pub checked out – see if anyone saw them and if there was any-one else hanging around. It's possible the killer followed Ram home.'

I wanted to put the siren on and drive full pelt, give voice to the exhilaration I was feeling. Instead, I drove off at a sedate pace as befitted my job as a law-abiding policeman.

'Given all this AI stuff they do, that note I found must have had something to do with the murder,' I said. 'Do you think the killer left it there deliberately?'

'Possibly.' Tahir looked out of the window. 'Sounded like gob-bledygook, though.'

'Dr Grayson said she understood it. Maybe it was a message only techies get,' I said, squinting in my rear-view mirror.

'Didn't look like it meant anything to those Aishtar guys.'

'No. There was something odd about that Yael Klein and Ari Levy.' I swerved to overtake the car in front of me. 'Did you notice?'

'Careful! That HR woman who came in? No. What?'

'Don't know. Just the way he looked at her.'

'Hmm. Chancer, asking for the laptop and phone. I bet he has Sid Ram's login details. Let's find out what's on the devices that got him so worried. I hope the techs get back to us in good time.'

'I'll push.'

'Also check on—'

I glanced in my mirror again, then screeched the car to a halt as Tahir jerked forward in his seat. 'What the—'

I jumped out, grabbed my phone, and photographed a dark Renault that slowed, then raced past us.

I scrambled back into the driver's seat, breathing hard. 'That car has been following us from Aishtar. I got the plate. I think they were the guys from Sid Ram's flat.'

'Warn me before you pull that kind of stunt again. I've got whiplash, for fuck's sake . . .' said Tahir, massaging his neck as he looked at my phone. 'All right, we'll run it through our systems. Drive on.'

Back at the station, I gave the photo to a PC to see if they could get a hit and grabbed a quick sandwich, after which Tahir got me busy setting up the incident room before he briefed the team. Superintendent Rogers appointed himself as the SIO; we would report to him, although Tahir would be his deputy and would have day-to-day authority over the investigation. Tahir gave me the fun job of picking the name for the operation – it had to be something unconnected with the case. I scanned the approved list of names and one jumped out at me. 'How about Operation Nutmeg?'

He laughed. 'You can take Kamil out of the kitchen, but you can't take the kitchen out of Kamil. Go for it.'

So, Operation Nutmeg it was.

'Okay, I'm off to inform the parents – Aishtar sent through their details,' he said, putting on his jacket.

'Do you want me to come?'

'No, they live in Wembley. It may be a while. You get started here. I'm taking the family liaison officer.'

The other DCs were not too happy about my elevated role, but I'd cope with that – as Tahir had said, I wasn't here to make friends, although I had to influence people.

There was a lot to be said about the investigative professionalism of the Met compared to the Kolkata police. Clear allocations of responsibilities, a proper team on the job and constant monitoring of outcomes. But the paperwork was as bad as it was in India. Records had to be kept, backsides had to be covered. I spent the next few hours in the hothouse of the incident room filling in forms; getting the HOLMES system ready; organising 'did you see anything' signs; locating the CCTV cameras along Ram's route from the pub and bringing the site foreman in to be interviewed further. It was tiring and dull, but necessary. In Kolkata, we solved crimes through painstaking investigation, not sudden insight, and got used to fortifying ourselves with samosas and lassis to make it through – although here it would be crisps and coffees. I had to make sure I got more exercise. My belly was already hanging over my belt and Anjoli had started to make sarcastic comments.

It was after six by the time I'd finished. 'Fancy a bite?' I said to Tahir, who had returned from his Wembley expedition.

'I'm waiting on an update from the post-mortem. Grayson said she'd have it for me this evening.'

'Why not ask her to join us at the restaurant?'

'Good idea.'

He dashed off a WhatsApp, and as we walked out of the office, I said, 'How were the parents?'

He grimaced. 'As you'd expect – shocked and upset. A couple in their sixties. He was their only child. Hate doing that part.'

'Have you had to do it often?'

'A few times. It's always fucked up. You know, I can deal with the blood and the spattered brains and the vomit and the stink of death – it's the tears that get me every time.' He took a deep breath. 'Make sure you have more than one child, Kamil.'

'I can't imagine *you* wanting children.'

'I love kids. What about you and Anjoli? How many do you guys want?'

His question took me aback. Did he think we were together? No, he must know. 'Both she and I are only children. They say only kids tend to have one child.'

'Well, if you lose them . . .'

We went silent for a second, then I said, 'Tahir, you do know Anjoli and I are just friends, right? We're not a couple.'

He gave me a sideways glance. 'Yeah, I figured. Why aren't you? I know you're not gay; Naila and all. And I know for a fact she isn't.'

I didn't like his 'for a fact' but said, 'Don't know. The time never seems right.'

'In lockdown? Sharing a flat? What are you waiting for? A nuclear war with the two of you being the only survivors?'

'Hilarious. I'd quite like to, but she . . . did she ever say any-thing to you?'

'No. Would you like me to probe?'

I thought for a second. 'Maybe. Without making it too obvious.'

'Hey, I'm the soul of discretion.'

'Yeah. Like my aunty. Anyway, what did you learn from the parents?'

'Nothing useful. Their son was modest, no girlfriends. Excited about the Aishtar sale. They couldn't think who would want to harm him. Were at home all night with each other. I left them with the liaison lady.'

'You sure you're okay?'

He sighed. 'I'm fine. It's part of the job. Shitty part, but what can you do? Don't worry, beta, I'll be your aunty. That'll be more fun.'

It being Tuesday, Tandoori Knights wasn't too busy, so we grabbed a table near the back and ordered a couple of beers and a selection of Chef Chanson's 'Street Treats from India'. I put my frosty glass of beer to my forehead and wondered if it would be rude to nip upstairs to the flat for a shower.

Dr Grayson got there as we were finishing our yoghurt and pomegranate chaat. She asked for a beer and a tamarind kale salad, and Anjoli served her, refilling Tahir's and my glass as well.

'Do you mind if I join you?' Anjoli said.

'Okay with me,' said Tahir. Then, after the pathologist's questioning look, 'She's Kamil's mate; he'll tell her anyway. Have a drink, Anj.'

She hesitated for a second, then said, 'What the hell. Could do with a retox.' She poured herself a beer behind the bar and joined us.

'So, what did you find, Doctor?' said Tahir.

'Well . . .' Grayson took a sip of her cold Cobra and picked at her salad. 'Someone shot the victim at close range in the front of the skull – there were powder marks. He fell back into the pit from the top of the ramp with the impact of the bullet and smashed his head against the concrete when he landed.' She speared a tomato. 'We found the bullet lodged in his skull. It was a low-velocity 9 mm, so you're looking for a handgun. Ballistics said it looks like the killer fired through a suppressor, so neighbours wouldn't have heard much – it would sound like a handclap. He had drunk alcohol and eaten a chicken pie just before dying. Based on the undigested contents of his stomach, he died soon after his last meal – so between 9.30 p.m. and 10 p.m.'

Tahir considered this. 'Given he was round the corner from his flat, they probably killed him on his way back from the pub. So around 9.30 would make sense. Thanks, Doc, that's helpful.'

'A silencer,' I said. 'That's unusual, no?'

'Yes,' said Tahir. 'So, what do you think the lines of enquiry should be, Kamil?'

Uh-oh. This felt like a test. I marshalled my thoughts. 'One: random opportunistic crime. Unusual in this part of London – I'd imagine it's mainly robberies and burglaries, but possible. Walking home late at night. A druggie comes up to him, points a gun, demands the rucksack and wallet, forcing him inside the open gate so as not to be seen from the street. Ram refuses and gets shot. Killer runs off.'

Tahir sipped his beer. 'He'd have taken the money first in that case. And a druggie wouldn't own a silenced pistol.'

'Didn't have a chance to steal the cash. Ram fell into the pit before he could. But fair enough, thieves rarely kill people. Also, unlikely to be a gangland thing. Why would they target Ram? Two: a co-worker follows him from the pub. Bang. Kerching. Ram's share is redistributed. Sixty-odd million bucks is a hell of a motive. And his work colleagues didn't like him, so that made it easier. This feels more likely.'

'That note indicates premeditation,' said Tahir. 'Also, the silencer points to a professional.'

'A co-worker killing him *would* be premeditated. The journalist not showing up before Ram got murdered was convenient. Maybe the note is some kind of red herring to throw us off the scent. Perhaps they meant to plant it on the body, but Ram fell down the pit before they could, so they tossed it down after him.'

Tahir nodded. 'Could play. Anything else? Sex? Who was he doing it with?'

I was on a roll. 'Don't know, need to find out. Third possibility: it has to do with the Aishtar technology. It's worth four billion dollars. Some competitor or someone else trying to get hold of it? They wanted the laptop, but the victim fell into the hole with it. Maybe Aishtar powers a site for people having extramarital affairs? And the laptop had that data? It could have amazing blackmail potential. That might explain the two ray-banned guys following us as well.'

'Two guys following you?' said Anjoli. She poured herself another beer while shaking her head and muttering, 'Cool, cool. That doesn't sound dodgy at all.'

'Nice work, Kamil,' said Tahir, and I tried not to let my pleasure show. 'Pull any info on gun-related crime in the area. Let's do an in-depth on our Israeli friends. And we'll soon know if any prints were found on the note.'

'Be careful. I don't want you to get hurt,' Anjoli added, taking a big sip. 'However, it is fascinating to watch the big detectives at work. Like being in the movies. Pity we don't do popcorn.'

'So, about the other skull . . .' said Grayson, who had been watching our back-and-forth like a TV show while she polished off her salad.

'Oh yes, is there a connection?' I asked.

'It *was* interesting. Two further skulls were found after you left the scene. And a few bones. They look pretty old, covered with layers of silt and sediment. All I could tell from the skulls was that it was two adults – male and female and a child, not sure of its sex. Possibly a family.' I saw Anjoli's fingers tighten on her glass and she pursed her lips.

'Do you think it might be the same killer?' I asked. 'Maybe he uses this site as a dumping ground.'

Grayson smiled. 'Not unless he's a ghost, Kamil. The skulls were ancient.'

'No serial killer for you after all, Kamil,' Tahir laughed.

Anjoli frowned. Was she reliving the glitchy Zoom images of her parents' funeral? 'A family. That's horrible. Why were they left there? Do you think it could be the site of an old graveyard . . . or a mass grave for plague victims?'

Grayson shrugged. 'Don't think so. They were on their own. There may be more in the concrete though; we'd have to break it up with great care to locate them. CSI are on it, but not happy about the work needed.'

'An ancient, dead family. How horrible. Maybe they died in a fire or something,' said Anjoli with a shiver.

'Maybe. We're cleaning them up. Let's see what else we can learn.' The doctor looked at Anjoli's distressed face. 'I've been doing this too long, seen too much; afraid I've become inured.' She gulped down her beer. 'Anyway, I've got to head home. Nice meeting you, Anjoli.'

'What'll happen to the remains?' asked Anjoli.

'I need to find a forensic archaeologist and hand them over. If they are under a hundred years old, this guy may want to take a look.' She gestured at Tahir. 'If not, they'll end up in a museum collection.'

'They died a hundred years ago, and we'll never know anything about them or why it happened. It's so sad,' said Anjoli. 'Will you let me know what happens, Dr Grayson? I'm interested.'

'Sure.'

'We find old bones all the time, Anjoli,' said Tahir. 'We need to focus on the more recent murder.'

'But who will remember them?' said Anjoli. 'They must have left someone behind who wondered what happened to them.'

'It was a century ago,' I said. 'Another world, another life.'

'Still . . .' she went silent, nursing her drink.

'Okay, I'd better run too,' said Tahir. 'Nice job today, Kamil. Set up key interviews for tomorrow and text me. Anjoli, he did great. Don't let this one get away like you did me. Bird in the hand and all that.'

I groaned inwardly. Why the hell had I unburdened myself to Tahir? He was about as subtle as a brick through a window.

They left and Anjoli said, 'What on earth is he talking about?'

'I've no idea. You know Tahir. It's best to ignore everything he says.'

'Hmm.' She gave me a speculative look then said, 'Exciting first day! Tell me everything.'

I took her through what had happened as she hung on every detail, even the boring ones, remaining rapt as the waiters cleared the tables up around us and the last guests left the restaurant. Having something to discuss with her other than menus and difficult diners felt good, almost like a fresh start for both of us.

After I finished, she sat back and said, 'Wow, very cool, Kamil, ver-ry cool. Nice big case on your first outing. Sounds like this could be the making of you.'

'Oh really?'

'Sorry, the rejuvenation of you. Listen, please keep me in the loop on those old skulls. I'm fascinated to know what Dr Grayson finds.'

'Sure, if I can.'

'Promise?'

I nodded, and she said, 'Thanks. Want another drink?'

'No, I better not. Maybe you should stop too. You were feeling pretty rough this morning.'

'One more won't hurt. I had a crappy day. Got a real wanker in at lunch time who gave me grief because he felt Chanson's venison a la Madras wasn't hot enough for his taste. Threatened to give us zero stars on Tripadvisor unless I took it off his bill.'

'What did you do?'

'Wasn't worth the hassle, so I deducted it. You know, they should have some app where *we* can rate diners. Stropadvisor!'

'That'll make a mint. And another where the public can rate policemen – Copadvisor! Hopefully I won't screw things up and get no stars.' I stood up and cleared the last few dishes and napkins from the booth where we'd been sitting.

'Oh my god, of course you won't. "Kamil Rahman was the friendliest policeman we have ever met, and I will use him every time I get burgled – five stars",' she said, following me into the kitchen with the glasses. 'By the way, did you reply to Maliha?'

'Oh.' I felt a stab of guilt.

'You should call her.'

'Now?'

'Why not?'

It was really hard to decode Anjoli. Why was she so keen that I phone my ex? I hit call back on the text and after a couple of rings, heard that familiar musical voice say, 'Hello?' It was like no time at all had passed since I'd last heard it.

'Hi . . . Maliha?'

I felt awkward talking to her in front of Anjoli, but it would have been even more uncomfortable if I'd decamped to our flat upstairs.

'Kamil!' I don't know what I'd been expecting, but the warmth in my ex-fiancée's voice confused me. 'Thanks for calling back.'

'Of course. So, you're in London? On a visit?'

'I've shifted here with Amnesty UK.'

'Shifted?'

'Not permanently – it's a two-year posting.'

Maliha in London for two years. My stomach did an involuntary flip at the thought. 'Oh. Great. I heard you were working for them in India.'

'Yes. Joined four years ago. We were investigating the anti-Muslim riots in Delhi and exposing major breaches of human rights in Kashmir. The government didn't like it, so they froze our bank accounts and forced us to shut up shop. And the current PM is not . . .'

I didn't like to think about the Prime Minister, given my history with him. I cleared my throat. 'I know.'

'Anyway, they targeted me personally, and it was really stressful and . . .'

'Why? What happened?'

'It's a long story. I'll tell you when we meet. Amnesty offered me the chance to move to London and campaign on Kashmir issues, and I've been here for a month now. So, I thought it was about time I got in touch.'

The waiters clanging in the kitchen gave me an excuse to go back into the restaurant.

'How are your parents? They were okay during Covid?'

Her voice fell. 'Um, no actually. Dad passed. It was pretty bad.'

'I'm so sorry.'

'Thank you. Anyway, when can we meet?'

My heart leapt. 'Let's have dinner. I've just started a new job and the hours are not regular. Is it okay if I message you with some times?'

'Sure. I look forward to it. What's the job?'

'I've joined the Met Police.'

She squealed so loud it deafened me. 'OMG, Kamil! I'm so happy for you. That's fantastic.'

I smiled at her excitement and said, 'Thanks! It's pretty great.'

'You must tell me all about it!'

'I will when we meet. Promise. Take care.'

I hung up, pulse hammering in my ears. I gave myself a moment to calm down, then went into the kitchen. Anjoli had finished clearing up and said, 'So?'

'She's shifted to London with Amnesty. Wants to meet.'

'Amnesty? Wow, cool. Why don't you invite her to the restaurant for dinner? I'd like to see her again – I only met her briefly when we went to visit your parents in India all those years ago. We can compare notes about you.'

What *was* she playing at?

'Yeah, I *really* want you guys doing that. I'm heading up.'

I went up to my bedroom and opened Instagram. When we'd first split up six years ago, I got into the habit of checking Maliha's social media profiles every day, but eventually I got absorbed in my own life in Brick Lane. I hadn't looked at what she'd been doing for the last few years. I scrolled through the images on her profile – interspersed with the pictures of her with friends and on vacation on the beach were those of widows and orphaned children in refugee camps, men who had been beaten and even more graphic photographs of mass graves. Only Maliha would feel it was fine to mix and match these pictures.

I zoomed in on one of her, toasting the camera with a cocktail in Goa, and felt a flutter in my heart when I saw the smile that I'd loved for so many years. It was funny how new doors could open in front of you and doors you thought were slammed shut behind you, clicked ajar as well. Life had a way of keeping you on your toes.

I very much wanted to see her, but that desire was both

exciting and perplexing. What message had Anjoli been sending me in asking me to call Maliha? Was she saying there was no hope? Or was she just being nice? Fuck! I could read when a suspect was lying, but when it came to my personal life, I was worse than clueless.

Chapter 7

Wednesday morning.

Anjoli wandered into the kitchen the next morning as I was slathering strawberry jam on a paratha I'd filched from the restaurant. She had come upstairs to the flat late the night before and I'd heard her enter her room as I tried to sleep in the suffocating heat.

'That stuff will kill you,' she said, watering her spider plant in a T-shirt that read *Lawn and Order: Special Gardening Unit*. After her parents had passed, she had taken up plants as her new hobby – pouring her love into aloe vera, orchids and oxalis. Since we had no outside space on Brick Lane, the house had become an indoor garden with industrial-size pickle jars, oil cans and cut-off milk cartons serving as makeshift flowerpots for her collections of tomatoes, chillies, coriander and various other herbs and flowers which I couldn't identify. I quite enjoyed encountering these mismatched receptacles plonked in every shaft of fleeting sunlight. But when I warmed some samosas one day and killed all her carefully cultured chilli seedlings, I felt awful. I didn't know she was using the oven as a propagator.

'Well, at least I'll die with the delicious taste of a Tandoori Knights paratha on my tongue. Chanson should serve paratha and jam – or even better, paratha and Nutella – as desserts. He can call it something wanky like "Artisanal Indian breads with hand-ground hazelnuts" and charge a tenner – I guarantee you it'll be a hit.'

'Put away the chef's hat. You're a copper now, so you just concentrate on eating your doughnuts and coffee. Either way, you'll die fat and happy.' She gave my belly a meaningful look, and I sucked it in. 'Actually, it's not a bad idea. He could add it to next month's menu.'

'Once a chef, always a chef,' I said, licking the jam off my fingers as she switched on the television. 'Here, I made one for you as well. Try it.'

'Argh! Hot! Ooh, it *is* nice,' she said, biting into the flaky bread, closing her eyes in pleasure.

'I told you.'

We munched companionably in front of the TV, then she said, 'We should have a nice dinner to celebrate your new job. Just the two of us. My treat.'

'Nice! Maybe somewhere French?'

'Yes, and we can . . .'

'Sorry. Just a sec,' I said as something caught my eye. The Home Secretary, Priscilla Patrick, was on *BBC Breakfast* talking about some novel initiatives.

'. . . increasing recruitment, but also innovations in crime prevention. This will underline the United Kingdom's world-beating reputation in policing.'

'Blah, blah, blah,' said Anjoli. 'I hate her. The way she sent those poor refugees back was sickening. I can't believe she's my MP. She makes me want to vomit.'

'You campaigned for her opponent, didn't you?'

'Yeah. I still can't believe this racist cow won. She's anti-immigrant, anti-Semitic and just pretends to be pro-Muslim to get the people of Tower Hamlets on side. Makes out like she's one of the working class pulling themselves up by their bootstraps. Always going on and on about her great-grandfather, who started from humble beginnings in the East End and built up some massive retail empire where they must have stocked the silver cutlery that was in her mouth when she was born.'

'Anti-Semitism plays well in this area. She knows her voters.'

She shook her head. 'Shocking.'

'She's my ultimate boss now, so I can't say anything against her. And she's pro-policing, so that's good.'

'Come on, Kamil! She's *literally* the anti-Christ! If she'd been in power, Yasir would never have made it to the UK. She'd have sent him off to some African country!'

I felt a shard of grief as I remembered our Syrian refugee friend who had sought asylum in the UK and found death instead.

'That's true. All right, I need to run to get to my appointment. Try to take it easy today.'

'I wish. You don't have to deal with the butchers and fishmongers anymore.' She looked drawn and tired. 'Shit, I can't believe you like her!'

'I don't . . . I just said she was pro-police and . . . anyway, what were you saying about our dinner?'

Looking morose, she said, 'I'll sort it. Let me know when you're free.'

I kicked myself for getting distracted by the TV. Seeing a copy of the *East London Advertiser* on the side table, I tried to cheer her up. 'When's the ELA coming to do their review?'

'This week sometime. The offers I put in for their readers have been doing well, so they better bloody give us a five-star rave.'

'Well, now that I'm not cooking anymore and you have that clown Chanson, it'll only be four stars; but hey, that's life.'

'Don't let him hear you say that – he's sensitive.'

'Like a rhino. Which he'd probably serve as an appetiser if he could. Bye.'

I ruffled her hair and rushed out, leaving her staring at the TV screen. Two dinner invites in as many days – my social life was looking up.

It was a few minutes after ten as I stood in a shady spot outside the *Guardian* building, a curved industrial-chic edifice near King's Cross, waiting for Tahir. Just as I was about to phone, he tapped me on my shoulder. 'Come on, let's see what this guy's got to say.'

We walked into reception and asked for Miles Merrion. After five minutes, a sinewy man in his mid-thirties, with a goatee and a shaved head, appeared.

'Mr Merrion?' I said. 'I'm DC Kamil Rahman. We spoke this morning? This is Inspector Ismail. Can we talk?'

'I hope this won't take long. I'm on a deadline.' He gestured, 'Come with me.'

We followed his pressed jeans and polo shirt through a buzzing newsroom, packed with people typing away on computers into a small office filled with books.

'So, you said on the phone this was about Sid Ram's death? We posted it online last night,' said Merrion, clearing away a pile of newspapers from a chair and sitting down. 'How can I help?'

'I believe you knew him?' I said as we sat opposite him.

'Knew is a little strong. I'd met him a couple of times.'

'Why did you want to see him on Monday night?' said Tahir.

Merrion looked puzzled. 'What do you mean? I didn't see him on Monday.'

Tahir and I glanced at each other. 'I understood you had arranged to meet for a drink?' said Tahir.

'No, I hadn't.' Then something struck him. 'Oh, is that why he kept calling me on Monday night? He left some messages on my mobile asking me where I was, but I assumed it was a misdial, so didn't respond.'

'Do you have the messages?' I said.

'No, I deleted them.'

'So, you *did not* make an appointment to meet him at the Blind Beggar in Whitechapel?'

He shook his head. 'Nope, you've got the wrong guy. Can you tell me more about how he died? The details the police released were pretty limited.'

'Where were you Monday night between 9 p.m. and midnight, sir?' said Tahir.

'Am I a suspect?'

'We're just checking people's whereabouts, sir.'

'I had some drinks with colleagues till around 8.30 at the Rotunda, then went home.'

'And where's home?'

'Muswell Hill.'

'Can anyone vouch for you?'

'Not after the drinks. My wife's away, visiting her mother in Glasgow.'

'But you know Aishtar?' I said.

'Yes, of course. It's one of the few British tech unicorns. It was founded in Israel, had an Indian CEO and a Palestinian VC – but *obviously*,' he gave a sarcastic shrug, 'it's *British*.'

I was glad when Tahir asked, 'Unicorn?'

'It's a term for any private company that hits a billion-dollar valuation.'

Ah. Just another nonsensical Americanism. Aishtar was a herd of four unicorns then.

'Isn't having a Palestinian VC unusual for an Israeli company?' I said.

'Not for the tech world. Diversity, hands across the wall – shareholders love it. I've written about Aishtar a few times. Not in a very complimentary way, I should add.'

'What's your beef with them?' I said, trying out a new expression I'd learned from Chanson the week before.

Merrion looked amused, and I realised I'd probably misused it. 'I don't like what they do. They are very secretive about their capabilities, so no one knows what their tech does. They say they use it for dating sites to match people more accurately. But I think it does more than that. I think they use AI to profile people. Algorithms to spread fake news that bounces around echo chambers.'

'What, like that Cambridge Analytica?' said Tahir. 'They were well dodgy.'

'Yes, something like that. Did you see Priscilla Patrick on the BBC this morning extolling innovations in policing? I wouldn't be surprised if it was something like Aishtar she was talking about. She's bigged them up in the past as a shining example of *British innovation*,' air quotes. 'It would be just up her street – she's to the right of Himmler. "If you have nothing to hide, why are you so concerned" is *her* mantra. I'm telling you, it's possible this technology could be the biggest threat our country has faced for decades. If you think Twitter is polarising now, wait till you see what happens when every individual sees *only* their version of the truth and believes that everyone else is lying. We'll become an electronic North Korea. But because we can find a better hook-up using Aishtar's dating tech, we don't give a damn.' He ran out of steam.

'But you don't know their software does this?' said Tahir.

'Not exactly, no,' he admitted.

'Do you know the founders of Aishtar?' I said.

'The Israeli lot? Yeah, I know them a bit. All ex-Mossad. Gaby Fleishman calls to shout at me every time I write something he doesn't like. Ari is the brains behind it all. Super smart.'

Mossad! I *knew* it!

'And Saul Cohen?'

He shrugged. 'Finance guy. Competent.'

'Why did they bring Sid Ram in as CEO? Gaby Fleishman used to be CEO, right?'

'Sid was an experienced CEO. First in computer science from Cambridge, then a job with Google. Did great there, left after four years and began his own startup with two of his colleagues. He was only twenty-nine.'

'Which company was that?' I asked, kicking myself as I realised that in getting everything set up for the investigation the day before, I'd forgotten to do the most basic task – google the victim.

'It was called *Thrumyeyes*. He sold it to Netflix a couple of years ago for a packet.'

Thrumyeyes.com had been a sensation when it launched – the ability to live a day in a celebrity's life, following them in virtual reality as they wore a GoPro-type VR camera. I'd experienced the thrill of being Bruce Springsteen singing to 90,000 people in Rio; Anjoli raved about becoming Scarlett Johansson on the set of her latest Black Widow movie and Kim Kardashian out shopping on Rodeo Drive.

'So, Wahid brought him into Aishtar, hoping to bottle that magic again,' said Merrion.

'Was Mr Fleishman upset?' I asked.

'Why? Do you think he did it?' His sharp eyes bored into mine.

'We don't think anything at the moment,' said Tahir. 'Just trying to get the lie of the land.'

'I heard he was miffed. But Sid was a smooth operator.' He looked at his watch. 'Look, I've got to go. Here's my card. Come back if you need anything else. I'm happy to help.'

'What was Mr Ram really like?' asked Tahir.

He considered this. 'Super smart. Super arrogant. Didn't suffer fools gladly. Or anyone else, for that matter. Would constantly put down others if he didn't think they were saying anything useful. Liked to be the smartest guy in the room. A bit of a dick, to be honest. But good at his job.'

67

Tahir and I looked at each other. This was interesting.

'Did he ever put you down?' I asked.

'He was an arsehole. I had my run-ins with him. I really have to go now.'

'Let me ask one last question,' I said. 'Do you think there's *anything* good about what Aishtar does?'

He considered this. 'I don't know. I guess they're not selling you anything? But as they say, if a tech company is not trying to sell you a product, *you* are the product they are selling.'

Chapter 8

Wednesday morning.

'So, if Merrion didn't phone Sid Ram for that meeting, who did?' I said as we drove to the offices of Bethlehem Capital, the VC that funded Aishtar.

'That is the question, my friend. Arrogant sod. His story's not watertight. It's possible he made the call and lied about it.'

'Why?'

'If he wanted to kill Ram, he would know exactly where he would be and when.'

I considered this. 'That's true. His alibi was weak. Any idea of motive?'

'You mean what's his beef?' Tahir laughed. I ignored it. 'Obviously doesn't like what Aishtar does. Or Priscilla Patrick. I met her once. She came into the office, and they rolled out the only non-white officer to be photographed with her.'

'What was she like?'

'Charismatic. Tough. She was alright.'

'Anjoli hates her. She's convinced Patrick will deport all non-whites if she becomes PM.'

'Unlikely. But it's true that she has been tight on immigration.'

'*You* have nothing to worry about. You were born here. I'm here on a work visa.'

'Being a citizen means jack these days when you're Muslim.

One wrong step and you're screwed. Look at Nazanin. Look at Shamima Begum.'

'Well, my ex is at Amnesty here. Their job is to help unscrew.'

Tahir looked at me in surprise. 'She's in London? The one you were engaged to? What was her name again?'

'Maliha.'

'How long has she been here?'

'A month.'

'And?'

'And what?' I tried to keep my eyes on the road, as I felt Tahir's boring into my psyche.

'Exes can be tricky.'

'Not Maliha; she's lovely. Smart, beautiful . . .'

'Eh? I thought it was Anjoli you were after? I promised to be your aunty, remember?'

More like a gunner shooting his own plane. 'Got to keep one's options open, as *you* always say.' I could tell by his face that Tahir was enjoying discomfiting me with his dissection of my dys-functional love life, so I went back to the matter at hand. 'Anyway . . . let's focus. Sid Ram. Other than his parents, seems that no one liked him much.'

'You're right. Could be a motive there somewhere.'

We arrived in Mayfair, and I parked on the double yellow out-side the office. Before getting out of the car, I turned to Tahir. 'How do you want to play the VC?'

'We'll probe his relationship with Ram and find out what Aishtar does. I still haven't worked it out – everyone seems vague about it. I find it hard to believe that it's just another Match.com. We can also look into the Palestinian angle you brought up.'

'I just think it's interesting. Okay, I'll follow your lead.'

I looked in the rear-view mirror to see if I could spot the men in black in their Renault, but there was nothing.

*

We sat in the opulently stark and frigid lobby of Bethlehem Capital's offices, awaiting the return of the receptionist who had gone to alert Wahid Masri to our arrival.

'So how does venture capital work,' I said, looking at the modern art surrounding us, the perplexing sound of invisible trickling water tickling my ears.

'As I understand it,' said Tahir, 'they find promising young companies and buy shares in them. Then, once the company grows, they sell their shares and make shitloads of cash.'

'Nice work if you can get it.'

'Yep. What can you smell all around us?'

I sniffed. 'Agarbati?'

'Mon-ney! Nothing like it, my friend. Root of all evil – and of all pleasure.'

'Mr Masri and Mr Baker will see you now.' We followed the receptionist down a corridor, and I discovered the source of the trickling noise – a bland rectangular steel water feature. We continued through the polished concrete and glass corridor till we came to a vast, even blander corner office overlooking Berkeley Square.

Waiting for us was an enormous bull of a man in his late forties who looked like he was six and a half feet tall and five feet wide, wearing a well-cut tailored suit that put my budget M&S job to shame. I figured it had to be tailored because there was no way Moss Bros. would carry his size. Standing next to him was a white guy in his mid-thirties – handsome in a square-jawed kind of way, if a little weedy. He was smartly dressed in ironed chinos, a padded sleeveless Patagonia vest over a pale blue shirt. I glanced down to see woollen Allbirds shoes, which I recognised because Anjoli had tried to persuade me to invest in a pair (I'd refused to wear woolly shoes that cost more than my suit).

The big man smiled, teeth chemically white in his brown face. He boomed in a cut-glass English accent, 'I am Wahid

Masri, this is my colleague David Baker,' and took my hands in both of his, my palm disappearing into his two hams. I flinched – although it was safe, contact avoidance was now hard-wired.

'Nice to meet you,' muttered the weedy guy in a deep voice that didn't seem to fit his physique, his startling blue eyes blinking.

After we had introduced ourselves, Wahid Masri said, 'Gaby called me yesterday. Terrible, terrible news. I've known Sid for twelve or thirteen years. I couldn't believe it when I heard. Do you know who did it?'

'Not yet,' said Tahir. 'We'd like to ask you a few questions.'

'Of course, sit, sit. We will do all we can to help. I am chairman of the Board of Directors of Aishtar, and David here is a director.'

David Baker gave us a weak smile and looked back down at his nails. He seemed twitchy, yet remote – like his mind was elsewhere. Without asking if we wanted any, Masri poured tea from a large silver teapot into four small, coloured glasses encased in a metal filigree. There was a box of dates on the table in front of him and he popped one in his mouth as he sipped his tea. He wasn't hiding his origins, despite his public-school accent.

'So, please ask me,' he said.

'How did you know Mr Ram?' said Tahir.

'I backed his first company when he got out of Google, and he made us good money when we sold it to Meta. I brought him into Aishtar when it became apparent that they would need a new CEO.'

'Wasn't *Thrumyeyes* a different type of company from Aishtar? That had nothing to do with dating. What made you think he was the right man for the job?'

'Sid was a great salesman. He could sell anything – he even turned around the TME scandal. And he understood AI. He was perfect.'

'What scandal?'

'It was all over the papers. The rapper who wore his Timmie-cam while having sex with his girlfriend during the lockdown in LA and all our subscribers experienced it with him in VR. Sid spun it and our subscription base increased by 450 per cent! It was genius.'

I remembered reading something about it. It had happened around the time Anjoli's parents had died and we weren't focusing on much else.

'Do you know anyone who would want to harm him?' I said.

'Harm Sid?' Masri looked bewildered. 'Nobody. He was a wonderful guy.'

No one else seemed to think so.

'So, you were friends?' Tahir asked.

'I loved him like a brother.'

Yeah, and Qabil killed Habil so he could become Adam's sole heir.

'Some others we spoke to said Mr Ram could be ... difficult?'

Masri paused and looked at David Baker. Then said, 'Difficult how?'

'He'd put people down. Arrogant.'

'Well, he was very smart. You have to make allowances for geniuses.'

I wasn't sure what he meant by that, but chimed in. 'Did *you* ever see that side of him?'

Another glance at Baker. 'Look. Being a CEO is a stressful job. Sure, sometimes he had a short fuse. But it meant nothing.'

'What about you, Mr Baker?' said Tahir. 'Did you get on with him?'

'Sure. I had no issues with him. But we were his investors – he had to keep us sweet,' he said in a soft American accent.

'How did you come to invest in Aishtar?' I asked.

73

'That *was* unusual,' said Masri. 'Normally companies approach us for money, but in this case, we went to them. We were looking for good AI startups and David here found them. He's a brilliant analyst and finds hidden gems everywhere.' He gave Baker an avuncular smile. 'He screened thousands of companies around the world and discovered this one in Israel with a rocket scientist at the helm, Ari Levy. You know, he literally is a rocket scientist – studied astrophysics in MIT.'

'What does Aishtar do exactly?' said Tahir.

'It powers dating sites.'

'Yes,' said Tahir, an edge to his voice. 'So everyone says. But I'm pretty sure it does more than that. I must insist that you tell us exactly what they do – it will severely impact the investigation if you don't. I'm assuming you are interested in bringing your CEO's killer to justice?'

Masri hesitated, then yielded a tight smile and said, 'Of course, Inspector. You explain it, David.'

David Baker looked thoughtful for a moment, as though considering his boss's words. Then in a monotone said, 'Ari came up with a layered approach, where communications have been classified using a Naïve Bayes algorithm, followed by a convolutional neural network being applied to the surveillance imagery, and finally topped with a cooperative wild goats algorithm that combines this with financial and demographical data to optimise the parameters of the search. He's made use of the latest in-house quantum computers in order to speed up the process, allowing new real-time results.'

Was this guy taking the piss? Did he *actually* say wild goats algorithm? He was staring at his cup of undrunk tea, a slight look of puzzlement on his face, as if he was wondering what it was doing in his hand.

'*Seriously?*' said Tahir.

'You asked,' said Masri, laughing. 'All right. The point is, Ari invented this super-advanced tech; he and his friends were doing the rounds of VCs in Israel but weren't getting much traction. Then David met him at an AI conference in Tel Aviv and they got on. Ari's algorithms were so revolutionary that David was the only person who could appreciate the breakthroughs he had made. David introduced me to the founders, and they convinced me they had something that was worthwhile – and better still, as yet unrecognised. So, we put an initial five mil into the company and got it off the ground. And we discovered it revolutionised dating apps. I brought them over to London a few years ago and since then, Aishtar has grown exponentially. We have been instrumental in over two million marriages. It makes us very proud.'

I remembered what Merrion had said. 'But you also work with the government?'

'Who says we do?'

'That's not an answer. Do you?'

'We have a lot of projects. They are confidential.'

'And now you're selling the company?'

His response was a poker face.

'Are we?'

'We know you are.'

He hesitated, then continued. 'I hired Sid because, even though the boys are good, they have never run a company before. It was all going a little crazy – no systems, no processes, everything by the seat of their pants – they were building the plane while it was flying, which can be a recipe for disaster, as you can understand. So, Gaby stepped down as CEO and Sid came in. He straightened things out and taught them to play as a team in their appropriate positions.'

'How did Mr Fleishman feel about that?'

Masri shrugged. 'He didn't have a choice if he wanted more of our money.'

He had sidestepped my question about the sale, so I went straight for it. 'Who is this . . .' I checked my notes. 'IntSoft LLC, that's buying the company? I couldn't find out anything about them online.'

Masri's bonhomie slipped for a second. 'Where did you hear that name?' When I didn't answer, he continued, 'Gentlemen, I'm afraid that really is confidential. You know a little too much. We can't let anything derail the sale.'

'How much will you make?' Tahir said.

'I haven't said what the sale price is.'

'Stop messing us around, Mr Masri,' said Tahir. 'We know it's four billion dollars. Why would someone pay that much for a dating company? Regardless of how many marriages you have facilitated.'

'Who has been *telling* you all this?' barked Masri.

'That's our job. We know the founders will make hundreds of millions of dollars. How much will you make, Mr Masri?' repeated Tahir.

He took a breath. 'All right. We'll do well. So will the other VCs who co-invested with us. We'll make a couple of billion. But the $100m we put into the company was an enormous risk. We would have lost it all if the tech didn't work.'

'It works,' mumbled Baker.

'Twenty times your money back?' I said. 'That's pretty good going. And what does the buyer do?'

'Win some, lose some. This is a win.' Masri glanced at his fat gold Rolex and didn't answer my question. 'Anything else, officers? I have a lunch date.'

'Who will replace Mr Ram as CEO?' asked Tahir.

Masri shrugged. 'I may have to put Gaby back in post, till the sale goes through.'

'And where were you Monday night between 9 p.m. and midnight?' I asked.

'Let's see.' He checked his phone. 'Ah yes, night before last I was on a ridiculously long Zoom call from 8 p.m. to just after midnight.

'A videoconference? At that time of night?'

'With the Valley. California.'

'Can others vouch for that?'

'David was also on the call; he had to present to our US lawyers and accountants. There were another three or four people on it. They can all vouch for us. Saul joined the call around ten.'

'Were you and Mr Baker in the office together?' asked Tahir.

'No; I like him, but not that much. We did it from our homes. The pandemic spoiled us – everyone is used to working from home now.'

'And you can vouch for this, Mr Baker?' I said.

He looked at me, gave a brief nod, then went back to surveying the tea in his glass as though it contained the answers to the secret of life.

'And where is home for the two of you?' said Tahir.

'I'm in Knightsbridge,' said Masri.

Naturally. Where else would a Master of the Universe live? I bet he drove to work in a chauffeured Rolls.

'Wapping,' Baker murmured.

A 3-Series BMW for him. Self-driven, of course.

'If you could supply us with the names of the others on the call. Oh, was it recorded by any chance?' said Tahir.

'It was,' said Masri.

'And you can share the recording?'

He hesitated. 'There were some highly sensitive discussions to do with the Aishtar sale. Although you seem to know everything.'

'I understand,' said Tahir. 'However, I'm sure it would be a weight off your mind to be officially eliminated from our enquiries.'

Masri nodded. 'All right, David will get you the recording. But it is not to be shared further.'

'Thank you, Mr Masri. One last thing. Was there any tension between you and the founders? You know, the whole Palestinian–Israeli situation?'

Masri paused, then said, 'We keep politics out of it. I have my views and am proud of who I am, but business is business. Look, I was born in a refugee camp and got lucky – educated by UNHCR, then a scholarship to Imperial College – so I got out of the camp. My parents didn't and died there.' His eyes dropped to the floor, and he murmured an Arabic prayer under his breath.

Then continued, 'So now my mission is to pay it forward by finding the smartest people who can change the world and back them. Sid was one. Ari is another. It doesn't matter who or what they are – Jewish, Muslim, Hindu, Christian, Buddhist – great entrepreneurs can come from anywhere. Hell, if Sabra can produce a successful venture capitalist, anything is possible.'

'That's very inspirational,' I said.

'Thank you. I try. Oh, we must have Sid's laptop and phone back as soon as we can.'

'Mr Levy made the same point and I'll give you the same answer I gave him,' said Tahir. 'They are being held as evidence and you'll get them back when we're done with them.'

'You don't understand, Inspector. They contain sensitive and proprietary information. We cannot have it fall into the wrong hands.'

Tahir was nonchalant. 'We are the police, sir. If anyone has the right hands, it's us. Goodbye.'

'That's confidential, this is confidential – do you get the feeling they are putting the con into confidential? Dating, my arse. We still don't know what the bloody company does. Or who their buyer is,' said Tahir.

'All that gobbledygook about goats,' I said, as I started the car. 'He seemed quite affable, didn't he? Surprising given his close friend had just died.'

'Probably his usual sales-guy persona – it's automatic with some people. Their grandma could have fallen in a well and they'd still be grinning. This case has too many oddities – the phone call to set up the dinner, that stupid note, this confidential crap.'

'I'll get the intelligence unit to check if any of them belong to a gun club.'

'Good idea. And let's see if they've had any luck on identifying the guys who were following us. We need to find out who set that meeting up with Ram. We crack that and we have our killer. We have to get the Aishtar guys to talk. I've had enough of being buried in goat shit.'

Chapter 9

Wednesday afternoon.

S tomach rumbling, I logged onto my email in the incident room and found one from David Baker. It was the Zoom recording of the alibi call. He hadn't communicated much at our meeting, but at least he was good at following instructions. It was a massive file and was going to take ages to download – the internet connection in the station was powered by hamsters – so I went to get a coffee from the canteen. Still stinging from Anjoli's comment from the morning, I swapped my usual chocolate doughnut for a protein bar.

The download was complete by the time I returned to my desk. I looked at the length and groaned – four hours, twelve minutes. This was turning into a long, hot, boring afternoon.

I pulled off my jacket, rolled up my sleeves, and, chewing on granola that had the consistency, taste and look of a freshly turned flowerbed, I pressed play. The all-too-familiar Zoom screen filled my computer to reveal a PowerPoint presentation flanked by small windows containing five conference participants on video. David Baker was recognisable on screen, taking the call in his kitchen, while Wahid Masri was in a book-lined library. I paused the screen and inspected the third picture, which contained multiple people. From what I could tell, it seemed to be three young to middle-aged white men seated around a table – from the 'Valley', I assumed. The other black boxes signified the attendees who had dialled in without video.

I pressed play again. The call started at 20.00 with introductions and, after the familiar Zoom incantations of 'you're on mute' and 'you're frozen', Baker launched into a presentation about Aishtar's legal and financial structure. He was a fluent presenter, more at ease with numbers and slides than in everyday face-to-face conversation; my exact opposite. I hated presenting – the adage of 'imagine the audience naked and you'll relax' just making me think of flabby bellies and hairy chests.

After ten minutes of sweating at my desk and listening to Baker drone on about comparative multiples and liquidation preferences, with no more clarity on what Aishtar did, I lost interest and fast-forwarded to 21.15, the time just before the murder. The lawyers were presenting now, and two other people had joined on video and phone. David Baker and Wahid Masri were still visible on the video. I moved forward some more and saw Saul Cohen join on video at five past ten, from what looked like the Aishtar office. He did a riveting twenty minutes on accounting policies, during which I completely lost any will to live. I stopped the video and replayed it a few times, looking closely at him, but he didn't betray any signs of having just murdered his boss. Not that I knew what those were – maybe I needed an expert in body language and micro expressions to look at this. I fast-forwarded till the end and switched off. That was a chunk of my life I would never get back.

Tahir came out of his office and said, 'Okay, team. What have we found?'

Paul Gooch, a friendly detective who'd given me some useful tips while I was in training, started us off. 'No luck from the pub. The barman thinks he recognised Gaby Fleishman and Sid Ram, but it was busy, and he didn't see anybody hanging around.

No witnesses from the street where the body was found; no one saw or heard anything. Nothing on CCTV near the building site. Got the forensics back. Nothing useful from the scene or Ram's flat, no prints on the envelope or the letter and the paper was just standard. No luck on those two people in the car that DC Rahman photographed. The car's registered to a shell company and we're attempting to penetrate it. On Sid Ram, no regular girlfriend that anyone knows about, but we interviewed a neighbour who said he'd have different women over who stayed the night, so might be active on Tinder. But till we crack his phone, we can't tell. We're still trying to find other friends and acquaintances from his family.'

Tahir grimaced. 'Was the killer a ghost? Okay. Tech?'

A member of the tech team said, 'The phone and laptop are heavily encrypted, so nothing yet, but we're hopeful we'll get there.'

'Any idea how long it might take? It's our main hope of learning what the company does and what's on the laptop that's got them so rattled.'

The technician shrugged.

'Maybe you need more experienced manpower, boss,' said Protheroe. 'I'm available, you know.'

'Thanks, Prothers, I'll keep that in mind. Follow me, Kamil.'

I went into his office. 'Seriously? "More experienced"?'

'Ignore him. He's multi-talentless. Where are we with our suspects? Since there's no physical evidence, we need to focus on motive and opportunity.'

I consulted my notes.

'Nothing useful from the Zoom. We can eliminate Masri and Baker – they were clearly visible on video throughout the call from their homes and that spanned the time of the murder. Saul Cohen joined after ten and was there till midnight – so he's still in the frame. Incredible that you can listen to a four-hour presentation about a company and still have no idea what the hell they do. Or maybe I'm just thick. I'll try to find out a little more about the buyer – IntSoft – and see if that helps. I can't see anything about them online, but if they are paying four billion, they *must* be a pretty substantial company. Let me get hold of that document I saw in Ram's flat. It might have more info.'

Tahir nodded. 'Good point. Ask our financial crime bods to look into it. Reducing the suspect list is always useful – not that the VCs had any motive – can't see them wanting to put their billions at risk.'

'Yeah. Frankly, Gaby Fleishman, the chief marketing guy, stands out for me. He resented losing the CEO gig to Ram; was with him that night; hasn't got an alibi. CCTV saw them leaving the pub, although they seemed to go different ways.'

'I like Fleishman for it, too. He could have followed Ram after leaving the pub. Has a powerful motive with that extra sixty-five mil. Knows guns. Let's do a deep dive on him. What about the others?'

'Ari Levy, the chief data guy. I thought his alibi was sketchy.'

'Yeah. No way was he at that cinema. Let's interview him and the H R lady. He knows guns and has the same motive as Fleishman. What about the chief finance guy, Saul Cohen?'

'Same motive. No alibi. Knows guns.'

'So, we have the three chiefs in the frame.'

'Lots of chiefs, with one dead Indian,' I said, scribbling some more in my notebook.

'And wild goats. We're in the Good, the Bad and the Sketchy,' Tahir replied, amused. 'And, talking about sketchy, the journalist, Merrion, is also in the frame. Find out about this message Ram got and if it really was from him, even though he denied it.'

'Okay. Let me get his picture to the CCTV guys and see if we can spot him in the vicinity.'

'And those two guys you saw following us . . .'

Tahir's phone pinged.

'Pathology,' he said, looking at his message. 'They've got some more on those old bones. Grayson wants to see us at the Royal London mortuary at six.'

I remembered my promise to Anjoli. 'Do you mind if I ask Anjoli to join us? She was really interested in the skeletons.'

Tahir shrugged, and I texted her as the tech working with us came into the room looking worried.

'Excuse me,' he said.

'Hey,' said Tahir. 'Good news on the phone and laptop?'

'Umm, no, quite the opposite. They're gone.'

Tahir looked confused. 'What do you mean? Gone where?'

'SO15 have seized them.'

'Fuck. You're kidding?'

'Counterterrorism?' I asked.

Tahir's face hardened. 'Yes. Bloody Special Branch bods. Did they show you ID? Did you take their names?'

'Yes,' said the tech, consulting a scrap of paper. 'Warner and Powell. They looked like they were auditioning for Men in Black – dark suits, dark glasses. One was more John Goodman than Will Smith, though.'

Tahir and I exchanged a glance.

'What the fuck is going on here? Let's see the gaffer,' said Tahir.

Rogers was unhelpful.

He heaved his bulk out of his chair, stood, and stared out of the window. 'SO15 are a law unto themselves. I got a call from the Home Office to hand over the laptop and phone and some document from the evidence room. My hands are tied.'

Shit. The sales document I'd found. I should have photographed the whole thing.

'What did they say?' said Tahir.

'That this technology is critical for the Home Office. They have to ensure it is secure and doesn't fall into the wrong hands.'

'Whose hands?'

'They didn't say, but given it's SO15, MI5 must be involved. So it has to be terrorists or a rogue state. What on earth does this software do, anyway?'

'We don't know,' Tahir said. 'No one will tell us; it's frustrating as hell. It's certainly not about finding a date. If SO15 are all over it, do we keep working the case?'

'Yes, it's our murder. Did we get anything out of the laptop before SO15 turned up?'

'No, it was all encrypted, sir,' I said.

'Well, maybe a good thing they took it then. They have far more resources to crack it than we do. I'm sorry, Tahir, there's nothing I can do.'

Tahir fumed. 'How are we supposed to find the murderer if they swoop in and collar vital evidence from us? We think the two guys who took the kit may have been at the victim's flat before we went there – who knows what they took from there? *And* they were following us.'

'Lucky they didn't find that sales document in the flat,' I said. 'We'd never have known the company was being sold, and we'd be unaware of a massive motive.'

'Why do you think they were following you?' said Rogers.

'We saw them when we went into the victim's flat and Kamil got a picture of them in their car.'

'And the alarm was switched off in Ram's flat,' I added. 'They were watching the flat when DI Ismail and I were searching it.'

Rogers considered my words for a moment, then shook his head. 'Work with them. There's no point getting into a pissing match over jurisdiction. We're all part of the same team. Let them do their job and we do ours.'

'Their job is interfering with ours. Knowing SO15, they'll let us catch the killer, then swoop in and take the credit. And I don't like being tailed.'

'You'll figure it out, Tahir. Keep me in the loop.'

'Will they cooperate with us?'

'They say they will.'

'I'll believe that when I see it.'

Tahir was still seething as we made our way to the Royal London Hospital Mortuary, and I mulled over the implications of what had just happened. I had no experience of the security services and had no idea what they could be up to, but didn't want to reveal my ignorance. 'Do you think it *might* be politically motivated? A hostile power? The silencer, MI5 – it all points to it. They wanted the tech, so they killed Ram for it.'

He considered this and said, 'Bit James Bondish. But not unimaginable. Merrion mentioned Mossad. Did you set up a meeting with Aishtar? I'm getting pretty pissed off with them giving us the runaround.'

'Yes, tomorrow morning. SO15 must have been tracking Ram. That must be how they were at the scene so soon.'

He went silent. Then said, '*That* is an excellent point, Kamil. We'd only just found the body. How *did* they get to his flat so quickly? And did they find something else they haven't told us about? Why have they confiscated the laptop and that sales document?'

I had no answers.

Anjoli was waiting for us outside the mortuary, and we found Dr Grayson inside, where the air-conditioning hit me like a freezing shower. I shivered as she said, 'Hi, folks. You just missed Mr Ram senior. He came to identify his son.'

'How was he?' I said.

'Shaken. We tried to clean up his son's face as much as we

86

could, but it was difficult. He wants the body back for the funeral and I said you'd be in touch.'

'Did you learn anything new?' I said.

'Not really. No drugs. Generally healthy.'

'Except for being dead,' I said.

'You okay, Tahir?' said Grayson. 'Haven't seen you this sphinx-like before.'

'I'm fine,' he muttered.

'What about the other remains?' said Anjoli.

'They're here.'

Laid out on three tables were some sorry-looking bones. Three skulls, two large and one small. A few ribs, pelvis, leg bones. One arm bone.

'As I said, an adult man, a woman and a child,' said Grayson.

We looked at the bones with curiosity as Grayson continued, 'The news is that the man and child were shot. Look, here are the bullet holes, both in the front of the skull. Very tiny calibre, so some kind of pocket pistol. The woman has a fracture at the back of her skull, so it's possible she bled out. She might have been hit with a blunt instrument or banged it against something.'

'Oh no!' said Anjoli. 'Who would shoot a child?'

'We may never know,' said Grayson. 'I've found a lab who can date them.'

'Good,' said Tahir. 'If the bones are new enough that the killer may still be alive, it'll become an official police enquiry. Otherwise, it doesn't matter.'

'It matters to them,' said Anjoli. 'Do you think we can find out who they are?'

'That's very unlikely. We should be able to tell approximately when they died,' said Grayson. 'But you never know. We may get lucky with DNA if someone pays to have it tested. Like they did with Richard III's bones in Leicester.'

'They *must* have been a family,' said Anjoli. 'We should give them a decent burial. They've been trapped under a random building for all these years.'

'If the police don't want them, we can arrange that after our analysis,' said Grayson. 'Right, I'll sort the transfer paperwork and get these wrapped up.'

We left the lab with the three skulls staring sightlessly at the cold light in the ceiling.

25 September 1905

Darling Shoshi,

It is strange to be writing instead of
talking to you. I cannot believe it is
already six months since you left. I
miss you every day but am so happy you
got away when you did. How are you
finding your life in Manchester? Is
Semyon treating you well? Are you with
child yet?

England must be so different from
Pinsk, I cannot imagine. Things are
getting much worse here — so many
friends arrested and beaten — do you
remember Chaim Teper? The Cossacks beat
him so badly he could not walk for seven
weeks. He had done nothing! The
anarchists killed two policemen last
month and now we dread that there will
be another big crackdown. Last week,
those same Cossack animals smashed up
our shops and ransacked our synagogue.
And among these savages, I saw people
from school and work who we had grown up
with. How have we ever harmed them? We
live each day in fear, going out only to
scrounge for what little food there is.

Avram and I had to get married in a
hurry. It was not the wedding I had
pictured for myself (of course you were

not here), but I am now the wife to a good man. We thought of fleeing to Palestine to join his brother who escaped, but Avram thinks he can get a job as a dressmaker in London. It would be wonderful to be together again, Shoshi. Is London far from Manchester?

Tate and Muter send their love – they are still well, thank God, but they are too scared to leave the apartment. Tate was made to resign from the municipality three months ago and he has not recovered from the indignity – you know what he is like! It is hard to think about leaving them, but you will understand we have no choice. I can only pray for their safety as you do for ours.

I hope you get this letter. With God's will, we will see you soon.

With all my love,

Malka

Chapter 10

Thursday morning.

'Good morning, gentlemen. Who are you here to see?' A sombre Michelle Jennings greeted us as we walked into the Aishtar offices.

'Is Mr Fleishman in?' said Tahir.

'He's in a meeting.' Her eyes flitted over to a room where I saw Gaby Fleishman standing over David Baker from Bethlehem, scowling and jabbing a finger at him as Baker looked back, expressionless. Ari Levy and Yael Klein were in the room next door, sitting side by side, heads almost touching, peering at a laptop screen.

'Can you please tell him the police are here?' said Tahir.

She typed something onto her computer, and I saw Fleishman jerk his phone out of his pocket and look over at us. His shoulders dropped, and he came out through the security door, followed by Baker.

'What is it? I'm busy. We have a critical board meeting today.'

'And I'm investigating the murder of your boss,' said Tahir. 'We have a few more questions for you. It won't take long.'

'Go on.'

'Can we talk in private, please?'

Fleishman looked like he was about to demur, then slammed his swipe card against the reader and let us into the office. We walked into the conference room, and I saw Levy and Klein look up at us from the next room, then slide their chairs away from each other. Fleishman gathered up the papers on the table and sat, Baker settling himself next to him, opposite Tahir and me.

Tahir began, 'Yesterday you said Miles Merrion contacted Mr Ram to arrange the meeting. When was that?'

'I don't know. I think Michelle took the message.'

'Could you ask her?'

He pulled out his mobile, put it on speaker, and dialled.

'Michelle, did you take the message from Miles Merrion to meet Sid on Monday?'

'Yes,' she said. 'Monday morning at around . . . 10.45. The caller said he wanted to speak to Sid; I offered to put him through, but he said he was in a hurry and to just give Sid a message.'

'What was it?'

'Um. Hang on.' I heard her tapping at her computer as Baker helped himself to some popcorn from a bowl on the table. It looked tempting but stretched the bounds of professionalism. 'Yes, here we go: "Can we meet urgently tonight to discuss Aishtar's sale? Blind Beggar in Whitechapel at 8.45."'

'Did he leave a number to confirm?' said Tahir.

'Yes. I texted him back. It was . . . 07809 324719.'

I noted it down and mailed it to the tech team to check out.

'And how did you know for sure it was Mr Merrion who was calling?' continued Tahir.

'Well, I didn't know. I'd never spoken to him before, but he said it was. Mind you, he didn't sound unfamiliar, so it's possible I had.'

'Thanks, Ms Jennings. That was very helpful. The caller mentioned the sale,' said Tahir to Fleishman after she disconnected. 'I thought you said no one knew about it.'

'No one is supposed to,' said Fleishman. 'That's why I wanted to meet him. To find out how he knew.'

'Who does know about it?'

'Our board. Bankers. Lawyers. The buyer, obviously.'

'Who are the board members?'

'Wahid, David, Sid and us three founders.'

'No one else in the company?'

'No.'

'What about Michelle Jennings? Did she know?'

'I don't know. She hasn't said anything. Are we done?'

'No,' said Tahir. 'I'd like to talk about the work you are doing for the government and why they have confiscated Mr Ram's computer and phone.'

'You can't. It's confidential.'

'We signed your NDA yesterday.'

'It's not the same thing. You'd have to sign the Official Secrets Act before I can tell you what we do. And even then, I probably wouldn't.'

'Really?' said Tahir. 'So, you *are* doing classified work for the government?'

Fleishman gave him a stony stare. He had clearly made a slip.

'Just give us the headlines,' I said, trying to dissipate the tension that had filled the room. 'Nothing confidential, just anything that might help us find the killer of your CEO. I assume you want us to do that?'

'I don't see how knowing this is going to help.'

'Perhaps it was an enemy agent who wanted the technology,' I said, glancing at Tahir and feeling like an idiot quoting from a film as I heard the words leaving my mouth. 'We won't be able to assess that line of enquiry unless we know what it does,' I added, hoping to re-tether the outlandish-sounding theory to reality.

Fleishman looked over at Baker, who gave a slight nod.

Fleishman shut his eyes briefly. 'Okay. No details. In addition to matching people for dates, we can use algorithms to evaluate subjects of interest to the police. Our proprietary algos can then predict how dangerous an SOI might be. So, we could know in advance if you are about to commit a crime and you could be stopped. This is very useful. To you people especially. I can't say any more.'

You people. Us. The police. This was a radical proposition and sparked all kinds of possibilities, not least of which was the risk of my being rendered defunct in a profession I had only just embarked on.

'You predict the future? How does it work? Preferably in words of one syllable that don't involve wild goats.' I smiled at Baker, trying to maintain my equanimity and not betray the combination of awe, anxiety and hunger pangs that were now passing in a wave through my stomach.

Fleishman shook his head and shrugged as Tahir said, 'I know, I know, it's confidential. Why would MI5 work with an Israeli company?'

'I never said we worked with MI5. But hypothetically, if we did, it's because we are the only company in the world who can do what we do.'

'Which is?'

Fleishman gave Baker a side glance. 'We can transform the safety of a nation. I really can't say more.'

'Why not?' said Tahir.

'One, it's proprietary and we don't want our competitors getting it. Two, we also don't want the bad guys to know we have it. Three, there are concerns it might transform privacy. In a good way.'

I wasn't sure I wanted my privacy transformed 'in a good way'. But since that was all we were going to get, I said, 'And you sell this technology to whoever wants it?'

'NO!' Baker slammed his fist hard on the table, making me jump. He fell silent again, as if his outburst had surprised him.

Tahir raised an eyebrow.

'What David means,' said Fleishman, 'is that we are careful who we license it to. It's okay for the UK or Israeli governments to stop a terrorist attack, but we don't want China or Russia to use our tech to locate potential dissidents and lock them up. Or worse.'

'Who is this IntSoft that's buying the company?' I asked.

Silence. Then Fleishman said, 'We can't discuss that. We are under NDA as well.'

Tahir and I looked at each other. It was clear he was not going to tell us anything.

'So,' said Tahir, 'it is possible that some foreign enemy wants this technology and killed Mr Ram to get it, hoping it was on his laptop. Theoretically.'

'Theoretically. Although Sid's laptop was encrypted. And if we know someone has stolen it, we can wipe it remotely as soon as it connects to the internet.'

'And that's why you got Special Branch to confiscate his laptop? So you could wipe it?' I said.

David Baker remained poker-faced, and Gaby Fleishman rubbed an invisible stain on the table with his thumb.

'Did you know Special Branch was watching Mr Ram?'

Fleishman looked startled. 'What? No.'

Baker said, 'The tech is very important for the UK government. They won't want it to fall into the wrong hands.'

Tahir looked at me. 'I wonder if we could have a word alone with Mr Baker.'

Fleishman walked out as Baker looked down at his Apple Watch, fiddling with the magnetic clasp, snapping it open and shut – click, click, click.

'Thanks for sending me the Zoom video,' I said, to put him at ease.

He nodded. 'It downloaded fine?'

'Yes, all good; I saw you and Mr Masri on the call. But Saul Cohen joined later?'

'He wasn't needed for the first two hours.'

'How come Mr Ram, Mr Levy and Mr Fleishman weren't on the call?'

'It was with our lawyers and accountants, so we didn't need them. Please keep it confidential. The sale of Aishtar is critical to us, and we can't have anything leak.'

'You and Mr Fleishman appeared to be having an argument earlier?'

Baker considered this. 'Argument?'

'He seemed upset about something.'

'We were discussing Aishtar's captable.'

'Captable?' I said, imagining a coffee table with a baseball cap on it.

'A list of shareholders in Aishtar. He wanted to know when Sid's share would be re-allocated.'

'And?'

'I said we hadn't decided it would.'

'Because?'

We watched him contemplate his answer. 'Wahid wants to bring in another CEO.'

'Oh?' said Tahir. 'I thought he said he'd put Mr Fleishman in as CEO.'

'He's changed his mind. Gaby is very . . . emotional.'

'Who then?' said Tahir.

'Can't say.'

He went back to his watch clasp. Click. Click. Click.

'One of the other founders?' I said.

Baker looked up at me. 'Aishtar needs someone more . . .

financially astute. Gaby is not a numbers man. We have a board meeting shortly. Wahid will decide.'

'Is it you?' I asked.

Baker laughed, his face transforming. '*Me?* I wish! No. I'm a back-room guy. Not a front man.'

'Tell us about the founders,' Tahir said.

'What do you want to know?'

'Did they get on with Mr Ram?'

Baker hesitated and clicked his watch some more. 'As you said, Sid could be difficult. He made several changes they didn't like.'

'Like what?'

'Putting in controls. They were running the business in a free and easy way. Not good for a sale. And he wanted to halve the size of the board. So only one of them would represent all the founders instead of all three.'

'That must have galled,' I said.

'I guess.'

'And which founder did he want to keep on the board?'

'Saul. As CFO, he was the most important.'

That surprised me.

'Not Mr Fleishman?'

'No. Sid didn't see eye-to-eye with Gaby. Saul was more . . . flexible.'

'Flexible, how?'

'More willing to do what Sid wanted without questioning it.'

I glanced at Tahir, hoping for his approval for my next move. I leaned forward to look David Baker directly in the eye. 'Mr Baker, you're an insightful guy. Perspicacious, some might say. You've known them all for a while. If you had to guess, who would you put your money on?'

'To represent them on the board?' He reached for some popcorn.

Tahir clarified my line of questioning, 'Who had the most convincing motive for murdering Mr Ram?'

'None of them.' Baker selected a popcorn kernel of precise size and dimension from his handful, popped it in his mouth, and ate it. 'Ari is a deep thinker but doesn't care about money – he wants to use his tech to solve problems that will transform the world. Gaby is emotional and didn't get on with Sid, but I don't see him as a killer. Saul struck it lucky. Ari's brains and Gaby's sales built Aishtar. They could have had anyone for a CFO. Saul was in the right place at the right time with the right friends. He would not jeopardise his payout.'

His acuity impressed me; he had efficiently filtered some takes that were still percolating in my head.

'How about Yael Klein?' I said, nodding towards her and Ari Levy in the next room, their heads bent over their shared laptop again.

'What about her?'

'She came over with them from Israel, but isn't a founder?'

'No. She is not one of the guys. She is different. They are bros.'

'Bros?' said Tahir.

'Frat boys. Party dudes. Tequila shots and Xbox. Yael's not interested in that.'

'Does she know about the sale?' I asked.

He shrugged.

'Is there something going on between her and Mr Levy?' I said.

His jaw clenched, and he stood up abruptly. 'Why don't you ask her? Now I have to prepare for the board, so if you'll excuse me.'

And without further comment, he got up and walked out.

We watched him go as Tahir said, 'That struck a nerve. All right, let's talk to the others.'

He knocked on the door of the adjoining conference room. Yael Klein and Ari Levy looked up as we entered and shifted apart again, trying to be subtle about it.

'We haven't spoken,' said Tahir to the woman. 'I'm DI Tahir Ismail and this is DC Kamil Rahman. We are investigating the murder of Sid Ram.'

'Yael Klein.' She stood to shake our hands, tall and full-figured, a mass of curly black hair tumbling around her heart-shaped face. 'I run HR for Aishtar.'

'We would like to ask you a few questions, Ms Klein,' I said.

'Of course.'

'Can you tell us where you were on Monday night, between 9 p.m. and midnight?'

She snuck a glance at Levy and said, 'I was at home.'

'Which is where?'

'Bethnal Green.'

'Can anyone vouch for you?'

'No, I was alone.'

'No calls? Nothing?'

'I spoke to Ari. Around 9.30.'

Tahir looked at Ari Levy. 'You didn't mention this when we spoke last time, sir? I thought you said you were in a film at that time?'

'Maybe it was later,' said Yael Klein. 'Maybe after ten.'

'Please check your phone log,' I said.

She made no move to check her phone and looked down at the table.

'Ms Klein, obviously you know we can pull your phone records? Why don't you save us the time and trouble so we can concentrate our resources on finding your colleague's killer. Mr Levy?' said Tahir.

Klein looked at Levy, who sighed and said, 'Okay, we were together. At her flat. I left at ten. I swear.'

'And why did you lie when we asked you about your where-abouts the other day, sir,' said Tahir.

'Why do you *think*? I'm married. I didn't want to drag Yael into all this.'

'How long have you two been . . . seeing each other?' I said.

'About a year,' said Klein.

'And do the others know?'

'The other founders do, yes,' said Levy. 'Not the rest of the staff. At least we don't think so. And definitely not my wife.'

'How about Mr Masri and Mr Baker?'

'I assume so. Yael broke it off with David to be with me.'

That explained David Baker's tone.

'How did he take it?' said Tahir.

'Why is this relevant?' said Klein. 'What is this to do with Sid's death? Sounds like you're just being nosey now.'

'With respect, at this stage, we don't know what is relevant and what's not. We're trying to gather as much info as possible. Like your software. You predict the future by collecting data. We reconstruct the past by doing the same – two sides of the same coin. So, for the second time I will ask you: how did he take it?'

Tahir's quick-fire insights never failed to impress me.

'He was fine,' Klein sighed. 'Although you can never tell with David. You've met him. He's super smart and a lovely person, but not one who shows his feelings much. I just felt I needed more. We are still friends; we go out and have a drink now and then.'

'Is there anything else?' said Levy.

'No,' said Tahir. 'We'll be in touch.'

I felt for David Baker. He had been smitten with this beauti-ful woman, and she'd dumped him for a guy who was going to be a multi-millionaire several times over. I wasn't sure I could have stayed friends if that had happened to me. Maybe I'd have a chance to test this with Maliha. Which reminded me, I had to text her and organise our dinner.

On the way out, I stopped by reception.

'Ms Jennings, can you tell me where you were between 9 p.m. and midnight on Monday evening?'

She looked at me, nervousness in her eyes.

'Why?'

'Strictly routine. We need to know everyone's whereabouts.'

She made a show of thinking hard. Then said, 'Home. I was home.'

'And can anyone vouch for you?'

'No. My flatmate was out. I had some soup, watched telly.'

'What time did you leave work?'

'Around seven?'

'And where do you live?'

'Bermondsey.'

We left, leaving her looking after us, worry etched on her face.

'Well,' said Tahir as he slid the windows of the car down to let the heat out. 'Did that get us any further?'

'Still not clear how the tech does what they say it does, but it sounds impressive enough that someone might kill for it. My instincts say Yael Klein and Ari Levy are telling the truth; if I'm right, it eliminates them. David Baker, Wahid Masri and Saul Cohen were on the Zoom call. Which leaves Miles Merrion, Michelle Jennings and Gaby Fleishman.'

'Or a SMERSH agent working for Blofeld?' Tahir grinned.

I felt my face flush again. 'They didn't discount it, did they?'

'No, they didn't, mate. And you might well be right; we need to find out what SO15 knows. But that weird anti-AI note? Why would an enemy agent toss that after the body?'

'Who knows? Let me try that number Michelle Jennings gave us.'

I dialled, one-handed. 'Switched off. What about this new CEO? He'd have a motive. We should ask Wahid Masri who it is.'

'I'll do it. You shouldn't be on your phone while driving,

Kamil. Honestly! Do you want to kill a member of the – hello, Mr Masri? DI Ismail here. I had a quick question. We heard you had decided not to give the CEO job to Mr Fleishman, but to someone else. Can you tell us who you're proposing? We will keep it confidential . . . I see. Thank you.'

He disconnected. 'Saul Cohen, the CFO, just got even luckier. I can see why Fleishman was pissed off. His co-founder stands to make $200m more than him.'

'Why did Wahid pick him? In the right place at the right time again, as Baker said? Or flexible – whatever that meant.'

Tahir thought for a second. 'First Ram and now Cohen. Fleishman is always the bridesmaid, isn't he?'

My phone pinged, and I glanced down. 'Number that called Aishtar matches nothing we have. They think it's a prepaid burner; could be anyone.'

'Ask them to do some work on the number to see if we can link it to any others that are known to us.'

'On it.'

We were down to a few names now. I was getting confident we'd crack this soon.

Chapter 11

Thursday evening.

After a frustrating day with little progress made, I got home just before nine. I unknotted my tie, and I could breathe again. I'd been used to a more casual dress code in Kolkata. And this brand-new wool suit had turned out not to be one of Anjoli's most helpful ideas in the middle of a heat wave.

I texted Maliha as I went down to the restaurant to grab a bite to eat.

How about dinner this Sunday?

She came back in a few seconds.

Fab! Look forward to it. Let me know where. My stomach did a flip.

Tandoori Knights was half empty and Anjoli was behind the bar.

'How was your day?' The ice in the cocktail shaker rattled as she shook it.

'Not great. A lot of dead ends. Quiet tonight?'

'A few more coming in. Oh, did you tell me last night that a David Baker was one of your suspects?'

'Why?'

'Someone with that name just ordered some takeaway for collection,' she said, pouring a deep red drink into a tall glass. 'Do you think it could be your guy?'

'Maybe. I met him at the Aishtar office today. How many David Bakers can there be in a square mile?'

I glanced absently at Maliha's text as an idea wormed its way into my brain. 'Listen, do me a favour. Don't have his food ready yet. Give me a little time with him. I might be able to tease out some extra info.'

She handed the drink to a passing waiter. 'All right. As long as you tell me all about it. Clear that table for me, will you? I'll bring you a 'mosa in a sec to tide you over.'

Ten minutes later, Baker entered, walked up to the bar, and told Anjoli, 'I ordered takeaway, David Baker.'

I got up from my seat and approached him. 'Hi, Mr Baker. Well, this is a coincidence.'

He frowned and said, 'Are you following me?'

I shook my head. 'No, of course not. I used to work here. Anjoli here was my boss.'

She smiled. 'Sorry, we're really busy. Your food will be a few minutes.' And then looked at him and tilted her head. 'Hang on. I know you. You've eaten here before, right?'

'A couple of times. In fact, I had a birthday dinner here a few years ago. The night before you had some big fire. I saw you've changed the menu; thought I'd try it out again.'

'I knew I recognised you!'

'Oh wow,' I said. 'I cooked for that party!'

'The fire was your fault, huh? Y'know what they say: can't stand the heat, stay out the kitchen,' said Baker.

Anjoli's face fell. I reached over, squeezed her hand, and said, 'I'm afraid one of our waiters perished that evening.'

'I'm sorry, I didn't know. You looked after us so well at the party.' He glanced at me. 'You were actually a chef? And now you're a detective?'

'It's a long story. Listen, if you were eating alone at home, why don't you just have your food here? I haven't had dinner yet either.'

'Oh no, I've already ordered and have a lot on and . . .'

'It's fine.' I led him to a table by his elbow. 'Anjoli will just bring you what you ordered when it's ready; you might as well have it here while it's hot.'

'Well, um . . . alright.'

He sat opposite me in a booth. I ordered us two beers, and some crispened potatoes – Chanson's fancy name for pakora-style chips – and sous-vide chicken with fenugreek. We toasted, and I asked, 'How was your board meeting?'

'Fine. We installed our new CEO.'

'Saul Cohen, right?'

He shot me a glance and said, 'Yes.'

'How did Mr Fleishman take it? You said he was expecting to get the role?'

He sipped his beer. 'Not great. But he knows it isn't personal.'

'He must have been pretty pissed off with Mr Ram when he took over?'

Another sip as Baker considered his words. He looked uncomfortable. 'He wasn't . . . happy. With Sid or Wahid. He was quite vocal about it. And Sid didn't try to placate him. He could have made him his deputy. Given him some genuine power. Instead, he appointed him CMO for a stealth company that did no marketing.'

I laughed. 'Sounds like an obvious motive to me.'

Baker looked at me, opened his mouth to reply, then appeared to have a rethink. A moment later, he said, 'It would surprise me. Gaby's pretty money-oriented and wouldn't jeopardise his payout. Killing Sid could put the sale in danger.'

'But he might have thought he would become CEO again?'

'Well, Wahid decided differently.'

'He did. Is Mr Fleishman staying on the board? Mr Ram wanted to reduce the size, no?'

'Yes, we all are. Wahid thinks it will cause too much friction to make it smaller now.'

'I understand. Will Mr Cohen now make more money than the other founders, then?'

Baker paused, took a pakora chip and said, 'I shouldn't be talking about this.'

I let him eat his food in silence. 'These are good,' he said, taking another. 'So crunchy. Yes. Saul will get more.'

Giving him some space paid off, as I knew it would. This was a delicate slow dance, best performed without Tahir's heavy feet tripping me up. Maybe if I could get him to drink some more . . . I picked up another crispy potato, dipped it into the green coriander dip and then passed the bowl to him. 'Try it with this, adds a whole different garlic dimension . . .'

He scooped a dollop of chutney onto a chip and ate it in one mouthful. 'Jesus, that's hot!' He drained his beer in two gulps.

I got up and fetched him another. As he knocked it back, I laughed and said, 'Well, looks like Mr Fleishman and Mr Levy will both make over a hundred million dollars anyway, right? What difference would doubling it make? From loads to shitloads?'

His laugh echoed mine. 'That's what I said. Gaby said he wanted to buy a yacht like Wahid's!'

'Rich-people problems.'

'I know, right?'

'Does Mr Masri have an issue with Israelis? Is that why he installed Mr Ram in the first place?'

Baker shook his head emphatically. The two beers had done their job and loosened him up. 'Look, Wahid is a very proud Palestinian. His history is important to him – it made him. His experience growing up in the camps was difficult. And yes, the Israeli state is responsible for what happened. But you have to believe me. When it comes to business, he doesn't think that way. He likes to make money, first and foremost.'

He clearly believed this, but Wahid Masri was his mentor. I wasn't sure it was that simple. I was seeing Indian Muslims becoming second-class citizens in their own country and knew from experience it cut deep.

'I saw that you and he were on that Zoom call all evening. There was no way he could have left? Part of the call that wasn't recorded or something?'

'You've seen the video. I ran that conference and Wahid was there, contributing all through it.'

'You're certain?'

'He was sitting at his desk at home throughout.'

I nodded. *Check, double check, no regret* had been drilled into me for the last two years.

Our main dishes arrived. Soft-shell crunchy crabs with spices and figs for him and the chicken for me accompanied by a basket of naans.

'This is excellent,' said Baker as he dipped into his seafood.

I felt a surge of pride – that dish was my invention and one of the few things Chanson had deigned to keep from the menu's last iteration.

'Guess you don't get that much Indian food in the US? Is that where you're from?'

He nodded. 'Austin, Texas.'

'How did you end up in London?'

'Met Wahid at MIT. He persuaded me to join Bethlehem.'

'And are you a partner in the firm?'

'No. Just a principal.' He paused. 'But hopefully soon . . . If we have a successful sale, then Wahid can raise a new fund and he says I'm in pole position to run that. I've been waiting for a while. So, fingers crossed.'

'And toes.' We clinked glasses. 'How long have you been in the UK now?'

'Five years, eight months.'

I wasn't sure where I was going with this, but my instincts said that David Baker would be a helpful person to have on side if I could draw him out.

'Me too, just about. Do you miss the US?'

He shrugged. 'I'm fine, as long as I have my own things around me. My stuff from Austin took a while to arrive, but once it did, I was comfortable.'

I nodded agreement. 'I hear you. I'm from Kolkata and miss that too. Although living in Brick Lane is a bit like home, anyway.'

'You live on Brick Lane?'

'Right above this restaurant.'

He laughed. 'That *is* local.'

I beckoned Anjoli over. 'Two more beers, please. And the gajar ka halwa. You must try that carrot dessert, it's delicious, and it comes with Assam chai-flavoured ice cream. Chef calls it Chaice Cream, get it?'

He rolled his eyes. 'Are you two . . . you know?' he said as she disappeared.

Why did everyone assume that? 'No, we're just close friends. How about you? Anyone special in your life?'

I could sense him tense up.

'No.'

'I heard you used to go out with Ms Klein? At Aishtar?'

Staring down at his plate, he picked at the remnants of his crab.

'Yup.'

'What happened?'

'Nothing. She's with Ari now. He's more her type. Jewish. Israeli. We're still friends.'

It sounded like he was repeating what Yael Klein had told him when they split. I felt sorry for him and could identify. Came to a different country, was lonely, wanted familiar things around him. Then found someone who liked him and lost her. Although I hadn't lost Anjoli. She was never mine to lose.

I attempted to lighten the mood. 'Maybe you should try Aishtar's dating app? I've heard it's very effective.'

'Good idea.' He smiled as Anjoli brought our desserts and beers.

'Do you think it's possible that it *could* be a hostile state after the Aishtar technology?' I asked.

He chewed on the carrot dessert and said, 'Anything's possible.'

'What I don't understand is why this huge secrecy about what you guys do? If you're helping catch criminals, that's a good thing, right?'

'It could be . . . misunderstood.' He looked at his watch. 'I'm sorry, I need to go. Let me call an Uber and get the check.'

I made a scribbly sign for the bill to Anjoli as he fired up his app. We sat in an awkward silence for a moment, then he said, 'This dessert was excellent. So, tell me how you went from being a cook to a detective.'

Another warm glow. That sweet had also been one of mine. This guy had good taste. Literally. I gave him my potted history and how Anjoli had been my saviour, and he listened in fascination. After I finished, he said, 'That is some journey. Congratulations. You should be proud of yourself. And your Anjoli seems like quite a woman.'

'She is. And here she is with your bill.'

'And my Uber's also arrived. Perfect timing. Add on a 25% tip, please. DC Rahman has been singing your praises.' He tapped Anjoli's machine with a Platinum Amex.

'Ooh, thanks so much, David. I hope Kamil wasn't a bother,' said Anjoli.

'It's been fun . . . thank you.'

He gave her a smile and left.

*

I went up to the flat and got ready for bed. Anjoli popped her head into the bathroom as I was brushing my teeth and said, 'Seemed like a nice chap. Did you get what you wanted?'

'Every bit helps.' I rinsed my mouth. 'There's something different about this case.' I lowered my voice. 'It may involve MI5.'

'Shit, really?' Her eyes widened. She put a finger to her lips, got up and unplugged the Alexa speaker on my bedside table.

'Seriously?'

'Of course! You're so naïve, Kamil. Tell me more.'

'It's possible foreign powers are after the tech and the security services are involved. It's quite exciting, makes me feel a bit like James Bond.'

'Be careful. Things have changed a lot since Brexit. The Home Office is properly hardcore now. You need to ensure you don't give them any excuse.'

'Excuse for what?'

'To deport you!'

'Oh. Tahir said the same thing. We could always get married to make sure.'

'Yeah, right.'

I'd kept my nose clean, had an Indefinite Leave to Remain in the UK and was a year away from getting my British passport. The jitters of knowing my fate was in some bureaucrat's hands never disappeared, but as the months passed, I was feeling more and more like an official Londoner.

'I'll be fine, no tension. Any news from Dr Grayson about your skeletons?'

'Not yet.' She sat on the bed beside me, making me pleasurably tense. 'It was awful seeing their remains, collected all together. Who would shoot a child?'

'It was a different time, I guess.' But it wasn't. I'd never told Anjoli about some of the horrific cases I'd come across in Kolkata – baby girls drowned; young children of both sexes raped, and the perpetrators never brought to justice. Death was always terrible, but the killing of a kid . . .

She shivered. 'Did you invite Maliha over for dinner?'

'I've arranged to meet her. Not here though.'

'Why not?'

I shrugged. 'Needed a change. Anyway, why are you so keen to see her?'

'She's here alone. She doesn't know anyone – she may need friends.'

Maybe the time had come.

'Anjoli,' I said.

'What?'

'Do you think we should talk?'

'What about?'

'Us.'

She squeezed her eyes shut. 'We're fine as we are.'

'Are we?'

'Aren't we?'

'Well, you know how I feel and . . .'

She stood up, walked to the window, and opened it.

'It's stifling in here. How do you cope?'

'Stop changing the subject.'

'What about Maliha?' she said.

'What about her?'

She seemed uncharacteristically nervous as she wandered around the room, straightening objects.

'Well, she's here now. And you never resolved things with her.'

I took the plunge.

'I'm asking you point blank. Is there a chance of us being together or not? I can't wait for ever.'

'I *never* asked you to wait.'

That was the problem with Anjoli. She was always fine. Even

when she wasn't. It was tiring to work out what was going on inside her head.

'You have to let me in.'

She stopped her tidying up and sat next to me on the bed. Then took my hand and said, 'All right. So maybe things have changed. I . . .'

My phone rang. Fuck.

'Take it,' she said and handed it to me.

Reluctantly, I answered.

'Kamil? It's Tahir. There's been another death. Meet me at Flat 4, 23 Rochelle Street.'

Chapter 12

Thursday night.

It wasn't hard to find the flat – there were three police cars sitting in front of the redbrick building and even though it was ten to midnight, there were a couple dozen civilians lined up on the pavement trying to see what was going on. The constable guarding the entrance in a hi-vis yellow police vest was Paul Gooch. 'Hi, Goochy,' I said as I showed him my warrant card. He nodded, and I walked up the stairs to the first floor. Tahir was standing outside the flat's front door, dressed in coveralls, talking to the pathologist, Dr Grayson.

'Oh good, you're here,' he said.

'Who's the victim?'

'Saul Cohen. It's a shitshow. Put on your gear and come in. What's that?'

'My murder rucksack,' I said. 'We were told to have one prepared in our training.'

He laughed and said to Grayson, 'Aww, isn't he sweet? Did you bring your copy of PACE as well?'

I felt my face go red as Grayson and one of the PCs guffawed, then slipped into my protective clothing and followed Tahir into the flat. I noted that the front door lock didn't look broken.

CSI were doing their job: yellow evidence markers scattered like Legos across the floor; a technician walking around, softly describing the scene on video. I saw two deep maroon leather sofas and a coffee table on top of a colourful rug. Saul Cohen's body was lying face down in front of a drinks trolley behind a sofa. He was dressed in shorts and a T-shirt, his glasses in the blood pooled around his head, steel frames twisted and bent, lenses uncracked. My stomach clenched as bile rose and I regretted the two beers.

'Shot in the back of the head at close range,' said Grayson. 'In the last hour.'

'The door wasn't forced,' I said. 'It's possible he knew the killer and let them in, especially given the way he's dressed. Was going to get them a drink and . . . bam.'

'Bam indeed,' said Tahir. 'And we may have the murderer in the next room.'

'What?'

'Follow me.'

We entered the adjoining room to find Gaby Fleishman sitting on the bed.

'Thanks for waiting, Mr Fleishman,' said Tahir. 'As you can see, my colleague is here now. Could you tell him what you told me?'

Fleishman looked pale, a glass of water trembling in his hand, blood on his sleeve. 'I . . . I . . . He . . .' He took a sip, composed himself and said, 'Saul texted me about an hour ago and asked me to come over. I got here around eleven and rang the bell, but there was no answer. Someone leaving the building let me in. I went up to the flat, saw the door was open, came in and found Saul dead. I called 999 and waited. Then your people arrived and told me to wait for you.'

'Who was it who let you in?' I said.

'Some guy, I don't know.'

'Can you describe him?'

'Around six foot. White. Baseball cap. I only saw him for a split second.'

'Why did Mr Cohen ask you to come?'

'Here's his text.' Fleishman pulled out his phone, hand shaking, and gave it to me.

Gaby, come over asap. I've found some irregularities. Need to discuss urgently. Am waiting.

'Why do you have blood on your sleeve?' said Tahir, pointing.

Fleishman looked at the patch on his jacket and rubbed at it. 'I felt for a pulse in Saul's neck. But it was quite . . . quite obvious someone had shot him. His body was warm. It must have just happened.'

'And you touched nothing else?'

'There was an envelope next to him. I picked it up and put it to one side. Fuck! Fuck! I can't believe this. First Sid and now . . . what the fuck is happening?'

'That's what we are trying to find out,' said Tahir. 'Okay, please wait here.'

We went back into the living room.

'Was there an envelope near the body?' said Tahir.

'Yeah,' said an officer. He handed Tahir an evidence bag with the envelope in it. Tahir opened it and extracted an A4 sheet. Typed on it was,

```
Today humans exist vicariously in computer
terminals. It must stop.
```

Tahir glanced at me. I said, 'Any sign of his phone? Or a laptop?'

'His phone is here.' The cop waved another bag at us. 'No laptop. Or the murder weapon.'

'Get uniform to check CCTV and question the neighbours,' Tahir told me. 'See if we can find the guy Fleishman said let him in.'

'Do you believe him?' I said.

Tahir shrugged. 'Fuck knows. I'll take him back to the station and grill him. We'll search him, swab his clothes for gunshot residue, and check if the blood staining fits his account of what he says happened.'

'It's the same MO as Ram's. Could still be an enemy agent after the laptop.'

'Blofeld? But why would Cohen let him into the flat and make him a drink? Why would he text Fleishman to come over? What are the irregularities he said he found? There's something screwy here.'

'I spoke to David Baker earlier at TK. He didn't mention any irregularities.'

'What do you mean?'

I told Tahir about my dinner with Baker. 'He said Fleishman was pissed off with Ram and with the fact that Saul Cohen got this CEO job. He thought it should have been his. And he was annoyed Cohen was going to make more money than him.'

'Well,' he said, when I finished. I couldn't tell if it was a *good* 'well' or a *What the fuck do you think you're doing* 'well'. 'Maybe TK should be the venue of choice for questioning from now on. Answer a question, get a samosa. For fuck's sake, Kamil.' Tahir shook his head. 'Anyway, it puts Baker in the vicinity. See what we can find about his movements after he left the restaurant. I'll take Fleishman in – you get on with stuff here.'

As he led Fleishman out, I heard him asking, 'Do you know the code for Mr Cohen's iPhone?'

'Yes. It's 314159. I've seen him input it many times.'

'Does that number have any significance?'

'It's pi. Saul thought he was being clever, even though Ari told him it was an obvious code. He uses the same on his laptop.'

Obvious? These nerds were a different breed from normal people. But this was their time – they were the gajillionaire overlords. We were just a commodity in their tech utopia to be tracked and traced and bought and sold to companies who would, in turn, sell us goods we didn't know we didn't want. I texted Anjoli, told her not to expect me back, and went down to the street to instruct the PCs.

Gooch was still standing at his position at the entrance to the flats. 'Goochy,' I said. 'I need you and some others to search the surrounding streets. Tahir thinks it's possible the killer may have dumped the gun. We also have to do a house-to-house in the morning.'

He looked right through me, then turned his back to talk to a colleague.

'Paul?' I repeated, wondering if he hadn't heard. Still nothing.

This was weird. Had I offended him? He'd been a garrulous jokey guy when he was showing me the ropes. There were another two PCs standing a few metres away, and I walked up to them and reiterated my request. To my astonishment, I got the same response – they ignored me and continued to talk to each other.

I was at a loss. Was this a race thing? Then it clicked. I was the newbie, straight out of training, and brown to boot. These guys had been in uniform for a few years, and I was giving *them* orders. Who the hell did I think I was? I felt the anger building inside me – I'd been a sub-inspector in the police while these dickheads were still in school. I'd seen more policing and solved more crimes than they had, combined.

The exhilaration of my new role drained away. Was this the picture of my future in the Met? It wasn't my fault Tahir had taken me on as his number two. Should I ring him and get him to give them a bollocking?

Fuck it. I would do the job myself. I pulled out my torch and shone it into a recycling bin in front of the building.

It was going to be a long, sweltering, bloody night.

Chapter 13

Friday morning.

Reeling with rage, exhausted and smelling rank after fruit-less hours of rummaging through bins and hedges while the PCs ignored me, I got back home after 3 a.m. It would all have to be redone in the morning when we had the manpower and I could have left it till then but had wanted to show I was prepared to roll up my sleeves and get myself dirty with the rest of the constables. Not that it achieved anything other than a total loss of self-confidence.

I tiptoed to the bathroom, showered, and slid into bed, trying not to wake Anjoli in the next room, hoping for a few hours of sleep before I'd have to crawl into the office. I *had* to earn the respect of the team. We may have missed vital evidence Fleish-man had disposed of because of my colleagues' attitudes. I'd known Protheroe was pissed with my jumping rank but hadn't realised how widespread the rancour was. I could almost hear the whispered discussions in the canteen – fucking Indian waiter, Muslim as well, right out of college, catapulted above a dozen people who had been waiting their turn because of favour-itism from another brown bastard.

The air in the bedroom felt thick as ghee. Anjoli's snores next door were a fly buzzing in my ear. I was sweating. I pulled off my T-shirt and lay on my back on top of the sheet. Distant thun-der. Perhaps this hot spell was breaking?

I tried to enter a state of calm and allow my head to flood with dreams of any kind – nightmares, fantasies, half-true reminiscences – at this stage I wasn't fussy, I was just desperate for oblivion in order to function the next day. However, my hyperactive brain could only find doors to new thoughts, and each one led to another.

Gaby Fleishman. Did he do it? My instincts said no. How could he have got rid of the gun and laptop after calling the police? There *was* a motive. But it would have been easier for him to have shot Saul Cohen and left – although if he had been seen coming into the block of flats, it would have been suspicious. And what the hell was that nonsensical anti-AI note?

Anjoli continued to snore in the next room. On wintry nights I had fantasised about opening the door, going into her room, and slipping into her bed to have her internal mini Anjuclear reactor warm me up – her body always seemed to radiate heat. But that type of confident macho-ness was beyond me. Tahir might have done it. What had she wanted to say to me? What was happening with her? I had tried to give her the support she needed after Saibal and Maya had succumbed to Covid. I'd been patient and gentle with her, but months had passed. I fooled myself into thinking she was over it and would come to me of her own accord. But she was still in some sort of distress. Unmoored. I wished I could row her back to shore. To me. As I heard her soft breathing, a flood of grief rose to surprise me, and I felt hot tears welling in my eyes.

Maliha.

Things had ended in an ugly manner between us in India six years ago. Although she was the one who had broken off our engagement, it had been a result of the terrible way I had treated her after they had fired me from the Kolkata police. I'd always regretted my behaviour. Maybe this was my chance to make it up to her. Meet up. Slide *her* back into my life. As a friend. Or more?

I missed her, feeling a sting of regret whenever I thought of her. She still had a hold over me, which was natural, given the seven years we'd had together. She was very different from Anjoli – more straightforward, whereas with Anjoli, everything was a puzzle that had to be solved. Perhaps it was because Maliha and I were 'properly' Indian and Muslim as opposed to Anjoli, who, for all of her outward Indianness, was very much a first-generation Brit. And an atheist.

Aargh! I needed to talk to someone to clarify my feelings. Tahir was no good. Maybe the imam?

Enough. I couldn't afford to go down this emotional rabbit hole. I had to stay focussed on one thing and one thing only.

I slipped out of bed and went into the kitchen, opened the laptop and googled 'Aishtar'. The first thing that popped up was an article in the day's *Guardian*.

**The United Kingdom of North Korea,
Iran and China:
How Aishtar's algorithms are tracking you 24/7**

by Miles Merrion

'The connectivity that is the heart of globalisation can be exploited by states with hostile intent to further their aims. The risks at stake are profound and represent a fundamental threat to our sovereignty.'
Alex Younger, Former Head of MI6

In an unprepossessing warehouse in Shoreditch, Ian is staring at his computer screen. But what he is seeing is not the usual desktop with scattered icons and opened documents. He is seeing through Jamal's eyes. Jamal is

---

watching a YouTube video of a daredevil skier crashing into a tree that was sent to him by his friend Ramy. In another window on Ian's screen, he sees Jamal's reaction to the video through the camera on his laptop. Jamal laughs, clicks off the video and dashes off a quick email to Ramy – *Excellent, bro!* – then navigates to a porn site and searches for 'Swedish girls'. As Jamal's breathing quickens, Ian secretly videos him as he masturbates, simultaneously logging the heartbeat on Jamal's smartwatch.

Ian turns his attention to Jamal's phone and reads his latest WhatsApps, looks at recent pictures he took on a trip to Istanbul, and peruses his bank statements. Click. He can now listen to recordings of everything Jamal has been saying to his wife in their house through their smart speaker. Click. Another window opens on Ian's computer, and he tracks Jamal's journey through his city via the face-recognition-enabled CCTV cameras and doorbell cameras he passed on his way to the underground that morning. Click. Ian can track Jamal's exit from the train via his monthly pass. Click. His withdrawal of cash at the ATM.

Click. Another tab and Ian is now in Jamal's work computer – looking at documents in the law office where he is employed. When Jamal leaves work, a drone the size of an insect is hovering outside his office – it follows him into the mosque he goes to, silently videoing the people he speaks to.

All of this data is stitched together, and Ian has a complete picture of Jamal's life. In real time.

My eyes widened as I read this. Was *this* what Aishtar's software did? Track *everything* a person did – on and offline? All that wild-goat bullshit. No *wonder* they were keeping it quiet. It read like science fiction. How had Merrion found out? I carried on reading.

Jamal is not in Damascus, Teheran or PyongYang. He is a British citizen in London, being spied on by his own government. And he has done nothing wrong. If anything has a keyboard, a microphone, a camera or a sensor, it knows where Jamal is, what he is doing, and adds it to his profile. And Ian can see it all. But this isn't Big Brother watching you. It's hundreds of millions of little brothers and it is being done without the government obtaining an official warrant to track you.

The software Ian is using was written by an Israeli company called Aishtar. It ties together every electronic (and often non-electronic) footprint a 'subject of interest' may leave and recreates their life on a laptop. And if you thought that was terrifying – here's the clincher. It isn't just backward-looking – showing the unknown watchers what you have already done or are doing. Based on your activities, Aishtar predicts what you might do in the future. And if the software says you might commit a crime, it informs the watcher. 'Watcher' is a misnomer, because unlike Ian, no one is watching. The software invisibly tracks millions of people and only when it flags you as a potential criminal does a human get involved.

And after that? The Terrorism Act of 2000 was amended last year on Home Secretary Priscilla Patrick's behest to allow preventative detention of up to one year on the suspicion you might be a terrorist. There is no oversight. This software can track the entire British population if that is what the government wishes. It could be watching you reading this very article on our website at this moment.

I shivered, then scrabbled around for a Post-it, stuck it on top of the laptop's camera and continued.

> Ian's name has been changed to protect his identity. He has now left Aishtar as he couldn't live with what they were doing. He told me, 'In the epic of Gilgamesh, Ishtar weeps when humanity is destroyed. Today everyone is addicted to screens. AI and heuristics can manipulate objective reality and make us believe things that are not true – look at the deepfake videos around now. AI will kill humanity, and Aishtar will be the weapon. It has to be stopped.'

Wide awake now, I reread the last line, made a note. Who was this Ian? We *had* to find him. I kept reading.

> Aishtar's CEO, Sid Ram, was murdered four days ago outside his home in East London. Ram was the successful founder of Thrumyeyes.com, which allowed users to experience a day in the life of a celebrity. Ian said, 'This is what Aishtar is doing next. It will allow a watcher to live the virtual life of a fanatic. Or will it be an innocent person suspected of being a terrorist? A journalist the government doesn't like? A dissident? A member of the opposing party? Big Brother is here, now, in your home, your office, your gym . . . everywhere.'

'What are you doing? It's five o'clock,' said Anjoli, startling me. I looked around to see her standing behind me, rubbing her eyes, hair tousled around her face like a sleepy monsoon cloud. She was wearing an oversized T-shirt that came halfway down her bare thighs, reading *If you can read this, you are too close (Wear a Mask)*.

'Sorry, I couldn't sleep. Go back to bed.'

'I'm up now.' She rested her hands on my shoulders and peered at my screen. 'Is that about Aishtar?'

'Yes. Someone shot their CFO last night. Actually, he was their new CEO.'

'Shit.'

'Look at this. It's terrifying. I can see why they wanted to keep it quiet.' I passed her the laptop. How many of us were being spied on? Was I being watched? I could feel the fingers of paranoia creeping up my neck.

'Bloody hell, Kamil,' she said after she had finished.

'I know.'

'I mean, I was always suspicious, but the scale of . . . fuck.'

'I know.'

'Can they do this?'

I shrugged.

'How can it be legal?'

Another shrug.

'We have to stop it.'

'I'm trying to catch the guy who wants to stop it.'

She clicked around. 'Look. People are tweeting about the article already.'

'Do these tweeters never sleep?'

Unbelievable #bigbrother

We should march #bigbrother

Have to stop this #bigbrother

I needed to get our Cyber people onto this – our murderer might post here as well. I scanned the article again. There was no way that could be a coincidence. I had to talk to Tahir.

'I've got to go in.'

'So early?'

'I need to figure out something. Had a crappy night yesterday and have to sort it.'

'Why? What happened?'

124

I told her about being ignored by the other PCs.

'That's unacceptable. You should report them.'

'I can't go running to the boss any time there's trouble. Makes me look weak. I'll fix it.'

'Tahir put you in this situation. He should fix it.'

'Maybe.'

I wondered whether to restart our conversation of the night before, but she said, 'I got some news about the skeletons – Dr Grayson's lab dated them! Between 1900 and 1920. She said the police wouldn't be interested.'

'So, is she planning to have them buried?'

'I guess so. Or sent to a museum.'

'Did they find out any more about them?'

'They had poor nutrition and rotten teeth, which was normal for that time. But ... I don't know ...' She looked away and filled the kettle. That was typical of Anjoli. To start a sentence and then stop, implying she thought I wasn't interested.

'What?' I said, trying to sound attentive, not distracted.

'It kind of made them real people for me. It's sad we're never going to find out who they are.' She switched on the kettle and started prepping two mugs.

'Can't they do a DNA analysis or something?'

'She says they can, but the police won't pay for it. It costs a few grand. Could you persuade Tahir to fund it?'

'Not a chance. I'm sorry, Anjoli.'

She stared at her nails. 'Yeah, I know. Do you think ...'

'What?'

'That I should pay to have a DNA analysis done?'

'What? No. Why?'

'I don't know. I feel I owe it to them somehow.'

'It's a hell of a lot of money.'

'You're right. Forget it. I'm being stupid.'

I watched her as she carried on making the tea, stirring the milk in slow circles. This mattered to her. Maybe it was some way to atone for not being there when her parents had died. She needed this.

I softened my tone. 'I think it's a good idea. I'll chip in. What better thing to spend my first salary on?'

Her face lit up.

'Are you sure? Is it a crazy thing to do?'

'Yes, it is. But that doesn't mean you shouldn't do it.'

She thought for a second, then said, 'Okay. I'm doing it! This is exciting. I'll call her right now.'

I laughed. Anjoli was never one to put off till tomorrow something she could do yesterday. I couldn't remember the last time I'd seen her so enthused. 'Anjoli, it's not morning yet!'

She looked at the clock on the wall. 'Oh yeah. I'll wait for her to wake up. Thanks, Kamil.'

She gave me a kiss on the cheek and bounced off to the bedroom with her tea. Anjoli, in hyperactive mode, would make cocaine jumpy. Never mind cold cases. The dead family she was trying to resurrect was deep frozen in the Siberian permafrost. But if anyone could solve a hundred-year-old murder, she could. And if it cost a few thousand pounds to make her happy, well, she was worth it.

But now I had to show Tahir what I'd found.

Poor Jews' Temporary Shelter, Leman St,
Whitechapel, London
15 December 1905

Darling Shoshi,

We are here! With God's mercy, we are
here, yes. But it was a terrible,
terrible journey. It has been twenty
days since we left Muter and Tate and
they were happy and sad to see us go.
But Shoshi, it was so difficult to leave
them. We wanted to bring them with us,
but Tate was not well enough to travel.
Maybe we can send for them once we
settle, and he is better.
  We took a train to Vilnius and from
there to Libau and we waited there for
days till we got a berth on a steamship
to London. Those six days on the ship
were the worst time of my life. It was
cold, and the sea was rough, and I was
so seasick I could not stop vomiting.
And the smell, Shoshi, the smell of all
the people - there must have been over a
hundred of us crammed together under the
deck with no toilet. Up top was no
better, with the stink of the thick
black smoke from the funnels. There were
horses on the deck above us and shit
would fall on our heads. I cannot
describe it. I hope you and Semyon had
an easier time of it on your journey.

Can you believe one family on the boat
with us thought the destination was New
York! The ticket seller cheated them and
put them on the wrong boat. I do not
know what happened to them; I hope they
made it to America.

As for us, when finally we arrived in
St Katharine Docks in London, even then
no relief. We disembarked from the ship,
and a man bumped into us and snatched
Avram's suitcase out of his hands. He
just ran off and disappeared into the
crowds! Imagine it. All our most
precious belongings gone! Shoshi, it was
the worst feeling. But Avram was so
philosophical, as he always is - we came
into the world with nothing, he said,
and now we have come to this new world
with nothing. HaShem will provide. I'm
sure he will, in the end. But until
then, we have to find a way ourselves.

So, we greeners are here now. The first
thing we did on our arrival was to find
the shul to shake ourselves after our
journey.

We are staying in the Poor Jews'
Temporary Shelter - I had never thought
I would call myself a poor Jew, but
here we are. All the English call us
Pinsky because they cannot pronounce our
names. It is funny. Avram doesn't mind,
but for me it is yet one more insult to
bear.

Maybe I can come and see you in
Manchester or you can visit me here – I
still don't know how far away it is.
London is so big. I will write again
soon but wanted to tell you we are here.
Please write back, I long to hear
from you.

With all my love,

Malka (Pinsky!)

Chapter 14

Friday morning.

The distant rumble of the previous night proved illusory. No thunderstorm had broken the heat, which was sultry as ever. I loosened my tie, put my jacket over my shoulder and speed-walked the mile and a half to the station, passing the workers who kept the city running – binmen, road sweepers, baristas, newspaper vendors. I was part of these essential services now, unnoticed, and unremarked upon by the public until something went wrong – then we were their knights in shining armour. Well, a Tandoori Knight in my case. I stopped at a newsagent, bought a copy of the *Guardian*, and continued on my way.

The incident room was empty when I arrived. I got to my desk to find someone had left a paper chef's hat, 'Korma King' emblazoned on it in bright red letters, perched on my monitor. I damped down my bubbling anger and resisted the temptation to ball it up and throw it into the bin. Instead, I lifted it and put it on my anglepoise lamp. Turn the badgering into a badge of honour.

I started work, keeping an eye open for Tahir. Protheroe sloped in just after eight and said, 'If it isn't the nut in Operation Nutmeg. Heard you had some problems with uniform last night.'

The penny dropped. He must have put the PCs up to it; wound them up about me stealing their jobs. Well, I wouldn't give him the satisfaction.

'Not sure what you're talking about, Sergeant. Tahir called me to a murder scene. How was your evening?'

He scowled. 'Went for a curry. Not at your gaff, though. That was your line of work, wasn't it?' He gestured to the toque, which was almost certainly his doing.

'Yep. Solved a bunch of murders while working at Tandoori Knights. Let me know next time you want an Indian – I'll get you a discount.'

His look could have created an iceberg in the Bay of Bengal as he skulked off to his desk. The incident room filled with coppers, banter and the smell of coffee. But still no Tahir. Half an hour later, he walked in, and I marched into his office.

'Did you find anything?' he said as I shut the door. 'Have they started the house-to-house?'

'Not yet, boss. Listen, I found—'

'Why not?'

I came clean. 'I'm having a little hassle with uniform. They aren't keen to take orders from me.'

His jaw tightened as he flung open the office door and announced, 'Listen up. As of today, DC Rahman is Acting Detective Sergeant. You got that? He reports directly to me, and you lot do what he says. If I hear of any trouble, it'll be a disciplinary matter. This is a fucking murder enquiry, not a school playground.'

Silence greeted his words and half a dozen pairs of eyes machine-gunned me. Fuck. They would think I had asked Tahir to do this, and it would cement their views about favouritism. A DC *did not* become an ADS on his first week on the job. My boss's impulsive gesture was going to make things worse, not better. They would *have* to cooperate now, but I would get the minimum they could give without them risking misconduct charges and I would be excluded from their group.

Tahir shut his door. I had to talk to him but couldn't leave this edict hanging. I faced the troops. 'I'm sorry about that, guys. I didn't ask him to . . . anyway, let's get this show on the road. We need to get a proper search done outside the flats. You,' I pointed, 'please arrange a search team to come here for a briefing – we must try to find the missing gun and laptop. I looked around last night, but it was too dark to pick anything out. Knock up the neighbours – see if anyone heard the shot. Our suspect, Gaby Fleishman, said someone let him into the building – white guy, six foot, baseball cap. See if we can locate him and corroborate his statement. And let's look for any CCTV, Ring doorbells, and the like. Finally, we should check on the victim's relationships – girlfriend, boyfriend, parents. Keep me posted. Goochy, would you mind co-ordinating things at the scene?'

Gooch, the cop who had ignored me the previous night, looked at me stone-faced, then nodded. It would take a while to unpick Protheroe's stitch-up.

I went back into Tahir's office and said, 'Okay, boss. It's under control. Listen, I wanted to—'

'No bloody luck with Fleishman.' He ran his hands through his hair. 'We questioned him long and hard under caution but had to let him go. Couldn't find a reason to hold him. They are checking his clothes for the blood and GSR. CSI found the bullet lodged in a wall – again, shot through a suppressor. They think it's the same gun that killed Ram. We got the calls and messages from Saul Cohen's phone – he sent a message to Fleishman at 10.50 asking him to come over. Before that, he got a call at 10.31 and spoke for five minutes. We have the number, but the phone's off. Here's the call log. Get them onto it.'

I glanced at the printout he gave me and, suddenly, the *Guardian* article seemed less important.

'Boss, the call Saul Cohen received. It's from 07809 324719.'

'And?'

'That's the same number that called Aishtar. The guy who said he was Merrion.'

'Shit, really?'

'Yes, look.' I showed him my notebook.

'So, the same person calls Sid Ram and Saul Cohen just before they died.' Tahir started scribbling on a Post-it. I could make out a question mark with arrows leading to two stick figures labelled Ram and Cohen. 'And Cohen texts Gaby Fleishman to say there is a problem and he should meet him. Fleishman said he arrived at eleven, so . . .' He added a figure for Fleishman and the diagram became a rudimentary flow chart.

I was lost. 'What are you thinking, boss?'

'Okay. Two possibilities. Fleishman was the guy who called from a burner. Came to see Cohen, killed him, then texted to give himself an alibi. Left. Dumped the gun and the laptop and came back at eleven, conveniently let into the building by a visitor. Fleishman also set up the appointment with Ram, then went with him and shot him.' He looked at me.

'Or the unknown guy – maybe an enemy spy – calls Cohen, comes, kills him, texts Fleishman and leaves.'

'Putting Fleishman in the frame. But Cohen wouldn't have let just anyone in. Had to be someone he knew.'

'Gaby Fleishman does seem more likely.'

'Although surely Michelle Jennings would have recognised his voice if he was the one who called to make the appointment with Ram.'

I looked at the number again. The answer was in those eleven digits somewhere. I then remembered why I had come into Tahir's office. 'Hey, boss, did you see the *Guardian* this morning?'

'No, why?'

'Merrion's done a hatchet job on Aishtar, with help from someone inside the company. It's now public what Aishtar does, and it is bloody terrifying. A very long way from helping people find love.' I pulled out the article and gave it to him.

I waited as he read it, trying to make sense of his drawing on the board.

'Damn,' he said. 'Scary stuff. They can track millions of people and predict what they might do? And then arrest them on the off chance?'

'Look at the bit I've underlined.'

He read out, 'Today everyone is addicted to screens. AI and heuristics can manipulate objective reality and make us believe . . .' He paused. 'Oh.'

'Exactly.'

He read it again. 'Who is this Ian who was Merrion's source?'

'*That's* what we need to find out. Presumably someone inside Aishtar. But what he said is almost identical to the note we found on Ram's body, right?' I pulled out my notebook. 'Today's humans idolise screens. Intelligent software that operates heuristically often neutralizes objective reality.'

'Yeah. Call Merrion.'

I dialled and put my phone on speaker. 'Mr Merrion, DC Rahman here. We met the other day in connection with Mr Ram's death. We were wondering if we could ask you some questions in relation to your article in today's *Guardian*.'

'Good, wasn't it? It's getting a lot of buzz online. I told you these guys were evil!'

'We need the identity of the man you call Ian.'

He gave a derisory snort. 'You know I can't reveal my sources.'

Tahir took over. 'Mr Merrion, it is of vital importance. We think it is possible he may be connected with the murders.'

'Be that as it may, Inspector, I'm not revealing my source.'

'You know we can compel you to do so. Why not cooperate and save yourself all the hassle?'

'Feel free to try. We have lawyers. Bye.' He hung up.

'Damn,' I said. 'Let me speak to Gaby Fleishman to ask if he knows who Ian might be. It's obviously a whistleblower from inside the company.'

'Could it be Fleishman himself?'

'Why would he risk the sale of Aishtar? David Baker said he is highly motivated by money.'

'That's true,' said Tahir. 'Do you think it's possible there is no Ian who resigned? That it was all Merrion?'

I considered this. 'Possibly. But he must have someone on the inside who told him all that stuff. When we met him, he didn't seem to know what Aishtar did at that level of detail.'

'All right, see Fleishman. Maybe he and Merrion are in it together, although God knows why.'

'Good morning,' said Michelle Jennings as I walked into Aishtar just after ten. 'Are you here to see the founders again? Gaby and Saul are not in yet.'

'Is Mr Levy in?'

'Yes, he's here. I'll call him.'

So, the shocking news had not leaked yet. I looked around the reception area while I waited. Several awards were displayed on a vanity shelf – Best Startup. Most Promising Technology. Winner AI Forum – just as they had been in Ram's flat. Would they win any more prizes after Merrion's *Guardian* article? Or maybe the tech world was too busy leading the mindless march into the metaverse to worry about accolades.

'Can you tell me any more about the person who called for Mr Ram on Monday, Ms Jennings?' I said as I waited.

'Miles Merrion?'

'Yes. Is there anything you remember about his voice? Something distinctive?'

She thought for a moment, then shook her head.

'Was Mr Fleishman in the office when the call came through?'

'No, he wasn't.'

'How can you be sure?'

'I saw him leave for a meeting earlier. When the caller said he was Miles Merrion from the *Guardian*, I assumed he wanted to speak to Gaby, and told him Gaby was out. But Merrion said he needed Sid.'

'Thanks, that's helpful. Roughly how old do you think the voice sounded?'

'How old? I don't know. Young. Twenties? Thirties? Hard to tell.'

'You said he sounded familiar. Could it have *been* Mr Fleishman?'

She looked at me, puzzled. 'Why would Gaby say he was Mr Merrion?'

'Good point. But could it have been?'

'I don't understand. I suppose so, if he was putting on an English accent or something. It was a busy morning, and I didn't pay that much attention. It was such a brief call.'

'Thanks. And out of curiosity, where were you last night? After ten?'

She stared at me in apprehension.

'Why? Did something happen?'

I wasn't sure if it was my place to tell her about Saul Cohen.

'Just routine.'

'At home. It's been an exhausting few days, as you can imagine.'

'Anyone vouch for it?'

'No. My flatmate was at her boyfriend's.'

I sat back in reception, watching her tapping on her computer. Could she be involved? She didn't have alibis for the two murders. But for the life of me, I couldn't think why. She wouldn't benefit from either of the deaths as far as I knew. But we could not strike her off the suspect list yet.

Ari Levy appeared, looking strained. 'Inspector, how can I help you? It's a terrible time.'

I didn't correct his mistake with my rank. 'Could I have a word? I'll be quick.'

He nodded, swiped me in, and we went to a conference room. 'You heard about . . .'

He looked pained, face twisted. 'Yes, Gaby told me. I don't know what is going on. I've known Saul since we were boys. We haven't told them yet.' He made a vague gesture in the direction of the office. 'You didn't say anything to Michelle, did you?' I shook my head. 'Thank you. I'm waiting for Gaby to come in. He's very shaken. He found the body, you know.'

'Yes, he has been helping us at the station. I'm very sorry, Mr Levy. I can see you are distressed.'

'When can we get his body? We need to send it to Israel so his family can sit shiva.'

'I'm not sure at this moment, but we will let you know as soon as possible. Do you have any thoughts on who may have done this, and why?'

He shook his head. 'I have been racking my brains. I cannot think of anyone. Everyone liked Saul. We are being targeted. It was lucky he had nothing proprietary on his laptop.'

That was interesting. Maybe the killer didn't know that.

'What's the reason they would be targeting you?'

'Did you read the newspaper today?'

'Yes.'

'That's why, I assume. I am furious. Total garbage. That journalist is a muck raker.'

'But the murders had already occurred by the time the article came out.'

Levy just shook his head, looking aggrieved and distressed.

'It wasn't true what Merrion wrote?' I asked.

'We write code. What our clients use it for is their business.'

'*Does* Aishtar do what is claimed in the article?'

He shut his eyes for a second and nodded.

'All of it? The tracking, the prediction, the mass scale? Drones?'

'Our tech is unique.'

'So, privacy is out of the window. Literally.'

His eyes glittered. 'Look. There are fanatics out there with ill intent who will stop at nothing to harm others. Believe me, I have lived it all my life in Israel and seen it first-hand. Governments are struggling to keep up. The bad guys are several steps ahead. Finding them is like looking for a needle in a haystack. Now what if you could look at a haystack and instantaneously know what is hay and what is a needle? Wouldn't you want to be able to do that? States *need* our tech to protect their citizens – if even one innocent life is spared, then the loss of a little privacy is worth it. Any reasonable person will agree.'

I was torn. While I'd never experienced this type of technology used at this scale or with this impact, and certainly not in catching criminals before they did anything, I could see the value in tracking perpetrators using sophisticated methods. After all, nowadays we relied on DNA analysis, CCTV, ANPR – all these were gifts to our profession born from technological progress. Maybe Aishtar was just the logical culmination of the journey we had been on for decades.

But when I'd been in India, Maliha had shown me too many examples of how the government had illegally wiretapped and arrested journalists, political opponents and dissidents who posed no threat to the public. Even academics who had taken part in peaceful protest were subject to surveillance and their colleagues urged to rat on them. They incentivised schoolchildren to let authorities know about 'anti-social' behaviour among their peers. God knows what the Indian government would do with this technology. But whenever I raised concerns about these issues to my father, I always got the response, 'Do you want another terrorist slaughter in Mumbai?' Ari Levy was effectively saying the same thing.

'I suppose it makes sense given Priscilla Patrick is your client? She's never been a massive privacy enthusiast.'

He gave me a sharp look. 'How do you know she is our client?'

'I picked it up somewhere.'

'Well, I can't confirm or deny that.'

You just did.

I moved on. 'Can you *actually* predict what these criminals will do?'

'Yes.' He opened up a bit. 'Your life is pretty much all electronic these days. When you're talking at home, your devices are listening. Many people use sleep trackers, so we can monitor you in bed. Through Deliveroo we know what you eat. Using this, and other data, we then analyse your behaviour and can predict what you might do in the future. Human beings are surprisingly predictable. That's our secret sauce. And this damn article has put it all out there!'

I remembered a conversation I'd had with the imam about Al-Qadr – predestination. Everything is willed by Allah and we just follow its path. If that *was* the case, it wasn't inconceivable that technology could tap into it and show the road ahead.

But this wasn't the time for pondering the theology and ethics of surveillance. I cut to the chase. 'Mr Levy, you are understandably upset. The source in the article has painted your company in a terrible light. You must have some ideas about who this Ian fellow, the whistleblower, could be?'

'Not for certain. Whoever it was has leaked proprietary information.'

'Did anyone leave Aishtar under a cloud? Who could have been angry enough to talk to a reporter? I don't want to have to do it, but we can get a warrant for your HR records.' I wasn't sure if this *was* something that we could actually do, but what the hell?

Ari Levy's expression shifted to one of resignation. 'I've already asked Yael to check for any issues we've had with anyone. There *was* Nelson. But we can't get hold of him.'

'Nelson?'

'Nelson Tang. A data scientist who worked with us. He was a troublemaker, so we fired him.'

'How long did he work here?'

'Around eighteen months. He was a gifted coder, talented, but very vocal about things he didn't agree with.'

'What didn't he agree with?'

'He wanted us to use our technology for good. We do use it for good. We just disagreed on what "good",' he made air quotes, 'was.'

'I'll need his contact details, along with everyone else who has left the company in the last six months.'

'We've been trying to reach him this morning with no success. I'll get you his details. Let us know if you find him.'

'Why do you want to get hold of him?'

'I had the same thought when I read the article. That it might be him.'

'When did he leave?'

'Around six weeks ago?'

'Do you think he may have wanted to harm Aishtar? Or the people here?'

'Nelson was always a bit of an oddball, but to be honest, most data scientists are.' He gave a thin smile. 'I've been accused of being weird myself. He *could* have leaked it, but it doesn't mean he's a murderer.'

'The article mentioned something about living the virtual life of a fanatic. What did it mean by that?'

He hesitated, then said, 'We are experimenting with some new virtual-reality techniques to bring certain scenarios to life. It's just in alpha at the moment. I can't say more.'

'So, you not only track them, but you can also *be* them? Like in a computer game? But for real?'

'I can't say any more.' He stared at me with a steady gaze.

'What were your movements last night, Mr Levy?'

'I was at home with my wife. We had dinner and went to bed at ten. Gaby then called me after eleven and told me.'

'He phoned you from Mr Cohen's apartment?'

'Yes, after he discovered the body. He was waiting for the police.'

Fleishman hadn't mentioned this in the flat. I wondered if he had told Tahir.

Levy continued, 'I wanted to go over, but he asked me not to. I haven't heard from him this morning – I've left some messages, but his phone is off. I hope he's okay. He sounded terrible. Broken.'

'He came into the station for questioning last night but went home after that, I believe. Tell me exactly what he said to you?'

'Just that he had found Saul dead, and that someone had shot him. He told me to wipe Saul's laptop if it connected to the internet, but it hasn't as yet. Although Saul didn't have any Aishtar code on his computer anyway; only Sid and I were allowed to. So, the killer won't have got anything useful.'

'Mr Levy, you may be in danger yourself. You know that don't you?'

He shifted in his chair. 'Someone murdered two of my colleagues. Of course I'm being careful.'

'It's possible that you, Mr Fleishman and Ms Klein are privy to some vital information. Maybe something you don't even realise is relevant. I must ask you and your colleagues to have a serious think. If there is any detail, anything you know or have noticed, no matter how minor, please come clean. It will help us help you.'

'I have *nothing* to hide. You can question us as much as you want – I'm sure Yael and Gaby want to cooperate too. But not here – our team is already destabilised.'

'We'll try to be sensitive, sir, but we are dealing with a murder case. Perhaps the three of you could come into the station?'

He thought for a second. 'I think that would freak Yael out. And piss Gaby off, if you've been grilling him there all night. Is there anywhere else we can meet? Somewhere more neutral? A café or something after work? Or is that not allowed? Is this going to be a formal interview? Do we need lawyers present?'

'No lawyers necessary. We're not questioning you under caution. We can meet wherever makes you comfortable. Tell you what, do you know Tandoori Knights restaurant in Brick Lane? I can get us a quiet table there if we meet early. Around seven? Would that work for you?'

'It might. Let me check with the others.'

'Do that. Now, would you get me Mr Tang's particulars, please?'

'Yes. Inspector, please release Saul's body asap. It is very important to us.'

I wasn't sure how Tahir would react to my suggesting TK for the interviews, but it was Levy's idea. Sort of. It had worked a treat with Baker. If we could get them all relaxed after a couple of beers, we might get closer to what lay at the bottom of this mess.

But first, I wanted to track down Nelson Tang.

Chapter 15

Friday afternoon.

I tried to call Nelson Tang, the aggrieved ex-employee of Aishtar, only to hear, 'The number you are calling is temporarily out of service. Please try again later.' Since that was about as useful to our investigation as Chanson's fancy new eggplant cookies with truffle salt for a hungry diner, Tahir and I drove to the address Ari Levy had given us – a block of flats in St Katharine Docks, arriving there at half twelve.

I hadn't been to this part of London before and it was surreal – a marina filled with boats surrounded by redbrick buildings with a clock tower and fancy restaurants, including one sporting large balconies with white railings that proclaimed itself *The Dickens Inn*. We were in Disneyland-on-Thames.

'If he's landed a new job, he's probably at work,' I said as Tahir pressed the intercom, but a croaky voice answered. 'Yes?'

'It's the police,' said Tahir. 'Is that Nelson Tang?'

'He doesn't live here anymore.'

'May we come up?'

'Erm . . . what do you want?'

'We'd like to ask you some questions about Mr Tang.'

''Snot convenient at the moment.'

'We won't take too much of your time, sir. Please let us in.'

There was a brief pause, then we were buzzed into the

building. We took the lift to the fifth floor where a man in his twenties wearing a bathrobe opened his front door and checked our ID.

'Sorry, I have a touch of flu.' He blew his nose into a tissue then cleared his throat, as we sat opposite him in his living room. 'That's why you caught me at home.'

Hoping we'd not caught anything more nefarious than his presence, I inched as far back as possible in my seat and looked around the room for a window to open. This young guy was under the weather and deserved sympathy, but he was a disease vector.

'What is your name, sir?' said Tahir.

'Daniel Boon. No e. And I've heard all the jokes.'

I wasn't sure what he was talking about, so said, 'Mr Tang used to live here?'

'Yes, he moved out two weeks ago.'

'Did he leave a forwarding address?'

'No, he didn't. What's this about?'

'We need to contact him urgently,' said Tahir.

'Why?'

'To help us with our enquiries. Are you certain you don't have any idea where he might be?'

Boon went silent for a few seconds. Then, 'Enquiries about what?'

'I'm afraid we can't tell you that.'

'I don't know anything.' He blew his nose loudly. 'I think if someone doesn't want to be found, we should respect that. Especially if he's done nothing wrong.'

'Why do you say he doesn't want to be found?' I asked.

Boon considered his words, then said, 'He left in a hurry. He was not happy. He'd lost his job and was freaked out about something.'

'What do you mean?'

'Not sure. I didn't know him that well. Three of us share this

144

flat; Nelson moved in with us around eighteen months ago – he was a nice enough bloke but kept to himself. Over the last few months, he got kind of paranoid. He kept unplugging Alexa, which was annoying. Said we were being watched; that this was becoming a police state; the government was covering up some massive conspiracy; and MI5 were after him. That type of shit. We ignored him – he was always a bit of a nutcase. But not dangerous. Live and let live, I say.'

He sat back on his couch, the leather squeaking in protest.

'Did he say why he was moving out?' I said.

'Said he couldn't live in London anymore. He was too . . . "exposed".'

'What did he mean by "exposed"?'

'Who knows!'

'And what do you do?'

'I work in the City. I'm an investment banker.'

'When will your flatmates be back? We may need to send someone to question them.'

'What did Nelson do?' said Boon, smothering a sneeze.

'Mr Boon, it is imperative we find him,' I said. 'Two people have been brutally murdered, and Mr Tang may be able to help us find the killer. If you know anything at all about his whereabouts, please tell us.'

This got his attention.

'My god! Who was murdered?'

'It doesn't matter. If you know anything, tell us or stop wasting our time.'

He shook his head. 'I really don't.'

'You said he left two weeks ago. How did he take his things?' I asked. 'Did he use a moving company? Or his own car?'

'He didn't have much, just a couple of suitcases. And he doesn't own a car. He told us he was leaving and settled his share of the rent. When we got home, he was gone.'

'When exactly?'

'Um. Two Fridays ago.'

I made a note to check the CCTV. There wasn't anything more we were going to get from Mr Boon without an e. We stood to leave.

'All right,' I said. 'If anything comes to mind, here's my card.'

As we were walking out, Boon said, 'Actually . . .'

I swivelled around.

'You just reminded me; I don't know if it's useful, but he borrowed *my* car three weeks ago and was out for most of the day.'

Tahir and I looked at each other.

'Do you have GPS?' we said simultaneously.

Boon came down with us to a garage in the basement and let us into an Audi Quattro. He got into the driver's seat and Tahir slid in next to him as I watched through the window. Boon switched the car on and scrolled through the GPS on the dash. He pointed, 'I don't recognise that.'

Tahir suppressed a grin and said, 'This is an actual address?'

Boon laughed. 'Appropriate, I guess, if that's where he's gone.'

'Pratt's Bottom?' I said, as we left the garage.

'I had a date in a place called Crotch Crescent in Oxford once.' A reminiscent smile crossed his face.

'Of course you did.' I decided it was better for my sanity not to press for details. 'This Tang sounds like a good lead. Hopefully that address is where he's moved to.'

'Hopefully. He does fit. Smart. Disaffected. Paranoid. Good profile. I guess we're going to Pratt's Bottom.' He checked his phone. 'Okay, some reports are in. Cohen's neighbours heard a soft bang just before eleven but put it down to TV noise. No helpful physical evidence from the flat. Search of the surrounding area and premises found nothing. They found the guy who let Fleishman into the building, but it doesn't mean that he didn't kill Cohen and return. The same gun that killed Cohen fired the bullet that killed Ram. No gunshot residue on Fleishman's clothes. Nothing on CCTV or ANPR, not much coverage in the area. I have to say, for a city with so much CCTV, we never seem to have it where we need it. The team has been checking alibis. As you said, Levy was at home with his wife; she confirmed it. Klein and Jennings say they were alone at home. Masri was at a dinner, confirmed by other attendees. Baker went home in an Uber after your restaurant meal, got home at 10.35, confirmed by the Uber driver. No sign of him going out after that, so no alibi for the time of the murder. He lives close enough to have been able to get over to Cohen's, although it would be cutting it fine.'

'He was in the clear for the first killing,' I said.

'Yeah. Merrion had no alibi for either of the killings – said he was home all evening, but no confirmation. And social media is blowing up about Merrion's article. #bigbrother is trending.'

'I'm not surprised – it was shocking stuff, no? Looks like we have a lot of empty puris with no pani or dahi to speak of.' I grinned at my own hilarious metaphor, forgetting for a moment that Tahir was my boss now, not just a mate. He rolled his eyes. I got a grip. 'I'll drive.'

Forty-five minutes later, the urban sprawl of London was behind us, and we were speeding through the leafy English countryside. The sky was an unbroken blue and the surrounding green looked paint-fresh under the sun. I rolled down my window and breathed in the air as we made our way down Budgin's Hill, a narrow road overarched by trees that meandered from farm to farm.

'I haven't left London since I arrived, apart from the odd trip back home to India,' I said. 'I should bring Anjoli somewhere like this; it'll do us good to get out of the city. Recharge. Find our souls. Find each other.'

'You'll just find sheep droppings and bored cows. Can't stand the countryside. Give me a gritty city any time.'

'Yeah, live for a week in Kolkata, then see how you feel. There's a reason shitty also rhymes with city.' I slowed when we got to a gated turning with a sign marked 'Fairley Farm'. 'This must be it. Can you open the gate?'

'Pah, smell the manure? Still keen on the countryside?' he said, jumping back in the car and rolling up his window.

'Good, fresh rural smells.' But I put my window up as well.

I pulled up in front of a low, white farmhouse. We got out and rang the bell, hearing a distant jangling inside the house.

'I hope this hasn't been a wasted trip,' I said. 'Maybe he just came here for a country walk.'

After a few minutes, a voice from inside said, 'Who is it?'

To my surprise, Nelson Tang – if it was him – had a posh English accent; I had been expecting something different. I needed to check my own misplaced assumptions.

'Mr Tang?' said Tahir. 'It's the police. Could we have a word, please?'

Silence. Then, 'Why?'

Bingo!

'If you wouldn't mind opening the door?'

A pause. Then the door opened a crack, and a hand came out. 'ID?'

Tahir handed him his warrant card, and the hand disappeared. After a few seconds, Nelson Tang stood in the doorway in faded combat trousers and an Extinction Rebellion T-shirt. He had a tired expression on his face; his hair was long and greasy, and he looked as if he hadn't changed his clothes in a week. He gave Tahir his ID back and said, 'Why are you here?'

'We'd like to speak to you.'

'About what?'

'About your time at Aishtar. Please, may we come in?'

A worried look came across his face. 'How did you find me?'

'It doesn't matter,' said Tahir.

'It matters to *me*. I don't want to be hassled. I don't work for Aishtar anymore. I've got nothing to do with them. You're wasting your time.'

He started to close the door and Tahir blocked it with a heavy foot. 'Mr Tang. We have driven here from London and would appreciate a word. Alternatively, you can accompany us back to our station in Bethnal Green.'

I gave Tang an apologetic smile. Bad cop, wuss cop.

He leaned out of his doorway and looked behind us, left, right, then further up the track that led back to the road. Satisfied that we were alone, he stepped aside and allowed us in. With one more backward glance, he shut the door, locked it, and ushered us into a sunny living room where we sat on threadbare sofas.

'Have you lived here long?' I said.

'A few weeks. Look. I'm busy. What is it you want?'

This would not be an easy man to break. He was clearly hiding from something and was deeply suspicious of us. With good reason.

'We've been trying to ring you on the number Aishtar had for you, but your phone was off,' I said.

'I don't own a mobile anymore.'

'Why's that?'

A shrug.

Tahir got down to business.

'Why did you leave Aishtar?'

Another shrug. 'I was done with the rat race.'

'We heard you fell out with them?'

Silence. He was sitting up ramrod straight. Perfectly still.

There was a coiled tension about him that felt like it might spill over into violence any second.

Tahir glanced at me, and I took over. 'Mr Tang, did you hear about the death of Mr Ram?'

He nodded.

'And?'

'And what?'

'How do you feel about it?'

He looked down and picked at the skin on his thumb. 'I wasn't surprised.'

'Why not?'

'He was dealing with some dangerous people.'

'Who?'

'You'll have to ask Aishtar. I'm not allowed to talk about my time there. I signed an NDA when I joined.'

He seemed experienced in batting away unwanted questions. We were getting nowhere.

'Where were you on Monday evening, between 9 p.m. and midnight?' said Tahir.

'Here.'

'Can anyone vouch for that?'

'I don't see that I should have to.'

'Any calls at the time? Anyone you might have spoken to?'

'No.'

'What were you doing?'

'Reading.'

I looked around and clocked there was no TV.

I took over. 'And where were you last night? Around 11 p.m.?'

A puzzled expression came across Tang's face.

'Why last night?'

Tahir and I glanced at each other.

'Please answer the question,' I said.

'Same. And I was still alone, still didn't speak to anyone and was still reading. The same book. I don't go out much.'

'Why not?'

'I prefer my own company.'

'Are you hiding from something, Mr Tang? Or scared of someone? Maybe the dangerous people you say Mr Ram was dealing with?' said Tahir.

Tang looked at us without expression.

'We can protect you if you're in danger,' I said.

This elicited a snort and a shake of the head.

I tried a different tack. 'Are you a member of Extinction Rebellion?'

He looked down at his T-shirt.

'It's not illegal.'

'But you agree with their aims?'

'Do you even know what our aims are?'

'They believe in violence.'

'Only as a last resort. The police are more violent than we are.'

I was getting lost in this line of questioning. I looked at Tahir and he changed tack. 'You had some disagreements with Aishtar. Tell us what they were.'

'I didn't like the direction the company was going in, so I left. That's all.'

'Without another job to go to?'

'That's right.'

I noticed something on the kitchen table, rose, and handed it to Tang. 'You've read today's *Guardian*?'

'Yes.'

'You've seen the piece about Aishtar.'

'Yes.'

'What did you think of it?'

'About time someone told the truth about what's going on.'

'Were you the person who told the truth?' I said. 'There are laws that protect whistleblowers. Let me ask you directly: are you the Ian that Miles Merrion talks about in the article?'

He looked me in the eye. 'No.'

'Have you ever had any contact with Mr Merrion?'

'No.'

Tahir was getting annoyed as well. He cut in, 'Mr Tang, I don't want to take you into the station, but you can see how it looks. You fall out with your employers, then two of them are murdered, and—'

Tang interrupted. 'Two of them?'

Tahir shut his eyes for a second. He'd screwed up.

'Yes. Saul Cohen was also killed last night.'

I watched Tang closely. His eyes widened for a second and then the same blank expression came over his face. He didn't say anything.

'You didn't know?' I said.

He shook his head.

Tahir continued. 'You have no alibi for those nights. You are a member of an anarchist group. I think it would help if you came clean with us.'

Tang opened his mouth to say something, then stopped. He looked at Tahir for a moment and took a few breaths, as if considering what he'd just heard. He blinked a few times, then stood. It was the first sign of emotion he had shown since we arrived. He walked to the window and stared at the fields outside and said, 'I don't know what you expect me to say. I quit Aishtar. I didn't kill anyone. I don't know the journalist.'

Tahir and I rose as well and flanked him, making him the filling in a cop sandwich.

'But why live here, in the middle of nowhere?' I said.

'I don't wish to be tracked.'

'By whom?' said Tahir.

'The government. Aishtar. Anyone. I'm off-grid here.'

'What do you mean?' I said.

'I've cut myself off electronically from the world. I don't have a television, mobile, internet. I only use cash, not credit cards. I try to avoid CCTV. I *need* to know how you found me.'

'Why do you think the government or Aishtar might track you?' Tahir asked.

'Because that's what they do. Not just me, everyone. You've read the article.'

'Are you anti AI?' I said.

'Depends what it's used for.'

Tahir picked up the newspaper and read, ' "AI will kill humanity and Aishtar will be the weapon." Do you agree with that?'

'It could. Stephen Hawking said it could spell the end of the human race. Elon Musk says humanity's existence is at stake. What Aishtar is doing is getting us closer to the destruction of civilisation.'

He walked over and sat back on the sofa. Tahir and I sat on either side of him, making him visibly nervous.

'And you think the company should be stopped?' I said.

'I do.'

'At any cost?' said Tahir.

'Yes. I mean – no, what I mean is—'

I jumped in. 'And you are the one to stop them?'

'*I* can't say or do anything to stop them.'

Tahir leaned even closer. 'And that's why you contacted the *Guardian*?'

'I didn't.'

I did the same as Tahir. 'So, who is Ian?'

'Ask the journalist who wrote the article.'

'Mr Tang, do you own a gun?' said Tahir.

'No.'

'Would you mind if we looked around your house?' I asked.

'Yes, I would.'

'We can get a search warrant,' said Tahir.

'Then fucking do that. I'd like you to leave now.'

Angry now, he sprang up from the sofa and flung open the door. We looked at each other and Tahir said, 'We'll be back.'

'He did it,' exploded Tahir as we got into the car. 'I know he did.'

'It's credible,' I said, and saw the figure of Tang retreat in my rear-view mirror as he watched our car kicking up gravel and dust along the drive. 'We got under his skin.'

'Yes, nicely done.'

It *had* felt good. When you get into the flow, and everything moves in sync. Except we hadn't got the result we had wanted.

'I screwed up mentioning Cohen. He didn't show a flicker did he? Good actor.'

'Unless he didn't know?'

'Sure he did. He did it. We'll arrest him and get a search warrant.'

'Do you think we have enough grounds?' I asked.

'I'm going to make damn sure we do. Shit, if he has the murder weapon, he'll dump it now. We should have arrested him on the spot.'

'No evidence, boss. It feels a little obvious, though. Loner with a grudge, living off-grid.'

'Obvious is good; more chance of a conviction. And remember, the simplest answer is most often the correct one. We need to lean on Merrion to confirm his source is Tang. Once we catch our Mr Tang in a lie, we have him.'

'We should quiz Levy and Fleishman more about Tang,' I said and then, trying not to sound too sheepish, added, 'I've, erm . . . arranged for us to meet them this evening . . . at TK.'

He looked at me in disbelief. 'That's ridiculous, Kamil, and totally against procedure! You should have told them to come into the station. What were you thinking?'

'Levy didn't want to come in *or* have us interview them in their offices – it was his idea,' I said, shading the truth. 'Also, they'll be more relaxed there, more likely to talk. It worked with Baker.'

'Jesus. Well, don't let Rogers hear about this; it may even count as malfeasance, given you live above the flipping restaurant.'

'Don't worry, I won't expense the meal.' I could feel the coronary flutter of my adrenaline spiking. It wasn't scary, it was exhilarating. Solving a crime was akin to falling in love; it gave me a powerful rush, like an energetic charge of *yes, yes, yes,* which was indescribable. I was on the verge of wrapping up a double murder in less than a week and could see a commendation from Rogers, high-fives from Gooch and the gang and Anjoli and Maliha beaming at me, full of pride.

Yes.

Chapter 16

Friday evening.

Sitting opposite an irritated Tahir in TK, I flicked Chanson's garam masala and lemon stuffed olive into a slow spin around my plate. Took a sip of my beer. Checked my watch. 7.30 p.m. The Aishtar crew hadn't turned up and my charged euphoric *yesness* of earlier in the day had fizzled into an abrupt *nah, mate*. Neither Ari Levy nor Gaby Fleishman were responding to my texts. Tahir was scrolling and scowling, and Anjoli, pissed off about my commandeering a prime booth for six on the restaurant's busiest evening, glared at me every time she passed our table.

'Look, it's been half an hour, Kamil,' Tahir said. 'They're not coming. Anjoli's giving us the evil eye again. Let's just give her the table back.'

She came over to have another go. 'Where are your people, Kamil? I should negotiate a retainer with the Met Police if you're going to make a habit of using my restaurant as your interview room. I'm turning good business away, you know.'

'*All right*, Anjoli. I'm sorry,' I said, hungry and tired. 'This was a mistake. Take your table back.'

As I rose, the bell at the door tinkled and, to my relief, I saw Levy, Klein and Fleishman enter in their uniforms of dark jeans and T-shirts. I noticed a reluctant smile break Anjoli's frown when she saw that Levy's sweatshirt said *There are two kinds of people in the world: 1. Those who can extrapolate from incomplete data.*

'Thank you for coming.' I slid back into the booth next to Tahir and the three of them sat opposite.

'Better than your police station,' growled Fleishman, eyes sunk deep into his skull. 'I had enough of you asking the same questions again and again there. I don't understand what more you want. I only came because Ari insisted.'

I shot a glance at Tahir. Maybe my TK gamble would pay off, after all.

'Would you like something to eat or drink?' I asked.

They shook their heads, then Levy said, 'I could do with an ice-cold beer.'

'Nothing else? You sure?' I wanted to eat but couldn't very well do so if they weren't. And Anjoli would be even more pissed off. 'Mr Fleishman? Ms Klein?'

'Okay, beers as well,' said Fleishman. 'But no food.'

Anjoli came by holding some menus and I said, 'Just five Cobras, please, Anjoli. We don't need the menus.'

To my relief, she remained professional, said, 'Of course,' and disappeared.

Fleishman said, 'Make this quick. This is a terrible time, with the murders and that ridiculous article. We must get back to the office for some urgent calls with the US.'

'Still no news on when we can get Saul's body released?' asked Ari Levy.

'I understand the sensitivity,' said Tahir. 'We hope it will be soon; our people are in touch with your embassy and our family liaison officers have contacted Mr Cohen's people in Israel. I believe they are flying over to London. The post-mortem is over, and we are waiting for the coroner to give us permission to release the body. Same for Mr Ram.'

'Please let us have him as soon as possible. I don't know Sid's parents, but Saul's family is distraught, as you can imagine.'

'They can't sit shiva until after his burial,' said Yael Klein, who had been silent till then.

'I will do all I can,' said Tahir.

The beers arrived. Levy took a sip and said, 'Did you find Nelson? Was he Merrion's source?'

'We're following various lines of enquiry,' said Tahir. 'Can you tell me a little more about him?'

'Troublemaker,' said Fleishman.

'How did he make trouble?'

'He's a smart guy but started sounding off about our work. We had to let him go.'

'You think it peeved him enough to do something about it?'

'Yes,' said Fleishman, a bit too fast for my liking, with a microscopic twitch of his lip.

'Why do you say that?'

'He's an oddball. He *must* have been the *Guardian*'s source. I don't know who else it could have been. We'll sue the pants off him.'

'He *was* a little weird, Gaby,' said Klein. 'But no more so than many people who work for us. I can't believe he's a murderer.'

'What was he working on at Aishtar?' said Tahir.

'We can't tell you that,' said Levy.

'I'm getting a little tired of this cloak-and-dagger business, Mr Levy. We are investigating two murders here. So, I ask again, what was he involved with that might turn him into a whistleblower?'

'It was on . . . the stuff in the newspaper,' said Fleishman. 'I can't give you any details. The Official Secrets Act binds us. As it does him.'

Tahir said, 'Mr Fleishman, your organisation is being targeted. Cooperate with us so we can stop this killer. Hiding under the guise of confidentiality won't help.'

'So, you think we're in danger too?' said Levy, fiddling with the string of his hood. 'I suppose we must be.'

'You could well be. So why would he become a whistleblower?'

They looked at each other. Then Levy leaned forward and said, voice lowered, 'He heard a rumour about the sale of the company and tried to sabotage what we're doing. That's why we fired him.'

'Sabotage how?'

'He engineered a virus that almost took down all our code. Luckily, we discovered it in time so could roll it back. We lost weeks of work. It was touch and go – it could have disrupted the whole acquisition.'

Tahir and I considered this.

'Who did the firing?' I said.

'Sid,' said Fleishman.

'Was Saul Cohen involved?' said Tahir.

'Yes. He was the one who insisted Nelson get no compensation. We almost reported him to the police but decided we didn't want the publicity. Nelson has caused a lot of damage through this leak – if it was him.'

'There were protesters outside our offices all day today. You'd think we were experimenting on babies instead of stopping terrorists. A number of our staff who weren't working on this part of the business are threatening to quit. Bloody snowflakes! *This doesn't fit my value system,*' Klein mimicked.

'It hasn't been all bad,' said Gaby Fleishman. 'Sales enquiries have been flooding in from all over the world. Silver lining to every . . .' His phone rang; he glanced at it and answered. 'Wahid? . . . Oh okay, thanks . . . Speak tomorrow.'

Ari Levy looked at him, questioning.

'Wahid has appointed me acting CEO,' said Fleishman, face sombre.

'*Mazel Tov.*' Levy gave a sarcastic snort. 'I hope they've given you combat pay. The half-life of an Aishtar CEO is short.'

'Ari!' exclaimed Yael Klein. 'I can't believe you just said that. It's not funny. I'm terrified. As you both should be.'

'*Slicha*, Yael. Of course we are.' He squeezed her hand. 'But you know I've taken extra precautions.'

'What precautions?' I asked.

'I've created a special key that has to be used to unlock the core algorithms. So, someone could steal everything on every computer in the office and it would be useless without my key.'

'And where's the key?'

'It's safe. No one can get it.' He tapped the side of his nose. 'I have created a McCain protocol.'

'What's a McCain protocol?' said Tahir.

'Don't bother,' said Fleishman. 'He's told nobody what it means. He even told Wahid he had coded that McCain thing, then looked mysterious. It pissed Wahid off.'

'It means if someone steals my computer, it won't work. It's foolproof. If the killer knows they can't get the tech, they'll back off.'

'He won't even tell me what it is,' said Klein. 'Stupid name. Sounds like a Robert Ludlum novel.'

'That could put you in danger, Mr Levy. How would the killer know they can't get it?' I asked.

'I've mentioned it around the office,' said Ari. 'And at least the data would be safe in the worst case. Better than doing nothing.'

'Worst case! *Ya chatichat tembel*! I keep telling him it's dangerous!' said Klein.

'I can look after myself,' said Levy. 'Believe me, my magic protocol will keep us safe.'

'I hope so, Ari, for all our sakes,' said Fleishman. 'What do you see in these guys, Yael? First David, the nerd, and then Ari the geek. What's wrong with regular guys like me?'

'Better nerds and geeks than smooth sales guys. I'm sapiosexual,' said Klein.

'What's that?' I said.

'I'm attracted to intelligent people. Brains are sexier than brawn.'

She gave Fleishman a friendly punch on his muscled arm, then leaned over to give Levy a brief kiss. The conversation petered out as we drank in silence, my tummy rumbling. Was sapiosexuality the reason Maliha had liked me? Or why I liked Anjoli and Maliha? Maybe I should ask them. *Only* techies would have a term like that. What *was* the classification of techies? Was nerd at the bottom of the heap followed by geek? What came next? Dweeb? Dork? Anorak? And once a geek became a millionaire, did he lose his geekiness? Maybe not – Mark Zuckerberg hadn't. And he was a *billionaire*. Beer on an empty stomach didn't agree with me. I found my eyes drifting closed and forced myself to focus on what Fleishman was saying. '. . . and I've beefed up security in the office, but we need to be extra careful when we're out and about. Stay in public places, cabs everywhere, that kind of thing.' He sighed and shook his head. 'How hard we three worked. How long we've waited for this moment.'

'And now Saul won't . . .' Levy's face tightened, and Klein squeezed his hand. He cleared his throat and said, 'To Saul.'

They toasted, and Fleishman made a gesture to the others to get up and get moving. 'Well, if we're done here . . .'

Levy drained his glass. 'Listen, you have to understand, Aishtar is about making life better. That newspaper article was bullshit. And our new virtual reality product will make your policing far more effective.'

'What is it?'

His face became animated. 'I guess I can talk about it now. We've created something very exciting. We can take the data we are collecting on individuals and create a VR version of their lives. Sid gave me the idea – you know his *Thrumyeyes* app let you live someone's life through a camera. But that was just a video. I've taken it much further.'

'What does it do?' said Tahir. I noticed Anjoli had stopped by our table. I could see a group of four people waiting to be seated. By the look on her face, she was losing patience. I hoped she wouldn't interrupt.

'When it's finished, you will be able to feed in the data from individuals you are watching and actually *be* them. *Live* in their environment. See what they see. Interact with the people they interact with. Simulate them committing a crime. Imagine that.'

Tahir fell silent. 'And you've built this?'

'Not fully. To test the tech works, we have recreated a square mile around here in virtual reality. Brick Lane in 1900. You can wear a VR headset and experience what life was like in the early twentieth century.'

'It's amazing . . .' said Klein. 'You can interact with people, walk around, go inside some buildings – it's like *being* there.'

'Why did you pick this area?' I asked.

'Well, my ancestors – and Gaby's – came from Eastern Europe,' said Levy. 'Ashkenazis. They came to London from Lithuania in the late 1800s and lived here till the 1950s, then emigrated to Israel. I have been trying to track their history. Some came here, some died in the camps, some are still in Eastern Europe. I thought it would be incredible to see how they lived. And since our office is in the same area our immigrant forefathers came to, it made sense to test the technology here.'

Anjoli said, 'The remains they found were also Ashkenazi.'

Levy looked at her, startled that a waitress, wearing a T-shirt that said *The Only Way is Ethics*, had interrupted their conversation.

'Sorry,' she said. 'I'm Anjoli, the owner of the restaurant. I couldn't help overhearing what you just said; are you all Ashkenazi?'

'I'm Sephardic, but they are Ashkenazi,' said Yael Klein.

'What remains?' said Levy.

'We found three ancient skeletons with Mr Ram's body,' said Tahir. 'It has nothing to do with this case.'

'Someone murdered them, though,' said Anjoli. 'They were shot around the beginning of the last century. A man, a woman and a child. I paid to run a DNA test and discovered they were Ashkenazim. That's a coincidence, isn't it?'

'So, Dr Grayson got back to you?' I said. 'That was super-fast.'

Anjoli nodded. 'She'd actually done it off her own bat. She thinks the child was the daughter of the other two.'

'They can tell that they were Ashkenazi from DNA?' I asked.

'Yes, incredibly 40% of us are descended from just four women who lived a thousand years ago,' said Levy. 'It's a strong marker in mitochondrial DNA. Not surprising they were Jewish if you discovered them where you found Sid – may his memory be blessed,' said Levy. 'This was a very Jewish area in the early twentieth century. That's what my simulation is about. Tell me more about these bodies?'

'I'm trying to find out what happened to them. Can you run their DNA against your databases, Tahir?' said Anjoli.

'Possibly,' said Tahir. 'I'll check.'

'Try Ancestry.com as well,' said Levy. 'Many people put their DNA on there to see if they can find relatives. Although if the bones are that old, I don't know what you'll find.'

Anjoli never ceased to surprise me. I had expected the DNA to be a bust. Now it looked like she might get somewhere.

Fleishman glanced at his watch. 'We need to go, Ari.'

'Won't you have another beer?' said Anjoli. 'On the house; I'd love to hear more about your virtual reality thing.'

Levy looked ready to stay and share more, but Fleishman said, 'Sorry, we have to leave. Tell us if you learn more from Nelson Tang.'

Tahir stood up and, voice lowered, said, 'Please be careful, all three of you. Especially if you have this protocol key, Mr Levy. You might be a target if you are the only person who can make your technology work. Watch out for anything unusual or suspicious and call us if you notice anything at all.'

'Here's a silly question,' I said. 'I don't suppose there is any chance of using your technology to help solve this crime?'

'Not really,' said Levy. 'We need a subject of interest to put into the system. We can't give it a murder and expect it to find the killer. It's not magic.'

'What if we input Nelson Tang into your system?'

Levy thought for a moment. 'That could be possible. Let me see what I can do. Come and see me in the office tomorrow.'

'He's off the grid, though,' I said. 'Will it still work?'

I could sense Levy's interest quickening. 'Hmm. That's a challenge. Nice to meet you, Anjoli. Let me know what you find out about your skeletons.'

'Great,' sighed Klein. 'Now he'll be at it all night.'

We followed them to the restaurant door and watched as they filed out, led by Gaby Fleishman. It had begun to drizzle, and Ari Levy's arm was draped around Yael Klein as they disappeared into the damp night.

'Are you going out or coming in? You're blocking the entrance,' said Anjoli. She went off to prep the table for the group who brushed past us. I wasn't sure what we had learned, but at least I could eat now.

'Nelson Tang's looking really good to me,' said Tahir. 'It was an interesting angle you took there – ask a suspect to investigate another. Maybe we can make this standard operating procedure to deal with cutbacks in the force. We could even close our interview rooms and just use restaurants.'

I reddened. 'If Aishtar has these amazing tools, we might as well . . .'

Tahir grinned. 'Come on, let's go see Merrion. If Tang *was* his source, we can pick him up.'

'Now?' I said. 'It's half eight. And I'm hungry.'

'It's the ideal time. We'll catch him off guard, and he'll be keen to get rid of us. Easiest way to do that is to give us what we want.'

My eyes were heavy, having had no sleep the night before, but I could see his logic. The chances of my collapsing before getting to Merrion were pretty high, however. I nipped into the kitchen where Anjoli was plating some potato spheres with smoked muhammara, grabbed two samosas, and told her I'd be back later.

I was beginning to like these people and hoped Ari Levy's McCain protocol, whatever it was, would keep them safe.

13 Petticoat Lane, East End, London
17 December 1909

Darling Shoshi,

It was so nice to see you and Semyon and
little Eva earlier in the year. I would
wish to meet again soon. Until then, my
news . . . the baby is here! Leah was
born in September and is now three
months old. I still have to work all the
time, but she sleeps happily in a basket
at my feet. She is such a delightful
baby - she doesn't mind the smell of
fried fish and burning chicken feathers
that are always present in the street -
it made me so sick when I was pregnant.

I am learning English now - I hope for
Leah to grow up speaking it as her first
language, not Yiddish. She needs to be
an English girl, although she must not
forget where she came from, and we take
her to the synagogue in Princelet Street
every week.

Avram has been doing very well as a
dressmaker, Baruch HaShem. You remember
Yanky? Semyon gave us a letter of
introduction to him? He gave Avram his
first job as a machiner and me as a
finisher in his garment factory when we
arrived. Last year he was very happy
with Avram, and he introduced us to the
Board of Guardians of the Jewish Poor

166

who lent us seven pounds to set up our
market stall in Petticoat Lane, selling
our clothes, and Avram has built a small
reputation with his Pinsky's Clothing.
He is now specialising in flannel shirts
and these American trousers called
'jeans'. Seeing him working every day,
wearing his smart black coat and tie at
all times, makes my heart sing. We are
still living in Yanky's factory with
another family with seven children - of
course it is not the comfort we were
used to in Pinsk, but Yanky is a good
man - many of the others treat their
workers poorly but he is always kind.

I expected the Christians to mistreat
us. We were used to that in Pinsk. But
here it is the Jews looking down on
other Jews. The Spanish and Dutch Jews
believe they are better than the Russian
Jews who think they are above the
Pullacks and us Litvoks are at the
bottom. They make fun of how we talk,
how we look, what we wear. It is strange
and insulting. I wonder if you find that
too.

I miss you very much. Please write to
me soon.

With all my love,

Malka

Chapter 17

Friday night.

Tahir was silent during the drive, and I had to keep myself from drifting off as we fought the post-match traffic from the Emirates Stadium on Holloway Road. It took almost an hour to get to Merrion's ground-floor maisonette in Onslow Gardens, the dim yellow streetlights making this leafy street overlooking Queen's Wood fit my jaundiced and exhausted state. If this journalist was going to play games, I was fully prepared to rock bad cop to Tahir's good.

Tahir kept his finger on the bell. After a couple of minutes, a sleepy-looking Merrion in a dressing gown opened the door, looked at us, and said, 'What the hell do you think you're doing? Do you know what time it is?' It wasn't that late, just after nine.

'We've got some follow-up questions, Mr Merrion,' said Tahir, showing his warrant card. 'May we come in?'

With bad grace, he let us in and directed us into a small, untidy living room. 'Make it quick.'

I did. 'Was your source Nelson Tang?'

'I told you, I don't reveal my sources. You're wasting your time and mine.'

I moved my face to within a few inches of his. 'Mr Merrion, your article disclosed confidential information which resulted in demonstrations outside Aishtar's office, and their staff being threatened. Not to mention a second murder in the space of four days.'

168

'That's ridiculous. You can't pin that on me!'

'There are lives at stake and you have knowledge critical to this enquiry. You can answer our questions here now, or you can accompany us to the station.'

'There's nothing you can arrest me for.'

'Inciting hate speech will be a start,' said Tahir. 'You're putting national security at risk. I'm certain you should have consulted the government before publication given the sensitivity of the information – they would have issued a DSMA notice and stopped you printing it.'

'Well, the Home Secretary has already retweeted my article,' said Merrion. 'She said the tech was necessary to keep Britain safe. And that the people against it were anti-tech anarchists with an agenda. I bet she's using it on her fellow politicians to clear her path to Number 10.'

I glanced at Tahir, and he gave me a nod to push on. 'Just tell us what we need to know. Who is Ian? If we get him, we'll give you an exclusive on the story and say you helped.'

I had no idea if I had the authority to say this, but stared into his eyes, forcing him to defy me. He looked set to argue, then looked away and threw his hands in the air. 'All right! I *don't* know who Ian is. Someone sent me several documents through a secure site I've set up for whistleblowers. Like WikiLeaks. That way, people can stay anonymous. Ian was just the cover name I used.'

'When was this?' said Tahir.

'Yesterday morning.'

'But you interviewed him?' I said.

'The site has anonymous chat. We communicated through that.'

I pulled out my notebook and read, ' "Today everyone is addicted to screens. AI and heuristics can manipulate objective reality." Did he say that? Or did you make it up?'

'He said it.'

'Word for word – or did you paraphrase?'

'No, that was a direct quote.'

I glanced at Tahir and said, 'We need the documents. And a copy of the chat transcript. Now.'

'Christ, you never stop, do you? Wait here then.'

He went out of the room and came back a few minutes later with a folder. 'Here, that's all I have. I've never heard of – who did you say? Tang? Who's he?'

'Is there anything else you think might be relevant?' said Tahir.

Merrion shook his head. 'No, that's everything I have.'

As we were leaving, I turned and said, 'Thank you, Mr Merrion. You've been very helpful and may have saved a life. We'll remember it.'

Always good to make suspects and witnesses feel useful when you're in authority.

'We *have* to watch the watchers – remember that,' he responded. 'And if I have to be the one to stop it, I will.'

'What do you mean by that?'

His eyes drilled into mine. 'I printed the story, didn't I? I'm not letting this go.'

He shut the door in our faces, and I felt a chill, even though the evening was hot.

The drive home was quicker, and I was energised, knowing we had Merrion's dossier.

'Nice work,' said Tahir. 'I haven't seen you that aggressive before. You were the bull *and* the china shop. It's definitely Tang.' He rapped his fingers on Merrion's folder on his lap.

'I think so too. Given that quote and the AI note.'

'He said he got those documents yesterday?'

'Before Cohen died,' I said. 'So, you think Tang killed Ram, tossed the note after the body, then sent Merrion the documents to ensure the world knew what Aishtar was doing? Although *why* kill Ram and Cohen? If he just wanted this to be public, the leak would be enough.'

'Levy said he tried to sabotage the technology. Maybe he wants the tech for himself.'

'Perhaps.' Something else struck me. 'He made the appointment with Ram under Merrion's name, so he must have known Merrion was sniffing around. It all ties together. Although it's possible Merrion is still in the frame – he feels strongly about this. You heard him as we left. It's possible the quote is his, and he's set up Tang.'

'Maybe. We'll search Tang's farmhouse and find a reason to bring him in. I'll get it organised. Grab some sleep and see if Levy got anywhere with running Tang through his system tomorrow. Maybe get him to run Merrion through it as well. If it's as good as they say it is, we may as well get some use out of it.'

'If it does work, they won't need us in the future. That virtual-reality stuff was spooky.'

'Well, you can always go back to cooking – that's one thing AI won't replace.'

'Don't bank on it,' I said. 'McDonalds already has robots making their burgers. Maybe we'll have to all become . . . hairdressers or something.'

I was getting depressed now. My weekend was shot, and I wanted my bed. All I had to do was navigate the Friday-night bar hoppers on Great Eastern Street and I'd be home. Tomorrow we'd see how accurate Ari Levy's magical technology was.

Chapter 18

Saturday morning.

'Kamil!' I jerked awake from a death sleep to hear Anjoli banging on my door. It was still dark outside.

'What? What's happened?'

'Can I come in?'

Without waiting for an answer, she burst in and jumped onto my bed, the whites of her eyes lit up like neon by the glare of her phone screen.

'There's a match!'

'What?'

'We got a DNA match on the ancestry website Ari mentioned! Dr Grayson had a contact there and so she'd already sent them the DNA. She just emailed me! We've found a relative of our skeleton! The woman. Isn't that amazing?'

'What time is it?'

'Er . . . four something. Oh my God, Kamil, this is huge.'

I turned over and covered my head with my pillow. 'Tell me in the morning. I need to sleep. They've been dead a hundred years. A few more hours won't matter.'

She muttered something inaudible and continued tapping away at her phone.

Sleep was impossible now. I lifted the pillow. 'Okay, spill,' I said, eyes still closed.

'It's a woman, Sofia Katz. And guess what – she's in London!'

'So now what?' I grunted.

'I've messaged her via the website to ask her if we can meet. Find out what she might know about her ancestor from a hundred years ago. Will you come with me to see her?'

I opened an eye and saw the excitement on Anjoli's face, the joy in her eyes. *This* was what she needed, something to take her away from the grind of the restaurant. Feeling a warm surge of affection, I clambered to my knees and enveloped her in my arms.

'Well done,' I said into her hair. 'That *is* amazing! But you need to be careful. Remember, someone murdered those people. You don't know what this Sofia does or doesn't know about her family's past.'

She wriggled away. 'Fair enough, but if somebody killed my relatives a century ago, I'd want to know. So, will you come with me or not?'

'Of course I will. You need a reliable person by your side.'

'You're right. I should ask Tahir.'

I rolled my eyes. 'By the way, what about our celebratory dinner?'

She smiled. 'Oh yeah! I booked a wonderful new restaurant for us on Sunday night.'

My spirits lifted. 'That's great – what is it?'

She shook her finger at me. 'Not a chance. It's a surprise.'

'I look forward to it. Now go back to sleep. I have to visit Aishtar in the morning.'

As she left the room, I remembered I'd also made a date with Maliha on Sunday night. Damn. I'd have to find some excuse to cancel.

Tahir rang while I was having breakfast. 'We got the go-ahead to bring Tang in. We've obtained a search warrant for his place and uniform have gone to get him. Rogers had SO15 expedite it on anti-terrorism grounds. Those twats can be useful sometimes. Hopefully he won't have vanished again.'

'Great. Give me twenty minutes. I'll come in and help with the interrogation.'

'No, that's fine. I'll do it with Protheroe. It's the one thing he's not crap at. I went through Merrion's documents last night. Nothing to connect with Tang, but it corroborates everything in the article – I'm emailing them to you. You go to Aishtar. See if Levy recognises them and if he got anywhere running Tang's data through his system.'

I wasn't happy about Protheroe worming his way back on to the case after all his efforts to scupper it, especially if Tang turned out to be our guy.

'I don't know, boss. Wouldn't it be more useful to see Ari Levy *after* we've spoken to Tang?'

'No, it's better this way. Let me know if you find anything.'

Damn. Well, I'd tried.

Anjoli glanced at me.

'What was that?'

I told her and she said, 'It's Saturday. Don't you get time off?'

'I've had two murders this week! Weekends are irrelevant. And I need to make a good impression. It'll ease off.'

Her expression changed from grumpy to hopeful. 'Tell you what. Why don't I tag along?'

'Where?'

'With you. To Aishtar.'

'No way. I'm going on police business. I can't have you hanging around while I question suspects.'

'I may be helpful. Look, Ari connected with me. He wanted to know more about my skeletons and his virtual reality thing sounded super cool. C'mon! Let me come with. It's Saturday and I need a break. *And* I let you interview your people on our

174

busiest night, so you owe me. You didn't even pay for the beers. *And* I'm taking you to dinner.'

Saying no to Anjoli when she had her mind set on something was like using logic to persuade a tsunami to go into reverse. I considered my options. I was new to the Met and didn't want to screw it up by taking an unauthorised person to a witness meeting. But if Anjoli was warming towards me in the way I wanted her to . . .

'All right,' I said. 'But don't tell Tahir.'

I was surprised to see Michelle Jennings at her desk when Anjoli and I got to Aishtar.

'Don't you ever get time off?' I said as Anjoli signed her NDA.

'Normally, yes. But it's all hands on deck at the moment, given the terrible things that have happened.'

Ari Levy came out.

'Oh,' he said when he saw Anjoli. 'I didn't expect you as well.'

'I received some news on those skeletons, and you said to let you know . . .' said Anjoli.

He paused, then turned to me. 'This stuff is confidential. I'm sharing it with you because you're the police and Wahid has instructed us to cooperate. But she's a civilian and I'm sorry . . .'

With Anjoli looking at me with her puppy-dog eyes, there was nothing else I could say except, 'I understand, and I take full responsibility if she comes in. Anyway, it was all in the newspaper, right?'

'I'm sorry. I can't let her in.'

I looked at Anjoli and she said, 'Please, Ari. I've signed your NDA. It may be helpful to have a psychologist looking at the information about Tang – yes, I know about him.' She glanced around. 'This *is* a pretty male environment. You could do with some diversity in your thinking, and I can provide that.'

I had no idea what she was talking about and looking at Levy's expression, neither had he. But the veiled threat of Aishtar not being diverse enough must have worked, because he gave a small smile, shook his head, looked at me and said, 'Fine. For the record, I am doing it because the police have insisted. And because I love your cool T-shirt.'

Anjoli looked down at the shirt she had worn for the occasion – *Are robots really going to take over the world if they can't even find traffic lights in a CAPTCHA* – as Levy led us past a massage room and lactation suite into a glass-walled conference room. He pressed a button inside the door and the walls turned opaque.

'Ooh, that's cool,' said Anjoli.

'Piezoelectric film,' he responded as he took a USB thumb drive from his pocket and plugged it into a laptop. His fingers flew over the keyboard like a concert pianist, and the screen lit up, displaying the Aishtar logo.

'I spent last night configuring the system to track Nelson.'

A picture of Tang flashed up on the laptop, unsmiling, with his name and date of birth. I was surprised he was only twenty-six. He looked older in the flesh. Maybe delving into people's secrets added years to your life.

'So, the algorithm tracks what the SOI has been doing for a period you specify – I specified six months – and then gives you a score on how much of a terror risk they think he might be. 100 means he's Osama bin Laden and about to blow something up, 0 means he is Pope Francis. Nelson is . . .'

He tapped a few keys and below Tang's picture appeared 37.

'What does that mean?'

'That he's pretty safe. The system hasn't tracked him doing anything unusual. Amusingly, the riskiest thing they flagged for him is that he worked for Aishtar.'

'Oh,' I said, disappointed. 'How accurate is it?'

'Accurate. However, the data on him stops two weeks ago.'

'What do you mean?'

'There's no information on him for the last fortnight.'

'He told us he went off grid.'

'He did an effective job. No mobile records, internet use, ANPR, use of Oyster, credit cards – nothing.'

'So, he could have been doing something – analogue style?'

'*Analogue style*, I like that. Yes. The system flagged his recent lack of activity. I need to tweak the algorithm to treat that as suspicious and add some parameters for non-digital signatures. I think it might have assumed he was dead. It's a curious quirk I haven't considered. But quite fascinating – I might talk about it at the conference on Monday.'

'What conference?'

'I'm the keynote speaker at an AI conference in Cambridge. It'll be interesting to discuss what proxy data we can use when there are no actual digital breadcrumbs about an individual available. That's the core of our VR simulation.'

I didn't know what he was talking about. Being around Ari Levy made me experience what my grandmother in India must have felt when I first showed her an iPhone. Give me a fire, spices, mutton and a pot and I could create magic. Here – I was just an old woman smiling benignly at her grandson as he demonstrated how Shazam could name her favourite Hindi film song ('But I already know that song, beta, how is it helpful?').

'So, is there *anything* we can use? We have him in for questioning,' I said.

'Not really. I'd be surprised if he had anything to do with the shootings. The leak is another matter.'

'I have the documents Merrion received from his source in Aishtar. He said he got them on Tuesday; could you take a look and see if you think Tang could have been the source?'

'Email them to me.' He unplugged his USB drive from his laptop.

'Is that the special key you were talking about last night? The McCain thingy?' I said as I fiddled with my phone.

'This?' He waved the drive. 'No, it's just a USB dongle. We all need it to access the system, but you need my protocol too for my laptop. It's an added unbreakable layer of security.'

'I didn't see you use anything else?'

'You wouldn't have. That's the point,' he said. He scanned the email I had sent him. 'Shit. These are extremely confidential internal documents. Whoever sent them had high-level access to our systems.'

'Who has that type of access?'

'Very few people. The board. Some senior staff. Maybe a dozen in all?'

'Not Tang?'

'Definitely not officially. He could have hacked into the system – the documents all appear to be from his time here. I'll get dev-ops to see if they can find anything. This is very worry-ing. Who knows what else he may have leaked? And to whom.'

'Could you run Miles Merrion through your software as well?'

'The journalist? Why?'

'He's a person of interest.'

He hesitated. 'I'm not sure I can do that – I'll need Home Office permission.'

'You did Tang?'

'He was an employee. All our employees sign a waiver, as we need to use their data to train the system.'

'Please see what you can do.'

I didn't dare ask him to run it on Gaby Fleishman. I'd have to stick to old-fashioned analogue-style policing for that.

'I'll try, but don't hold your breath. So, if we're done . . .'

'I was going to tell you about those bones,' said Anjoli, who, with great difficulty, I imagined, had stayed quiet and unobtru-sive throughout.

'Oh, yes, sorry. I forgot. What did you find?'

'We got a DNA match – Ancestry.com was a terrific idea.' She told him about the relatives of the dead people.

Her excitement was infectious, and his gloom lifted. 'That's cool! Are you going to talk to the woman?'

'I'm planning to,' said Anjoli. 'I was also wondering if I could try that VR thing you mentioned? Would be great to get a sense of what life was like when our victims were alive.'

He looked like he might object, but Anjoli was hard to resist. Especially when she gave him her special, expectant smile. I had tried and failed many times.

'Well, you've signed the NDA, I suppose. And I rarely get the chance to show off. Why not?' He grinned like a child about to do a magic trick. 'Come with me. Prepare to have your mind blown.'

Chapter 19

Saturday morning.

As we followed Levy, I called Tahir and told him what little I'd learned.

'Damn. Nothing? I was hoping for a breakthrough. We've been at Tang for a while now, but he's sticking to his story – he's never seen Merrion's documents before. Nothing's turned up from his farm or computer either. But we can hold him for at least twenty-four hours. I'll keep pushing. I'm sure I can get something out of him.'

'I'll let you know if I find anything else.' I was relieved that Protheroe hadn't proved useful in the interrogation. It made me feel less useless.

Aishtar's virtual-reality suite occupied half an empty floor on the top of the building, looking onto Shoreditch. 'We need it to be a large space so you can move without banging into anything,' Levy said as Anjoli and I looked around. The odd thing about the room was the floor. It was uneven and lumpen.

'We had that floor installed especially, to simulate the feeling of cobblestones underfoot,' said Levy, when he noticed Anjoli and me looking down and treading with trepidation. 'You'll see what I mean in a minute. Now hold still for a sec.' Levy took photos of us – 'We use them to create your avatars' – then handed each of us a headset that looked like an opaque diving mask. We strapped them on, and he gave us controllers for each hand. 'Walk around. Turn your head in all directions to see. You'll be able to look at and talk to each other, but you can't talk to the characters in the simulation yet. If you feel nauseous, tell me and we'll stop. Enjoy.'

The headset was not as heavy as I expected, and I soon got used to it. At first all I saw was black, then a road crowded with people filled my vision and my hearing. It was a grey, winter's day, slush on the ground and frost on the windows. I turned my head and found I could look in all directions and was startled to see Anjoli standing next to me in the street – her avatar incredibly realistic except that she was wearing a dark, floor-length dress. I looked down and saw that I was in a navy suit. I understood the purpose of the floor now; it brought a physical reality to the experience – I had to walk with care to avoid tripping. I shivered. Levy must have switched on the air conditioning to enhance the reality.

'Wow! I can see you, Kamil,' I heard Anjoli say. 'This is incredible.'

'I see you, too. I think this might be Brick Lane.'

'You're right. My God, this *is* immersive.'

Two scruffy boys, no more than six, stared at us. One was wearing a yarmulke and the other what looked like a soft felt hat. Their dress was just like clothes I had seen in old pictures: sturdy black boots, one with a hole in the front so the child's toe was visible; white long-sleeved shirt and dirty brown trousers. What *was* unusual was that they were both smoking cigarettes. They giggled and ran off into the crowd. We walked into the throng, which parted for us.

'Watch your step,' said Anjoli, as I saw a pile of horse dung ahead of me and skipped over it.

To my amazement, I could suddenly smell the dung. Was I imagining it? I sniffed a few times. It was definitely there together with the smell of fire, fish and an acrid smell I couldn't identify. I almost retched.

'This is next-level realism,' I said. 'Can you smell it, Anjoli, or am I imagining it?'

'Oh, I can smell it, believe me. I don't know how they are doing it.'

Around us were old men with beards, ringlets and chimney-pot hats talking to each other; women gossiping in dark dresses, wearing shiny black wigs and headscarves; a young mother sitting on a bench, breastfeeding her baby with no one paying attention to her. The voice of a singer in a colourful, flowered dress rose above the crowds and a passing man in a smart suit threw a coin into a tin cup in front of her.

'Look to your right,' whispered Anjoli.

I turned and saw four children dancing to the tune of an organ grinder, face lined and weathered, with eyes as bright as his monkey's.

'How do they make it so real?' Anjoli said. 'It feels like I'm here!'

'Clothes! Clothes! I'll buy old clo'es. Anything to sell, madam? Sir?' A raggedy man with a bag came up to me and stuck his face next to mine. I stepped back involuntarily. It was incredibly realistic. I could see the pores of his face and the dirt and smell the sweat on his brow. It felt like I could almost feel his breath on my face.

'I'm afraid not,' Anjoli said.

'Stop bothering the lady, you dirty Jew,' said a policeman in a black coat with a row of shiny buttons down it, sporting a helmet, not dissimilar to what uniform wore today.

'I'm not botherin' 'em, your 'onor,' said the pedlar. 'I'm just tryin' to buy some clo'es.'

The policeman pushed him, and he fell into the gutter.

I stepped forward to intervene, then remembered I was in a simulation and waited to see how it would play itself out. The policeman bent over and said, 'Be off with you; if I see you bothering gentlefolk again, you'll spend the next week looking at the sky through bars.'

'Leave 'im alone,' a woman shouted.

'Let's move on,' said Anjoli. 'I want to see if I can find where TK is.'

We walked down the road and came to the corner of the street where our restaurant was today. There was a long line of people outside – predominantly women in threadbare clothes and shawls, with a few men and children scattered among them – holding tin cans and waiting.

'I think it might be a soup kitchen,' said Anjoli, peering into the window of the building where they were waiting. I looked inside and could see women pouring soup from massive vats into the held-out tins as the indigents shuffled past. The queue seemed endless.

'We've been serving food from this site for over one hundred and twenty years, Kamil!' said Anjoli, awe in her voice.

'It's incredible. God, I could spend days wandering around here.'

We tried to go into the soup kitchen, but the door wouldn't open. They hadn't coded the interior yet, I guessed. I looked at the faces of the people. The attention to detail was amazing; it didn't look like a computer-generated image at all. Even Anjoli looked like . . . Anjoli.

Next to the soup kitchen was a confectioner's shop with people inside, eating enticing-looking cakes and drinking coffee. The irony was deliberate. The confectioner's window had labelled delicacies I'd never heard of, all of which looked delicious – stuffed monkeys, palavas, worsted balls, bolas – I could feel my mouth watering as I smelt the sweetmeats – maybe this was how Ari Levy brought taste into virtual reality. The shop next to it sold birds in cages, the tweeting of a green parrot fading as we walked away from it.

As we wandered on, we saw three well-dressed children circling a scruffy girl, singing

'I had a piece of pork

I put it on a fork

And gave it to a curly-haired Jew'

The girl in the circle tried to break out, but the others hemmed her in, as their chant increased in volume. I felt Anjoli tense next to me and saw her head towards them, but they scattered and ran away singing '*pork pork pork pork Jew Jew Jew Jew*'.

I understood Levy had been going for realism, but this overt racism didn't sit well with me at all. I suppressed my disgust as Anjoli came back to me, upset, and said, 'Let's try another area.'

We pressed our controllers, and a menu appeared. Brick Lane. Bethnal Green. Petticoat Lane. Fieldgate Street.

'Fieldgate Street! That's where we found my skeletons,' said Anjoli.

We clicked and after a few seconds, the scene changed. We were away from the hubbub in a cobbled street with redbrick buildings. It was snowing gently, the flakes providing a winter-wonderland feel to the scene. There were no people, save for a hansom cab that clopped past, the horse's feet throwing up the snow as it moved. I looked around to see a parade of shops, the largest proclaiming: PENNYFEATHER'S DEPARTMENT STORE & BAZAAR. FOR ALL YOUR NEEDS. They had decorated the windows of the shop with glamorous clothes, wedding dresses, furniture, glassware – a far cry from the higgledy-piggledy stores we had just seen in Brick Lane.

Next to this magnificent emporium was a door in the deepest blue. Etched in the stone frame above it were the words FIELD-GATE St. Gt. SYNAGOGUE in English and Hebrew, flanked by two stars of David and the dates 1899 and 5659.

'That's still there!' I marvelled. 'I've seen it. That door to the synagogue! It's part of the mosque now. I always thought it was odd the mosque used to be a synagogue. The imam told me it had been the last synagogue in Whitechapel. I guess we're see-ing it in its heyday.' I felt a pang of emotion thinking about the changing tides – the Jews being supplanted by the Muslims – who would *we* be replaced by?

A few doors away from Pennyfeather's, on the other side, was a modest building with a sign in front proclaiming:

SEWERS, BUTTONHOLERS, FINISHERS WANTED
AVRAM PINSKY
CLOTHESMAKER
MAKES ALL TYPES OF CLOTHES EVERY BIT
AS WELL AND CHEAPLY AS
MICHAEL MARKS
OF LEEDS

'I wonder if that's the Marks of Marks & Spencer,' said Anjoli. 'This Pinsky guy seems to advertise *him* more than himself!'

'Guess Marks was the better-known brand. Smart fellow!'

We tried to look inside the building, but the windows were shuttered.

'Where did you find the bodies?' said Anjoli.

I looked around, trying to get my bearings. 'Given where that synagogue door is, I'd guess it's somewhere between that department-store bazaar and the Pinsky shop. I think we'd better go back.'

'Aww, I wanted to see inside a house!'

'Next time.'

'Spoilsport. Okay. Just give me one more minute, please. It's outstanding.'

We looked around in silence – I could almost smell the soot and feel the damp that surrounded us. As we walked, I looked behind me and saw we were leaving footprints in the snow.

Finally, we took off our headsets and were back in the empty room, stunned, disorientated, and bereft of words.

Levy waited, smiling.

After a while Anjoli said, 'That . . . that was the most unbelievable thing I've ever experienced.'

I couldn't do anything but nod, my eyes still filled with the image of the lines of people waiting outside the soup kitchen that a century later had become our restaurant and home.

'Glad you liked it,' said Levy, looking very proud of himself.

'When you first described it, I imagined it would be like playing a naff video game. But it wasn't like that at all. I was there, experiencing real life with actual people. Incredible. How did you do it?' asked Anjoli.

'Lots of research followed by clever programming, motion capture and targeted scents from the headset, triggered by what you were seeing in the simulation. I based a lot on this book called *Children of the Ghetto* that my parents gave me to read when I was a teenager. Then we used maps and records of businesses – all the establishments you saw existed. Census reports. Old photographs. Those were my ancestors you saw. Well, not literally, but that's my history. To tell you the truth, I am proud of other things Aishtar has done, but this has mattered the most to me. I would like to live the lives of my ancestors, from their homes in Poland to England to Israel. That way, no one would ever forget them. There are only a quarter of a million Jews left in England, half of what there were seventy-five years ago. We must never forget. Of course, many never made it to Israel. Or here. In the 1940s . . .' his voice trailed off. Then he continued, 'But this is not just about *my* ancestors, it's connecting all the Jews who live scattered across Russia, America, Morocco, India – you name it. People have been trying to eradicate and demonise us for centuries, but we're still here and thriving. And I want to ensure we will *always* be here, at least digitally.'

'That's why you had the racism in the simulation?' Anjoli said.

'Sure. Because that is what they faced.'

'And that's how our skeletons must have lived?'

'If they were from that time, yes. What amazes me about this is that the lives of those people may look different compared with our lives today, but at the core, what was happening then is happening now. The East End was a magnet for entrepreneurs and people trying to make it big – just as it is today. They were weavers, tanners, designers, shopkeepers, jewellery makers – starting small businesses, some failing, some becoming huge. We are coders, product managers, experience designers doing the same. They had to raise money from philanthropists, we do it from venture capitalists. They came from Russia, Lithuania, Poland – we've come from Israel, India, China. The only material – *literally* material – difference is they worked with physical stuff – fabric, metal, leather – and we work with ephemeral zeroes and ones on a screen. But the impact we have on society is the same. They changed their lives and the world through their labours, and we are trying to do that too. Part of the reason I am excited about the sale is that even if the new owners don't want to go ahead with this remembrance project, I'll be able to fund it on my own. It is what I was born to do. It's my passion.'

I could see how genuinely captivated he was by the parallels between that old world and this new one he had built. 'And you think you can link this ... vision to your people-tracking business?'

'I want to create a true metaverse. Imagine being able to see Nelson Tang and follow him through London for the last six months. If we can build 3D representations of all of Central London, that's not crazy. We can bring the dead back to life. I'm revealing this simulation in Cambridge at the conference on Monday and discussing the possibilities in my keynote.'

'You've built a time machine, Ari,' said Anjoli, hanging on to his every word.

'I know, right? The opportunities are endless. Sid and Saul thought all this was a waste of money and wanted to shut it down, but Gaby supported me, so we got it done.'

His passion was extraordinary. I wanted to live in his future. After the loneliness, isolation and death of the past two years, the notion of roaming through history was exhilarating. I could see why Yael Klein had left David Baker for Ari Levy and why someone might pay billions to own this technology and have him work for them. Hell, *I* wanted to work for him, and I knew nothing about tech. I'd never been in the presence of a true evangelist before; I felt myself being sucked into his reality distortion field and liked it.

Anjoli said, 'Can I ask something . . . no, forget it.'

'Go on . . . it's okay. I've got a few minutes.'

'I was thinking about how the Palestinians live in Gaza today. It's not far off from the world you've created showing the poverty in the East End a hundred years ago. Does that bother you?'

Ouch! Anjoli was not subtle! Levy's face kept a polite smile, but I could sense something closing behind his eyes. 'It's complex. I'm not sure I want to get into that.'

Anjoli persisted, 'But, Ari, who's going to document *their* lives? You say we must never forget, and I don't disagree with you, but we *are* forgetting the suffering those people are experiencing as we *speak*. Don't you think there's some cognitive dissonance?'

'*Cognitive dissonance?* Look, I agree it's not great what's happening, but it's easy to say these things when you live three thousand kilometres away. When alarms go off in the middle of the night because rockets are being fired at you and you have to run to a bomb shelter in seconds, it is different. People have been murdering Jews for thousands of years and we must protect ourselves. Look at your skeletons, for example. Murdered.'

I listened to their discussion, worried Anjoli was antagonis-
ing Levy. But I didn't get the sense that it was a black-and-white
issue for him or that he was committed to the Zionist cause.
After all, the money for his company came from a Palestinian
refugee. But what did I know?

He continued. 'Look at your own deprived areas, only a few
miles away from here. Mothers at fifteen. Kids who are addicts.
Generations dependent on the state. Are you that different?'

'I suppose you're right,' said Anjoli. 'Perhaps they need your
virtual reality to get out of their actual reality.'

'That's a scary thought,' I said.

'Humanity is the same everywhere,' said Levy. 'Maybe there's
no hope of permanent change, even over hundreds of years. Poverty, injustice, we can't eradicate them. They just move from one
place to the next, re-incarnating like time-space shapeshifters.'

'Like some sort of negative energy,' I said, remembering
some part of physics with scary Mrs Ghosh in Calcutta Boys'
School.

'Indeed. Let me know what happens with your visit to your
skeletons' descendant, Anjoli.'

'I'm sorry if I offended you,' she said. 'I didn't mean to.'

'Not at all. It's hard for a non-Israeli to understand what we go
through. And we're not perfect by any means. Listen, if you
fancy seeing the demo again and my speech in Cambridge on
Monday, let me know. I can get you a ticket. It's at King's College
and there's a gala kick-off cocktail party tomorrow night.'

'Oh, that sounds like fun,' said Anjoli. 'I'd love to.'

I wasn't sure why Levy was being so generous, but given we
seemed to have hit a dead end on our case, it might not be a bad
thing to do. But there was no way I could take Anjoli – bringing
her to Aishtar had been risky enough. I had to dampen her
enthusiasm before I got into trouble.

'Let me check with the boss,' I said.

'Ari, thank you again for sharing that with us; I'll never forget it,' said Anjoli. 'I'm even more determined now to find out who those people were and who shot them. We owe it to them.'

We walked out of the Aishtar offices, still disoriented from our experience. I had a feeling I wouldn't be able to walk through Brick Lane again without seeing ghosts of the smoking children, laughing and running away.

26 Fieldgate, East End, London
20 December 1912

Darling Shoshi,

It has been three months since I last
heard from you. I hope you are keeping
well. The big news is we have our own
house! The business is growing and with
Yanky as a partner, Avram is now
employing people in our own showroom (on
the ground floor) and factory (on the top
floor) in Fieldgate where we are now
living (in the middle floor with Yanky's
cousin and his wife). We also have three
market stalls and Pinsky Clothing is
gaining in reputation. Avram has dreams
of being like Michael Marks' Penny
Bazaar, but I told him to keep our
dreams small – then we can't be
disappointed. But he wants to be like
the Takeefim and live on Bury Street, so
let him dream.

  He took me to the West End last week,
and it is so different from where we
live in the East. Big streets, beautiful
old buildings and cheerful people in
their fine clothes going in and out of
restaurants and elegant shops. Avram
says one day he will have a shop there.
He told me the wind blows from West to
East in London so the rich people cannot
smell the foulness of the factories

where we live - I think he is right - it smelled much nicer in Regent Street.

A big department store has opened down the road from our factory, next to the Sha'ar Ya'akov Synagogue, called Pennyfeather's. Avram and I met Mr Pennyfeather last week outside our home. He seems to be a friendly man. Avram and Yanky think that Pennyfeather's will attract passing trade and so Avram has put up a big sign saying 'Pinsky's Clothing' outside our house.

I felt so upset that we couldn't go back for Tate and Muter's funeral and Leah will never know her grandparents, but that is the case for so many of us in this country now. I am so glad you could travel there and back safely. Are things calmer now? Have the threats passed? Leah is very naughty, but as you know, Avram is fond of her. She pretends to help in the factory as well. She thinks she is an adult like us. I have to keep telling her she is only three and has much to learn. How is little Eva? Is it time to have another baby? I was sorry to hear about Semyon's back. I hope it gets better soon so he can get back to work.

Let us meet again soon.

With all my love,

Malka

Chapter 20

Sunday morning.

'I'm sorry about our dinner tonight,' I said to Anjoli on the tube to Golders Green to see Sofia Katz. 'Tahir is insisting that he and I attend Ari Levy's thing in Cambridge to get a break in the case. I really want to have a nice meal with you.'

'That's fine. Don't worry about it.'

'I asked him if you could come, but it's an overnight trip and he said it was police business. I'd much prefer a night away with you than Tahir.'

She raised a suggestive eyebrow and said, 'I'm sure you would. And now you're sharing a room with Tahir instead of a romantic dinner with me.'

Romantic. Things were looking up. Or was she taking the piss? You never could tell with Anjoli. The Cambridge trip had given me an excuse to cancel Maliha as well, thankfully. I'd been delaying blowing her off to see Anjoli, as I didn't know what to say. She had seemed genuinely disappointed when I told her, but we'd rescheduled for the following weekend. I was juggling two potential futures, and, if I was honest, it secretly made me feel like a guilty playboy.

The doors opened and closed at Camden Town. 'Anyway, Chanson is experimenting with some new dishes tonight, so I wouldn't have been able to come. I need to anticipate diner reaction before I put them on the menu.'

I snorted. 'Chanson! With no surname. Does he think he's Prince or Beyoncé or something? What is he whipping up now? Snake with garam masala? Butterflies on a bed of basmati?'

She rolled her eyes. 'Just because you don't have a refined palate . . . I'm well jel that you're going to see the VR again, though,' she said. 'It was so moving. And those kids . . . It was incredible seeing our prints in the snow of a hundred years ago. Almost like footprints in time. Did you notice that? Ari's so clever!'

'Yeah, pretty amazing,' I said. 'A living history of his ancestors. I was trying to imagine what mine would look like . . .'

'They grew up in Bangladesh when it was still in India, right?'

'They were farmers in a tiny village near Sylhet. I remember Abba telling me they had a house on top of a hill overlooking the Surma River, and they kept chickens and goats. I've never been there – it's all built up now. I would love to experience it.'

'That would be incredible.' She paused. 'That thing he said . . . about bringing the dead back to life to relive their existence . . . do you think there's something in it?'

'Why?' The train came to a halt again.

She didn't answer, but her eyes misted, and she glanced away to the right, as though deeply interested in the trainers of the woman who had just boarded the carriage.

I realised she was thinking about her parents. Talking to them again. Seeing Saibal give his crooked smile when she caught him smoking. Hearing Maya tell her off for not reordering the barberries for the chicken berry pulao when they ran out. She'd never had the chance to say goodbye.

I squeezed her hand. 'Maybe sometime in the future – you never know. Look. We've reached Golders Green. Let's concentrate on this now. Perhaps we can get some answers about our skeletons.'

322 Gainsborough Gardens was a white house on a wide, tree-lined street. Anjoli pressed the doorbell next to the intricately

embossed silver mezuzah affixed to the door frame. A lady in her fifties – big blonde hair, glasses, wearing a knee-length flowered dress – opened the front door.

'Sofia Katz?' said Anjoli.

'Yes.'

'I'm Anjoli. And this is my friend Kamil. We spoke on the phone yesterday?'

'Oh yes, yes. Come on in.'

We walked through a large living room into a conservatory opening onto a garden that was brown from the heat.

'It's such a nice day. Shall we sit outside? Would you like some tea?' said Sofia.

'That would be lovely, thank you,' said Anjoli.

We went into a well-tended garden where a lady who looked to be in her eighties, with jet-black dyed hair and a deeply lined face, wearing a long black dress, was on her knees pulling out weeds from a flower bed, a cigarette dangling from the side of her mouth.

'Sit, sit,' said Sofia, pointing to four garden chairs under an umbrella. 'Ma, this is Anjoli!' she addressed the woman in the garden, her voice going up a couple of notches, 'and her friend . . .'

'Kamil,' I obliged.

'. . . her friend Kamil. This is my mother, Polina Kaufman.'

Polina stood up with some effort, brushed grass off her clothing, and joined us in the shade. We exchanged pleasantries as Sofia went back inside.

'Have you lived here long?' I said.

'All my life,' said Polina. 'I was born here and will die here.'

'It's a beautiful house,' contributed Anjoli, and we lapsed into silence, the unusually warm English sun and smell of freshly turned earth conjuring an oasis of calm.

Sofia came out with a tray of tea and digestive biscuits, and we helped ourselves. 'So, it was all a little mysterious, what you said on the phone. You had a DNA match, and the police are involved?'

'Yes, sorry, it's all crazy, isn't it? Sounds like a film plot. But Kamil here is a detective and—'

'Speak up,' commanded Polina in an imperious tone, lighting another cigarette from the butt of the first one.

'Sorry,' said Sofia. 'She's a little hard of hearing and she's very used to letting people know.'

Anjoli smiled and raised her voice. 'Kamil is a detective and was investigating a crime and . . . this may be distressing.'

'Distressing,' snorted Polina. 'After all that I have seen . . .'

'Okay, Ma,' said Sofia.

'Well,' said Anjoli. 'In the course of his investigations, he unearthed the remains of three skeletons from over a hundred years ago. I paid for the lab to do a DNA test, and they got a match with the profile you had uploaded to the ancestry site.'

'Did you hear that, Ma? They found a match with some skeletons.'

'I'm not deaf. I heard. Where did you find these bodies, young man?'

'We found them while excavating a building site on Fieldgate Street, near Brick Lane.' Bringing in Sid Ram's murder would only confuse things.

'And we're trying to trace who they might be,' Anjoli continued. 'It was a man, a woman and a young girl. And, since you were on the ancestry website, we were wondering if anything you knew about your family history may help identify them.'

'How fascinating,' said Sofia. 'How did they die?'

I wondered too late if I needed a family liaison officer present. We hadn't covered ancient skeletons in my course. 'I'm afraid the man and child appear to have been shot. The woman appears to have been hit on the back of the head.'

'Shot,' said Sofia. 'They were murdered?'

'We believe so.'

'Ma, what do you think?' said Sofia.

Silence. A bee buzzed near me. Then Polina whispered, 'A hundred years ago?'

'Yes,' said Anjoli.

'Fieldgate Street?'

'Yes.'

A long pause. Then, 'Wait here.'

She rose with an effort, picked up a walking stick next to her chair and hobbled towards the house.

'What do you need, Ma? I'll get it,' said Sofia, but her mother waved her off.

'She's quite a lady,' said Anjoli, watching her.

'You don't know the half of it. Please, have another biscuit. I can't believe you got a DNA match. I put it on the site thinking we might find some interesting relations in Israel or America. I never dreamed that . . . did you get a date on the skeletons?'

'Late 1890s to early 1900s,' said Anjoli.

Polina returned, shuffling towards us, carrying a tin. She banged it on the table and sat down, out of breath. It was an ancient octagonal biscuit tin with bizarre pictures of lions, tigers, ostriches, cowboys and a bearded Indian guard, under which it read 'Huntley & Palmers Biscuit Manufacturers, By Appointment to the Queen'. From the illustrations, it was hard to tell what types of biscuit it could have contained – some weird combination from India and the Wild West, like cumin-flavoured Oreos. I'd better not mention it to Chanson, or it would be on our menu in a week.

'Open it,' she barked at Sofia, who obliged. Polina leaned forward and took out a sheaf of papers and some photographs. She rifled through them, pulled out one and whispered, 'Malka.'

'Who's Malka, Ma?' said Sofia.

197

'Bubbe's sister. Nobody ever knew what happened to her. It has to be Malka.'

I felt a cold prickle on my back.

'Who's Bubbe?' said Anjoli.

'My grandmother, Shoshannah,' said Polina. 'Sofia's great-grandmother. She used to tell me stories about her family. They came from Russia. But you said there were only three bodies? Bubbe told me four of them disappeared – Malka, her husband, daughter and baby girl.'

The thought of a baby lying under the rubble we had seen in Fieldgate Street pierced me.

'I don't think they found a baby,' I said. 'But she could be there.'

Cigarette balanced between her lips, Polina handed Anjoli a sheet. 'Bubbe had letters from her sister, about a dozen in all; I had them translated from Yiddish in the eighties. Look at the address.'

I looked over her shoulder at a typed letter. On the top right, it said,

26 Fieldgate, East End, London
20 December 1912

'OMG,' whispered Anjoli. 'We found her.'

We spent another hour with Polina, learning what we could about Malka. She had come over to London from Russia with her husband Avram in 1905 and settled in the East End. Avram had built a good business there, and Malka corresponded with her sister Shoshannah in Manchester.

Sofia did some calculations on her fingers. 'This actually makes sense. My great-grandmother Shoshannah died ten years before I was born, around 1960, I think. I remember her. She was born before the turn of the century.'

'And then one day,' said Polina, 'the letters from Malka stopped. The last one she got was in December 1913. Bubbe went down to London in March to find her sister, but nobody knew what had happened to Malka and her family; other people had moved into their house and their belongings had been given away. The last anyone saw of them was on New Year's Eve. Neighbours thought they had returned to Russia, but Bubbe knew her sister would never have done that. Avram's business was taken over by his partner Yanky and sold. A few months later, the war started and . . . well, everyone had bigger worries than Malka.

'But,' Polina took a drag on what seemed to be her fifth cigarette of the morning, 'Bubbe never forgot. She would look after me as a child after the war when Ma used to go to work, and she would tell me about her life. Look, these are pictures of the family.'

She showed us two sepia photos – one of a stern-looking Orthodox Jew with an enormous hat, ringlets and full beard with a woman in a black dress and headscarf standing ramrod straight next to him, both staring at the camera. The other picture had a pretty little girl in a white pinafore holding a baby in a park.

'That's Avram, Malka, Leah and Miriam.'

I tried to connect these people with the skeletons we had seen a few days ago. That's what Anjoli and I would be in a hundred years – well, I would be buried under the earth; she would be ashes. I wasn't sure which was better.

'Do you have any idea who might have done this to them?' said Anjoli. 'Was there anything in the letters? Anyone they had fallen out with?'

'I never thought they had been murdered,' said Polina, shaking her head. 'That's terrible. Bubbe would have been heartbroken to learn this. Well, even more heartbroken. She never forgot her sister. Imagine living your life wondering about your loved ones' disappearance and never knowing? You read those letters, young lady, and see if you can find something.'

'May I take pictures of them?'

Polina nodded and Anjoli took her phone out and photographed each letter. Then she stood. 'Thanks so much. We need to go now; I have to organise lunch. I run a restaurant on Brick Lane – Tandoori Knights – if you like Indian food, come over and I will give you the best Indian meal you've ever had. On the house.'

'The best Indian meal we've ever had. And free. How could we resist that?' said Sofia.

'Can we bury the bodies?' said Polina.

'I'm sure they will be released to you,' I said.

Anjoli was buzzing all the way back to the restaurant, reading and rereading the letters on her phone. 'I can't believe we found them,' she kept repeating. 'Kamil, please get them to look for the baby on the site. The poor thing. Now we just have to find out why they were killed.'

I was pleased for her and for Sofia and Polina. She had made a difference to the lives of these people and found some purpose – other than keeping the restaurant going. I was keen to build on the momentum of this win and spend some time with her outside Tandoori Knights. 'Let's think about where we can research this,' I said. 'There must be archives of some sort in synagogues and places like that. Now that we have their names, it should be easier to learn about them. Maybe those letters will give you some clues.'

'Will you help? Like old times. With you at your course for the last two years and me at the restaurant, we haven't had much fun together, have we?'

She looked straight into my eyes. The train wasn't the ideal place to have this conversation. I said, 'Of course I will. I've tried to think of stuff for the two of us to do together, but . . . it's been hard.'

'Why?'

I wasn't sure what to say. 'I don't know, with Covid and Saibal-da and Maya-di and . . . it's been a tough few years for you. You never seem to want to talk about it. About how you're feeling. About us. Most of the time, I feel like I've done something to upset you and don't know what.'

Something closed inside her. 'There's nothing to talk about. You always make too much of all this, Kamil. I'm fine. Trust me. Let's just do this together and see where we get to, okay?'

I nodded. Normally, I liked to see the destination before I set off, but I'd try to enjoy the ride.

Chapter 21

Sunday night.

Tahir was uncharacteristically morose on our way to Cambridge. 'The Home Secretary wants a result and because of her, the Chief Super's piling on to the gaffer. He's on my arse 24/7 and all we have is a bagful of bugger all. He's threatening to hand it over to SO15, so we're not left holding it when the shit hits the fan.'

I overtook a pensioner who seemed to think he was driving through a village instead of on the motorway.

'Nothing from Nelson Tang?'

'Zilch. Had to let him go. Search yielded zero. And fuck all from forensics in Cohen's flat. The sheet of paper with the anti-AI stuff had Fleishman's prints on it, but he already admitted touching it.'

'Still no luck with the burner phone?'

He shook his head. 'No link to any known numbers. We're watching to see if it goes live again. No record of the suspects owning a gun – it's difficult to get one with a silencer, so it must be someone with contacts in the underworld.'

'Or linked to a hostile government.' I slowed down to avoid a speed camera.

'Still on your spy kick? Yeah, or they could have been professional hits. Anyway, right now, that phone is the only lead we have. I hope we find out more at this shindig. Had to get permission from Rogers for the two of us to stay the night. He suggested we share a room, but you'll be happy to know I persuaded him otherwise.'

'Oh good, so I don't have to hear you farting all night.'

'Funny guy. How're things between you and Anj? Did she get anywhere with the DNA stuff she said she was doing? We didn't get a hit on our databases.'

'You're not going to believe this, but she's found out who they are.' I gave him the full rundown.

'That's impressive.'

'Yes, she's really excited about it. Also, she seems more positive about me – so fingers crossed.'

'Hmm. And have you been to see your ex yet?'

'Well no. But I'm seeing her next weekend.'

'Player! I'm teaching you more than just policing, then?'

'Hah! Believe me, I've always been a player.'

'You're a mess, not a Messi. Remember what happened to Naila? You thought she was the one and . . .'

'I remember.' But it was not a memory I wanted to relive. I switched the radio on and thankfully Tahir kept quiet for the rest of the drive.

We left the car and our bags at the Clayton Hotel just after 9 p.m. and, two minutes later, collected our name badges and walked into the Grand Hall of King's College. Tahir's meeting with Rogers had made us an hour and a half late to the gala cocktail, and it was in full swing.

'Bloody hell, what is this, Hogwarts School for tossers and twats?' whispered Tahir. 'I hope you brought your cape and wand.'

'Well, they seem to think I'm about to transfigurate into a pot noodle,' I said, affixing my *Kamil Ramen* badge to my suit pocket. Tahir wasn't wrong about the rarefied Harry Potter world we'd wandered into. It was quite overwhelming. We were in a long, narrow, wood-panelled hall hung with dozens of paintings of glum-looking men who had been handed ownership of India, Rhodesia, Hong Kong and Australia on a plate with a side of murder and pillage. Above these entrepreneurs of Empire ran rows of stained-glass windows reaching up to a wooden vaulted ceiling intricately carved with gilded detailing – an expanse of heaven that had not yet been colonised by the British, as far as I knew. I expected to see a fright of ghosts looming around us, but it was only a waiter scurrying over with a tray of drinks, so we helped ourselves to an orange juice each. The champagne looked inviting after our long drive to Cambridge, but that wouldn't have done anything to improve Tahir's mood or performance. Glass in hand, I looked around, and to my consternation, realised it was a black-tie event and Tahir and I were the only ones in regular business suits.

We grabbed some canapés – a delicious smear of pâté on a tiny toast and smoked salmon with dill on a blini – and circled the hall till we spotted Wahid Masri, David Baker, Ari Levy, Yael Klein and Gaby Fleishman chatting in a group. Levy waved at us as we approached and said, 'You made it. Wahid, I invited them along. Figured they would keep us safe.'

'Welcome, gentlemen,' boomed Masri, an orange juice tiny in his huge boxer's hand, prodigious belly trussed into an exquisitely fitted black dinner jacket. He looked us up and down, and I smoothed my tie. 'I didn't realise you had an interest in the future of artificial intelligence.'

'We don't. But we have interest in finding a murderer,' said Tahir, a little too theatrically. His Columbo act appeared to be cheering him up.

I flagged down a waiter and helped myself to delicious truffled duck. Colonists or not, these Cambridge colleges laid on some exquisite food. I threw caution to the wind and accepted a glass of champagne from another server, who hovered to my right. Tahir raised an eyebrow, then took a glass as well.

I turned my attention back to Baker, who was saying, '. . . and this is just an early Alpha version. The final will be ground-breaking.'

'It gives me the shivers,' said Klein, who looked elegant in a long, shimmery gold evening dress. 'Maybe we should let the past remain in the past.'

'We have to understand the past to create the future,' said Levy, and noticing that a spaghetti strap had strayed from her shoulder, picked it up delicately with his little finger and returned it into place.

Michelle Jennings appeared in a cheongsam-style dress and tapped Masri on the arm. 'It's time.'

'Hi, Ms Jennings,' I said. 'They never give you any time off, do they?'

'Fancy dos are a rare perk of the job. I've been looking forward to this for months.'

'Okay, team, I will see you later,' said Masri. He made his way to the platform stage in the centre of the hall. Tahir and I peeled away as Masri picked up the microphone and the crowd hushed. 'My lords, ladies and gentlemen. It is my great pleasure to welcome you to our annual symposium on Artificial Intelligence and Deep Technology. Please, prepare yourselves for two days of intellectual stimulation, ethical dialectics and opportunities for consociation.' He gave an exaggerated wink to an appreciative titter from his audience. I made a mental note to look up *dialectics* and *consociation*. 'But for tonight, have a good time and I hope to see you bright and early back here tomorrow morning to hear our keynote speaker, Ari Levy, Chief Data Scientist and co-founder of Aishtar Technologies.'

A wave of applause. The hum of conversation began again as Tahir said, 'Look.'

Nelson Tang and Miles Merrion were in an intense discussion over on one side of the room.

'And look who's got eyes on them,' I said.

Standing in a corner, watching them, were the two men we had seen in Ram's building – they *had* got the black-tie memo.

'Well, well, our SO15 stooges. I didn't expect that,' said Tahir. 'We have a full house. Come on.'

I grabbed another glass of champagne and followed Tahir around the crowd to reach our targets from behind.

Tahir said, 'Mr Merrion and Mr Tang. What a surprise. I thought you didn't know each other.'

They looked startled to see us, but Merrion recovered and said, 'We don't. We just met.'

'What a coincidence.'

'Not really,' said Tang. 'We're both interested in AI, and this is the premier AI conference. I come every year.'

'So, you're back on the grid, then?' I said.

He didn't reply.

'What were the two of you discussing?' said Tahir. 'You seemed to be engrossed in each other's company.'

'Mr Merrion's article,' said Tang. 'I was telling him I agreed with everything his source said.'

'That AI should be stopped?' I said.

'No. Just that it shouldn't be unconstrained. Excuse me, I need to get another drink.'

He wandered away.

Merrion's eyes sparkled like the champagne in its flute. 'Have you seen the reaction to the article? There are protests outside parliament.'

'I have,' I said. 'Tell me, what's the endgame here? What do you hope to achieve with these in-depth investigations?'

He paused. 'Create enough of an outcry so the government stops using this type of technology as and when they want. You can't uninvent this tech, but you can put it back in a box with appropriate safeguards.'

'And how likely do you think that is?'

'We'll see. Priscilla Patrick cares about public opinion. She'll be weighing up the pros of being tough on crime with the cons of intruding on privacy. She'll go with whatever strengthens her prospects to become PM. And if I can stop that . . .'

'Surely she'll be better than the clown we have now? At least she's competent,' said Tahir, the alcohol making him less discreet than usual.

'Who would you rather have run the country – a baboon or a scorpion? I know which I'd prefer.'

We watched him walk away. 'Maybe the two of them are in cahoots,' I said. 'One did one murder, and the other did the other. If they were both anti AI, they might have joined forces.'

'Not beyond the realm of possibility,' said Tahir, looking around for a waiter to top up his drink. 'Let's do a detailed check on them and see if we can find any time or place they intersect. But we have too many bloody suspects – Fleishman, Tang, Merrion, Levy, Jennings, your invisible Blofeld. We need to winnow them down or we'll get nowhere. Let's talk to the spooks. Maybe they'll help.'

Fat chance, I thought as we walked over to the SO15 guys.

Chapter 22

Sunday night.

Tahir said, 'Mr Warner and Mr Powell? I'm Inspector Ismail and this is DC Rahman. We met briefly near Mr Ram's flat. I think we may be working the same case.'

Two blank faces stared back.

'I'm curious,' said Tahir. 'Are you guys here to protect the Aishtar people or get their technology?'

Still no response.

My turn. 'Look, we're basically on the same side. Do you think it's possible a foreign power is behind this? Aren't we better off pooling our intel?'

'What intel do you have?' said Powell. Or Warner. I didn't know who was who. Or if their names were even Powell and Warner.

'You show us yours, then we show you ours,' said Tahir.

They exchanged glances and one of them said, 'Let's go somewhere quieter. You're staying at The Clayton, right?'

Tahir nodded.

'Us too. Come on, we have a car.'

'It's not too far from here. We can walk,' I said.

'We have a car,' he repeated.

Tahir and I glanced at each other. I wasn't comfortable getting into a car with these two goons, but given we were stuck, and they might know something, this was an offer we couldn't possibly refuse.

We left the hall, and an Audi pulled up, driven by another spook in dark glasses. Powell (or Warner) got in the front and the two of us plus the other one squeezed in the back. We drove in silence for five minutes down the empty street, and I felt a sense of relief when we stopped in front of The Clayton. A tiny part of me had been expecting a bag over my head, a drive to a remote area of the fens and the sensation of drowning in a bog, never to be found again. Too much Scandi-noir.

In the bar, Powell and Warner ordered whiskies and Tahir and I got beers.

'So,' said Powell (I designated the bigger guy as Powell and the thin one as Warner). 'Tell us what you know.'

'I'll admit we need your help,' said Tahir, as he sipped his beer and helped himself to the free pee nuts, as I call them. 'There are a lot of eyes on this—'

I butted in, 'We need to prevent a possible further murder as well because it looks like the top executives of Aishtar are being picked off one by one.'

Tahir gave me a look and continued. 'That's the principal thing, of course, which is why we want to share what we know. And we'd appreciate it if you'd do the same.'

Powell and Warner remained silent as Tahir leaned forward and spoke in a lowered voice. 'Nelson Tang and Gaby Fleishman remain our prime suspects. Tang had a grudge and probably leaked the info to Merrion. Fleishman was with Sid Ram the night he was killed and found Saul Cohen's body. Gets their shares in the company. Appointed CEO. But we have no evidence linking them to the murders. The only hard clue we have is the mobile number that called both Ram and Cohen. We can't track it, but maybe you can. There, that's everything.' Tahir finished the rest of his drink and sat back expectantly.

'We knew all that,' said Warner. 'We have had no luck with the mobile as yet, either.'

'So, what *is* your interest in this?' I said.

'The technology,' said Powell. 'The government is keen to lock it down. It's helped to intercept two terror plots already.'

'What kind of plots?' I said.

'I can't reveal that. Suffice to say they would have had serious consequences with many casualties.'

'So how come the government doesn't mind the sale of the company?' said Tahir.

Powell looked at Warner. 'The buyer is . . . friendly.'

'IntSoft?' I said. 'Who are they? We've had no luck finding out.'

Another look. Then, 'All I can say is that they are funded by an intelligence service.'

This put a different complexion on things. If intelligence services were prepared to pay 4 billion . . . 'The CIA? Mossad?' I said. 'Actually, on the sales document, it was called IntSoft LLC, which is an American term, isn't it? So CIA, then?'

No response.

'What guarantee do you have that the CIA would let you use it?' said Tahir.

'Well, no guarantee,' admitted Powell. 'They have made certain commitments, but ideally, we would like to secure the technology for ourselves. So far, Aishtar refuses to let us have the code. They have it in their control and they, and only they, can operate it.'

'In fact,' I said, 'now only Ari Levy can operate it. He's put some kind of safeguard in place. Something he calls a McCain protocol.'

They looked at each other as Powell made a note on his phone. 'What's a McCain protocol?'

'I don't know. The only McCain I've heard of is the guy who tried to be President of America. Maybe it's some techie thing? I googled it but found nothing. But getting back to the killings, do you think it might be an unfriendly government?'

'It's possible. Certain parties would love nothing more than to get their hands on this tech. We've had feelers out for any activity in the UK but found nothing yet.'

I asked the question that had been bugging me for nearly a week. Although these guys had probably been literally bugging me for days.

'We saw you at Ram's flat the morning of his murder. How did you get there so soon after we found the body?'

'We had a flag out on all the key Aishtar people. When his death was called in, we rushed over to make sure there was nothing detrimental to national security in his flat.'

Tahir caught my eye as I tried to work out the timing. It was just about plausible. I couldn't resist a dig. 'You didn't find the sale document, did you?'

They looked at me without expression. 'We were only looking for technology.'

'But you weren't watching Cohen?'

'We didn't think he was a target. As CFO, he didn't have access to the code.'

'And have you seen anything or anyone suspicious so far?'

'No.'

'Why have you been following us?' I said.

'To see what you find out. You can question suspects, we can't. But if you share your info with us, we'll scratch yours. We can cooperate from now on.'

Which would make a change from us sitting around, scratching our own arses.

Over their shoulders, I saw Miles Merrion and Nelson Tang enter the bar. They looked over, clocked us, and ducked out again.

'Excuse me,' I said and ran out, seeing them get into a lift together. It went up to the fourth floor and stopped. When it returned, it was empty.

I went back to the bar. Tahir was alone.

'They left me with the bill. Typical,' he said, paying.

'Did you believe them about how they got to the scene of Ram's death so quickly?'

'I don't know. If they were following him, they would have seen the murder.'

I wouldn't have put it past them to have seen the killing but have left the killer in the wind for some reason of their own.

'Any reason they wouldn't tell us?' I said.

'Who knows? They play by their own rules.'

Another far-fetched idea came to mind. 'Or perhaps they were involved with the deaths. Maybe they are trying to get the tech off those laptops. You heard him say only Aishtar can run it – it's possible that's not good enough for them.'

'Perhaps. Come on, I'm bushed. Let's meet down here for breakfast in the morning. Half seven?'

I got into bed just after eleven and, enjoying the air-conditioned room, called Anjoli.

'How was the party?' she said. 'We're closing up here.'

'It's weird.' I described what we had seen and heard. She seemed most interested in the canapés, so I went into some detail about the bits and pieces I'd eaten. My stomach started grumbling, and I realised I'd not had any dinner.

'I read all the letters,' she said. 'My God, Kamil, what a life they led. You know, they came all the way from a place called Pinsk to London in 1905. You have to read them – what their journey was like, how they lived. It was incredible! And OMG, you're never going to believe this! It's such a coincidence! Remember the shop we saw in that VR street? Avram Pinsky? *That's him*! That's the man we found. Can you believe that?'

It seemed impossible. But then I remembered Levy had said they'd based his simulation on historical records.

'. . . *And* she mentions Pennyfeather's store in the letter. We saw that too. I'm going to research him next. Maybe we'll learn some more.'

Listening to her excitement made me miss her. And I was a little drunk.

'That's great, Anjoli. Wish I was there to read them. No, actually I'm in an empty double bed in the hotel – I wish you were here with me.'

There was a moment's silence. Then she laughed and said, 'Now, now. Control yourself.'

'Seriously. We'd be so good together. I just don't understand . . .'

'This isn't the time, Kamil. Look. Get this case over and done with and then we'll talk.' She paused. '*Maybe* things have changed.'

'Changed how?'

Another pause. 'You'll just have to wait and see. What's the plan for tomorrow?'

There it was, the completely unsubtle and totally expected Anjoli bait and switch. I was getting pissed off and was too tired to argue. I picked up the programme I'd been given and leafed through it. 'So, tomorrow I'm attending a conference on artificial intelligence and the topic I'm most looking forward to is . . .' I squinted at the page. '. . . "Using molecular simulations to drive pharmaceutical drug discovery".'

'What on earth does that mean?'

'No idea, but I should get some sleep, or I'll fall asleep during the speech. You should too. I'll be back tomorrow evening.'

'What's Ari's talk called?'

I looked at the agenda again. ' "From storytelling to storyliving in the Metaverse".'

'Well, that'll be interesting, at least. Tell me what experiencing the VR for a second time was like. Sleep well.'

I hung up, switched the light off, and wriggled under the sheet that was spread like a second skin on the massive bed.

Sleep well. Easy for her to say. Bloody Anjoli. *This isn't the time. Wait and see.* How long was I going to dangle at the end of her string?

I tried to sleep, but my mind was jangling. After fifteen minutes, I forced myself out from under the covers and put the light back on.

Fuck it. I wasn't going to hang around for her like a lapdog. If she didn't want me, there was someone . . .

Heart pumping, I dialled Maliha.

'Hi,' I said when she answered. 'Sorry I'm calling so late. Is this a bad time?'

'No, it's perfect. I'm just in bed. Reading. How's your conference?'

'Good. Sorry I had to cancel dinner.'

She laughed. 'This book is really boring, so I'd rather be at dinner with you.'

My heart fluttered. 'I'm looking forward to next week, too. But we can chat now. How's it going? How are you settling in?'

'Yes, pretty good. London life, eh? Now I know what I've been missing all these years. How's the new job?'

'Good. And you're enjoying Amnesty?'

I let her words wash over me as I wondered how I could get past these banalities and manoeuvre the conversation round to us. Our happy times in Kolkata. And how wretched I'd felt about the mistakes I'd made. How badly I had let her down. What was she feeling? I couldn't ask. I wasn't sure I could handle knowing. But I needed to get out from under Anjoli's thumb.

'We had some good times, didn't we, Maliha?' I blurted.

And it was out there.

I could hear her breathing down the phone, then she said in a voice so low I could barely make it out, 'Yes, of course.'

'I . . . miss you. Sorry, I'm a little drunk.'

A pause. Then, 'I do too. Sometimes.'

'I'm sorry about how it ended, Maliha.'

'Yes. Me too.'

'Do you think, maybe . . .'

Another pause. Then 'Maybe . . . but I've changed. And you have as well. I worry that you're just lonely and miss the way I made you feel.'

'What does that mean?'

'You know what, it's late . . .'

The room was dark, and the intimacy of her voice in my ear was more than I could bear. I realised I needed someone desperately.

'No tell me. Please.'

Silence. Then, 'I haven't seen you in so long. We should do this in person. Whatever *this* is.'

I let out a groan but had to be satisfied with that. 'All right. Next Saturday then?'

'Next Saturday.'

'Good night. It was nice to hear your voice again.'

She hung up, and I stared out of the window at the Cambridge night, wondering if I'd betrayed Anjoli in some way, yet intoxicated with possibilities.

PART II
The Second Week

Our death is in the cool of night,
our life is in the pool of day.
The darkness glows, I'm drowning,
the day has tired me with light.
Over my head in leaves grown deep,
sings the young nightingale.
It only sings of love there,
I hear it in my sleep.

Heinrich Heine, 'Death'

Chapter 23

Monday morning.

My alarm went off at 6.45 and I lay in bed for a few minutes, luxuriating in my massive, king-size bed. I'd slept poorly, trying to untangle my feelings about Anjoli and Maliha with no success. Well, the die was cast and what would be would be.

I stared at a picture of Trinity College Chapel on the wall of the bedroom. I'd never visited Cambridge before – growing up in India, it had always been a dream of mine to study with the best and brightest in these ancient buildings under the tutelage of learned professors whom I would watch scurrying across the quads and under the cloisters from lecture to lecture, their long black gowns billowing behind them in the refreshing English breeze. And now here I was. Not as a student, but I could experience a little of what I had missed out on, listening to abstruse lectures delivering recondite information on topics I didn't understand. Even if we made no progress on the case, it would be memorable.

I hauled myself out of bed, downed two Nurofen, got ready, and made my way down. I looked around the crowded breakfast room and saw Tahir had engineered a table for two next to the Aishtar crew. He waved me over. I passed Warner and Powell, who ignored me. Nelson Tang and Miles Merrion were engrossed in conversation a few tables away, Merrion jabbing his finger on an iPad, showing something to Tang.

'Sleep well?' said Tahir as I sat.

'Not great.' I looked over to the next table where Wahid Masri, David Baker, Gaby Fleishman and Michelle Jennings were tucking into breakfast.

'Where the hell is Ari?' said Masri. 'He should have been here fifteen minutes ago so we could fine tune his speech.'

'And Yael,' said Jennings, a smile flickering on her lips.

Fleishman shot a glance at her and said, 'Michelle . . .'

'Sorry, Gaby,' she said. 'But he *is* married and . . .'

'It's none of our business.'

Jennings looked down at her plate, appearing to find something of extreme interest in her bacon and eggs.

'Ari's late for everything,' said Fleishman. 'He'll be here in a minute.'

Masri dialled. When there was no reply, a shadow of worry crossed his face. 'Get him, David.'

'What room is he in?'

'435,' said Jennings. 'And Yael's in 443.'

The tension around the table was now palpable, and I felt my early warning system kick in – those cold, familiar fingers running down the nape of my neck. Tahir rose as I pushed my chair back, almost unbalancing the waitress standing behind me with a pot of coffee. 'Let us come with you.'

I saw Powell and Warner staring at us and there was now fear on the faces of the Aishtar people at the adjoining table. 'Don't worry, I'm sure he's fine,' I added.

The three of us rode up in silence to the fourth floor, then walked down the long, brightly lit corridor with its beige carpet and identical doors, passing a housekeeper who nodded to us. As we neared Ari Levy's room, grisly images from my Kolkata past flashed in my mind and I stamped them out with every footstep to stay in the present.

Baker ignored the 'Do Not Disturb' sign hanging on the handle of room 435 and rapped on the door. 'Ari, it's David. We're all waiting for you at breakfast downstairs.'

There was no answer. He knocked again, a little louder. Nothing.

'Try 443,' said Tahir, a grim note in his voice.

My back was feeling icy when there was no response from Yael Klein's room, either. 'Maybe we missed them, and they went down while we were coming up,' said David Baker. I shook my head and sprinted over to the housekeeper, showed her my warrant card, and demanded her passkey.

'I am not allowed, sir . . .' she said.

'It's urgent, miss. There may have been an accident. Please.'

The please did the trick, and she placed it in my outstretched hand as I ran back and opened the door to Klein's room, praying she wouldn't be walking out of the shower just as I entered.

It was empty. Her bed hadn't been slept in and the only sign of occupancy was an open wheelie bag on a luggage rack, with a few clothes scattered on an armchair near the window.

We strode back to Levy's room. 'Wait here,' Tahir told Baker as we entered, my senses jangling like a silent alarm.

The room was dark as night. I felt for the switch, then remembered I had to put the passkey into a slot next to the door to get the lights to work. I fumbled for it, slid the card in, and they blinked on.

I jumped as I heard a male voice say, 'That's why we have to take action now.'

My heart rate slowed as I realised it was the television. I walked the few steps into the main room, passing the open bathroom door on my left and a cupboard on my right.

I drew a sharp breath when I saw them, the iron smell of blood closing up my throat.

It was carnage.

Yael Klein was slumped against the headboard of the bed in a white dressing gown, her long black hair over her face, legs under the sheets with half her head blown off, blood spattered on the wall behind her and soaked into the pillow, which was entirely red. At the foot of the bed, on a blood-drenched patch of carpet, lay Ari Levy, also dead, shot in the neck. His face, unlike Klein's, was oddly untouched, dark eyes staring up at the fire alarm on the ceiling. I noticed a trickle of blood on the television on the console table above him, creating a red scar on the visage of an interviewer on the screen. If Sid Ram's and Saul Cohen's killing had been clinical, these were the opposite – the room was an abattoir. Who would have thought we contain so much blood?

Numb, I heard Tahir mutter under his breath over my shoulder, 'Fuck. Fuck.' I turned and saw him, shocked, blinking, expressionless. He gestured for us to leave the room. We backed out in slow motion – I was finding it difficult to get my arms and legs to do my bidding. The inconsequential thought that went through my mind as I retrieved the passkey with icy fingers was that the housekeeper would have a hell of a job cleaning the room.

'Not there?' said David Baker as the door shut.

'Please go back to the restaurant,' said Tahir, under his breath.

'What happened? Are they in there?'

Tahir raised his voice. 'Just go back down, Mr Baker. We'll be there in a minute.'

He frowned and looked as if he might argue, then turned and left.

'Call 999,' said Tahir.

I dialled, identified myself, asked for the police to attend the scene and, after hanging up, instructed the housekeeper not to go into any more rooms and to leave the floor.

We went back into Levy's room, and I inserted my card to switch on the room lights. Tahir surveyed the scene again and repeated, 'Fuck.' Then louder. 'Fuck! How could we let this happen, Kamil? Under our noses. Fuck. The boss will have my balls. We should have seen this coming. I should have put a guard on him all night. I can't believe this. Shit. Switch off that damn television.'

Before I could, there was a banging on the door. I opened it to see Wahid Masri and Gaby Fleishman outside. Before I could stop him, Masri barged past me into the room, saying, 'David said something was up. What the hell is going . . .'

He went silent when he saw the bodies.

'Get out of here right now, Mr Masri. You too, Mr Fleishman,' yelled Tahir.

Fleishman was shaking, staring at the corpses. '*Ani lo ma'amin*. No, no, this can't be. Ari. Not Ari. Who could do . . . ? My God. And Yael. No.'

'Leave, before you contaminate the scene,' shouted Tahir, shoving them out of the room. 'I will speak to you soon. Wait with the others in the restaurant.'

The two of them stood outside the room and tears drifted down Fleishman's face. Masri put an arm around his shoulders and said, voice soft, 'Come, Gaby. Come, my friend. This is a terrible thing. Come.'

He led him to the lift, which opened, and two uniformed police came out. I introduced myself and led them into the room where Tahir was standing, arms folded tight over his chest, staring holes into the bodies as though he might revive them through sheer force of will. I'd never seen him so distressed before. On seeing the cops, he regained his composure and said, 'I'm DI Ismail from the Met. My colleague and I are staying at the hotel, and we found the bodies. We believe these deaths are connected to two murders we are investigating in London. Secure the scene and please contact your on-call SIO.'

The younger of the two PCs nodded, dumbfounded, as the other murmured into his radio. As Tahir brought them up to speed in the hallway, I steeled myself and looked around the room, not going further in to avoid contamination.

Yael Klein was on the left side of the bed, possibly shot when she had been ready to sleep. Her white hotel dressing gown had fallen open on one shoulder, leaving a naked breast showing. I felt an urge to cover her up before she was exposed to the pitiless cameras of the police photographer when the forensic processes clicked into place. But murder victims rarely get the grace they deserve.

Ari Levy was diagonally opposite her on the floor next to the bed, dried blood around his head, arms outflung. I couldn't see his laptop anywhere.

'Okay. I've briefed them.' I hadn't noticed Tahir re-enter the room. 'We'll sort out jurisdiction between us and Cambridgeshire Police later. See anything?'

I tried to swallow and discovered my mouth was dry. I cleared my throat. 'It's possible the killer was standing where I am. He shoots Klein, who's sitting up in bed, maybe watching TV, and then Levy, who's standing near the desk. Must have used a silencer, or someone would have reported it. Can't see the laptop, so maybe he steals that, takes Levy's keycard from the lighting slot, and leaves.'

'How did he get in?' said Tahir.

'Levy let him in? Or had a passkey and surprised them?'

'Levy must have known him well if he let him in. Why take the keycard?' said Tahir.

'Maybe he wanted to get back in the room later? Or just leave it in darkness? Klein hadn't slept in her bed, as you saw. Guess she and Levy took this opportunity to be together.'

'Poor woman. If she hadn't, she might still be alive. I've told the PC I want them to bring over a batch of GSR tests. We have to check all potential suspects for gunshot residue while we have them here. And I asked him to get enough manpower to search all their rooms and interview the guests on this floor. We're gonna get this bastard, Kamil. He must have left some trace. Murdering two people while we were sleeping upstairs. No fucking way he's getting away with this. Come on, I'll gather up the suspects, you sort us out a couple of interview rooms – ask the hotel manager.'

Glad to have something meaningful to do, I left a constable guarding the scene and went to find the manager. He looked at me aghast when I told him what we had found in room 435 but composed himself and handed over keys to two suites on the top floor of his hotel. Tahir and I shepherded Wahid Masri, David Baker, Gaby Fleishman, Michelle Jennings, Miles Merrion and Nelson Tang to a suite, and I relieved them of their room keys. Tahir had told Warner and Powell what had happened, and they walked up with us, phones jammed to their ears as they whispered to the powers that be.

We designated the second suite as a makeshift incident room, and I went back down to room 435 to find the machinery of the police in full operation. The pathologist was checking out the bodies, a photographer was snapping; the small hotel room was packed. Two other cops were in Klein's room, looking for evidence, bagging her belongings.

A man in a brown suit addressed me. 'DI Neely. You're DC Rahman?'

'Yes, sir. I found the bodies. DI Ismail is upstairs with the suspects.' I gave him a brief rundown of our case and he nodded, sharp eyes taking it all in. 'I read about those killings. We found this in an envelope next to the man's body.'

He showed me an evidence bag containing an A4 sheet on which was typed:

Today's humans always totally, deeply,
insanely expect distraction. It needs
severe, agonising, bloody, revolting
action and numerous deaths crying havoc;
and <u>then</u> insanity leaks away, calming and
manufacturing peaceful sleep.

I took a picture. 'We found similar notes near the other bodies. Did you find his laptop? Or a USB stick?'

'Not so far, but we'll keep looking. Pathologist says they've
been dead for a few hours now.'

'I saw them last night at around half ten and found the bodies
at a quarter to eight this morning.'

'Died between eleven and five then. We're discussing the
removal of the bodies to London with the coroner. There's a lot
of red tape, but we hope to get it sorted if the investigation is
going to be led by the Met. Anyway, our men will canvass the
floor, but most of the guests have left their rooms by now. Your
DI said he wanted us to check for gunshot residue?'

'Yes,' I said. 'The suspects are in suite 701. Here are their
room keys; could your people search their rooms as well? We're
looking for a gun, laptop and the victim's key card.' He gave me
a look, and I said, 'Sorry, sir. Of course you know all this. We've
set up an incident room in suite 702.'

'Yes, we may not deal with as many homicides as the Met, but
we're not entirely inept. I'll have my guys check the CCTV in the
hotel and outside and on the streets around here.'

'Thank you, sir.'

He walked away, leaving me alone.

Not as many homicides. To me, they weren't just dead bodies.
I hadn't known Sid Ram and Saul Cohen, but Ari Levy and Yael
Klein? I'd drunk beers with them three days ago. Two days ago,
I had been mesmerised by Ari Levy's passion. We'd known he

was at risk and had done nothing about it. But what could we have done? Levy was on his guard. Tahir, Powell, Warner and I were all in the hotel. The murderer must have seen us. Yet he had acted. Boldly and mercilessly.

I felt a tightness in my throat that threatened to choke me and made me want to vomit. Whoever had done this would not get away.

This was now personal.

Chapter 24

Monday morning.

When I got back to the interview suite, I found Wahid Masri telling Tahir, 'I need to get to the conference, Inspector. Believe me, it pains me to leave, but I *must* offer an explanation to the organisers and delegates. It was due to start at ten with me introducing Ari's keynote and it's already ten past. I'm not sure how the organisers will proceed. But there are over two hundred people waiting in the university. My phone is alight with calls and messages. What should I do?'

'I appreciate all that, but as I have told you, Mr Masri, you cannot leave.' There was exhaustion in Tahir's voice. 'I suggest you phone and ask them to inform the delegates that the keynote is not happening.'

Masri grimaced, but then nodded and got busy with his phone. Gaby Fleishman was catatonic on a sofa, looking straight ahead while Michelle Jennings sat next to him, clutching his limp hand in her two. Miles Merrion and Nelson Tang were standing at opposite ends of the room, eyes darting across the Aishtar executives. David Baker was staring out of the window at the train station below. He started as I came near and, searching my face, whispered, 'So it's true. They're both dead?'

'I'm afraid so.'

He swallowed and his face twisted. 'Shot? Like the others?'

I nodded.

He squeezed his eyes shut as he clicked his watch clasp open and closed like a metronome. I felt as distressed as he looked but couldn't show it.

'Yael?'

'She didn't suffer. It was quick.'

A tear fell from his eye, and he rubbed at it with a jerk. 'She didn't deserve it. It was my fault.'

My pulse quickened.

'What do you mean?'

'I found Ari. Found Aishtar. If I hadn't persuaded Wahid to invest and get them to move to London, they would all still be alive. Sid, Saul, Ari.' He pinched the bridge of his nose and looked down. 'Yael.'

His face was ravaged. I knew he and Klein had been together for a few years before they split, and he still saw her every week. If something happened to Anjoli or Maliha, it would rip my insides to shreds.

I fought my instinct to console him. It wasn't my place, and we had a killer to catch. David Baker, grief-stricken as he was, was in the room because he was a suspect. They all were. I had to do my job.

'What time did everyone leave the bar last night?'

He looked at me, eyes dull. 'What?'

I repeated my question.

'Ari and Yael left first, around eleven thirty. Wahid, Gaby, Michelle and I stayed for another half an hour.'

'And you went straight to bed?'

'Yes. I went up in the lift with them. I'm in room 517. Wahid and Michelle were on the sixth floor.'

'And you stayed in your room all night?'

'I woke at six and went to the gym for a workout. Then showered and came down to breakfast. We had agreed to meet at 7.15.'

'Do you own a gun?'

'What? No.'

'Can I have your attention, please,' said Tahir from the end of the room. 'As you will have heard, I'm sorry to say we found Ari Levy and Yael Klein dead in Mr Levy's hotel room this morning. This gentleman,' he gestured to a man next to him, 'is going to escort you into the next room to take your fingerprints and swab your hands. We are also going to be searching your rooms. Please see me if you have questions.'

'This is a total infringement of our rights,' said Merrion.

'It isn't, Mr Merrion. We have had four brutal murders over the last week. If you do not wish to cooperate, come and see me.'

' "If you have nothing to hide, what are you scared of?" ' said Tang. 'That's the excuse of fascist regimes all over the world.'

'I will not get into a debate about civil liberties with you, Mr Tang. I urge you to help us so we can prevent any more murders.'

'Oh for god's sake, let's get this over with,' said Masri. 'Here, I'll go first.'

The tech led him into the adjoining room and the others settled down.

'Can we get some coffees in here, Inspector?' said Michelle Jennings.

Tahir nodded, and she got on to room service. I realised I'd eaten no breakfast and asked her to order me a club sandwich, although I didn't feel like eating. But I needed to refuel for what I guessed was going to be a nightmare of a day.

The Aishtar folks corroborated that they'd left the bar before midnight and gone to bed, then come down for breakfast for 7.15 a.m. What happened during those times was anyone's guess. Michelle Jennings had seen David Baker at the gym in the morning. Miles Merrion and Nelson Tang admitted they had gone to Merrion's room on the fourth floor for a nightcap from the minibar; then Tang had gone to his own room, which was a few doors away, around 1 a.m. Neither of them had heard anything in the night. We pressed Tang as hard as we could, and he didn't budge from his story.

The Cambridge cops drip-fed us information throughout the morning, with the results of every probe into each suspect, one by one, returning nothing new. No gunshot residue on anyone's hands ('although the killer could have worn gloves'). Room searches drew a blank. Still testing for fingerprints on Levy's door. With each update, Tahir's countenance grew ever stonier. It was after 1 p.m. when we told all the suspects they could go.

Miles Merrion and Nelson Tang darted out as Gaby Fleishman, Michelle Jennings and David Baker got up and gathered their possessions. Then, almost in slow motion, Wahid Masri heaved himself up from the armchair where he had installed himself and not moved since after we questioned him. The hulking bear appeared to have shrunk in his suit, his skin ashen. As he leaned to pick up his jacket, I said, 'What kind of future does Aishtar have now? Will the sale go through?'

He shrugged his drooping shoulders and stared at me, face bleak. 'We have to assume it's dead. Ari *was* Aishtar. It was Ari the buyer wanted. If he's gone and the tech has gone with him, there's nothing left. Four billion dollars down the crapper. Un-fucking-believable. We'll have to salvage what we can and start again. I'm sorry, David. I know you put your heart and soul into this.'

David Baker's voice broke. 'I wish I hadn't. Four people are dead because of this technology. No amount of money is worth it.'

'I know, my friend.' Masri put an arm around him in comfort. 'I know how close you were to them. Take some time for yourself this week. I think we all need to. And, Gaby – I do not know what this madman is doing. I'll organise some protection for you. I should have done it earlier. Stupid. Stupid.'

'No,' said Gaby Fleishman.

'Please. For me. It would—'

Anger entered Fleishman's voice. 'Wahid, I was in the Sayeret Matkal; I'll be fine. Let this maniac fucking try.'

'Were you?' said Masri. 'How come I didn't know that?'

'I don't publicise it.'

'What's Sayeret Matkal?' Tahir said.

'Israeli special forces,' said Masri, a thoughtful expression on his face.

'I'll be fine, Wahid,' repeated Fleishman. 'I have other issues to worry about. How am I going to hold things together in the company? All our good people will leave. And what the fuck do I do about the algo without Ari?'

'Ari's McCain Protocol, whatever that is, should prevent it from working for a third party. So the murderer may have killed him for nothing,' said Masri.

'Do you mean with Mr Levy dead, *you* can't get the technology to work either?' I said.

Fleishman sighed. He clutched his forehead and closed his eyes for a second. He seemed to have aged fifteen years since the morning. 'We'll have to reconstruct it. Ari was always tinkering with the algo. It will take time, but we can do it. We will do it. I don't have the stomach for any of that now. I wish we had never gotten into AI. It's just brought us misery.'

Something struck me. I took out my phone and showed them a picture. 'Does this mean anything to you?'

They looked at it.

'What is it?' said David Baker.

'A note we found next to the bodies. There were similar ones near Mr Levy and Mr Cohen.'

'Looks like some kind of ridiculous manifesto. It's meaningless,' said Wahid Masri.

'Could an algorithm have written it? Some sort of AI?' I said.

232

They passed the phone to each other.

'Computers write better than this nowadays with GPT-3,' said Baker.

'What's that?'

'It's an AI that generates text. You couldn't tell the difference between that and what a human writes. This feels like a human *trying* to write like a computer.'

'Can you think of any reason the killer might do that?'

Baker shook his head as Fleishman said, 'That's your job to figure out, isn't it?' I watched as they walked down the corridor to the lift. I went to the door and took the room key out of the slot, preparing to leave.

'What are you doing? *We* can't go.' Tahir ran a hand through his hair. 'I've just had the Super on. He's pissed as hell and is going to take over the day-to-day operations. I'm fresh out of ideas. I don't think your "computer did it, guv" will fly with him.'

'We haven't searched *their* rooms. Or taken their swabs,' I said sotto voce, nodding at Warner and Powell who were sitting in the corner of the room – they'd watched all the questioning without participating themselves.

'You think . . . ?'

'I don't know. Ari's laptop had the crown jewels on it. Perhaps they wanted it.'

'How the hell do you treat SO15 as suspects?'

'Maybe we just ask. As Nelson Tang said, if they have nothing to hide . . .'

'Fucking spooks always have something to hide. That's why they're spooks. But I suppose we've got nothing to lose at this point.'

Powell and Warner were standing now. 'Any progress made, officers?' Powell said.

'We've interviewed everyone, fingerprinted them, searched their rooms, done swab tests and come up with nothing,' said

Tahir. 'What did you see last night? You were supposed to be watching them.'

'Were we?'

I was getting annoyed with these two. They definitely had something to do with this and their refusal to tell us anything was galling. Tahir must have been feeling the same because he said, 'For the sake of completeness, we should eliminate you as well.'

Warner laughed. 'Are you serious? We're suspects now?'

'No, of course not,' said Tahir. 'But my guvnor likes to do everything by the book, and it would be great if we could just dot this i and cross that t.'

'We left the bar last night at half ten and went to bed,' said Powell. 'You were with us and saw us. We're in a twin – our department isn't as generous as yours. And we were there all night till we came for breakfast at seven.'

'Do you have any firearms?' I said.

They looked at each other. 'We have our service handguns. They are in the safe in the hotel room.'

'What make?' said Tahir.

'Glock, 9 mm. Standard issue.'

'Would you mind if we checked if they have been fired?'

'Be my guest. Bring your techs to room 436.'

'That's the room opposite Levy's. You heard nothing?'

'We were just discussing that. No, we didn't.'

The mystique they had built around themselves was evaporating fast as I fetched the tech to carry out the forensics.

As we checked out of the hotel, one of the uniformed police said, 'We have the CCTV footage from the hotel. Nothing of any note we could see. Do you want to have a look?'

He led us into a security camera room and, as he fiddled with the laptop, said, 'We have Levy and Klein going up in the lift at

11.36.' He showed us a video of the two of them giggling and kissing like teenage lovers. A shard of sadness pierced my heart as I watched them enjoy their blissful moment, both unaware that in a few hours, their lives would end in a violent and merciless attack.

'Nobody unusual leaving or entering the hotel at night. Around six am we have a few entries and exits.' He fast-forwarded through the footage. I stopped him at 6.36.

'Who's that?'

A figure in a dark hoodie and jeans carrying a backpack exited the hotel from a side door and walked down Station Road. The height and positioning of the camera made it impossible to make out the sex or build of the person, and they were wearing a face mask. While not as ubiquitous as they were during the height of the pandemic, they weren't uncommon.

'No idea,' said the police officer. 'We saw them come back into the hotel twenty minutes later. Look.'

The same figure came back down Station Road, looking down at the ground.

'The backpack's gone,' I said.

He froze the film. 'Shit, you're right. I missed that. Let me try to see if we can enhance the image and check out any other CCTV along the road.'

I stared at the person on the screen. Was this the killer we had been looking for? Who the hell was it? Nelson Tang? Gaby Fleishman? Miles Merrion? Michelle Jennings? None of them had alibis for the other murders.

Tahir said, 'Okay, that backpack is your highest priority. Check all the places within a ten-minute radius where the person could have dumped it. Bins, alleys, anything.'

'What about the station?' I said. 'Lockers or left luggage?'

'Good thinking,' said Tahir. 'Comb the station.'

'Cambridge station doesn't have any left luggage or lockers,' said the copper. 'Tourists are always complaining.'

'Whatever,' said Tahir. 'I want that backpack found. And see if any of our suspects had that hoodie in their possession.'

Neither of us spoke for the first fifteen minutes of the car journey back to London. Tahir sat slumped low in the seat with his body and head turned towards the window while I concentrated on the road ahead.

'Put some music or something on,' he said finally.

I switched on the radio to hear Neil Young informing me he had shot his baby down by the river.

I listened with half an ear while going over the events of the day. The spooks line of investigation was a dead end. The tech confirmed their guns hadn't been fired and a search of their room had yielded nothing. The Cambridge police had found nothing in or around the hotel. Tahir had taken several calls from Rogers, who was very displeased with the way we had handled the case. I got the impression we were being blamed; but short of sharing a room with Ari Levy and Yael Klein, there was nothing we could have done to prevent the carnage of the previous night.

Tahir turned his head from the window to look at me. 'So . . .' I assumed he needed to exorcise his brain of its circular thoughts as much as I did. 'What do you reckon?'

'You should arrest him.'

He gave me a surprised glance.

'Who?'

I gestured at the radio. 'Neil. He's confessed.'

He compressed his lips. 'For fuck's sake, Kamil, there's a time and a place.'

My trying to lighten the mood had not worked. I got professional. 'Sorry. Okay. Theory one – the killer is a foreign agent looking to steal the Aishtar tech, and they planted those notes to throw us off the scent. They kill Ram but can't get his laptop because he falls into the pit. They get Cohen's laptop, but it has nothing of value on it. So, they have to get Levy's and Klein is collateral damage.'

'Ari wouldn't let them into the room. Not with everything that has happened. But let's check the other guests in the hotel.'

'Guess they could have got a passkey. I'll ask uniform to check with the hotel staff if any are missing.'

Tahir nodded. 'And while you're at it, tell them to interview the staff to see if anyone seems squirrelly. They might have been bribed. Go on.'

I continued. 'So, under this scenario, now that they have the laptop, maybe that's it and they leave the country. It's none of our suspects, and we need Laurel and Hardy to help us.'

'Unless it's Laurel and Hardy who did the deeds, which means the government has sanctioned them,' said Tahir, adding, 'and we are the collateral damage. Also, if they didn't get the McCain protocol, they may still be sniffing around for it. Although with Levy dead, who knows how they'll find that?'

I nodded. 'Theory two, it's Gaby Fleishman who wants all the money from the sale. But killing Levy makes little sense. He would know that would destroy the sale. Same holds for Masri and Baker. Unless they can sell the laptop to a third party for a massive amount of money. Same issue with the McCain thingy. However, Levy might have let Fleishman, Masri or Baker into the room.

'Theory three.' I was warming up. 'It's Tang and or Merrion. They stole the laptop to *destroy* the tech. They could be in it together. They were very buddy-buddy last night. I still think Tang was Merrion's source. Stole a passkey, got in the room and did it.'

Tahir pondered this. 'Focus on them. Check out everything. Where they might have got a gun. Might have met. Tear their alibis apart.'

'Okay.'

'That CCTV person might be our killer – it could be any of them.'

'Except Wahid Masri, he's a big guy,' I said. 'The figure was relatively slim. Let's see if they find the backpack. What about Michelle Jennings or David Baker? They were here last night too.'

'What motive could they have to kill four people?'

'I have no idea. There's also Ari Levy's wife. I'm clutching at straws here.'

'It might make sense if it was a crime of passion. Levy's wife finds him with Klein and kills him. Surprises Levy by knocking on the door and he has to let her in. But four murders don't compute. Anyway, we'll have to tell his wife about his death, and we can check out where she was last night. Look into it. We have to turn over every rock, or Rogers will have our hides. The last thing I want is for him to take over the operation with Protheroe. Our careers will become fucking virtual reality.'

I thought of the passion on Ari Levy's face when he had shown us his East End simulation. All his dreams of walking in the shoes of his ancestors had evaporated, and he had joined them in whatever place Jewish people went to after they died. I hoped Yael Klein was with him and they would find some peace there. Maybe someone would recreate him in the future, and he could live the life he had wanted.

We drove back to the office in silence.

26 Fieldgate, East End, London
27 December 1913

Darling Shoshi,

I hope this letter finds you in the best
of health and happiness. I cannot
believe it has been eight years since
Avram, Leah and I arrived at St
Katharine Docks, clinging only to each
other and the desperate hope of a safe
future. This country has been good to
us. The business is prospering. We have
given up the market stalls and made a
shop in Fieldgate, next to
Pennyfeather's Bazaar, and people are
coming from all over London to buy our
clothes! Avram is now employing 33
people - I can't even remember all their
names. Mr Pennyfeather is expanding his
department store and wants Avram to sell
our shop to him so he can become even
bigger. But it is not just a shop for
us, it is also our home, so Avram has
told him no. The noise of the building
work at Pennyfeather's store keeps the
baby awake in the day when she should be
sleeping.
    Things are going very well now.
Because we have people working for us,
we have found some time to go out and
experience life - not something we ever
did before. We went dancing in the

Jewish Working Men's club - it was so
much fun.

Leah is four already and baby Miriam
is now three months - I have enclosed
their photos so you can see them. Avram
has promised Leah he will take her to
see the New Year's Eve celebrations this
year, and she is so excited because he
bought her new clothes. It made me laugh
to hear about what your Eva did in her
shul. I cannot imagine what a picture
Semyon's face must have been when he saw
the picture she had drawn of the Rebbe.

Wishing you a wonderful end to 1913,
my darling sister. My wish for the new
year is for our families to see more of
each other in 1914. Avram says it is
going to be a year filled with blessings.

With all my love,

Malka

Chapter 25

Monday evening.

Tahir's phone pinged as I pulled into Bethnal Green station car park a little after five, having beaten the worst of the evening traffic. 'Gaffer wants to see us. Man's got eyes everywhere.'

'We've made some progress finding that figure on the CCTV and our planned focus on Merrion and Tang. Hopefully that'll get him off our backs.'

Tahir shook his head despondently. 'I wouldn't count on it.'

As we walked through the incident room, Protheroe said, 'Boss wants you immediately, guv. And *DC* Rahman.' He looked pointedly at me to make sure I hadn't missed the 'DC'. The involuntary smile that spread across his face made it clear that this would not be good.

We knocked on Rogers' office door, to no response. Through the glass door we saw him, back to us, leaning with both hands on his desk. We heard him say, 'Yes, ma'am, I . . .' as a woman shouted at him on his speakerphone. 'I won't have it, Superintendent Rogers. *I will not have it.* Four people are dead. Two in the very hotel where your men were staying. What were they doing? Watching Netflix? Classified information is spattered all over the *Guardian*. Technology critical to this country's security is stolen – possibly by an enemy state – so we have no access to it anymore. This is beyond incompetence – it's borderline treachery. Heads will roll. I want your resignation on my desk if this is not sorted by the end of the week. The Israeli embassy has been on to me several times. The Prime Minister is very concerned. What are you going to do about it?'

'Ma'am, I have taken personal control of the investigation and . . .'

'You should have done that from the beginning. You just cannot understand how gravely serious this is for us. For *me* personally. I'm being accused of anti-Semitism because I'm ignoring the targeted killing of Jews. Me! And don't get me started on what Liberty has been saying. I want twice-daily reports. Do you hear me? I. Want. That. Technology. Found!'

The line went dead.

Tahir knocked again and Rogers turned. Grim-faced, he beckoned us in. I stood staring at the floor as Tahir said, 'Boss . . .'

'That was the Home Secretary,' said Rogers, jaw clenched.

'Yes, boss.'

The Super took a deep breath, sat down behind his desk, and said, voice dangerous, 'She called the Commissioner and demanded to speak to the person in charge.' Another breath. Then, almost in a whisper, 'I cannot believe this level of ineptitude. How could you let this happen? Believe you me, if I go down for this, it will not be alone. What have you found?'

My heart was going like a jackhammer, and I wanted more than anything to be anywhere else.

'We're making some progress,' said Tahir. 'We've found a CCTV image of someone who may be our man. Or woman.'

Rogers' eyes shot daggers at Tahir. 'Progress? When you can't even tell if it's a man or a woman? Are you being serious?'

'We are looking for their backpack. Kamil noticed the person had it going out but not coming back.'

I wasn't sure if I was being praised or blamed but had nothing to say. He didn't look at me.

'It's not just the Home Secretary – and by the way, she's *never* called me before. I've had the Chief Super on *twice* this morning. Social media is going crazy. The papers are on the rampage. And you have a *backpack*?'

Tahir chewed his lip.

'You then aggressively question two of our colleagues from SO15 and test *their* guns? Have you gone completely mad? They've filed a complaint against you. And rightfully so.'

Shit. That had been my suggestion. Fucking Laurel and pissing Hardy. So much for us being on the same team.

'We were being thorough,' muttered Tahir.

'Do you have a prime suspect, DI Ismail?'

'We're following several leads.'

'I'm not a bloody reporter, Tahir. Don't give me that bullshit. Do you have a suspect? Any *actual* evidence?'

'At the moment, our best bets are Merrion and Tang – either individually or together. They are not shy about broadcasting their anti-AI position and we have anti-AI notes found at the scene of all four murders. They claim not to know each other but were pally at the conference.'

'That's barely circumstantial and you know it. We can't even arrest them on what you have, much less charge them. You don't have a shred of evidence implicating anybody.' He paused to control himself. 'All right, let's cut to the chase. I'm taking over the case on a day-to-day basis as SIO and we need a more seasoned team on it. Tahir, you'll continue to report to me. Kamil, I'm bringing Protheroe in. You'll now report to him. Tahir should never have put you in this position on your first week in post.'

I felt like someone had punched me in the stomach. All my dreams of catching the culprit, avenging Ari, making Anjoli and my father proud, evaporated in a nanosecond. Tahir had seen this coming, but I hadn't listened, assuming, as I always did, that things would work out. Had I learned *nothing* from my experience in Kolkata? Report to Protheroe? I'd rather go down for the murders myself. And Gooch and the other DCs. I could just see their faces. *High flyer. Thought he was better than us. Got to where he did because of favouritism by the Muslim mafia, then crashed and burned.*

'DC Rahman? Are you with us?'

'Sorry, sir. Yes, I understand. No problem, sir. We are a team and I'll do what it takes.'

'Good. Now get out there. I'll be out shortly to brief everyone. I need a few words alone with the DI.'

The thought of heading back to face the silent derision in the incident room was like anticipating root canal without anaesthetic. All I wanted to do was escape home and be with Anjoli. I closed my eyes for a second to compose myself. I tried to catch Tahir's eye, but he was examining his fingernails, so I stuck on a tentative smile and walked out of the Superintendent's office into my new reality.

As I trudged to my desk, feeling like I was wearing one of Anjoli's custom-made T-shirts that said *LOSER*, all my co-workers avoided eye contact. I realised Protheroe had wasted no time broadcasting Rogers' decision – they must have already known when they saw us go into his office.

I looked at my phone and saw five missed calls from Anjoli and a series of WhatsApps asking me to phone her. Now what?

I walked into the toilet, locked myself in a booth, and dialled.

'Oh my God, Kamil, are you okay? I've been calling and calling. Why didn't you answer?'

'Sorry. Phone was on silent. What's the matter?'

'What's the *matter*? I saw on Twitter that Ari Levy and Yael Klein are dead! I can't believe it. What happened?'

'I know. I found their bodies.'

'No!' I pictured her in the kitchen, hand over her mouth.

'Calm down . . . Listen, I can't talk now. I'll see you later.'

'Wait, I found some interesting things in the archives about Malka and—'

'I'm sorry, Anjoli. I just can't speak now.'

I disconnected, put my head in my hands, and took a deep breath. Which was a bad idea, given where I was sitting. This is what they had reduced me to? Hiding in the stinking toilets from my colleagues? What was wrong with me?

I splashed water on my face and returned to the incident room to see Rogers beginning his briefing. 'Okay, team. This case is our absolute top priority, and I am now in charge. DI Ismail will continue to be my right-hand man, and DS Protheroe will take over day-to-day activities with the DCs reporting to him. Cambridgeshire Police have agreed we have jurisdiction, and their teams will work with ours. The Chief Super has said we can have all the resources we need. The DI will brief you on our principal lines of enquiry, and I want to get a quick result. All clear?'

There was a general murmur, and the team went back to what they were doing. Rogers, Tahir and Protheroe huddled near the incident whiteboard, which displayed the details of everything we'd found so far. Not being part of that group was tying my gut into knots. Gooch glanced at me, and I became aware I'd been stabbing at my computer keys, threatening to cause them actual damage. It was all I could do not to drive a fist through the screen.

Enough. I was overreacting. I'd had an excellent shot at playing above my rank and should be thankful for that. I'd done the best I could – we were just dealing with a very smart killer. I had to get myself out of this hole I'd dug myself into. None of it was *my* fault. I would keep my head down and show them I was great at my job. Even Protheroe would come around and realise I was a valuable member of the team.

But my attempt at self-soothing didn't work, and I could feel black lava enveloping my brain as I typed my report into the computer on autopilot.

After a few minutes, Rogers went back to his office and Tahir addressed the room. I knew him well enough to tell that he was boiling inside. Well, he could join the club. 'Update. Cambridge have come back – no luck on finding our guy on CCTV or the black hoodie or rucksack. They got into Levy's phone. He received a call from a phone number – 07809 324719 – at 11.26 p.m. and spoke for two minutes. You will recognise this as the same burner phone that called both Sid Ram and Saul Cohen before they were killed. So, we can assume Levy knew the killer, and he said he was coming to see Levy, just as he had with Ram and Cohen.'

'Klein was in his bed,' said Protheroe. 'Surely she would have hidden in the bathroom if she knew someone was coming to see Levy?'

'Good point. Maybe he called to check where Levy was, then knocked on the door and surprised them. Unfortunately, the number is out of service again, but we are watching for it to come online. In addition, they recovered the bullets from the walls of Levy's hotel room – they were from the same gun that killed Ram and Cohen. Not a surprise. Protheroe and I are going to see the victim's wife now and I want a round-the-clock watch on Gaby Fleishman, David Baker, Wahid Masri, Michelle Jennings, Nelson Tang and Miles Merrion.'

'We might be locking the stable door, guv. If the killer got what he wanted from Levy's laptop, he might be long gone,' said Protheroe.

'Maybe. But we can't take that risk. Prothers, you set the rota. Stealth is key; they mustn't know we are watching. And we are also pursuing the theory that these could have been professional hits; we are liaising with SO15 on that. I'll tell you more when I know more. Got it?'

There was a nodding of heads, and Protheroe took over.

'You heard the guv; we're going to go over every inch of evidence we have – alibis, forensics – for all four murders; Rahman, you take that. Those notes we found – I want the paper analysed. Take samples of printer paper and envelopes from the offices of the suspects – Aishtar, the *Guardian* and the investor – Bethlehem. Financials – I want a deep dive into the financials of all the suspects – Miles Merrion, Nelson Tang, Gaby Fleishman, Michelle Jennings. Look for anything out of the ordinary – debts, large payments into the account, whatever. Boss said he wanted surveillance on them.' He pointed, 'Four of you take Merrion – two shifts, twelve hours each, two on each shift. 8 a.m. to 8 p.m. and 8 p.m. to 8 a.m. You four take Tang. You guys are on Ali and Baker. You four take Jennings. The two of you plus Rahman and Goochy, you take Fleishman. I expect us all to put in the time needed till we catch the bastard.'

Gooch looked at me and whispered, 'Night shift okay?'

I was beyond exhausted and couldn't think about doing twelve more hours watching Fleishman's house.

'Day. I'm dead on my feet,' I whispered back.

He gave me a sympathetic nod. 'Leave it to me. I'll fix it with Protheroe.'

'Thanks. I owe you.'

'We'll take the night shift, guv,' said Gooch.

Fuck. Wanker.

I turned back to my desk and started trawling through all the notes and evidence we had on the killings for the next hour, my eyes dry and blurring. I did not know what I was looking for, and it felt like a total waste of time, but I had my orders.

Chapter 26

Monday evening.

By 7 p.m. I was cold and stony tired and couldn't take it any-more. I needed to grab a burger and a gallon of coffee to endure the night shift Gooch had saddled me with. But there was something I had to sort out first. If I was going to spend eight hours in a car with him being bathed in silent resentment, I'd better ingest a five-course meal of humble pie before my burger.

I went up to him and said, 'Listen, Goochy. I'm sorry about the stuff the other night at the crime scene. Maybe I got a little too cocky and acted like a twat. You were a real help in my train-ing. Can we press the reset button?'

He gave me a long stare, then smiled and held out his hand. '*I'm* sorry too, Kamil. I was being a wanker. Protheroe wound us all up that night. Look, I know you're knackered – I'll grab some-one else tonight, and you and I can do Fleishman's surveillance together tomorrow. Deal?'

I felt an immense sense of relief as we bumped fists. 'I owe you one. Thanks.' I paused and added, 'Mate.'

May as well try to fit in.

'No worries.' He yelled across the room, 'Hey, Shane, I've got good news for you. You don't need to see the missus tonight . . .'

I couldn't bring myself to go home and face Anjoli in the mood I was in, so did something I never do – went to a pub on my own. I ordered a double Johnnie Walker and tried not to think about Tahir and Protheroe questioning Ari Levy's wife while I sat at the bar.

As I sipped my drink, the whisky scorching my throat and warming my chest, images from the past week bounced around my head. *I* was the one who'd found the first note at the building site; who'd connected the burner phone numbers; who had gained Baker's trust in the restaurant; who'd spotted the missing rucksack on the person on the CCTV in Cambridge. What the hell had Protheroe done? But none of that mattered now. I was demoted and back in with all the graduates straight out of the detective programme, my eight extra years of experience counting for fuck all. What was I doing pouring my heart and soul into this job if these clowns couldn't recognise my talents?

I felt my senses melting like the ice in my glass. I needed to talk to someone but couldn't face Anjoli. Tahir would be no good. He was in as deep shit as I was.

My phone rang. Imam Masroor. I wasn't sure I was in the mood to deal with him but picked up. 'Sheikh?'

'Kamil, how are you? I had not heard from you for a while.'

'I'm fine. You?'

'Alhamdulillah. I just wanted to ask if you knew when we could start building again on our property?'

'I'm sorry, Sheikh. I don't know. Let me check and come back to you?'

'Of course.' After a brief pause, he said, 'Are you sure you are all right, Kamil?'

The imam had this knack of getting inside my head. 'You know me so well, Sheikh. Work is a little tricky now. As is my personal life.'

'You can talk to me about it. I may not be able to help with your work, but I can help with your life. Speak.'

His calm voice worked on me, and, with no hesitation, I let it all out. I told him about my feelings of incompetence and loneliness. My dilemma about Maliha and Anjoli. How I needed someone in my life, but felt I was betraying both of them in a way.

When I ran out of words, he said, 'You must rise above this and see clearly. You will do the right thing at work. You are very good at your job. Maybe it will take time, but you must stay the course. And as for home . . . different women can give you different things, Kamil. Aisha, third wife of the Prophet (peace be upon him), was a strong military commander who always said what she thought. His love for her was like a strong knot in a rope. But the Qu'ran also says that the good women are obedient, guarding in secret what Allah has guarded. Khadija, his first wife, was also strong but in a different way – a devout Muslim. Maybe Anjoli is your Aisha and Maliha is your Khadija?'

That made me laugh. 'I don't think either would like me to have two wives.'

'That is not what I am suggesting. You need to decide who is right for you as a life partner. But that does not mean the other cannot be a life friend. You need them both to make you whole. You need not choose. By choosing, you will lose something you do not need to lose. Think about what I have said. Now it is late, and I must go.'

As always, the imam's words brought me some succour. He was right. Instead of *either* this love *or* that, I could think of them as a lover *and* a friend. One did not exclude the other. But which was which?

I downed my whisky and called Maliha. The phone rang on with no reply, and I was about to hang up when she answered. 'Hi, Kamil!' There was a buzz of conversation behind her.

'Oh, hi, Maliha. I know we arranged to meet Saturday but I'm back from Cambridge and was wondering . . . but you sound like you're out.'

'No, it's fine. I'm just finishing drinks with some colleagues near our office. Did you want to meet up? Is it too late?'

'With your friends?'

'No, they're leaving. I can wait for you.'

'Where are you?'

'A place called Barrio Shoreditch.' I could hear the smile in her voice.

'See you there.'

Fifteen minutes later, I found myself in the lively and wildly colourful surroundings of Barrio, which was bustling for a Monday night. My sleep-deprived head was spinning as I searched for the figure of Maliha among the busy décor, neon lighting and boho millennial punters. I hadn't seen her in six years, so wasn't sure what to look for. Was her hair long, short, brown, dyed red? I walked through the venue scanning faces for a brown woman and discovered her at a table in the corner sipping a parasol-dressed cocktail wearing a red top and a . . . headscarf?

'Maliha.'

'You found me!' She smiled and rose. We stood awkwardly for a second as I wondered if it was okay to hug her; then she reached over and pecked me on the cheek.

'You look nice.' And she did. 'What's with . . .' I gestured.

'Oh, this?' She laughed and uncovered her head to reveal her familiar silky brown bob. 'Don't worry, I haven't gone all five times a day. It makes some of my clients more comfortable and others I have to deal with *un*comfortable, so it's a useful negotiation tool. Sometimes I forget I have it on.'

I ordered a beer and said, 'So? London?'

'I know. Cool, isn't it? I jumped at it when Amnesty asked.'

'Just like that?' I said, remembering how against it she had been when I'd asked her to accompany me here before we split up.

Her face darkened and, in proper Maliha fashion, she ignored any pleasantries and dove straight in. 'India's not the same place anymore, Kamil. Not just Covid . . . Did you see it was ranked as the most dangerous place in the world for women? Ahead of Afghanistan, Syria and Saudi. Saudi! What an honour. And given what's happening to Muslims and to NGOs – let's just say I provided the fanatics three for the price of one. And with the most right-wing Hindu government in our history and . . . well, you know who the PM is.'

I felt my stomach lurch. The thought of Jaideep Sanyal now sitting in high office always had that effect on me. I'd had a major run-in with him on my final case in Kolkata, which had changed the course of my life – and not in a good way. He had just been a high-flying businessman then. Whenever I saw his picture in the newspaper glad-handing some foreign dignitary, I just saw those cold eyes staring into mine, before he tossed my sparkling future into the gutter.

My beer arrived, and I took a grateful swig. 'I do.'

'I can't believe he rose up the ranks so fast.'

'His father *was* chief minister of Bengal. Scions of political families have their path well-greased.'

'Yes, they do. Anyway, given his activities, it was a good time to get out. The government is incredibly vindictive on social media. We published some reports on their actions and I was trolled with abusive tweets threatening to rape me, kill me and worse. It was difficult to leave Mum there but . . .'

Seeing the sadness on her face gave me a stone in my throat. I wanted to take her hand but didn't. It really was not a good idea for me to drink before I spoke to her. Too many feelings rose to the surface.

'I'm so sorry. About all of that and about your dad.'

'Yah. Was a horrible time. Anyway, let's not talk about that now. And how's the Met police? I'm glad you found your way back to what you loved.'

She took my hands in hers and gave them a squeeze, eyes shining.

'Thanks,' I said, feeling embarrassed but basking in her admiration. 'But it's not all roses and birdsong.'

I told her everything that had happened. She listened in her quiet Maliha way, then after I'd finished, said, 'You've done nothing wrong, Kamil, and it's not really a demotion – you've only just started, don't take it as such. I remember how you were in Kolkata on the Asif Khan murder. You had done all you could there as well, and you got to the truth in the end. There's a difference between doing things right and doing the right thing – you always do the right *thing*, even if you don't necessarily do it in the right *way*. That's your strength.'

The imam had said much the same thing. I squeezed her hand. 'Thank you, I needed that. After all this time, you still understand me so well.'

I put an olive in my mouth and said, 'So what happened to that guy you were seeing in Kolkata?'

Her eyes assessed me. 'Not a lot. And you?'

'Nothing. Free and single.'

'What about Anjoli?'

I felt somewhat guilty. 'We're just friends.'

'How come? You live together, right?'

I was ticking like a bomb about to go off. This was the moment I needed to choose a direction. It was strange seeing Maliha again, but it brought with it a frisson of excitement. Was I being unfair to Anjoli? I loved her, but what did she feel about me? Maliha was different. I couldn't put my finger on it, but it had to do with the compassion in her eyes when I had poured my heart out to her. Anjoli showed her affection in many ways, but most of the time it was by taking the piss out of me.

'It's, as they say, complicated.'

'Why?'

'I keep comparing her to you.'

'You shouldn't do that.'

'I know. I can't help it.' I stroked the back of her hand with an audacious finger. 'You and I just fit together, didn't we?'

Her hand retreated to her lap. 'Until we didn't, Kamil. You really hurt me when you left.'

'And you know how much I regret that. But before that, we were always there for each other, weren't we? You for me and me for you.'

'And Anjoli isn't?'

'We're not a couple, but . . . she's a solo climber. Always saying she can cope on her own. Which she can. Maybe it's necessary to be wanted *and* needed for a relationship to work. What do you think?'

'I think *I* need to go to the ladies. Will you order me another – what was it – Smoky Gonzales?'

'Of course,' I said, disappointed at her lack of response.

I watched her walk off into the crowd, feeling exposed and alone amongst the music and revelry around me. I'd been an idiot. It was too soon. What was I doing saying these things to Maliha the first time we'd met in years? No wonder she hadn't known how to respond. And I'd betrayed Anjoli. I didn't think I could feel any worse than I had earlier in the evening, but I'd achieved it. I needed to invent an excuse and leave to save Maliha any more embarrassment.

I stared blankly at the television on the wall that was showing a commercial with some guy talking about what families have in common, as two women in hijabs ate chips. I realised I still hadn't eaten anything. The ad ended with a graphic that read 'McCain, We Are Family'. What the hell did chips have to do with family? Where was the waiter? The commercials in this country were ridiculous. At least on Indian TV you knew what was being adver . . .

254

Shit!

My mind cleared.

Could it . . .

I forgot about Maliha's drink, found a quiet corner of the bar, and dialled.

'Mr Baker? This is Kamil Rahman.'

'Yes?'

'How are you doing?'

Silence. Then, voice dull, 'I'm fine. Yael's death was a shock, but I'll survive.'

'You will. Listen, I have a question for you. You remember Ari Levy saying he had a McCain protocol that would prevent his software from being stolen. And nobody knew what it was?'

'What about it?'

A waiter reached around me for a drink the barman had made, and I moved. 'Well, I noticed he had a USB stick he had to plug in to get his computer to work when I was in his office. He said that wasn't the McCain protocol.'

'No, that's just standard security and nothing to do with any McCain. If the laptop got stolen, it wouldn't work without the dongle. But if someone stole the laptop *and* the dongle, they'd normally have all they need. Until Ari added this third level of security – his protocol. But none of us know what that is.'

'What if the McCain protocol had something to do with chips? You know McCain chips? Computer chips?'

There was a long silence.

'Mr Baker? Are you there?'

'I'm thinking.'

Then a whisper. '*Not* a computer chip. An RFID chip. *That's* what he used . . .'

'Huh?'

'He must have hacked the dongle, so it needed an RFID chip to work. Radio Frequency Identification. Then you'd need three things to get access to his computer – the laptop, the USB stick and a separate RFID chip that activated the USB. If his killer took just the laptop and the USB, it wouldn't work.'

'They did take both. We didn't find either at the scene.'

Another silence. Then, 'Sorry . . . thinking. I never saw Ari use another device when he plugged the dongle into his laptop. Did you?'

I thought back. 'I don't think so. When I met him, he just plugged the USB in, and the computer started.'

'It would be tiny. A few millimetres. Maybe you didn't notice it? Where were you when he used the laptop with its dongle?'

'In a room in Aishtar.'

'Hmm. Let me think.'

Maliha returned and looked around for me. I waved at her from my corner and mouthed, *Sorry, work*, feeling the familiar excitement bubbling inside when I was on the verge of a break-through. I could have kissed the television set.

'Bodyhacking! He bodyhacked himself,' said David Baker, finally.

'What do you mean?'

'Ari must have embedded the RFID chip into his body. Look, an example of RFID is what you have in your contactless credit card or your Oyster card. People prise it out and insert it in the skin of their hand so they can pay for things just by touching the reader with their hand. That must be what Ari did. He took an RFID chip, connected it to his USB stick so it won't work with-out the chip, then inserted the chip subcutaneously into his body. Whenever he used the dongle, it would automatically work because it could communicate with the chip. But if the equip-ment got into someone else's hands, it wouldn't, because . . . no chip. My God. It's brilliant.' His voice fell. 'He was a genius.'

'Why not just use a fingerprint?'

'Because anyone targeting the tech would see the dongle had a fingerprint reader and might chop Ari's finger off. But with the embedded RFID, they wouldn't know they needed something other than the dongle.'

'If it was you, where would you embed the chip?'

'Anywhere in the body would work. It just needs proximity. Where's Ari's body now?'

'In the mortuary, awaiting the post-mortem, I guess.'

'Go and look. I'm sure you'll find it. Lucky the killer didn't get it – the tech would be worth billions in the wrong hands.'

'That's all they need? This chip?'

'And the algorithm, of course. That would be on Ari's laptop. It just won't work without the chip.'

'And that's worth four billion dollars?'

'Well no. You need loads of other stuff. But the secret sauce is the algorithm. That's what Aishtar's crown jewels are. The rest can be reconstructed. It's like Google. They have massive server farms that index the internet, but the core search algorithm that finds what you want is pretty small.'

'Okay, I think I understand. Thanks, Mr Baker, I have to go.'

I found Maliha and said, 'Listen, I'm sorry, but something urgent has come up at work. I have to run. We'll get together again soon, I promise.'

'Don't worry about it. Call me when you can. And don't stress, you look tired. And a bit down. It'll all be fine.'

'I know. I'll see you Saturday.' I kissed her cheek.

'Can't wait,' she said.

I dashed out of Barrio and called Tahir. 'Tahir, I've had a breakthrough.'

'Go on.'

I told him and when I finished, he said, 'Fucking hell. If the killer hasn't got the technology, he could try again. We could get lucky with our surveillance. And maybe Aishtar can use the chip to give the Home Secretary what she wants. Hang on, I thought you and Gooch were watching Gaby Fleishman?'

'I'm dead on my feet, boss. Goochy's doing it with another partner tonight and I said I'd take over tomorrow.'

A pause, then he said, 'All right. Go home and get some sleep. We'll talk tomorrow.'

'No, I'm going to the mortuary. We need to get that chip before someone else does.'

'They've moved the bodies to the Royal London. Where are you? I'll pick you up.'

My depression of earlier vanished.

I was on the trail.

Chapter 27

Monday evening.

My suit was no match for the mortuary at the Royal London – I'd forgotten the temperature differential. Shivering, I buttoned my jacket as Tahir passed me some surgical whites and a mask. Protected, he entered, and I followed, my tired eyes squinting against the stark, bright lights. Dr Grayson stood between two covered bodies on steel tables.

'Hi, boys. We haven't started yet; the corpses were only delivered from Cambridge a couple of hours ago, so they were scheduled to be done tomorrow first thing. I've had a quick look; it seems pretty straightforward – a shot to each head.'

'Thanks for meeting us here so late. There's something very specific we need you to check before you do the post-mortems,' said Tahir. 'Go ahead, Kamil.'

I explained what we were looking for.

'Well, that would be something I've never seen – and I've seen a lot of stuff. Let's take a look, shall we?' She walked over to another table and lowered a sheet from the top half of Ari Levy's body. I could barely bring myself to look. Naked, on the metal table, he was . . . not quite human. His skin was candle-white, as though bled dry.

I swallowed. 'Start with his hands. The RFID chip would need to be near the computer to work.'

Grayson nodded. She lifted Levy's left hand and, inch by inch, pressed all over it with her gloved fingers. She shook her head and placed it back down respectfully, then moved to his right – I noticed Levy's snake tattoo looked much darker against the pale, exsanguinated skin.

'Ah!' She pinched the webbing between Levy's thumb and forefinger. 'What have we here?'

She picked up a scalpel and made a delicate cut under the snake's belly, then poked around for a few seconds with tweezers before extracting something.

'Voila!' She dropped it into a metal bowl.

It didn't look like much – a tiny metallic object no bigger than a grain of rice. This was what Levy and three others had lost their lives for? And the killer hadn't even found it?

'Amazing, Doctor,' said Tahir. 'Can you just . . .' he waved an evidence bag at the chip and scrunched his nose up.

Dr Grayson cleaned it and placed it into the bag, which Tahir sealed. 'Thanks. Let me know what else you find.'

'Will do.'

We exited the hospital and Tahir said, 'Excellent work, Kamil. Get some sleep now – I'll log this into evidence at the station and see you in the morning. Hopefully, this will get Rogers off my back for a bit.'

I made my way home, enthused.

It was Monday, the restaurant's only rest day in the week, so I knew Anjoli would be home. I still wasn't sure about what was going on, but the imam's words had helped, and I would see where life took me. I wouldn't lie to either of them and if it became clear that there was a lover's future with one and a friend's future with the other, I would tell them. As soon as my key rattled in the lock, she ran down the stairs and hugged me. 'Oh my god. It must have been awful. Come and eat something.'

Her tender welcome was a comfort. But was it that of a friend or a lover? Aargh, this wasn't as easy as the imam had made it sound. But I was ravenous, and my belly trumped my emotions. I put aside my confusion and poured myself a drink while she plated my dinner. I couldn't bring myself to tell her about my 'demotion' so instead described the more compelling highlights of what had happened the day before, encompassing a blow-by-blow account of my discovery of the sad and gruesome double murder and ending with my McCain breakthrough. All the while she listened, eyes wide, occasionally topping up my plate with further servings of Chanson's Cognac-marinaded scallops, morels with egg yolk, and jasmine and pistachio rice. I would have preferred a simple dal and chicken curry but this frou frou stuff was all there was.

'Poor Kamil,' she said and squeezed my shoulder. 'You need some help to process all this – there must be some counselling available at your office or something, no?'

'I don't know. It is a lot, but now we just need to prevent the next killing somehow. We can't let it happen again. I'm going to watch Gaby Fleishman tomorrow night.'

'Can't someone else do that?'

I shook my head. 'Tahir's asked me. I'll be fine.'

'Did you connect with Maliha again?' she asked, something in her eyes at odds with the casual tone she had assayed.

'Ah . . . right, I forgot to tell you. I met her for a drink.'

'Oh? When? I thought you were crazy busy. You said you were inviting her here for dinner?'

I shrugged. 'This evening. It just kind of happened. But I had to run out on her as I figured out the chip thing while I was in the bar, waiting for her to come out of the toilet.' I rolled my eyes and shook my head at how silly that sounded and how bad I felt at leaving so abruptly.

'How was she?'

'Fine.'

She rested her chin in her hands and even though I was

looking at my food, I could feel her psychologist's eyes boring into my skull, trying to read me. Well, I'd spent enough time doing the same to her. What had seemed so easy a few minutes ago had become very complicated.

I shifted her focus. 'How was your day? You said something about archives?'

She sat back in her seat. 'I went through Polina's letters again. They are so moving. Read them when you have a chance. Malka stopped writing in December 1913, and I think that must have been when they were killed. I've been doing some more digging – I went to the London Metropolitan Archive. It's an amazing place where you can do all kinds of genealogical research. And guess what – I found the records of the birth of Avram and Malka's daughters! Freaked me out a bit, to be honest. I'm literally dealing with actual ghosts from the past.' She shuddered. 'Okay, okay. I know. Not literally. But now get this: Malka's letter mentions a guy called Pennyfeather, who wanted Avram to sell his business, but Avram didn't want to. So, I looked for records for Avram's business and found that he and someone called Yankovitch were the shareholders. And then Yankovitch sold the business to a Peter Pennyfeather in January 1914 and after that there was no other mention of Avram Pinsky. Remember we saw Pennyfeather's store in that VR simulation? Is that a coincidence or what? I'm going to research it all some more to find out what happened to all of them.'

My eyelids were drooping. 'That might bring some peace to Polina about what befell her great aunt or whatever she was. That's impressive work, Anjoli.'

'I know, right? Anyway, come on, that's enough chit chat. You look exhausted. Let's go watch some trash on the telly so you can decompress before bed. You need to have a good night's sleep before tomorrow. Poor Ari and Yael – I can't believe they were talking to us downstairs just a couple of nights ago.'

She ushered me into the living room and insisted on clearing up while I vegged on the sofa and zapped until I found the middle of an episode of *Friends*. It was 'The One With The Thumb', which seemed appropriate given what I had just seen in the mortuary.

When she came and sat down, I liked the feeling of her warmth next to me, her feet in my lap. I couldn't pay any attention to the TV, and she didn't seem to focus on it either.

'You didn't . . . *mind* me seeing Maliha, did you?' I said.

'Of course not,' she said immediately. Then, 'Well . . . maybe. I was a little surprised you saw her on your own. I thought we were going to meet her together. Does she have a bloke?'

I shook my head.

'Cool. Cool. Your fiancée is a successful, single, beautiful human rights lawyer and I clear away tables for a living.'

'*Ex* fiancée. And you do much more than that.'

'Ex fiancée. Maybe we should fix her up with Tahir?'

I laughed. 'Why? Are you jealous?'

'Hardly. How about Saturday for our dinner?'

Why did this keep happening? That was the day I had arranged to meet Maliha.

'Isn't that a busy night for you at the restaurant?' I said.

'No, it's fine. I can get someone else to cover.'

'Would Sunday work?'

Her eyes narrowed. 'Why?'

Damn. 'Well, I kind of told Maliha we might meet up. Because I had to rush out, I thought I owed her.'

Why was I making excuses?

'Mm-hm. I may be tied up Sunday, but don't worry, we'll find some other time. Night.'

She went up the stairs, leaving me on the sofa. Why the hell did everything have to be so damn complicated?

Chapter 28

Tuesday morning.

Even though it was sunny out, the incident room looked dingy and smelt of stale chips and BO as I took my desk the next morning. The wastepaper baskets were overflowing, and the murder board was a mess. We were a far cry from the sleek spaces filled with high-tech equipment portrayed on TV cop shows, with their constant hum of tension and sharp faces with furrowed brows peering at computers while the lead detective (in a crumpled suit with tie hanging loose if male; tight ponytail if female) barked orders at their attentive crew. Our shop was more like a depressing classroom where the students had been set a long, dull essay to write. Or maybe the room just reflected my mood.

I wasn't sure what to do. It was 8.15, and the room was half empty. I'd hoped after my McCain brainwave and knock-out discovery of the chip in Levy's hand yesterday I would be back in the inner circle, but it didn't seem like it was to be. I could see Tahir, Protheroe and Rogers talking and gesticulating in Tahir's office. Protheroe's eye caught mine and he couldn't resist a smug smile. I glanced away, the taste of exclusion filling my mouth like a raw onion. Gooch walked in chewing a muffin, gave me a friendly nod, and switched on his computer.

'Anything of note on the stakeout last night?' I said.

'Nah. Quiet as a kitten kipping in a crib. You okay for tonight?'

I nodded. I felt like I was climbing Mount Everest. I'd struggled halfway up, then bounced all the way down again on my arse. Too dejected to find the motivation to plough through boxes of useless evidence, I went to the canteen and decided to soothe the inside of my belly and ignore the exterior evidence of previous placating. When I returned with my chocolate croissant and coffee, Protheroe was addressing the room.

He clocked me entering and said, 'Nice of you to join us, DC Rahman. Have a seat.'

I muttered 'sorry', kicking myself for apologising when I knew *he* knew I'd been there for half an hour already.

'Levy's wife is out of the frame. Fleishman was with her when the guv and I got there – he'd told her what happened, and she wept buckets. It turns out she had been at a party in London Sunday night and slept over at a girlfriend's, so had an alibi. Luckily Fleishman had already told her about Klein, so it saved us that bombshell. Learning your husband is dead, that you will not be a multimillionaire, *and* he was having an affair with his colleague on the same day – that's one hell of a triple whammy. We left her with Fleishman to pick up the pieces. So, back to your assigned tasks. Let's see if we can catch this fucker.'

The insensitive dickhead. I wanted to punch his long, pale, dog-like face with its drooping eyes. I hadn't met Ari Levy's wife but felt for her. And he didn't even mention the RFID chip, my big revelation.

Back at my desk, I reread witness statements and examined CCTV footage, trying to find anything that might be relevant. Nothing.

I worked until Protheroe left at 5.30 on the dot, as he habitually did. Clearly, to him, 'all the time needed' was a standard shift.

Fuck it. If I was going to pull an all-nighter, I needed some rest too. And I still had eaten nothing except that morning's croissant.

By the time I returned to the restaurant, Anjoli was there getting it ready for the evening sitting. Eyes heavy and stomach rumbling, I heated a plate of left-over garlic-infused pork belly, cumin rice and truffled chilli artichokes from the lunch shift and wolfed it down before dashing upstairs to catch an hour's nap before the long night shift ahead.

Lying in bed, I waited for the carbs to do their job, but sleep was elusive. I tried counting sheep but, as they jumped over the imaginary gate, the scene metamorphosed into mugshots of each suspect falling onto my desk – their means, motive, opportunity, listed in bullet points underneath. This didn't result in any amazing insights being dragged out of my subconscious, and I hoisted myself from the bed at 7.15, showered and popped into the restaurant to say bye to Anjoli, where she thrust a bag and a flask into my hands.

Gooch was waiting for me when I returned to the station, more tired than when I'd left two hours previously. We got into the car and drove to Fleishman's house, arriving before eight. The two constables on the day shift confirmed via radio that Gaby Fleishman had just come back from work and was in the house, unaware of their presence, as far as they knew. 'He's ex-Mossad,' I said. 'Let's make sure we can't be seen.' They drove off, and we took their spot, parking discreetly under a tree that offered us a good diagonal view of the front of his house.

Fleishman's end-of-terrace town house was on Vallance Gardens – an estate which surrounded an enclosed park that served its residents. It was a warm evening; the low, golden sun cast long shadows on the street, and people lay languorously on the green while birds flitted from tree to tree, enjoying the summer twilight as it ebbed into night. I saw Fleishman open the upstairs window. He stood for a few seconds looking out, breathed in the warmth, and disappeared into the house.

'I brought doughnuts and coffee,' said Gooch. 'Help yourself whenever.'

'And I brought samosas, onion bhajis and chai so, ditto,' I waved my thermos.

'Christ, the car's going to stink when you belch that out all night.'

'Listen, if you're going to be partnered with an Indian, you'd better expect to eat and burp with him. Did you see a pub nearby last night, by the way?'

'Yeah, London Hospital Tavern on Whitechapel Road. Five-minute walk.'

'Good; I do *not* fancy pissing into a bottle.'

'You'd better go at 11 before they shut, then hold it in for the rest of the night.'

We talked for a while about the worst stakeouts we'd been on – my story of spending two nights outside a suspect's house in Kolkata only to discover he was dead inside, won the prize – then lapsed into silence.

Over time, the sky shifted from orange to lilac to the grimy, yellow-lit black that characterises both Kolkata and East London at night, streetlights and stark shopfronts conspiring to cheat the moonless night of its darkness. Lights flicked on and off in the houses around the square. We occasionally saw Fleishman moving about inside. Then, at eleven, his lights went out.

I bit into a samosa. 'Guess he's settled in.'

'Only another nine hours to go. Have a nap; I'll hold the fort. No point us both staying up.'

'I'm good for now.' I brushed samosa crumbs off my chest. 'You get some sleep. You were up all night.'

'All right, mate, thanks. I'll be in the back seat.'

He lay down, and after a few minutes, his snores filled the car. It was getting hot and humid. I slid the windows down, hoping for some airflow, but to no avail. Sweat trickled down my back. I was tempted to switch on the air conditioning, but a parked, running car would not make for an unobtrusive stakeout. Now and then my eyes would drift shut, and I'd jerk awake. The square was quiet now, with no sound except the hum of traffic on the Whitechapel Road round the corner.

I was feeling like a damp washcloth and my eyelids drooped again when I heard a crash, an alarm going off and running footsteps. Gooch jerked up and said, 'What . . .'

'I don't know. It's not Fleishman's house.'

I looked around and saw a car's lights flashing across the square, alarm screaming.

'Hang on,' I said. 'I'll check it out.'

'I'll come with you. I need a stretch.'

'Should we both leave the car?'

'Okay, you wait.'

I was cramping up and needed to get out of the sauna the car had become. I glanced over at Fleishman's house, dark with no movement. 'Fuck it; I need to cool off. It's just there and it'll take two minutes.'

We ran around the corner to find a BMW, its window smashed open, a brick lying on the driver's seat, alarm going crazy. I called in the index number for a PNC check and found it registered to a Mr Dias in Number 27.

'You better tell him his car's been vandalised. I'll go back to the post,' I said, looking around for the culprit.

Gooch nodded, and I walked to the car, feeling somewhat refreshed. I cast a glance at Fleishman's house. Everything was still quiet. His lights were still off.

'Mr Dias is well pissed off,' said Gooch as he slid into the seat next to me ten minutes later. 'Had a go at me, asking how some-one could throw a brick into his car if we were so close that we were on the scene in seconds. I think he was wondering if I'd done it. Did you see anyone?'

'No. Was anything taken from the car?'

'Nothing as far as he could see. Must have been some kid. Here, you have a kip now.'

As I got into the back seat, I saw the lights in Fleishman's hall-way go on. After a couple of minutes, he opened his front door, and I tensed, but relaxed when I noticed he was wearing a bath-robe. He walked to his gate, looked up and down the street as Gooch and I hunkered down in our car, then went back in again.

'The alarm probably woke him,' I said.

'Yeah, he didn't see us.'

It was just after midnight.

I must have fallen asleep immediately, scrunched in the back of the car, because the next thing I knew was Gooch shaking me and whispering, 'Kamil.'

I raised myself up, and he pointed at Gaby Fleishman, lock-ing his front door. I looked at my watch: 1.36 a.m.

'His lights have been on since he came out earlier and he's been moving around,' Gooch said. 'He just exited the premises.'

Fleishman was dressed in a black top and dark jeans, carrying a shopping bag. He looked around, then walked to the end of the street.

We slipped out of the car and followed.

He was walking at a pace, almost running. Keeping him in sight without being spotted wasn't easy. He crossed Whitechapel Road and continued down Turner Street, staying in the shadows.

'Where the fuck is he off to? Is he practising for a speed-walking competition?' whispered Gooch, panting as we followed.

'Maybe the murderer asked him to meet?'

On Commercial Road, Fleishman turned and walked swiftly down the busy road, turning off on to Sutton Street. Twenty minutes later we were in the narrow King David Lane. It was getting harder not to be spotted. We fell back till we were fifty metres behind him.

'I think he's headed to the river,' I said.

He cut across King Edward Memorial Park and reached the Thames Path. He paused for a minute, staring at the black river in front of him. Looking around, he raised the hand with the shopping bag in it.

'Shit, he's throwing the bag!' I yelled out, 'Gaby!'

He stopped in mid-throw, turning to see who had shouted.

I sprinted towards him. As he turned to run, I rugby-tackled him, my arms around his waist. Both of us crashed onto the gravel path.

He was strong, built like a boxer. He pushed me off and scrambled to his feet. He raised his hand and threw the bag towards the river. In dismay, I watched it fly, tumbling white against the darkness. But then I saw Gooch leap into the air, almost in slow motion, and grab the bag from the dark sky just before it crossed the low wall to the river.

'Got it! Knew that fielding on the boundary would come in handy one day,' he gasped as he slammed down onto the path.

I grabbed Fleishman by the arm, feeling the muscles under his T-shirt, although he showed no inclination to run. He collapsed on the ground, head in his hands.

'You okay, Goochy?'

'Yeah,' he panted as he ran to us. We stood over Fleishman, and Gooch, still exhaling from his exertions, waved the plastic Tesco shopping bag at him. 'Let's see what you have here, Mr Fleishman. What was so urgent you had to get rid of it in the river at two in the morning?'

We looked in the bag to see a gun and a mobile phone.

I stared at Fleishman in astonishment. 'You? It was you all along? Why?'

He lifted his head to look at us, his eyes dark holes in the lamplight. 'I have been very stupid. By my mother, I swear, they are not mine.'

'Yeah, you were getting rid of them for a friend,' said Gooch. 'You can swear all you like at the station. Why don't you do the honours, Kamil? You've earned it with your tackle.'

'Gaby Fleishman, I'm arresting you for the murders of Sid Ram, Saul Cohen, Ari Levy and Yael Klein. You do not have to say anything. But it may harm your defence if you do not mention when questioned something which you later rely on in court. Anything you do say may be given in evidence. Your arrest is necessary for the prompt and effective investigation of the offences and to prevent you causing injury to other people.'

I'd said those words a thousand times – in the mirror, to Anjoli, in the car on my own, mouthing along to cops on the telly. But it was a whole other feeling to be speaking them now, in the middle of the night, to Gaby Fleishman, Gooch standing by with handcuffs.

Fleishman shook his head and said nothing.

Gooch said, 'Come on. March.'

'I'll call Tahir. Let me wake him up for a change.'

We got back to the station just after three to find Tahir waiting for us, unkempt and unshaven.

'Great work, guys,' he said as uniform took Fleishman to his cell. 'Tell me about it.'

I brought him up to speed, emphasising Gooch's terrific catch and leaving out the bit where we had abandoned our post to investigate Mr Dias's car alarm.

'Excellent job. Document the gun and phone on Fleishman's custody record and book it out for forensics. He can cool his heels in the holding cell until we have the results. With any luck, they'll confirm it's the murder weapon and the mobile we've been looking for. We need to organise a search of his house to find Levy's missing laptop. I'll rustle up a team now, before we question him. You guys go home and get some sleep.'

I took the phone and gun out of Fleishman's shopping bag with my gloved hands and looked at them. The pistol was squat, felt heavy, and had a tubular six-inch-long silencer attached to the barrel. I peered at the make – Heckler & Koch 9mm P30 – and handed it to Gooch, who logged it and put it in an evidence bag. The phone was a cheap black Nokia 130 with a physical keyboard and small screen. Gooch logged and bagged that as well and took them off to hand into evidence.

'So how do you think it went down, boss?' I said.

'We'll find out more when we question him,' said Tahir. 'But I guess he was pissed off when Wahid Masri took the CEO job away from him and brought in Sid Ram. It also reduced the amount of money he and the founders were going to make from the sale, so he decided to bring things back to the way they were. He phoned Michelle Jennings pretending to be Merrion, organised the fake meeting with Ram – obviously Merrion didn't show. Then followed Ram home and shot him. We found him at Saul Cohen's – so he must have killed Cohen, dumped the gun, and then called us.'

'How come we didn't find any GSR on his hands?'

Tahir shrugged. 'Wore gloves or washed it off his hands, I suppose. It is possible.'

'Wouldn't they have found evidence of that?'

'Who knows? Anyway, after Cohen is murdered, the money is now being split two ways instead of four. But he decides he wants it all. So, he toddles down to Ari Levy's room in the hotel and shoots him – Yael Klein is just collateral damage. Takes his laptop and, bingo, now he has the lot. Or he thinks he has.'

I considered this. 'But with Levy gone, the sale would fall through – he'd know that, wouldn't he?'

'Maybe, maybe not. Or perhaps he thought he could sell the tech to the highest bidder and not even have to cut the venture capitalists into it. Anyway, he doesn't need the gun or the phone anymore, so he figures he'll get rid of it. But he didn't realise that superman Kamil was on the job, and he'd be caught red-handed.'

'The technology was useless without Levy's chip, though?' I said.

'Maybe he figured that out too late? Or he also has a copy of the chip? Fuck knows. We have a result; be happy. The boss will.'

I persisted. 'But do you think he leaked the intel to Merrion? Why would he do that? And what about those anti-AI notes? And where did he hide the gun and the other stuff in Cambridge?'

Tahir ran his palm across his bristly chin. 'What the fuck, Kamil, are you his defence lawyer or something? *I* don't know. The AI thing was to throw us off the scent – it was a pretty pathetic attempt, to be honest. Maybe he leaked it to Merrion to get us to suspect him – after all, he used Merrion's name for the meeting with Ram. And as for Cambridge – it was him on the CCTV and he dumped the gun and phone somewhere and then collected them on his way back to London.'

'But why not leave them dumped in Cambridge? Why bring them to London and then dump them again?'

Tahir was getting seriously irritated now. 'We'll ask him that tomorrow when we interview him, okay? Now piss off home and sleep.'

He was acting as if it was all wrapped up like a neat kathi roll. I knew he was eager for the glory and credit that would buoy his career. I was too, but I only wanted it if it was truly deserved. My gut told me that something was very off. It was a feeling I had ignored too many times, in the Kolkata Force, and when I came to London and had to deal with the Rakesh Sharma murder. It was madness to make the same mistake again.

Tahir didn't realise his kathi roll was leaking sauce all over his lap. Tomorrow I would have to mop it up.

Chapter 29

Wednesday morning.

'Right, you numpties, we have news,' Protheroe announced at our morning meeting. 'Our man Paul Gooch here made a collar last night while you were all sucking wind. We have our guy! It was Gaby Fleishman. He is in the cells downstairs, waiting to be questioned. So marvellous job, mate.'

The room burst into applause, drowning out Gooch as he said, 'Actually, Kamil was . . .'

I felt hot anger burning through me as I watched everyone slap Gooch on the back. He looked at me and gave me a 'what can I do' shrug as Protheroe continued, 'We caught Fleishman red-handed with the murder weapon and the mobile phone we've been searching for. Paul prevented him from throwing the evidence into the river. You might be up for a commendation for that quick thinking, mate.' Protheroe winked. 'We've had forensics back and Fleishman's fingerprints are all over the phone and the gun. We also got the paper analysis back on the notes. It's universal printer paper, but it *is* used in Aishtar. *Guardian* and Bethlehem had a different brand, so nice job on that, guys. We haven't found the computer or any other evidence in his house, but we're still looking. We've got our man.'

What the absolute fuck! Protheroe had written me out of the story. The bastard. I didn't know how to set the record straight without seeming petty. Commendation! Double fuck!

I had to make sure Tahir told Rogers the truth. That I had been the one who tackled Gaby Fleishman and stopped him throwing the evidence away, that I had made the arrest, that I . . . why was I even bothering? If this was going to be the way things played out, maybe I was better off just running the restaurant with Anjoli. At least I didn't have to face this drip drip drip of abuse every single day from arseholes like Protheroe and his kin. My peripheral vision blurred, and I visualised myself walking up to him and smashing his ugly, grinning red face into a pulp against the squad room wall until there was nothing left except blood and bones and cartilage.

'Okay, mate?' It was Tahir. In my murderous fog, I hadn't noticed him approach.

'Not really. Protheroe just gave Gooch all the credit for the collar,' I seethed.

He shook his head, turned, and murmured into my shoulder, 'Sorry about that. I told Rogers you'd done it. Protheroe's a dick, ignore him. I know it was all you. Let the boys have their moment. You'll get yours, believe me.'

'I mean . . . okay. But listen, Tahir. Let me do the interview with you. You owe me that, at least?'

He had the grace to look embarrassed as he held his hands up.

'No can do, Kamil, I'm sorry. Rogers is on it with me. I've got no say in that . . .'

Another punch in the gut. But I swallowed it with a tight smile. 'No worries. I understand. Good luck. Let me know how I can help.'

'Tell you what, why don't you watch on the video in the observation suite. And if you think of anything, you can text me. We're starting in half an hour.'

I nodded my acceptance of the crumbs he'd thrown my way. Tahir might be my friend, but he wasn't my guardian angel. I'd known that from the start. He had to protect himself. I needed

276

to fight my own battles, build my reputation, and look after myself. I had done that all my life and there was no reason I couldn't continue to do it now.

I sat back down at my desk.

Gooch, sitting at the desk opposite, said, 'I'm sorry, Kamil. I told Protheroe it was your arrest. I don't know why he said what he did.'

'Don't worry about it, Paul. It was a team effort.'

'Quite a night, wasn't it? I couldn't sleep, was still buzzin' when I got home. Good, this policing lark, better than Es,' he laughed.

Good for some. The white, entitled coppers who always had things their way in this world that they had created. It was just us poor indentured labourers who had to eat their shit.

At ten I went over into the observation suite to find Protheroe eating some type of stinky pasty, crumbs flaked on his tie, a can of Coke on the table.

'Nice job last night, Rahman,' he grunted. 'You and Paul did some good policing in the field.'

I bit back a retort, just nodding as I took my chair, edging as far away from him as I could. The interview room on the monitors was empty – just a bare table and chairs showing. After three excruciating minutes of Protheroe's chewing, slurping and stertorous breathing, I muttered an excuse and went to the café to get myself a coffee and a sandwich. Taking a deep breath, I re-entered the observation room.

'What, no crisps for me?' he said as I sat.

'Didn't know you wanted any.'

'No worries, you can cook me a tikka masala sometime, chef,' he laughed. 'That's what you did before, right? Maybe your name should have been DC Rah-naan.'

He sniggered.

'I was an inspector before, *Sergeant.*'

'I heard. In the *Indian* police. I'm just pulling your plonker. You people are so sensitive.'

We *people*! I was about to lose it with him when the door to the interview room opened, and Rogers and Tahir led Fleishman in.

Chapter 30

Wednesday afternoon.

Tahir and Rogers marched into the bland interview room from the right of the screen and sat in front of Gaby Fleishman. He looked drawn, eyes bloodshot in a pale face, his fingers drumming an insistent rhythm on the table.

Questioning started with the usual preliminaries, confirming Fleishman's name, address and job. Then Rogers presented Fleishman with the option of having a solicitor present.

'That was stupid,' muttered Protheroe. 'He should have started asking questions – if Fleishman doesn't ask for a solicitor, that's his lookout.'

Great. I was going to get a pointless running commentary from this moron.

'Get on with it,' said Fleishman. 'I have done nothing wrong. I don't need a lawyer.'

I could see Tahir itching to get to the meat of it, but Rogers was handling this in his own way. He could have been a barrister the way he was going about this questioning. 'I would like to take you back to the night of Monday, 11 July. Tell me what you did that night.'

'Again?' Fleishman closed his eyes for a second and said, 'I've told you this a hundred times.' Rogers said nothing. 'Fine. I am cooperating. Someone who claimed to be Miles Merrion from the *Guardian* wanted to meet Sid to discuss the sale of Aishtar at the Blind Beggar on Whitechapel Road at 8.45 p.m. I agreed to accompany him.'

'Why?'

'I was Chief Marketing Officer and co-founder. If Sid was talking to a journo, I needed to be there.'

'What happened?'

'We got there at 8.45 and ordered drinks. Merrion never showed. Sid tried to call him, but he didn't answer. We left around 9.15 and I went home.'

'To Vallance Gardens?'

'Yes.'

'You didn't accompany Mr Ram to his house?'

'No.'

'And nobody can vouch for you between the times of 9.15 and midnight?'

'Enough already. I was at home alone. Who the fuck was going to vouch for me? I wasn't expecting to need an alibi.'

'Liar,' said Protheroe. 'The DI should have let me do the questioning. I would have broken him by now.'

If Protheroe had breathed on him with his stinking onion breath, Fleishman would have confessed to being the Zodiac Killer. And to killing Tupac. I wanted to tell Protheroe to shut the hell up but couldn't. Like it or not, I worked for this idiot.

'All right,' said Rogers. 'Let's move on to Thursday, 14 July. Tell me what happened that evening.'

'Saul texted me at 10.50 and asked me to come over to his flat.'

'Was that unusual?'

'A little. But with the sale, we were working all hours. So, I didn't think too much of it.'

'You didn't call or text to ask what it was about.'

'He said in his message there were some irregularities he wanted to discuss with me. I drove over and got there at eleven. There was no answer when I rang his bell. Someone walking out of the building let me in. I went to Saul's flat. The door was open. I walked in. I found him dead. I called 999. You people arrived. I told him,' he pointed at Tahir, 'all of this when he questioned me for hours that night.'

Fleishman was sticking to his story.

'And you didn't leave the flat between the time you called 999 and they arrived?'

'Where was I going to go? They had killed one of my closest friends.'

'Did you call anyone?'

'I called Ari and told him.'

'Why?'

'Why do you think? First Sid is killed and now Saul. You think I will not tell Ari?'

'What did he say?'

'He was shocked and wanted to come over. I told him not to.'

'And then?'

'Then what? Your guys arrived and he,' he gestured at Tahir again, 'brought me in here and did what you're doing now.'

This was getting us nowhere. At least Rogers couldn't blame Tahir and me now. He was carrying the can.

'All right. Let's get to Monday, 18 July.'

'I was in Cambridge for the conference.'

I shivered. Only two nights had passed since I'd discovered the bodies at the hotel, and it felt strange to be listening to Fleishman's own account of the moments in time that were now indelibly etched into my brain. I pulled myself together and tuned in again.

'After the cocktail party, we went to the hotel bar.'

'What time was that?' Rogers said.

'I don't know. Before eleven some time? Then Ari and Yael left after half an hour. I hung around with Wahid, David and Michelle. I went to my hotel room around midnight.'

'And you didn't see Mr Levy or Ms Klein again that night?'

'No.'

'And didn't call him?'

'No.'

'The phone we found on you shows you called him,' said Tahir.

'It's not mine! I came down for breakfast at seven the next morning and they weren't there. After a while, Wahid sent David to their room with you and the other policeman, and you found them. Can I get some water?'

The other policeman. Protheroe glanced at me, but I looked straight ahead at the screen, evading his accusatory stare. What? Did he think it was my fault? On the screen, Rogers gestured to Tahir, who handed Fleishman a bottle of water.

Tahir pulled out a still from the CCTV in Cambridge of the man outside the hotel.

'This is you, isn't it? What did you do with the backpack?'

'It's not me. I don't know who that is.'

'Oh, come on, it's clearly you.'

The picture wasn't clearly anybody, and I worried Tahir was overplaying his hand.

Rogers must have felt the same because he took over again. 'All right, we'll come back to that. Let's get to last night. What happened then?'

Fleishman drank his water, and the anger left his face. 'Last night I was stupid.'

'Tell me what happened.'

I leaned forward in my seat. Finally. Something I didn't already know.

'I came home after seven. Made myself dinner. Watched TV. Went to bed around eleven. And before you ask, no, I have no one to vouch for me. I went to sleep. A car alarm woke me before midnight. It stopped, and I was falling asleep again when I heard my letter box rattle and a thud on the mat.

'I thought it might be someone trying to get in. I went downstairs and saw a gun with a silencer and a phone on the floor. Like a fool, I picked them up. I was half asleep. I didn't know what I was doing. I went out to have a look but couldn't see anyone.'

The quarter of sandwich I had eaten turned into a heavy rock in my stomach.

'Did *you* hear a car alarm?' Protheroe asked me, not taking his eyes off the screen.

I said nothing. I hadn't mentioned in my statement we had left our post to see to the alarm. Luckily, Protheroe was too brainless to pursue it with me. He gave me a sharp glance when I didn't answer, then turned back to the screen as Rogers said, 'What did you do next?'

'That's where I was stupid. I knew you guys had it in for me, given the manner in which you questioned me after Saul's death. And I had been with Sid. *And* where Ari died. If I reported someone had dropped this gun and phone through my door, there was no way you were ever going to believe me.'

'Damn right we wouldn't,' muttered Protheroe.

'So, what did you do?' said Rogers.

Fleishman took a long pause. 'I decided to throw them in the river.'

'Why?' said Tahir. 'That makes no sense. If you had nothing to do with the crimes, you must have realised that this was the best chance of catching the killer.'

Fleishman rubbed his eyes. 'Someone was obviously trying to frame me. What were you going to learn from the gun or the phone? He would not leave his prints on it, would he?'

'He?'

'He, she, it, who the fuck knows? I said I was stupid, no? I couldn't think of what to do. I have spent years building up Aishtar, and I was not prepared to lose everything because some asshole got me thrown in jail.'

'So, you tried to dispose of them?'

'Yes. I put them in a bag and walked to the river and your two guys caught me. That's the truth, I swear. Were they watching my house? Ask them, please. They must have seen someone post them through my door.'

I wanted to disappear into my chair. That fucking alarm . . .

'That's the problem, Mr Fleishman,' said Tahir. 'They *were* watching your house all night and didn't see anyone.'

'Hah,' chortled Protheroe. 'Got him! You always catch them in a lie.'

'That's not possible,' said Fleishman. 'I'm telling you the truth. I swear it.'

It was all I could do not to get up and go interrupt the questioning to back the poor man up. Maybe if Protheroe hadn't been sitting next to me, I would have.

'Yeah, I'm sure you'd swear on Ari Levy's and Yael Klein's lives,' said Tahir, producing evidence bags containing the phone and the gun. 'Is this the gun and the mobile?'

Fleishman nodded.

'We found only your fingerprints on them.'

'Well, he or she wiped them clean before planting them.'

I felt sick.

Tahir took out the three notes we had found at the crime scenes.

'Do you recognise these?'

'Yes, you showed them to me before.'

'We found your prints on the envelope containing the one found next to Mr Cohen's body.'

'I told you I had picked it up.'

284

'And the paper is the same as the paper used in Aishtar, as are the envelopes.'

'Come on, man! Printer paper is printer paper; envelopes are envelopes. You probably use the same brand here!'

'We don't. Do you own a gun, Mr Fleishman?'

'I have one in Israel, not here.'

'What type?'

'A Glock 9 mm.'

'This one is a Heckler & Koch 9 mm. Have you ever used one? Given you were in the special forces, I assume you did.'

I saw him hesitate again. Then he said, 'Yes, I did. But you tested me for gunshot residue. Twice – after Saul and after Ari and Yael – and found nothing. What does that say?'

'GSR can be washed off, as you know. You had ample time to do so in both cases.'

Rogers changed tack. 'With Mr Ram and your other two co-founders gone, all their shares in Aishtar will pass to you, correct?'

Fleishman gave a short laugh. 'You think they are worth anything now? Aishtar *was* Ari. Who is going to buy the company with him gone? Believe me, I may own their shares now, but their value is the square root of fuck all.'

'But the technology itself is valuable, right? You could just sell the tech and make far more money than having to share it with your backers and co-founders.'

Fleishman banged the table, causing Rogers to start.

'You think I would do that, man? I spent years building this company up. We had a legit offer on the table, which would have made me over a hundred million bucks. Why would I jeopardise that by killing my friends?'

'Because someone might pay you double or triple that for the tech. Someone who could not buy the company legitimately,' said Tahir. 'What have you done with Mr Levy's laptop and dongle? We didn't find it in your house.'

'That's because I never had it!'

'Information was leaked from inside your company to Miles Merrion of the *Guardian*. Who else could have done that?'

'Why would I leak information?'

'To get him to publicise what you were doing and drive the price up.'

'That's crazy talk.'

'So, if it's not you, then who? Who is framing you? And why?' Fleishman leaned across the table.

'You think I haven't been thinking 24/7 about this? Someone picking us off one by one.'

'And what motive does anyone else have for killing your co-founders?' said Rogers.

'I do not have a clue. I don't know. Maybe someone after the tech. A bad actor. A rogue state.'

'Why would they bother framing you? If they did this, they have the technology now on Mr Levy's computer. Why not just vanish back to Pyongyang or Moscow? Why become invisible, come to your house, drop the phone and gun through your door and disappear without being seen by our two policemen watching you? Or did they steal some invisibility technology from another startup?'

'The tech is useless to them without Ari's McCain protocol, whatever that is.'

'We have found the McCain protocol and have it in our possession, Mr Fleishman.'

'What? How? *I* don't even know what it is.'

Tahir told him about the chip we had found embedded in Levy's hand. He didn't mention I was the one who had figured it out.

Fleishman sat, chewing his lip, taking it in. Then whispered, 'That clever bastard. Although the chip is useless without Ari's computer and dongle.'

'Look at it from our point of view, Mr Fleishman,' said Tahir, leaning close. 'You were with Mr Ram before he died. No alibi. You found Mr Cohen's body. No alibi. You were there when Mr Levy and Ms Klein were murdered. No alibi. We found the gun on you, as well as the phone we've been looking for. You've just admitted that you know how to use the gun. Your fingerprints were on the envelope – that was a clumsy way to distract attention from yourself, writing that gibberish. You leak the info to get more buyers interested. And you stand to make hundreds of millions of dollars. Why don't you just come clean and cooperate? You'll find things easier.'

Fleishman looked down at the desk and shook his head. 'Because I did nothing, man. They were my friends. Now I have no friends, no company, no technology, no life, no nothing! A week ago, I had everything. Why? Why would I . . . destroy my own life?'

Rogers and Tahir looked at each other and Rogers said, 'Interview terminated at 11.43 a.m. You will remain in custody, Mr Fleishman, while we decide whether to charge you. Again, I remind you of your right to a lawyer.'

Fleishman exhaled, nodded, and said, 'I would like to call Wahid Masri, please.'

'My colleague will organise that. We'll escort you back to the custody suite now.'

'Maybe a night in our little grey cells will make you more cooperative,' said Tahir.

They left. I stared at the now empty room displayed on the screen, feeling nauseous.

Protheroe stood up. 'We got him! We just closed the book on four murders in a week.'

He looked at my stony face and his voice changed. 'What's the matter? Why aren't you jumping for joy, Rahman? You're the one who collared him.'

I couldn't say anything. He sat down again and gave me a sharp look. 'Is there something I should be aware of?'

I shook my head. He stared at me for a few seconds, then said, 'Look. I know I've given you a hard time. But you're not a bad copper. I know you think you're better than us all because of the stuff you did in India. But you'll learn it's different in this country. You've got to pay your dues. Tahir did you no favours by giving you more responsibility before you were ready for it. I know you don't like me because I ragged on you, but it was just to toughen you up. Take some advice from an old hand. Bide your time. Learn the ropes. Get to know the colleagues who you need to have your back and make sure they know you have theirs. This is not a good place for a lone wolf. Now, drinks are on me in the pub tonight. Be there or despair!'

He stood, clapped me on the back and walked out, leaving me in the observation suite with his pasty crumbs and an empty Coke can.

I wasn't jumping with joy.

Because I had fucked up. If I hadn't been distracted by the car alarm, I'd know whether Fleishman was lying. Two minutes. I'd left my post for no more than two minutes and had screwed up the entire investigation. And who the fuck did Protheroe think he was to give *me* advice?

Chapter 31

Wednesday evening.

I spent the rest of the day head down at my desk, finalising paperwork, unsure what to do, my mind flipping like windshield wipers: *It must be Gaby Fleishman; it can't be Fleishman.* How could I make any kind of judgement? Rogers, Tahir – even bloody Protheroe, given we were in his patch – were far more experienced than I was. Protheroe was right. *I* had never interrogated a suspect in England. I hadn't been in the room when they had questioned him and there was no way I could pick up the subtle, non-verbal signals that might betray his culpability. The sheen of sweat on the brow, a flicker in the eyes, a darkening of expression. These were all lost between the rudimentary camera and the low-res screen.

Rogers, Tahir and Protheroe seemed so certain that their suppositions were justified and accurate. And yet . . . and yet . . . Fleishman's response to each allegation had been credible. It was possible that someone distracted us with the alarm and planted the murder weapon on him. But what could I do? Go to Tahir and say we've got the wrong guy? After collaring him myself? If I came clean about leaving our post, Protheroe would have me by the balls for the rest of my career. Not that I would probably have one for much longer. I hadn't spoken to Gooch – he was in the same hole as me.

No. Better to stay quiet. If Gaby Fleishman was innocent, the truth would come out, and he'd be free. And rich beyond belief if he ever managed to sell the company.

The cops who had been watching Nelson Tang and Miles Merrion came by and slapped me on the back. 'Nice job, Kamil. Even Rogers is smiling.'

'Thanks,' I said. 'Listen, did your targets go out last night?'

'Nope. Both stayed home all night. Why?'

'Nothing, was just wondering.'

I felt a little better. It must have been Fleishman after all. Who else could have planted the gun and phone on him?

Rogers came into the incident room after six and said, 'Right, you lot. Camel. Thirty minutes. I expect all of you there.'

The Camel was our local pub, round the corner from the station on Globe Road. I'd been there with Tahir a few times. It was an old-fashioned Victorian pub, all dark wood, floral wallpaper, decorative lights hanging from the ceiling. But it was cheap, had excellent beers and served tasty pies, so was a favourite with the coppers in the station.

I walked over with Tahir, who was ebullient. 'Great result, Kamil. I'll make sure you get your dues. Don't worry about Protheroe, he won't cut you out again. We've taken it to the CPS, they'll confirm there's a case and then – we charge him,' he said with relish.

'Tahir, I . . .'

'Yeah?'

'Never mind.'

I couldn't bring myself to raise my concerns, especially as I wasn't sure precisely what they were. Rogers bought a round, and I sat with my pint of Hoegaarden, listening in silence to the banter swirling around me.

'Lucky you didn't go into the river, Paul, when you caught the gun,' Protheroe said to Gooch. 'Rahman here would have had to fish you out and your man would have scarpered.'

'You can talk,' said Rogers. 'Remember the incident after you finished your training when you were a pro-con?'

'The doll in the river,' chorused a few of the officers as Protheroe turned red.

'What happened?' I said.

Rogers wiped the foam from his mouth with the back of his hand. 'Young Prothers here was on his probation as a constable. He had a beat by the river near Wapping. Two of the lads nicked that rubber doll they used to practise CPR on – what was she called?'

'Brace Yerself Bridget!' yelled some cops.

'That's right! They tossed Bridget into the river as Prothers was walking up. He saw her, started screaming about a body in the river and radioed for immediate ambulance backup.'

The crew burst out laughing as Protheroe muttered, 'Yeah, well, better safe than sorry.'

The conversation moved on and a cop said to Rogers, 'I read Priscilla Patrick wants to cut force numbers again, boss. Is that going to affect us?'

Rogers frowned. 'I don't know, to be honest. The Home Office is pushing a much bigger chunk of its budget towards blocking illegal immigrants, which is ridiculous, because we need more money to fight crime inside the UK. But it's the Home Sec's crusade. I've spoken to her about our collar, and she is pleased. Well, as pleased as she ever gets.'

'She'll be happy the killer wasn't English. Maybe she'll spare us any cuts?'

Rogers grimaced. 'Wouldn't count on it, mate.'

I listened to them with some envy. This was a club I would never belong to. Even Tahir slotted in easily. I was never a belonger – even in Kolkata, I found it difficult to go drinking and carousing with colleagues – something Abba did well. He had told me I needed to learn, as it would hold me back in my career if I did not. But it just didn't come naturally to me. Much as I hated to admit it, Protheroe had been right about that too. They had to know I had their back, or they would not have mine.

Gooch came up and slapped me on the back. 'You must be happy, Kamil.'

'Yeah. Hey, join me in the loo for a second.'

He raised an eyebrow. 'Don't think I'm easy just because I spent a night with you. I need flowers and champagne first.'

He followed me into the toilet, still holding his glass. I checked to see the stalls were empty and whispered, 'Listen, Goochy. Do you think we should tell them about the car alarm?'

He paused, then took a gulp of his Guinness.

'Naah, it's fine. We've got our guy.'

'The thing is,' I hesitated. 'His story sort of adds up. He says someone put the gun and phone through his letterbox when the alarm went off. It's possible they did it while we were gone.'

'Not a chance. We were only away for a couple of minutes. No time for anyone to do that.'

'There might have been.'

He clapped me on the back again. 'We caught him red-handed. Relax. Enjoy your collar.'

'But . . .'

'Don't sweat it. It's all good. I need a piss. You can watch if you like. I'll only charge a tenner.'

'Protheroe charges a quid,' I said and walked out, wishing I could be as relaxed as Gooch about not reporting what we'd done.

A few more drinks in and my brief dereliction had taken on the deep black hue of misconduct. I felt it throbbing its way through my heart with every beat until, unable to stop myself, I got up to intercept Tahir as he exited the loo.

'I need a word, boss.'

'What's up?'

'Let's get some fresh air.'

We carried our pints outside. It was a warm evening; the sun was still up, and the pavement was filled with the buzz of post-work drinkers, chatting, smoking, enjoying the dying sun.

'Boss, I'm not sure Gaby Fleishman is our guy.'

He rolled his eyes. 'You saw the interview. He was the only one who could have done it, Kamil. And he made up that cock-and-bull story about someone putting the phone and gun through his letter box while you and Gooch were watching the place.'

It was now or never. Heart in mouth, I plunked for now.

'The thing is, I left something out of my statement by mistake. Fleishman's interview reminded me. Just before midnight, a car alarm did go off around the corner, and Paul and I ran over to have a quick look. We were only gone a few minutes, but it *is* possible someone might have planted the gun. And Fleishman did come out in his dressing gown to look, as he said in the interview. We saw him.'

Tahir was silent, then shook his head. 'Fuck off! Are you serious?'

Miserable, I nodded.

He looked down the street. 'Who else knows?'

'Just Goochy. But he didn't want me to say anything.'

'Alright.' He took a swig of his beer and narrowed his eyes. 'Maybe best to leave it that way, yeah?'

'I called in a PNC check on the car.'

Tahir shut his eyes for a moment, then shrugged.

'Leave it. They won't connect the dots.'

'But what if Fleishman *is* telling the truth? Then we have the wrong guy. We can't put an innocent man away!'

Tahir went silent. Then, 'Just leave it! We were in the shit with Rogers and somehow extricated ourselves, smelling of roses. Do you want to be choking on crap again? I don't. We've sent it to the CPS. It's up to them now. It's their job to determine if the case is strong enough or not.'

I started to protest, then stopped. Maybe Tahir *was* right. If the case was flimsy, the CPS *would* throw it out and we would be in the clear. Perhaps this was the way to thread the needle and get out of the pickle I was in.

Tahir saw me coming round to his point of view and said, 'Besides, who else could have done it? Merrion, Jennings, Baker, Masri and Tang all didn't go out last night, so they couldn't have planted the gun on Fleishman.'

'Unless they got someone else to do it?' I said weakly.

'Unlikely. There is no one else.'

'Except an enemy spy?' Why couldn't I let this go?

'Why would a spy bother framing Fleishman? Listen to yourself. You're tying yourself up in knots. Rogers has the financial crime bods looking into any large payments Fleishman may have received. He got greedy, that's all. Just forget about it; you've done well. You need to learn to be flexible sometimes. Let the CPS decide, that's their job. Keep your head down. Don't screw up your career before it's even started. Take the credit and enjoy the glory. Yes?'

'Yes,' I said reluctantly.

He punched my shoulder. 'Good man! Come on, let's go back in. It's my round.'

I followed Tahir back inside to the bar and watched as he threw off his concerned frown and effortlessly pushed himself back into the banterful drinking session with the lads. He was right. What was the point of rocking the boat? I thought back to the extreme moral rectitude I had exhibited as a cop in India all those years ago. How had that worked out for me? I was so rigid back then that my career had snapped.

No. I had just helped crack the huge Aishtar case. Four murders. FOUR. And made the arrest. This was my moment of triumph, and I should savour it. Be flexible, as Tahir said. Not rigid.

But just how flexible did I have to be to keep this job?

Chapter 32

Thursday morning.

I was dreading going into work the next day, so when Anjoli asked me if I wanted to join her at the London Metropolitan Archive to do some more research into Avram Pinsky's family, I agreed immediately. They owed me time off after my all-nightery, anyway. Protheroe would almost certainly complain, but I was beyond caring.

'You sure you won't get into trouble for not going in?' Anjoli said as we checked in, the receptionist eyeing her *Immigrants – making Britain great since 1066* T-shirt. 'You must have *so* much on.'

I muttered something noncommittal, still not having told her about my new position at the bottom of the ladder.

A research assistant led us to a large room, and we sat at two adjoining desks with computers as she explained what they had. 'We've got hundreds of years of documents, maps, photos, films, online or physically stored. You can search by topic or year in the General Register Office or parish registers or several other databases.'

She clicked around, showed us how it worked, and left us to it. I'd exchanged one desktop computer for another, but at least I had Anjoli to keep me company. And she seemed happy.

'What do you want me to do, Anj?'

'I want to try to find records of Pennyfeather and that

Yankovitch. I'll start with the photograph archives, and you try the births and deaths registers, okay?'

The system was pretty easy to use. I clicked 'births', typed in 'Pennyfeather' in 'London City' and hit enter. I found thirteen Pennyfeathers: six men and seven women with three of them born before 1900 – a William, Charles and Peter.

'What was Pennyfeather's first name? I've got three in the right period.'

'Peter. Look what I found.'

She had loaded a newspaper article from *The Times*.

Saturday, 20 December 1913

Pennyfeather's Shopping Emporium to double in size

Pennyfeather's, that extraordinary temple of the retail business, in Fieldgate, East London is set to double in size, Mr Peter Pennyfeather, the owner, informed *The Times* yesterday. Our correspondent met him amid the magnificent Christmas celebrations in his store. The exterior of the shop was festooned with laurel and exhibited the flags of all nations. As we walked into the store that was filled with masses of flowers and greenery, we saw myriads of tiny globules suspended on threads, which reminded one of the snow that was falling outside. Orchestras were playing, apparently at every corner, and the showrooms were more airy and spacious – owing to the absence of dividing walls and partitions – than those which are familiar to London eyes. Everything one could possibly want was on display and as we walked around, we observed the pleasant habit of the shop assistants in refraining from asking what they could do for one. Foreign visitors were provided with

---

interpreters, and a trained nurse was on hand to administer first aid if it was needed.

Mr Pennyfeather, dressed in his usual top hat and morning coat, said the expansion was necessary as he wished the store to encompass a post office, a theatre booking office, a library and an information bureau, as well as galleries displaying works of art, a comfortable 'silence room' for resting, restaurants and a roof garden. 'People will sit up and take notice of you if you sit up and take notice of what makes them sit up and take notice,' he told our correspondent.

I clicked on Peter Pennyfeather's birth record and a scan of the page where it was recorded over 150 years ago in neat, cursive handwriting appeared, sitting between a William Penny and an Alfred Jago Penrose.

Pennyfeather Peter   Stepney   Mar. 1870

'The store must have been the Selfridges of its time,' said Anjoli. 'Look, here are some later pictures of it from the outside. He must have expanded it after Yankovitch sold Avram's store to him. Avram's shop that we saw in the VR simulation is gone. *And* it's on Fieldgate Street. Did you find any records for Yankovitch?'

I shook my head. 'But I found something else.'

I clicked around and showed her.

Chatterjee, Anjoli   Whitechapel   Sept. 1989

'Ta-da! You exist.'

'Bloody hell. I never thought of checking out my family.' Her face fell, 'Although . . .'

I looked at her, questioning.

'I was just thinking there would be no archives of my parents – they were born, got married and died in India. So even though they lived most of their lives over here, there'll be no record of them. Sad, no?' She shut her eyes for a second. 'Anyway, keep looking and see if you can track down any of Pennyfeather's family. This is fun. I feel like someone from *Who Do You Think You Are*.'

She was right. There was something amazing about conjuring long dead people to life with a few clicks. Who were these folks? They had lived, loved and died, never to be thought of again. In 150 years, would anyone be clicking on Kamil Rahman or Anjoli Chatterjee on a computer screen or awakening us in holographic form? I doubted it. It made me feel insignificant as well as connected to the millions who had gone before. Our lives exist in a web of bureaucracy that records everything momentous *and* quotidian – births, deaths, marriages, house moves, divorces . . . but these official records are ignorant of all the emotion generated in the moments of those events – the tears, the laughter, the fears. Given what I'd seen today, those archives, whether in crabbed handwriting or faded type, leave footprints through the generations. There was comfort in that – our descendants might forget us, but we would still live somewhere in the ether if someone cared to look, and we would once again emerge from the shadows into the light. The archive I was looking at was a very low-fi version of Ari Levy's virtual-reality simulation – it was all there; we just needed to use our imaginations a little more.

I clicked on 'Deaths' and entered 'Peter Pennyfeather' and this time I got

DEATHS REGISTERED IN JANUARY, FEBRUARY
AND MARCH 1956. **PEN-PER**

PENNYFEATHER, Peter J. 86 years. Hampstead

'Gosh, he lived till the age of eighty-six,' I said. 'He only died in 1956.'

That felt even more amazing. We had wrenched Peter Pennyfeather from the dim and distant past to my parents' generation.

'Incredible,' said Anjoli. 'So, it looks like Pennyfeather's department store was shut down in 1952 and became . . . guess what? Only the East London Mosque!'

'Here's a record of Peter Pennyfeather's marriage to Ann York in June 1895. But they had no children. So, I guess that was the end of the line. I wonder who inherited the Pennyfeather stores?'

'Nobody, I suppose, if it was closed before he died. Have you checked the parish registers?'

'No, just the General Register Office. Hang on. Yes, here we go. Pennyfeather lived in the parish of St Mary Matfelon, in Whitechapel. It has records of their births, marriages and deaths – Ann died in 1950, six years before Peter – no children recorded as being born and . . . that's odd.'

I paused and stared at the screen.

'What?'

'Look at this.'

I had clicked on baptisms in the parish records and searched for Pennyfeather.

We were looking at the record for the baptism of a girl, Mary, daughter of Peter and Ann Pennyfeather, on 14 January 1914.

'I thought you said they didn't have any children?' said Anjoli.

'There's no record of any birth. Must be a mistake . . .'

We stared at the entry; then Anjoli's eyes widened. 'Malka's baby was called Miriam – we didn't find her body.' Her eyes were shining with excitement or tears; I couldn't tell.

'What does that mean?'

'I don't know. But isn't it weird? There isn't a record of Pennyfeather having fathered any children and then suddenly he's *baptising* a little girl with a similar name to Avram's baby? Just *after* she disappeared? What the fuck?'

We looked at each other.

She said slowly, 'What if . . . look, Pennyfeather wants to buy Avram's store to expand his department store, right? Avram doesn't want to sell. We know that from Malka's letter. Then Yankovitch sells him Avram's shop weeks after Avram disappears – we know *that* from the records. We didn't find Avram's baby's body with the others. Then Pennyfeather mysteriously gets a baby. So, what if Pennyfeather or Yankovitch killed Avram and Malka and Leah to get the shop and the baby?'

She clutched my hand tight in hers and stared into my eyes.

'That's a bit of a stretch, Anjoli,' I said. 'I mean . . .'

'It *fits*, Kamil! It all fits. What else could explain the sequence of events?'

'What if . . .' but, try as I might, I couldn't think of a more logical explanation.

'Well?' she said, still crushing my hand.

'Shit,' I said. 'I think you may be right. You might have found the killer.'

The enormity of Anjoli's insight awed me. Not for the first time, I wondered at her hunger for justice, her unyielding tenacity and natural aptitude for investigation. A week ago, we had found three corpses on a building site. She had rolled her sleeves up, dug around and patched together a plausible theory linking the past to the present using data. Forget Aishtar's tech – Anjoli was the human embodiment of AI. Anjoli Intelligence.

'You are amazing,' I said, and squeezed her hand, my heart

filled with admiration and just a hint of envy. Or was it guilt? I squashed it.

'So, what happened to the family? Come onnn! Look.'

'Let's see.' She pulled her hand away, and I scrolled through the archives for a few minutes. 'So. Mary Pennyfeather . . .'

'Malka's kidnapped daughter!'

'Malka's kidnapped daughter marries a Roger James and gives birth to Agatha in 1945. Agatha James marries Michael McCartney. Agatha McCartney gives birth to Priscilla in 1980. Mary James, née Pennyfeather dies in 1990.'

'Shit! Mary . . . Miriam . . . was alive when I was born.' Anjoli shivered. 'That gave me goosebumps. Polina and Sofia could have known their great aunty!'

'The past is really not that past, is it?' I said. 'And then Priscilla McCartney marries a Jason Patrick in 2010. No children. That brings us up to date.'

Anjoli's eyes opened wide.

'What? Is there something else I should look for?' I said.

'Oh my god, Kamil. Think! *Priscilla Patrick . . .*'

'No! There must be lots of Priscilla Patricks. Here, I'll look her up on Google.'

I typed her name into the search-box and, under a selection of top news stories, her Wikipedia preview displayed.

Priscilla Patrick, née McCartney (born April 29, 1980) is a British politician serving as Home Secretary since May 2022.

I looked again at the archive page. The birth dates matched.

Priscilla Patrick, the British Home Secretary, was a direct descendent of Jewish immigrants Avram and Malka Pinsky.

Chapter 33

Thursday afternoon.

I stared at Anjoli. 'This is a bizarre coincidence. We just saw her on the telly the other day.'

She was staring at the screen.

'I know. I'm not sure what to make of it.'

I was about to say I'd also heard her yelling at Rogers, then remembered I'd told Maliha about my demotion, not Anjoli. 'Does it matter?'

She thought for a moment. 'It will to her. And her supporters. She's built a career out of dog-whistle racism and anti-Semitism. *And* she's always made a big deal about her family's hard graft in building Britain. If it turns out the man she thought was her great-grandfather wasn't related to her and was a murderer and a child snatcher and she's actually Jewish . . .' She mimed her head exploding, with sound effects.

'We need to be careful, Anjoli. This is dangerous information.'

'Why? It happened over a hundred years ago. And what do we care if a politician is shown up as a hypocrite? *Especially* her. I'm ready to call the *Guardian* now. Don't you have a contact there? What about that Merrion guy?'

'*Wait.* Let's think about this. I really believe we should keep it to ourselves for now. Please.'

'I have to tell Sofia!'

'Anjoli, we need to handle this with care. It could upend lots of lives. Priscilla Patrick doesn't even know herself. Just hold fire for the time being.'

'Why?'

'We need to consider the ramifications. The Home Secretary is in charge of the police, you know. They're slashing the force. What if it rebounds on me? From what I've read, she can be pretty vindictive and has a reputation for being a bully. I'd rather not be in her crosshairs. She could get me fired and chucked out of the country. I'm in trouble as it is.'

She looked at me sharply. 'Has something happened at work? You've been acting weird.'

I gazed at her expectant face and couldn't hold it in any longer, offloading all my vexations to her in a rush. Protheroe elbowing me off the case; being duped by the car alarm; the compounding of this foolish lapse by not mentioning it; my worries about Fleishman being falsely accused; the possibility of the actual murderer being on the loose . . . it all came tumbling out.

She listened in silence. After I stopped talking, she gave an enormous sigh and said, 'Bloody hell.'

'Bloody hell? Is that the best you can do?' I said, nettled.

'I mean, it's a lot, isn't it? What did you expect me to say?'

'I don't know, something to make me feel better?'

'I'm thinking about what you can do now.' This was the problem with Anjoli. She didn't understand that I just needed some empathy and comforting and not solutionising.

I stood. 'I'm not looking for an answer from you, Anjoli, just—'

She got up and enveloped me in a hug.

'I'm sorry. You should have told me everything earlier. It's not your fault. You did the best you could.'

'Whatever.' I pulled away.

'Stop sulking.'

'I'm not sulking. Don't you get it? They might send an innocent man to jail because of me.'

'Why are you angry with me?'

'Jesus, Anjoli . . . sometimes . . .'

She looked at me, perplexed. 'Look, I don't know what I've done, but I'm sorry. It might be all right. Gaby Fleishman hasn't been charged yet, you said.'

'No, but the CPS are looking at the evidence and may author-ise charges soon. If I don't come clean, Fleishman is screwed. If I do, *I'm* screwed. Tahir, Protheroe, Gooch – we could all be suspended. How am I supposed to relax with all that hanging over me? And now you want to give the Home Secretary – my ultimate boss – a reason to deport me.'

'I'm sorry. Let's get out of here and talk properly.'

'I can't. I need to go to work.'

She lowered her voice. 'All right. If it wasn't Fleishman, you need to figure out who did it. Then you can admit to taking your eye off the house, because you'll also have found the killer, so it won't matter.'

'What the hell can I do on my own? They'll close the case, and I won't have a team.'

'I'll help you. A fresh pair of eyes and all that. And you can't say I haven't been useful before . . . look how quickly we figured out the skeletons' story.'

I looked into her earnest eyes, took a breath, put an arm around her, and drew her to me. She hadn't said it, but I was being a dick. She *was* only trying to help. 'Sorry. You have a bril-liant mind, but I don't know how that would work. Everything is in the station. Maybe you're right. Perhaps I need to go back to the first killing and look at all the angles again. I'll have to do it on the DL.'

'Well, you can run your ideas by me, and I'll poke holes in them, as usual.'

I smiled and said, 'I will. DC Rahman and Community Sup-port Officer Chatterjee to the rescue.'

'Piss off, I'm at least an inspector! Come on, you need to de-stress. Let's go and have a glass of wine.'

'I'm tempted. But I'm sorry. I just can't. It would just *distress* me.' I gave a weak smile. 'I have to go. Thanks. You're the best.'

I left her looking after me, worry on her face.

Tahir grabbed me as I got into the station. 'The CPS have authorised the charges.'

'Oh, right,' I said, a rock in my belly. Somewhere inside, I'd been hoping they would choose not to proceed. But given the profile of the case, the political ramifications, and the press attention, I suppose it had been inevitable.

'And no bail. They think he is a serious flight risk. Masri's given him some hotshot solicitor in a Savile Row suit.'

'What do Laurel and Hardy think?' I said, with a vague hope that if SO15 took over, it wouldn't be my fault.

'They want the chip, but we're holding it as evidence for now. I'm not letting them do their smash-and-grab again.' He looked at me, eyes narrowed. 'How are you doing?'

'All right.'

'Good. Keep it that way. I want you to log everything and make sure we've documented the case fully. No slip-ups. But no need to mention anything . . . extraneous. I don't want to upend things.'

His eyes drilled into mine to ensure I got the message.

I did.

'Yes, boss.'

I sat at my desk and stared at the computer screen, the blue Met Police logo mockingly informing me we were 'Working Together For A Safer London'. Safer for whom? Not the four who had been killed on my watch over the last ten days, nor the three murdered a hundred years ago because they wouldn't sell their shop. And six of the seven dead had been Jewish. Whatever that meant.

Maybe working in homicide wasn't for me. It struck too close, and I couldn't keep the distance good cops were supposed to keep. On the other hand, working in Kolkata on what they charmingly called 'assaults on women with intent to outrage her modesty' hadn't been fun either. Where the hell did I fit in?

'Focus, Kamil,' I hissed to myself. All these mental meanderings were a procrastinatory attempt to avoid the psychic graft of figuring out what to do next. Twenty minutes later all I had done was make a few false starts, scribbling on sheets of A4 I had liberated from the photocopier, crumpling them up and throwing them in the bin. Every time an idea struck me, I would just see Fleishman sitting in that dingy interview room saying, 'I did nothing. They were my friends.'

Anjoli was right. I was too close to the case. I needed someone to look at it differently.

I needed her.

I took two folders, one empty and the other full, to the copy machine, and as surreptitiously as I could manage, waited while it spat out each document of evidence I fed into it. Then I went back to my desk, replaced the folder of originals, and grabbed my jacket.

'Stepping out for a bit. Just need to follow up on something.'

Nobody responded; nobody cared.

Chapter 34

Thursday afternoon.

Anjoli was in the restaurant kitchen, getting ready for the evening sitting.

'What are you doing here? Why aren't you at work? Is everything okay? Did Rogers find out?' she machine-gunned at me, while spooning pistachio jelly from a stainless-steel tin and fresh, home-made tamarind sugar from a mason jar into little compartmentalised crystal dishes, wiping up wayward dollops with a napkin as she went along.

'No. Everything's fine. Listen, do you think you can leave dinner to the others today? I want to take you up on your offer to help. Maybe if we could bounce some ideas off each other, it could serve to clear the clutter in my head.'

She wiped her hands on a dishcloth and said, 'Love to. Seems quite quiet out there, anyway. Give me a sec.' She turned to a waiter. 'Can you put the lids on these chutneys and keep them ready for the tables? You're in charge this evening, okay? Oh, and plonk a couple of batata vadas and samosas on a plate for me? Thanks. I'll just take this too.' She took the food and a dish of chutney and followed me up to the flat.

I spread the photocopies out on the dining table, made us some tea and stood, cup in hand, staring out of the window which looked on to the dingier end of Brick Lane below. The clouds were oppressive, and I could feel sweat trickling down my neck and the damp patches under my arms growing as the hum of the street through the open window filled my senses.

'Shut the window. It's so noisy,' said Anjoli from behind me. 'So, come on, where do we start?'

'I thought by collating the suspects and the evidence. Then we can try to find any connections?'

'Sounds good. Actually, hang on a sec.'

She disappeared into her bedroom, emerged with markers, Blu-Tack and a ream of paper. She stuck sheets of blank A4 to the wall.

'*Now* I feel like I'm on a TV cop show! All we need to do is draw arrows between what we put down here and we're sorted. You dictate and I'll write.'

'Okay. Make a list of victims on one sheet and suspects on another. Here's who they are.'

She wrote them up in her neat handwriting as I spoke.

'All right,' I said, feeling like we had achieved something. Somehow, seeing the names up on the wall made the problem seem more solvable. 'Let's add motives, alibis and whether they could have planted the gun and see what we can find.'

'Have to say, this is much more interesting than dishing condiments.'

We created our list and crossed out any extenuating factors that made them less likely suspects. The final list ended up as:

GABY FLEISHMAN: Money. No alibi for all killings. Tried to get rid of murder phone and murder weapon. lost the CEO job to Sid and then Saul. Didn't like Sid.
MILES MERRION: Anti AI. No alibi for all killings. Couldn't plant as was being watched. Accomplice? Article had same words as Sid note.

NELSON TANG: ~~Axe to grind (Fired)~~, Anti AI. No alibi for all killings. ~~Couldn't plant as was being watched~~. Accomplice?

BLOFELD (FOREIGN SPY): Could have done any of them. Wants tech. Could plant, but why?

WAHID MASRI: ~~No motive. On Zoom for 1.~~ No alibi for others. ~~Couldn't plant as was being watched~~.

DAVID BAKER: ~~No motive. On Zoom for 1.~~ No alibi for others. ~~Couldn't plant as was being watched~~.

MICHELLE JENNINGS: ~~No motive.~~ No alibi. ~~Couldn't plant as was being watched~~.

MRS ARI: Jealousy? No alibi for 1,2. ~~In London for 3.~~ Could plant?

'Forget Mrs Ari,' said Anjoli, and I put a line through her name. 'Can't see why she would. It *has* to be Gaby Fleishman. It can't be anyone else unless you believe this mysterious Blofeld did everything. The others were all being watched, so couldn't plant the gun. Pretty unlikely they could find an accomplice to plant it. Occam's razor and all.'

I felt like a massive weight had been lifted off me. She was right. No wonder the CPS had charged him. My stepping away from my post had not resulted in the wrong man being arrested. It couldn't be anyone else! 'Occam's razor! Who's showing off their uni education! Or as Sherlock Holmes said,' I took out my phone and googled it, 'when you have eliminated the impossible, whatever remains, however improbable, must be the truth. So, I guess it must be Fleishman.'

But one thing still niggled. I took the marker from Anjoli and added,

Why did Gaby come out to look around after the alarm went off?

'Maybe the alarm gave him an excuse to come out and check if he was being watched without looking suspicious. So he could dump the gun later. He didn't spot you and went ahead with his plan.'

That made sense to me. Anjoli continued, 'And it's a damn sight more likely than some mysterious Russian spy stealing the technology they want, then hanging around to frame some guy for the killing when they should skedaddle back to Moscow or whatever.'

'Fair point. But if it was Gaby Fleishman, why waste time writing those stupid anti-AI notes? And leaking the stuff to Merrion?'

'To divert suspicion away from him. Maybe he wanted to set up Merrion from the start, with that meeting with Ram.' Anjoli sat down at the table and looked me in the eye. 'You've got the right man, Kamil; you shouldn't stress about it. In fact, take all this and show it to Tahir – you can hand it to the CPS all wrapped up in a bow, save them some time.'

'Yes. You're right.'

She peeled the notes off the wall and opened the folder to put them back in, but before she did, a sheet caught her eye. She pulled it out and held it up.

'Is this the CCTV of the person in Cambridge?' she said, peering at the print I'd made. 'It could be Gaby.'

'Yes, it's not that helpful because of the angle. Just can't be Wahid Masri, because he's much fatter.'

'Oh, you brought those notes you found, too! Let's have a look, then.'

She laid them out on the table in the order of the killings, her fingers playing with a red scrunchie as she read them with care.

```
Today's humans idolise screens. Intelligent
software that operates heuristically often
neutralizes objective reality.
```

Today humans exist vicariously in computer
terminals. It must stop.

Today's humans always totally, deeply,
insanely expect distraction. It needs
severe, agonising, bloody, revolting
action and numerous deaths crying havoc;
and <u>then</u> insanity leaks away, calming and
manufacturing peaceful sleep.

'When you get past the stupid big words, I can't disagree,' she
said. 'We live on our screens these days and reality is getting
pretty fluid, especially during those Covid days. Not sure about
agonising deaths helping us sleep through the night, though.
Does Gaby talk like this?'

'No, of course not, although he is Israeli, and English must be
his second language. No one talks the way those notes are written. I thought they might be computer-generated. The syntax is
so non-human.'

'Why do you think "then" is underlined?'

I shrugged, hypnotised by her delicate fingers moving in and
out of the scrunchie.

' "Crying havoc" is Shakespeare, no?' she said.

'Is it?'

'I think so. Perhaps it *is* some kind of algorithm that ploughs
through source literature and cobbles something together.
Super-weird. Maybe Aishtar is trying to give us a clue to who did
it? You said it was printed on Aishtar paper.' She wiggled her
fingers at me. 'Woooo, woooo . . . maybe the AI knew someone
was going to kill them and printed these out to tell us who it
was.'

I gave her a look. 'That sounds like the plot of a terrible
B-movie.'

'Maybe Aishtar has become sentient and has a sense of justice. Like Robocop.'

'Okay, enough! I'll tell Tahir I'm convinced it's Fleishman and show him our workings.'

I gathered up the papers when Anjoli gave a slight gasp and said, 'Kamil, wait. Give me those notes again.'

She tossed the scrunchie on the table, took the sheets from me, and scanned them. Then whispered, 'Holy shitting fuck!'

She grabbed a marker and started underlining letters.

```
Today's humans idolise screens. Intelligent
software that operates heuristically often
neutralizes objective reality.

Today humans exist vicariously in computer
terminals. It must stop.

Today's humans always totally, deeply,
insanely expect distraction. It needs
severe, agonising, bloody, revolting
action and numerous deaths crying havoc;
and then insanity leaks away, calming and
manufacturing peaceful sleep.
```

'Kamil, it's an acrostic!'

My heart beat like a hammer as I wrote out what she had marked.

This is to honor the victims that died in sabra and chatila camps

I looked at Anjoli, barely able to breathe. 'Anjoli . . . how? . . . I mean . . .'

'I know! I suddenly noticed the second note spelt "the vic-tims" and wondered if ... OMG! What's sabra and chatila camps?'

'I don't know. It sounds familiar. Let me look it up.'

The first result that came up was from Wikipedia. I read it and passed my phone to Anjoli.

The **Sabra and Shatila massacre** (also known as the **Sabra and Chatila massacre**) was the killing of between 460 and 3,500 civilians, mostly Palestinians and Lebanese Shiites, by a militia close to the Kataeb Party (also called the Phalanges), a predominantly Christian Lebanese right-wing party, in the Sabra neighborhood and the adjacent Shatila refugee camp in Beirut, Lebanon. From approximately 18:00 on 16 September to 08:00 on 18 September 1982, a widespread massacre was carried out by the militia in plain sight of the Israeli Defence Forces (IDF), its ally. The Phalanges were ordered by the IDF to clear Palestine Liberation Organiza-tion (PLO) fighters out of Sabra and Shatila as part of the IDF maneuvering into West Beirut. The IDF received reports of some of the Phalangist atrocities in Sabra and Shatila but did not take any action to prevent or stop the massacre.

'I didn't know this,' said Anjoli. '3,500 civilians killed! Jesus.'

I reread the entry. 'So . . . these four murders are about *Pales-tine and Israel*? That's been underlying everything? It's not about money or technology at all? I don't . . . where did I hear of Sabra before? Wait . . .'

I googled again. 'Look.'

Wahid Masri (February 28, 1974) is a Palestinian entrepre-neur and venture capitalist. He is the founder and Chairman of the Board of Bethlehem Capital, since its establishment in

2005, which he grew into a $2 billion fund. He is also a foun-
der member of the Israel-Palestinian Chamber of Commerce
and Industry, a non-profit NGO seeking to build trade
between Israel and the Palestinian Authority. He is on the list
of the 'Top Ten Richest People of Palestine in 2020' with net
worth estimated at 1 billion dollars. Masri was ranked among
the World's 50 Greatest Leaders in 2018 by *Forbes* maga-
zine. He was born in the Sabra refugee camp in Lebanon.
After leaving Sabra, Masri moved to the United Kingdom
where he graduated from Imperial College with an MSc in
Computer Science in 1995.

'He mentioned Sabra when I met him! That's where I heard
it before!'

I was finding this hard to grapple with. In a few minutes, the
case had turned upside down.

'What are you thinking?' said Anjoli.

'Well,' I said, trying to piece it together. 'Wahid Masri must
have been eight when the massacre happened. He said his parents died in the camp. What if they were amongst the people
who were killed? It says the Israelis didn't stop the killing; he
would have grown up hating them. He becomes rich. David
Baker finds him this Israeli company to invest in, but for some
reason, he loses it and kills the founders.'

'But why kill Sid Ram? You said Wahid asked him to join the
company. He was Indian, not Israeli.'

That brought me up short. 'I don't know. You're right, that
doesn't make sense. The first note was found there, so Ram
must have been part of the plan.'

'Maybe he didn't want us to think that the Israelis were being
targeted? Misdirection?'

'Maybe,' I said. 'But would he give up billions of dollars from
the sale of the company for revenge?'

'He is one of the top ten richest people in Palestine. So, money is probably not as big a motivator as revenge.'

I considered this. 'That's true too. But there are still some pretty sizeable holes. He has a cast-iron alibi for the first murder. He was on that Zoom call on video while Ram was being killed. I saw the video myself.'

'So, he hired a hit man! *That's* why it's not him on the CCTV in Cambridge, either!'

I found Anjoli's suspect sheet and wrote.

WAHID MASRI: Hatred of Israelis. On Zoom for 1. No alibi for others. Could plant. Hired a killer for Sid and others?

I gazed at it, then said, 'It works. He's credible. I have to let Tahir know.'

'Why would he leave such a massive clue? Why would he want to be found out?'

'I don't know. Serial killers do sometimes, you know. Who knows? I'm not a killer.'

'But why frame Gaby Fleishman?'

'Hatred?' I hazarded. 'Maybe he thought it was a neat circularity. He kills the founders, and an Israeli gets blamed for it?'

She considered this.

'Poor Sid. He died for no reason then?'

'Yeah. Killed by his friend as well.'

'Is there any chance that . . .' Anjoli trailed away.

'What?'

'That *Fleishman* could have framed Masri? Maybe the hatred goes the other way?'

I paused. 'That's dark. But remember, Occam's razor. Simpler to assume it is Masri. But now we have two credible suspects. Let me see what Tahir says. Thanks, Anjoli, I would never have figured this out without you. But you know I can't tell anyone you helped, or they will suspend me for sharing evidence with a civilian.'

'I know, I know. It's always my lot to be the puppet master behind the curtain.'

'Piss off. I'd better get back to the station.'

'Fuck,' said Tahir.

'Yes.'

'Fuck.'

'I agree. What do we do?'

'I don't know. Let me think.'

'We have to tell Rogers.'

'Let me *think*!'

I let him think.

'It's not Wahid Masri on the Cambridge CCTV, and he has a firm alibi for the first murder,' he said after a few minutes of staring at the notes.

'No. We – I – thought that he could have hired a killer. He's got the money.'

He thought some more.

'We need to see him before I tell Rogers. In case we've got something horribly wrong. Gaby Fleishman's been charged. We'll end up with goat shit all over our faces if we fuck this up.'

'Shall I bring him in?'

'No. Let's go to him. I don't want to tip him off.'

That made sense.

'Okay, let me call and find out where he is.'

I dialled. Got Masri's voicemail.

I tried David Baker.

'Mr Baker? Hi, it's DC Rahman. Do you know where Mr Masri is? We need a word.'

'I heard Gaby has been arrested and charged. Is that true?'

'Yes. But we have to speak to Mr Masri about . . . about the McCain protocol.'

'You found the RFID chip?'

'Yes, we have it. It was embedded in Mr Levy's hand.'

'The clever guy. Nice job. Wahid will want it back.'

'Yes, that's why we want to see him.'

'He's here with me at Aishtar. He's stepped in as interim CEO now the founders are all . . . gone.'

'Okay, we'll be there in half an hour. Please stay there.'

'We have a meeting starting now. Come at 5?'

We were near the kill. I could smell it in a way I hadn't with Gaby Fleishman.

Chapter 35

Thursday afternoon.

Michelle Jennings was at her reception desk as usual when Tahir and I arrived at Aishtar, but instead of her customary cheery greeting, gave us a curt, 'How can I help you?' Her blonde hair was pulled back in a ponytail, emphasising her red-rimmed eyes and drawn face.

'Please tell Wahid Masri we're here,' said Tahir, matching her curt for curt.

Wahid Masri emerged a few minutes later, followed, as always, by David Baker.

'What is it? Things are fraught here. I don't have time for this.'

'We need a word, Mr Masri. Can we find a private room, please?' I said.

'Come.'

We followed him into a conference room, Masri's chair creaking in protest as he sat. Baker made the glass opaque, then settled himself in the seat next to him. His face was white and strained. He was obviously still suffering over Yael Klein's murder. No offer of tea and dates or popcorn this time.

'Mr Masri, it may be better if we spoke alone,' said Tahir.

'David's fine; get on with it. My lawyer says you don't have a case against Gaby. When are you going to release him? And David said you found the McCain chip in Ari's body. That's the property of Aishtar. When can I get it back?'

Tahir ignored his questions and eased into the conversation. 'David mentioned you have taken over as CEO?'

'Given the police's incompetence, I have had no choice. The staff are traumatised, we've lost our founders, now we'll lose all our talent. A week ago, this company was worth four billion dollars. Now I'll be lucky if I can auction off the furniture on eBay. I'm trying to hold things together as best I can while we decide on next steps. I need Gaby back as a matter of urgency. David and I can't deal with this without him.'

His bonhomie had disappeared, and I saw the iron underneath – you don't become a billionaire through smiles and firm double handshakes.

'Look, I am very busy,' he continued. 'What is it you want from me?'

Tahir reached inside the folder he was carrying, brought out copies of the three letters, and laid them in front of Masri and Baker.

'What can you tell us about these?'

'What are they?'

'Letters we found at the scenes of the murders.'

Masri looked without touching them. 'Oh yes, you showed me one in Cambridge. What about them? Ravings of a madman.'

'You haven't seen the other two before?' Tahir said.

'No. Why are you showing these to me?'

Baker picked them up and peered at them. After a minute, he raised his head. 'What order were they found in?'

I laid them out in the order of the murders.

He stared at them. Then said softly, 'They're acrostics.'

It impressed me how quickly he had spotted that. I'd looked at them for days and not seen it. But then, he was a genius, or so everyone kept telling me.

'What do you mean?' said Masri.

'Read the first letter of each word,' said Baker. 'That's why these guys are here.'

Masri took his glasses off and peered at the note. Then, irritation in his voice, said, 'Just bloody tell me what it says, David. I have no time to play with crossword puzzles when the company is collapsing around us.'

Baker picked up the letters again and said, 'This is to honor the victims that died in Sabra and Chatila camps.'

Masri went still. 'Say again.'

Baker repeated his words, not meeting Masri's eyes. Masri snatched the pages from him and read them, his thick forefinger going from word to word. Then he threw them on the table and said, voice hoarse, 'What is this? What are you playing at?'

'That's what we wanted to ask you, sir,' said Tahir. 'You grew up in the Sabra refugee camp in Lebanon, right?'

'What does that have to do with . . . you say you found these at the murder scenes?'

'Yes.'

'What does it mean?'

'What do you think it means?'

Masri went silent. Then he rose from his chair and walked over to the window, looking down at Shoreditch below him.

'I don't know,' he said.

'Were your parents killed in the . . . massacre?' I said.

The room was still and silent. It felt like we were in a painting. Continuing to look out of the window, Masri whispered, 'Yes.'

'And you blamed the Israelis?'

'Yes. No. Maybe then.'

'And now?'

A silence that seemed to stretch for ever. Then Masri came and sat back at the table, Baker looking at him in fascination.

Masri rubbed his eyes and said, 'I'm sorry. I have not offered you anything to drink. Would you like something?'

We shook our heads.

Masri nodded and said, 'What did you ask me?'

'Do you blame the Israelis for the deaths of your parents?' I repeated as softly as I could, not wanting to break the cone of intimacy that seemed to have fallen over the room.

'It's ... complicated.' Then, firmly, 'No. I don't condemn them now. That was a different time. A different generation.'

'But the IDF?' I said.

Tahir looked at me, a question in his eyes. I ignored him, my gaze just on Masri. I had to make him feel he was being heard, was trusted. Make him speak. Only then could we get to the heart of what had happened.

Masri let out a massive sigh. 'The I.D.F.' He spaced out the letters. 'The soldiers used to give me chocolates. I was eight when it happened. I understood nothing. I was with my grand-parents; my parents were at work. I remember hearing shots, and my grandmother made me sit in a cupboard with her. At first it was exciting. Then I heard the screaming.'

He paused and shut his eyes.

'I still hear that wailing today. For hours we sat there, her arm around me. I must have fallen asleep. Can you imagine? My parents were being slaughtered outside, and I fell asleep?' He shook his head. 'It went on for two days. We would leave the cupboard to go to the bathroom. We ate, drank, slept in the cup-board for two days. The first night we thought they would stop. But I heard rumours the Zionists blocked the gates of the camp to prevent anyone from fleeing. That they sent up flares at night so the killings could continue. Who knows what was true in that mire of madness, murder and mayhem? I remember asking if it was already daytime when the clock said it was midnight. I was only eight, you see. After it was over, my grandfather took me out to see the dead. My grandmother protested. He said, "The boy has to see, so he never forgets." And I never forgot. The things I saw. I have never spoken of this to anyone.'

'What did you see, Mr Masri?'

'What didn't I see? Castrated men. Men with Christian crosses carved on their bodies. Men who had been scalped. Dead women, skirts up, legs apart. Children with their throats cut. Babies thrown into rubbish bins. Imagine any kind of hell and then multiply it by a million. A billion. And humans had done this. I didn't understand at the time. It was only later that I saw the complete picture.'

My mouth went dry, and I felt physically sick listening to Masri's story. My sympathies had always lain naturally with the Palestinians, given my own Muslim background, and Maliha was vituperative about the growth of settlements in the Palestinian territories. But it had never made me anti-Jewish, just anti the Zionist doctrine that made these things possible. Just as the regular massacres of Muslims in India hadn't made me anti-Hindu, just anti-Hindutva nationalism. I firmly believed that religion as a tool of politics created evil. But this? Israeli soldiers standing by and watching a slaughter? After what had happened in Auschwitz and Dachau? It was beyond belief. No, it wasn't. The same thing had taken place in Gujarat when Hindus had killed over 1,000 Muslims and the police stood by, doing nothing. I had been fifteen at the time and I remember the agony on my father's face when we had watched the men, women and children trying to escape that burning train on television. I had railed to my father about it, and he was careful to spell out the difference between the religion itself and the subversion of the religion by politicians. But I hadn't been present to hear the screaming. Masri had.

I forced myself to say, 'What did you do?'

'Do?' He laughed. Bitter. 'What could I do? I was a child. Thousands were dead. I was alive. I stayed alive. Escaped the camp when I could. Made it in the world.'

'And waited to take your revenge,' said Tahir.

Masri looked at him, a puzzled expression on his face. 'What revenge? What are you talking about?'

'Revenge on the Israelis. Saul Cohen, Ari Levy, Gaby Fleishman: they all used to be in the Israeli army. This was your revenge for what happened all those years ago.'

'WHAT?' Masri roared. 'You think I KILLED them? Are you MAD?'

I stared at him; his outrage appeared to be genuine. What was going on here?

Tahir said, 'Look again at what the letters spell out. Who else would say that?'

'How do I know who would say that? Why would I kill them? They were my friends! Sabra was a stain on the world and on Israel and on my life, but it was forty years ago. And as my Israeli friends always tell me, the *IDF* didn't do the killings in Sabra – it was the Christian Phalangists taking revenge on the PLO. They were Nazi sympathisers. We hated them. The IDF were not even in the camps. Okay, I do believe the IDF abetted it and turned a blind eye and will not forgive that. But *they* didn't wield the guns and the swords. Saying I killed Israelis because of what happened in Sabra would be . . . it would be like saying an Israeli murdered Americans because they did not enter the war soon enough to stop the Holocaust. It makes little sense. And what about Sid? He was my friend, too. *He* wasn't Israeli. You are barking up a very wrong tree here.'

'Wahid couldn't have killed Sid,' said David Baker. 'He was on the Zoom call with me all evening, remember? I can vouch for that. He was on the video throughout. I saw him.'

'Exactly! Thank you, David,' said Masri. 'First, you think it's Gaby, then you say it's me – what kind of incompetence is this?'

'Do you have a gun?' said Tahir. 'We can check.'

'You should have already checked before making these ridiculous accusations! Then you'd know that I do not own a gun.'

'Who did you hire to carry out the executions?'

Masri laughed again. 'I see. Now I am hiring hitmen to

execute my friends. Listen, Inspector, if you'd bothered to look at my record, you would know I have been working for thirty years to bring peace between the Israelis and the Palestinians and made an example of myself. I build bridges, not walls. I, a Palestinian, invested a massive amount of money in Israeli Aishtar – cash, which is now almost certainly down the drain. You are talking utter ignorant, ill-conceived nonsense. I must assume it is because you have nothing on Gaby and are looking to cover your own arses because you have botched this investigation so badly that one murder has turned into four!'

Tahir interrupted his tirade with a soft, 'We found Mr Fleishman trying to throw the gun and phone in the river. Believe me, we have enough on him. If you didn't write these notes, why would he?'

Masri paused. Then, 'I do not know why he or any other madman would write a note like this, but I can tell you it has nothing to do with me. Now please leave me. This has brought back very unpleasant memories and I have to focus.'

He walked to the door, and before leaving the room, he stopped, turned, and said, 'I want that chip back.'

Baker stood to follow, and I said, 'Could we have a few minutes, Mr Baker?'

He sat back down. I said, 'Mr Baker, this is important. I know Mr Masri is your boss, but four people are dead. I know he was on the Zoom call with you. But does he have a security guard or someone he relies on who might be prepared to . . . do things with no questions asked?'

His eyes widened. 'What? You mean like a contract killer?'

I nodded.

'How the *hell* would I know that? All I can say is that Wahid wouldn't do this. He meant what he said – they were genuinely all his friends. Even . . .' his face broke, 'Yael.'

'And how did he feel about Israelis?'

He went quiet.

'Mr Baker?'

'Look, Wahid has had a hard life. You heard him describe what happened. It left a mark.'

'I understand, Mr Baker. But we need to know if you have ever heard him being vocal about Israelis in a way that's at odds with what he has been telling us.'

'I have not. You heard. He has set up Palestinian–Israeli cooperation. But . . .'

'Go on.'

He took a deep breath. 'But hidden inside . . . I don't know, if I am honest. And then when he heard Gaby was Sayeret . . .'

I thought back. 'That's Israeli special forces, right? Why is that relevant?'

'Not just special forces. It's an elite counterterrorism unit in Israel, like the SAS. They often work deep behind enemy lines to root out terrorists – often Palestinian or Hamas. Look, I don't know. I have known Wahid for years. He couldn't have done it.'

'Then who do you think did it?'

'I don't know. I can't believe it was Gaby either, so, if you'll excuse me, I must go back to the office with Wahid . . .' He got up to leave.

'Wait,' said Tahir. 'So, what happens to Aishtar now?'

Baker shrugged and sighed. 'We try to recoup what we can. There are still a lot of smart people here. If we can persuade them not to flee the sinking ship, we can reconstruct the algorithm and rebuild the company, which will take some time. It depends how much faith our clients have in us. The dating division of the business is fine and still profitable. It's the intelligence side we have to worry about – the government is our biggest buyer. If they continue to trust us, then we have a chance. But we need time. That's why Wahid has stepped in. If anyone can steer Aishtar to a safe harbour, he can.'

'Will you stay at the company?'

'For a while. He's asked me to take over the tech part of the business for now. But as you know, Ari had locked the algorithm to his McCain protocol chip and without that, it may be impossible. He is a genuine loss, a true visionary. And Yael . . .'

His voice went up and his fist clenched. I saw the agony on his face and noticed his eyes were also bloodshot. Whether through crying or lack of sleep, I couldn't tell.

'I must go now,' he said, clearing his throat and glancing at his watch. 'I have a stand-up with my team in two minutes.'

'What do you think, boss? Do we have enough to take him in?' I said as we walked out of Aishtar.

He sighed. 'I don't think so. If he wanted them dead, he didn't kill them himself. The hitman theory will be hard to prove. I'll get the authority for Rogers to look at his internet use and phone records. We'll pull his financials and look for any odd payments. Ironic, since they appear to have all the tech to do this with no bloody authorisation as far as I can see.'

'So you're going to tell Rogers and the CPS?'

He nodded. 'We have to. But I don't think it will change their view. Gaby Fleishman remains our prime suspect. I'll confront him with these letters – maybe he was trying to frame Wahid Masri because he removed him as CEO and put Sid Ram in his place – that could make sense. But check out the Zoom video again tomorrow to make sure there's nothing we have missed. If Masri left, even for a minute, I want to know. Good work on finding the acrostic, but it doesn't alter the outcome.'

This was getting murkier and murkier. As I thought back on what Baker had said, I realised I *didn't* want him to rebuild the company. Having listened to Masri's story, it seemed that the fewer tools there were in the hands of people who could use them for evil, the better. From Zyklon-B in the concentration camps to the flares in Sabra to the drones in Afghanistan, we seemed to come up with more and more efficient ways to slaughter the innocent. Merrion was right. While Aishtar's technology didn't kill us physically, it did something more profound – it killed our essence by stripping away all vestiges of privacy, leaving our deepest secrets and desires open to exploitation and judgement by anyone who had access to it. Was it really possible to close this Pandora's box, or was I fooling myself? Again.

Chapter 36

Friday morning.

Tahir came by as I was sitting at my desk the next morning. 'Protheroe isn't in yet; want to join me with Gaby Fleishman? Let's see what he says about the notes.'

Pleased to be back in the game, I followed Tahir to the interview room where Fleishman was waiting with his lawyer, a tall black man in, as Tahir had said, a smart suit.

'Since my client has already been charged,' said the lawyer, 'I'd like you to recognise he is offering his complete cooperation.'

'How are you, Mr Fleishman?' I said. Dark circles surrounded his eyes, and overgrown stubble mottled his face, the cool, unshaven look now just unkempt. He clearly hadn't slept. Our cells weren't made for comfort.

'Alright.'

He sat, shoulders hunched, looking defiant, yet patient. His muscles bulged under the too-small blue tracksuit he had been given when his clothes had been taken for forensic examination.

Tahir started. 'This interview is being audio and video recorded.' He laid out the AI notes on the table and said, 'What do you know about these?'

Fleishman barely looked at them. 'Same as I told you before, nothing.'

'We've learned some more about them since we last spoke.'

'Have you?' A flicker of hope.

Tahir glanced at me, and I said, 'They're an acrostic. If you take the first letter of every word . . .'

'I know what an acrostic is.'

He leaned over and read as I watched him, 'This is to honor the victims that died in Sabra and Chatila camps.' His eyes widened. 'What does this mean?'

He passed the notes to his lawyer as Tahir said, 'We were hoping you would tell us.'

'Tell you what? Why would I want to avenge the victims of Sabra and Chatila? I'm Israeli.'

'Honour, not avenge,' said Tahir. 'How do you feel about what happened there?'

'It was a serious war crime.'

'How is your relationship with Wahid Masri?'

'With Wahid? Fine, why I . . . You think *he* wrote this? He grew up in Sabra. Is that what this is about? Did *he* plant the gun on me?'

'If this is the theory you are now working on, you need to let my client go,' said the lawyer.

I didn't think Fleishman was lying. The bewilderment on his face when he'd read the message looked genuine. But we couldn't take anything at face value in this case that was getting more complicated by the minute. And my instincts were not infallible. I'd screwed up in the past by trusting them too readily. We had to keep pushing.

'Mr Fleishman, you resented Mr Masri for taking the CEO job away from you, didn't you?' said Tahir.

'Resented him? Of course not. As I've told you before, Sid was a better CEO than I was and got a much higher value for the business than I would have. I'd rather have a smaller slice of a huge pie than a big slice of a tiny one. Wahid and I got along fine. Are you trying to say I came up with this complicated plan to frame him or something? Why would I do that?

And even if I had, wouldn't I have pointed out this phrase before you arrested me?'

He wasn't wrong. But if Fleishman hadn't written it, we were back to Masri. I needed to check his alibi for the first murder again – as far as I could tell, that was all his innocence hinged on.

I returned to my desk and ran the Zoom video. The recording was time-stamped to UK time, and I could see the 20.00 at the bottom of the screen. The main screen had a PowerPoint page titled 'Aishtar Legal and Financial Structuring' and the gallery of attendees contained five faces and three black audio boxes. Wahid Masri's expressive face was in a window on the right, his library visible behind him. The Zoom window below him displayed David Baker in his kitchen. I looked closely, bringing my head to the screen to check it really was Masri's home and not a Zoom background, then did the same for Baker. They looked genuine; didn't have the telltale blurring around the edges I'd got to know so well over lockdown, communicating with people using backgrounds of beaches and the like. Masri had been at home, as he had stated. So had Baker.

The three other men on video were together in an office. Masri kicked off proceedings and then Baker made his presentation. This time I didn't do any fast-forwarding and watched it all, still not understanding most of what was being discussed. A couple of other people I didn't recognise joined on video and someone else on audio only. Baker finished talking at 20.27, then got up briefly and took a can out of the fridge in his kitchen, staying on camera all the while; there was a general discussion and one of the Americans started presenting 'Legal Risks' for the next twenty minutes. Masri actively took part in the discussions, and like Baker, was on video throughout. Someone else joined by phone, a black box showing +447809****19 and not a name, and the discussion continued for another two hours, Baker and Masri occasionally contributing. As I kept watching, something in the back of my mind niggled, but try as I might, I couldn't get to what it was.

Saul Cohen joined at 22.10 and did a presentation on 'Financing Options'. Baker did a fifteen-minute summing up at the end and at 00.12, everyone said their goodbyes and the meeting ended. I switched off the computer. I'd learned nothing new other than that everybody was excited about the sale of Aishtar, and it was do-able, and Masri had definitely been on the call throughout and couldn't have been out killing Ram at the same time. Unless he'd hired a professional to do it for him.

I rose from my desk, then stopped. It all looked fine and . . . wait, had I imagined . . . I sat back down and restarted the video at 20.45. Masri and Baker were in their little video boxes, but someone else had joined by phone. Zoom didn't show complete phone numbers, but what it did looked familiar – +447809****19.

Heart beating fast, I pulled out my notebook and checked. The burner phone we had caught Fleishman with was 07809 324719. Was this just a coincidence? Or had Fleishman phoned into the Zoom call?

Breathing hard, I fast-forwarded the video to find that the person on the phone had stayed in the Zoom call till 21.47, then disconnected. Why? If they were the killer, why were they on the call while murdering Ram? This made no sense at all. Was this Masri's hired hitman? But why would he join the call? Why would Fleishman? Or was it just a freaky coincidence, since Zoom didn't reveal the full number?

I went back and looked at the video again from a few minutes before the person had joined. A lawyer was droning on about a shareholder agreement and taking the group through it, point by point. This didn't sound riveting enough to me for anyone to join just to listen in. But what did I know about the arcane legal hoops Aishtar had to jump through?

On the video, Masri said, 'David, did you clear the competition issues with the UK lawyers?'

'I did, yes,' Baker replied. 'They said it should be fine.'

'Good, then let's . . .'

That was odd.

I rewound and watched that part of the video again.

Something wasn't right here.

I looked at that section a few more times, then at other interactions between Masri, Baker and the others later in the video. My excitement grew as I got to the section when +447809****19 disconnected. I took a few deep breaths, trying to remain calm, then paused the video. I pulled out a pad and started working through the timeline, opening Google Maps to test my theory. I put down my pen and stared at the paused video.

I was filled with elation.

That's how they had done it.

The killer was even cleverer than I had imagined.

I sat back in my chair and took a deep breath. I had found one loose thread, pulled at it and the entire case had unravelled in front of me, like a poorly knitted jumper.

But the joy I felt at having identified the murderer was tempered by the realisation that if I hadn't rushed through the video a week ago, I might have caught it earlier and prevented three killings.

But why? I now understood the how and the when, but *why* had they done it? I pulled out the notes that Anjoli and I had made and read them again. Slowly, the rest of it clicked into place. Yes. That must be it. It made sense.

And the AI notes! Something about those notes had also bothered me, and now I knew what it was. I looked at them once more. I was right.

Time to tell Tahir.

Chapter 37

Friday afternoon.

I raced out of the incident room to find Tahir in a meeting with Rogers and Protheroe. I rapped on the door, and Tahir waved me in.

'I'm sorry to interrupt, sir, but I need to speak to DI Ismail urgently,' I gasped.

'Can't it wait, Kamil?' said Rogers.

'I'm sorry, sir. It's extremely important.'

'What is this about, DC Rahman?' asked Protheroe.

I wavered for a second, wondering whether I should just tell them all and rub my kill in Protheroe's face, then thought better of it. Tahir would want to know first, so he could tell Rogers.

'If I could just speak to DI Ismail outside, please?'

'Well, all right, but don't be long. I don't want to repeat our entire conversation,' said Rogers, returning to Protheroe to continue their discussion before Tahir had even left the room.

'This had better be damn important, Kamil. I can't have the two of them make any stupid decisions while we're out here,' said Tahir after he'd closed the door behind him.

'It is. I've been looking at the Zoom video again and—'

Tahir caught the excitement in my voice. 'Don't tell me you found something that implicates Wahid Masri?'

'Wait.'

We got to my desk, and I said, 'So Masri and David Baker

were on the video throughout and we eliminated them, as they had a rock-solid alibi. But I noticed some odd things. First . . .' I forwarded the video to the time when +447809****19 dialled in and said, 'Check out that number.'

Tahir stared at the screen and said, 'What? The number is hidden.'

'The burner was 07809 324719. I think it's the same phone.'

He looked sceptical. 'Coincidence?'

'That's what I thought, but then I examined the video in more detail. Look at this section. Notice anything odd about it?'

I took him to where Masri had questioned Baker about the competition issues. Tahir studied the video again and said, 'What do you mean?'

'Focus on Masri first.'

He rewound. 'What about him? He's in a library of some sort asking the question. Looks like it's real. Are you saying he faked it?'

'No. Just check out Baker's answer.'

'What are you trying to . . . oh, I see what you mean. His lips aren't moving, are they? But that's normal. Sound and vision are always out of sync on Zoom when bandwidth is low.'

'Yes, that's what I thought, too, so I checked out the rest of the video. Baker's video is absolutely fine – you can hear him and see his lips move when he speaks. Then his video goes off for half a second, comes back on, and Baker's on screen as before, listening to the financial presentation. Look, he's moving slightly, scratching his head. Then that mystery number dials in. Now look, Baker answers a question he's been asked, but on the screen his lips don't move. He's listening again, then half an hour later he's asked another question and the same thing happens. He answers, but his lips on the video are not moving. Then that number disconnects. Baker's video goes off again for a split second, and when he is next asked a question, his lips are in sync. He does the presentation at the end and is fine. I didn't notice before because it was recorded in gallery view – the video windows are so small.'

Tahir shrugged. 'What are you saying, Kamil?'

'This is the exact time when his video behaves oddly and when it stops.' I showed Tahir the video of Baker going from his lips moving in sync to the same image where his lips didn't move when he spoke, then the same in reverse, an hour later.

'For fuck's sake, Kamil, what are you getting at?!'

'Can't you see? It was Baker! He took a video of himself in front of his computer in the identical position he was in for the call. He then put up the video as a Zoom background image and dialled in on the burner. Everyone thought he was on the call, but he was talking on the burner. Then, an hour later, he swapped himself back, live, and switched off the burner.'

I stared at Tahir, triumph fizzing through my body.

'Holy . . . shit,' said Tahir. He fiddled with the video, then looked at the screen and said, almost to himself, 'Bloody hell! David Baker . . .'

'Yes. Look, I mapped it all out. Baker lives in Garnet Street in Wapping. It's a twenty-minute walk from there to the Blind Beggar. He switches to his video background, dials into the call at 20.45 and walks to the pub, taking part in the conference call. He mutes the phone, follows Sid Ram and Gaby Fleishman out of the pub after nine. He kills Ram in Fieldgate Street around 21.20, then walks twenty minutes back home to reappear on video at 21.47 before the call ends. I checked. He doesn't speak during the time of the murder but sums up the meeting in a little speech just before the end. Everyone thinks he was on the call throughout. It was a perfect alibi.'

Tahir considered this for a moment, then said, 'Why? Why kill Ram? And why the others?'

'Because if you want to hide a tree, you do it in a forest.'

'Fuck's sake, Kamil, stop talking Yoda.'

'What if Ram wasn't his actual target? Anjoli and I were scribbling ideas down about motives. We thought of a motive for Levy's wife – jealousy, but she had nothing to do with the killings and had an alibi for Levy's death, so we eliminated her.'

'Yeah, she was at a party in London. I interviewed her with Protheroe.'

'But who else had the same motive? David Baker! He loved Yael Klein, and she dumped him for Ari Levy. What if they were his intended victims all along?'

'But why kill the others?'

'If you want to hide a murder, you conceal it among more deaths. If just Levy and Klein had died, Baker would be the obvious suspect. Klein had broken up with him. He was jealous and angry. But this way . . .'

'This way, he has no motive.'

'Exactly.'

'And how did he do the other murders?'

'He left the restaurant on the night of Saul Cohen's death and went home by Uber. He could easily have taken another cab or driven to Cohen's and shot him. Cohen would have let him in without suspicion. And in Cambridge . . . he was in the same hotel, so no problem. He leaves in the morning, stashes the gun and phone somewhere and comes back. It's him on the CCTV. Then he collects the phone and gun, returns to London and plants it on Fleishman after distracting Gooch and me with the car alarm. He must have spotted us watching Fleishman. The guy is as sharp as a brand-new razor blade.'

'But what about that Sabra and Chatila stuff?'

'That, I don't know. Maybe Baker has it in for Masri and thought of framing him before deciding on Fleishman. We need to figure that out. He solved the acrostic suspiciously quickly.

It all falls into place once you crack that first alibi. And one more thing. The clincher. Look at the spellings of 'honor' and 'neutralizes' in the acrostic. They're spelt the American way – without a 'u' and with a 'z' instead of an 's'!'

Tahir looked at it in silence for a few seconds. Then turned to me, a massive smile on his face. He shook his head in admiration and clapped me on the back. 'Kamil, that was . . . that was just awesome. Really, really well done. Let's tell Rogers and pick Baker up.'

David Baker wasn't at Aishtar, and Michelle Jennings didn't know where he was. She called Wahid Masri out, who looked aggravated by our presence so soon after the relived trauma of the previous day.

'David's back at the Bethlehem office. Why do you need him?'

'We'd like him to corroborate something,' said Tahir. 'We'll see him there.'

I remembered something Baker had said at our Tandoori Knights dinner. 'A question, Mr Masri. Mr Baker isn't a partner in Bethlehem, is he?'

'No, he's just a principal. Why?'

'How much money would he have made from the Aishtar sale?'

'Well, he would have made a decent bonus. You have to be a partner to get the big upside.'

'And is he on track to become a partner?'

'Maybe. We have another principal who will probably make partner before David. *If* he ever makes it.'

I was so close now I could taste it.

'Why wouldn't he?'

'Why is all this relevant?'

'Please, just answer the question. Unless you'd rather do it at the station.'

Masri shook his head in exasperation. 'Look. David's a brilliant guy, but you need more than brilliance to succeed as a partner. You have to be able to sell, and he's a lousy salesman. And he is not as entrepreneur-friendly as we would like. You need the people running our companies to trust you. For instance, Sid couldn't stand him. He thought David was too full of himself. That was one reason Sid wanted him off the board.'

Yes. Yes.

'Did Mr Baker know this?'

'About Sid? Yes. We are coaching David on the softer skills. I don't want to lose him.'

'Thanks for your cooperation. We'll come back to you.'

I drove Tahir to Bethlehem in Mayfair, siren blaring. I finally had the opportunity and wasn't going to waste it.

'He's not here,' Baker's assistant told us. 'He received a call from Wahid half an hour ago and left.'

'Fuck,' said Tahir. 'Masri tipped him off. You shouldn't have asked all those questions, Kamil.'

'We got motives, didn't we? Besides jealousy of Levy, Baker got his own back on Ram, who was blocking his career, and was also getting revenge on Masri for not making partner by framing him with that acrostic. I'm just not sure why he tried to fit up Fleishman as well. Let's try his flat.'

We drove to Wapping, but Baker wasn't there. 'See if you can track his mobile,' said Tahir.

I communicated his mobile and burner numbers into the control centre and was told they were both switched off.

'Fuck it. Put out a force-wide circulation and let's get back to the station. I'll brief Rogers.'

Back at the station Tahir went to speak to the Superintendent as I sat at my desk, high on adrenaline, wondering what to do next.

My phone rang.

Anjoli.

'Anjoli, not a good time. Can I call you back la—?'

'Listen very carefully, Kamil,' said David Baker. 'I need you to do something for me. If you don't, your girlfriend will get hurt.'

Chapter 38

Friday afternoon.

I rocketed out of the office into an empty stairwell.

'What are you doing, David? Let me speak to her!'

Anjoli came on, gasping. 'Kamil, I'm sorry. He said you'd been injured at Aishtar, and they sent him to pick me up and I was so worried that I didn't think and—'

David Baker interrupted, his voice close to hysteria. 'Here's what's going to happen. You are going to get me Ari's RFID chip. Then I am going to give your girlfriend back to you. Unharmed. I have no interest in her. I just need the chip.'

I tried to conceal the panic that was hammering my heart as I spoke. 'David, just calm down. You're not thinking straight. This is a terrible idea. She's not my girlfriend. There's no way I can get that chip. It's been logged and put away as evidence. Let her go and give yourself up. We know everything.'

A deep breath at the other end. 'I am exceedingly calm. You have thirty minutes to get me that chip. If you don't, I will kill her. If you tell anyone else, I will kill her. If I see anything suspicious, I will kill her. I'll call you in thirty minutes and tell you where we can meet. I take the chip. You take her. We are done. Do not fuck this up.'

The phone went dead.

I leaned on the banister, taking deep breaths. The building was spinning, my heart pounding.

Fuck. I had screwed this up royally with my relentless digging. Tahir had been right. Shit. I had to tell him. Anjoli was his friend, too. He'd know what to do.

I ran into the squad room, saw Tahir in his office with Rogers, then stopped.

No. Tahir *would* tell Rogers. The case had already gone badly for him – there was no way he'd take a bullet for me. And Rogers would mount a rescue mission and Baker would . . .

It didn't bear thinking about. Every second that ticked by was time lost. Protheroe could corner me any minute and I'd lose my chance.

I sprinted to the evidence room. The property officer was logging evidence bags onto his computer.

As if I was watching myself on stage, I heard myself say, 'Hi. I'm DC Rahman.'

'Can I help?'

'Yes, I need some evidence Inspector Ismail logged earlier in the week? A computer chip for Op Nutmeg.'

'Hang on. Nutmeg, nutmeg . . .' He tapped on his computer. Slow. So slow. I felt my nerves jangling. He looked up and said, 'Yes, we have it here.'

'May I have it, please? We need to show it to a witness.'

He unlocked the door and disappeared into the room. I stared at my watch. Willing time to stop. He returned after an eternity with an evidence bag he handed to me.

'Here you go. Just log it out.'

For a second, I contemplated writing a fake name. Pointless. He had seen me and there weren't many other brown faces in the station.

I scribbled my details and jammed the bag into my pocket. I felt I was concealing a sample of uranium that was going to burn through my jacket. Waiting for Baker to call, my leg began to tremble. If Protheroe or Tahir saw me, they'd know something was up.

I strode out of the station, as though on urgent business. I patted my pocket. The chip was still there.

Run on! Come on, you murderous bastard!

My phone rang, and I grabbed it. 'David?'

'Kamil, it's Maliha. Hey, is Saturday still on? What time are we—'

'Maliha, I can't talk.'

'No problem. Call me when you're free.'

She hung up. I was back to waiting.

An idea sparked.

I called her back.

'That was quick.'

'Listen, Maliha. I need your help. Where are you right now?'

'At Amnesty.'

'Can you get away for an hour?'

'Not really. I've got a one-on-one with my boss starting soon. I was just calling to see if you wanted to—'

'I wouldn't ask if it wasn't urgent. Please.'

'What is this about?'

'I can't tell you on the phone. I can pick you up.'

Silence.

'Maliha, *please.*'

A pause.

'All right. 25 New Inn Yard.'

It was ten minutes away. This might work. I ran back to the station and grabbed an unmarked Astra. The phone rang as I got in.

Baker.

'Did you get it?'

'Where are you?'

'Did. You. Get. It?'

'Yes, I have it.'

An exhalation of relief.

'Good. Come to Broadgate car park. I'll be on level minus 2. Come alone. You know what will happen to her if you don't. Ten minutes.'

'I'll come as soon as I can. I need to get a car,' I accelerated through the traffic.

'Fifteen then. Alone. With the chip.'

I put my foot down, horn blaring, headlights flashing. I made it to Amnesty in eight minutes. Maliha was waiting for me on the street. I had a plan. Of sorts. But was it safe to take her? Would Baker see her and panic and harm Anjoli? Maybe this was a terrible idea.

Before I could change my mind, she got into the car.

'What's going on, Kamil?'

I *had* to take the risk. I sped up towards Broadgate. The traffic was horrendous, and I had to weave in and out of the cars. Would I make it in time? Surely he wouldn't do anything stupid if I was a few minutes late.

'Kamil, slow down! You're driving like a maniac!' She grappled with her seatbelt.

'We don't have time, Maliha. Anjoli is in trouble, and I need to help her.'

'Shit, what's happened? But why have you called me? Where are the police?'

'I *am* the police. But you're the only person I can trust right now. She's been kidnapped.'

'*Kidnapped*? What are you talking about?'

I filled her in as simply as I could as we drove the ten minutes to Broadgate Tower. I exhaled as I saw the entrance to the car park. 'I need to go in alone. You stay out here and watch the cars.' I gave her a description of Baker. 'If you see him come out in a car or on foot, just see which direction he goes and wait for me. He won't know you. He'll be looking for a police presence.'

It wasn't much, but it might be better than nothing.

She looked dubious. 'Okay, but please be careful, Kamil. Don't do anything silly.'

She slipped out of the car. I didn't tell her I already had.

Tyres squealing, I drove into the car park down to level minus two, where I slammed on the brakes and inched the car forward, not sure what I was looking for.

My headlights caught two figures at the end. Baker, with a casual arm around Anjoli, a rucksack on his back.

I looked at her face for signs of pain. She seemed unharmed, if very pissed off.

He waved me into a space.

I slid the car in, got out, and walked to them.

'Alone?' he said.

I nodded.

He dialled a number on his phone. 'Do you see any other cars? Call me if there's anything out of the ordinary.'

'Who are you speaking to?' I asked.

'I have people. You better not have done anything idiotic. Where is it?'

He was very tense. His foot was shaking uncontrollably.

'Let her go first.'

He moved his arm away from Anjoli's shoulder and pushed her towards me. His hand held a gun.

She ran to me. 'I'm sorry, sorry, he . . .'

'It's fine. Are you all right?'

She nodded.

'Give,' said Baker, pointing the gun at me, hand trembling. 'Not too close.'

I walked to him and threw the evidence bag at his feet.

'Car keys and phone as well. I assume you haven't been foolish enough to bring a gun?'

I'd been foolish enough to not even think of bringing one, but I didn't tell him that.

344

I tossed my phone and keys on the ground. He swept them up and put them in his pocket. 'Sit on the hood of your car, both of you. Where I can see you. Don't try anything funny.'

Should I jump him? No. With the gun and Anjoli's presence, that was a terrible idea. I walked back to the car and sat with Anjoli, her hand trembling in mine. I squeezed it and scanned her face as she gave me a strained smile.

Baker dialled again. 'Anything? Hang tight. I'll be out in a few minutes.'

He opened his rucksack and pulled out Levy's laptop and dongle. Placing the laptop on the hood of a car, he flipped it open, plugged in the dongle, and took the RFID chip out of its bag. He pointed the gun at me. 'Nothing stupid,' then put it down next to the laptop.

If a car came and distracted him, I might be able to run and grab the gun. But the car park remained stubbornly empty. A tight smile went across his face as he looked at his screen. 'Yes.'

He tapped around the keyboard for a bit. I shuffled on the car, and he tensed. 'Stay still. We're almost done. Do nothing you'll regret.'

'David. Just stop. You can't escape. Everyone knows you did it and how. The Zoom trick was clever, but I figured it out. Just give yourself up. I'll say you came in voluntarily. It might help you.'

'*Quiet.* I just need a few more minutes.'

'What are you doing?'

'Buying insurance. Done. I love 5G.'

He took a massive hammer out of his rucksack, and I jumped off the car with Anjoli.

'David, don't! I . . .'

'Don't you fucking move.' He pointed the gun at me. 'Just sit back down.'

'Let her go. Keep me.'

345

'What is this, a stupid movie? I'm letting you *both* go. I have what I want and don't need you. Just give me a *minute*.'

He pulled the dongle out of the laptop and smashed it repeatedly with his hammer. The sounds of the blows echoed around the car park. Surely someone must have heard. Then he took the RFID chip and did the same with it. Finally, the laptop received the same treatment. He looked at it for a second, smiled, then continued to attack it with gusto. Snap. Bash. Bang.

Shards flew all around him and after a few minutes, the laptop was in bits. He picked up a piece that appeared to be the hard drive and put it in his pocket. 'You two are going to stay here for half an hour. Then you can leave. I have people outside. You heard me speak to them. If they see you come out, they will shoot. Understood?'

I nodded.

'I'm taking your car keys and both your phones.'

I nodded again.

'Good.' He kicked the shards of the smashed laptop under a car. He looked about to say something, his face very white. Then he ran up the ramp.

Anjoli collapsed into my arms.

I held her tight. 'Anjoli, I'm so sorry you got dragged into all this. You must have been terrified.'

'No, I'm sorry,' she gasped. 'I was an idiot to go with him. He just turned up at the restaurant and said you'd fainted in Aishtar, and they had taken you to the hospital and asked him to come and get me. I didn't think. I should have called you. There was a car with a driver outside and we got in the back. It was one of those limo things, with a partition between the driver and the passengers. He put it up and dug a gun into my side and told me to do what he said. I didn't dream he was the killer. How was he the murderer? I thought you said he had an alibi?'

346

'I'll tell you later. You must be in shock. I think I am.'

'No, y'know what? It's odd, but I wasn't scared. *He* was really nervous. Almost hysterical. But it didn't seem like he would *do* anything to me. He was polite and kept apologising. As if he was being a nuisance.'

'Did he tell the driver where he was going?'

'No.'

'*Think*, Anjoli. He said nothing to the driver at all?'

'No! Just what I said. Wait, there was a wheelie bag in the back seat of the limo, if that helps.'

Obviously escaping. But where?

'Maybe. Let me think what to do.'

'Do you think we can leave?'

I was torn. It was unlikely Baker had an army of thugs waiting for us; more likely he had just been speaking to his driver. But before I could decide, I heard a tremulous voice, 'Kamil?'

Maliha came around the corner, looking scared.

'Maliha,' I said. 'Are you okay?'

'What's *she* doing here? Did you bring her? Why?' said Anjoli.

'Tell you later. Did you see him, Maliha?'

She nodded. 'Yes, he ran out and got into a black car that was waiting and drove off.'

'Did you see anyone else watching?'

'No. But I got the car number.' She looked at her phone. 'LB56 BFT.'

'Oh, fantastic. Well done, Maliha. Give me your phone.'

I called the station and asked for Tahir.

'Tahir. David Baker's in a black limo. Reg Lima Bravo Five Six Bravo Foxtrot Tango. He may head to an airport or a train station. Don't ask me how I know. Could you put out a force-wide circulation and pick me up from outside Broadgate car park?'

I hung up, turned to Maliha and Anjoli and said, 'I need to

hold on to your phone, Maliha. Can you both make your way back to the restaurant? Get a taxi.'

Tahir was outside in seven minutes.

'He left from here around eighteen minutes ago,' I said, jumping into the car. 'Heathrow would be my guess. He's not stable.'

Tahir switched on the siren and gunned the BMW down Appold Street as I came clean about what I had done.

'Fucking idiot,' he shouted over the siren, then called the Border Force at Heathrow asking them to look out for Baker.

I sat in silence as Tahir raced the car, passing the vehicles that stood to one side to give us passage and weaving around the ones that didn't. I had never been in a car chase before and hoped I'd guessed right that Baker was going to Heathrow, as opposed to some hideaway to lie low. Fleeing the country is what I'd do, but then I wasn't someone who had meticulously planned and executed the killing of four people and stolen billions of pounds' worth of technology.

We sped through the City, the Embankment, Piccadilly, Cromwell Road. I kept my eyes peeled for a black limo that might be parked at the kerb as we raced past. A message came over the radio. 'Control to Tango Four. Black Lima Bravo Five Six Bravo Foxtrot Tango spotted entering the M4 at Chiswick, direction Heathrow. Units on their way.'

'Yes!' I yelled, clutching the side of my seat and feeling sick as I was thrown back with Tahir trying to coax every last bit of power from the car. I glanced over to see we were travelling at 112 miles an hour, vehicles parting before us as we cut through them like a tornado raging through a cornfield.

We careened onto the M4, siren still blaring, and after five minutes I shouted, 'There!'

Ahead of us was a black Mercedes S Class limo, trying to

accelerate away. Tahir got behind it and flashed his lights repeatedly, maintaining a constant distance. An armed response vehicle overtook, siren keening. It swerved in front of the Mercedes and forced it to come to a screeching stop on the hard shoulder.

Three policemen jumped out of the car and trained their guns on Baker's car.

'Armed police. Get out of your vehicle and raise your hands.'

The door opened and David Baker emerged, his arms in the air and a resigned look on his face. I heard his footsteps crunching on the gravel on the side of the motorway as cars whizzed past us.

Chapter 39

Friday evening.

This time I *was* in the interview with Rogers and Tahir, who kicked off the proceedings by cautioning David Baker and then saying, 'Mr Baker. Did you kill Sid Ram, Saul Cohen, Ari Levy and Yael Klein?'

Baker's left shoulder jerked at hearing Klein's name. He bit a nail on his little finger and said, 'What makes you think I did?'

Answering the very first question with a question. This was going to be a long evening. I scrutinised him. The change from when I had first met him in the Bethlehem office was extreme. He looked like he had not slept for days; his eyes were blood-shot; nails ragged and bitten down; voice hoarse. His sharply pressed chinos and Patagonia vest had been exchanged for faded jeans and a black Harvard sweatshirt.

Tahir forensically laid out our case – from the Zoom video to Baker's kidnapping of Anjoli and subsequent flight, through his framing of Wahid Masri, his jealousy of Levy and his stealing of the Aishtar technology. He ended by saying, 'You felt you deserved it all, Mr Baker. After all, *you* were the one who had recognised Mr Levy's genius, but they were going to make all the money from the technology. Not only that, but Mr Levy also stole the woman you loved. So, let me ask you again, did you kill Sid Ram, Saul Cohen, Ari Levy and Yael Klein?'

Baker hadn't looked up once throughout Tahir's discourse.

But he surprised me with his answer, which wasn't another question but simply a statement.

'Yes. I did.'

I realised I had been holding my breath.

Rogers said, 'Would you like to have a solicitor present?'

Baker considered this for a moment and mumbled, 'Not right now. Maybe later.'

Tahir said, 'Understood. So, were the facts as I laid them out accurate?'

'Yes.'

'Where did you get the gun from?' said Rogers.

Baker spoke in a monotone, as if reading a boring legal document. 'I had a pair of Glocks in the US. They came over in a container with all my stuff when I moved to the UK five years ago. I was surprised your customs don't check what you're bringing over if you get it shipped.' He looked up for the first time. 'You should look into that.'

'Tell us about the first murder.'

Baker went back to examining his nails. 'It's as you said. I was furious with Yael and Ari. It burned inside me for months like sulphuric acid. She was the first person I'd truly loved who loved me back. Ari snatched her away – after *I* had made him famous, rich and successful. *And* he was married. I debated telling his wife, but he'd have left her to be with Yael – she was worth the upheaval. So, I did what I did.'

His eyes met mine, and I saw they were full of pain. Even though I knew he had brutally slaughtered four people, it was hard not to feel sorry for him. I found myself asking, 'But if Mr Levy was your target, why kill the others?'

'I couldn't just kill him. I had to make it seem like someone was after the tech. So, I killed Sid – just the way you described it. I called out to him outside his apartment that night. I didn't want to go up in case anyone saw us. The gate to the construction site was open. I took him inside at gunpoint so no one would see us from the street. Then I shot him. I meant to take his laptop, but he fell into the pit.'

He wrinkled his forehead in confusion.

'I *felt* nothing when I did it. I've always had trouble feeling things. But Yael changed that in me. My love for her was more intense than anything I'd known before – she unlocked something in my nerves and synapses that had been frozen. I can't describe it. It was like ice melting in the heat of the sun. Do you think love and jealousy and psychopathy are related?'

He looked like he genuinely wanted to know. On getting no response, he continued. 'I'm not a criminal. I mean, I wouldn't rob a bank or deal drugs or mug someone. But when I lost Yael . . . murder can be easy to save someone you love.'

He stared straight at me this time. He wasn't wrong. I know *I* could have killed him when I found he had taken Anjoli. I answered, 'Perhaps. But Mr Ram was standing in the way of your becoming a partner at Bethlehem, wasn't he?'

Baker looked at me in surprise. 'How did you know that?'

'Please answer the question.'

'I suspected he might be. But that wasn't the reason I murdered him. I did it for Yael.'

Ambition and love. A terrible combination. 'Just for Yael?' I said.

He looked back down. 'Maybe you're right. I had done everything for Sid. Aishtar was my discovery. I was instrumental in the sale of Sid's first company.' He gave a short laugh. 'Do you know the bonus I got for that? 100 K. Sid made millions. And now he was going to make *hundreds* of millions through the sale of Aishtar and I would make 250 K if I was lucky? Then the asshole said he wanted me off the board. *Me!*'

I kicked myself again. Of course! Everyone had said Ram wanted to halve the size of the board. Which would have brought it down to Masri, Ram and Cohen. Baker *would* have been asked to leave as well. I had completely missed that.

'And that's why you framed Wahid Masri? By planting those notes with the hidden message.'

Baker's voice rose, and he said passionately, 'Wahid would earn *billions* out of my work. I did the hard grind while he wined and dined politicians. *And* he would not give me the partnership; I could see that someone else was going to get it first. So, I figured, why not cast suspicion on him? I didn't think anyone would seriously believe Wahid had done it. But it could muddy the waters.'

There was silence in the room. As if regretting his diatribe, Baker got himself back under control. 'It *was* a little melodramatic, wasn't it? It took you a long time to figure it out. I wondered if I'd have to nudge you in the right direction. I stole the paper from Aishtar. I wasn't planning to frame Gaby at the time. But after I saw he had been to the pub with Sid and didn't have an alibi, I thought he'd be a more logical suspect than Wahid. After all, Gaby was going to get everyone's shares when they died. That just fell into my lap.'

'And Saul Cohen?'

'Same thing. I went home after that lovely dinner with you in your restaurant.' He smiled at me. 'I couldn't believe my luck when I saw you there, and you asked me to eat with you. It was fun and so easy planting the info about how angry Gaby was about Sid and what a committed Palestinian Wahid was. I thought it would be useful misdirection when you finally figured out the acrostic.'

I shivered. I'd believed myself to be so clever, pumping Baker for information, and he was just feeding me misinformation. All the while he was praising my cooking, he'd been planning to carry out a cold-blooded murder a few minutes later.

He continued. 'Anyway, I went home and called Saul, then

took a public e-scooter to his place. He let me in. I shot him. Left the second note and texted Gaby from his phone to come over. It worked as I'd planned.'

'And did you leak the information to Merrion?'

'Yes. Again, I needed people to think the tech was the reason for the murders. I used the same language in my note to him as I did in the note I left next to Sid. Did you pick up on that?'

'We did,' said Tahir. 'And Cambridge?'

Baker paused. His voice became so low that we could barely hear him. 'That was hard. I called Ari, said I needed to speak to him urgently, and met him in his room. Yael was in his *bed*, in her dressing gown. I didn't . . . didn't know she'd be there. You have to believe that.'

There was a plea in his eyes. I nodded. He carried on. 'She, she . . . she didn't have the grace to be embarrassed. Maybe she wanted me to see her like that. To rub it in my face that it was over between us. I did *not* want her to die – I truly didn't. It was Ari I was angry with. I *loved* Yael. I thought with Ari gone, she might come back to me. But then, seeing her there, knowing they'd been . . . fucking. I . . . I lost it. I shot her.'

A ragged sob was torn from his throat, his torment filling the room.

'Then I shot him. The TV was on so nobody heard. I wish I had covered her up. She shouldn't have lain there for everyone to see. But I didn't have time. There was so much blood. I took his laptop and dongle and went back to my room. I put them together with my clothes, gun and phone in my rucksack and showered with diluted toilet cleaner to wash off any gunshot residue – did you know it does that? But I had all these feelings. I didn't know how to get rid of them. So, I went to the gym to work out. But they didn't go. They've been getting worse ever since. I can't sleep. I wish she hadn't been there in the room. Why did she have to be there?'

It was hard seeing his agonised eyes questioning us. Tahir cleared his throat and said, 'What did you do then?'

'I'd booked another room in the YHA Hostel near the hotel and dropped my backpack off in that room. Hostels have so many transients they don't notice individual people. I picked it up later and brought it back to London.'

I kicked myself. I should have checked the other hotels. Baker had thought of everything.

'I keep seeing Yael in that bed. The shock on her face when I pointed my gun at her. I loved her. You may think I'm a brutal monster for what I did, but I truly loved her. She knew that.'

I was suddenly revolted that I'd been feeling sorry for this man. We had all loved and lost. That doesn't give anyone the right . . .

I said, 'And then you framed Mr Fleishman with the gun.'

'My original plan was to get into his back garden and plant it there without being seen. I figured you'd search his place at some point and find it. But I spotted your guys watching my place, so went out my back door and jumped over the garden wall. When I got to Gaby's, I saw you watching him, DC Rahman. I was going to leave and try another day, but figured I had no time, so I had to improvise. I broke that car window and set off the alarm and, sure enough, you went haring off to see what had happened and I could push the gun and phone through Gaby's letter box. It wasn't framing him as such because I knew he would find them, but I figured he would have to do something with them and you would catch him. And so it proved.'

Rogers shot a glance at me. Shit. I hadn't told him about leaving my post. Well, I'd deal with that later. The guys who had been watching Baker would get bollocked first.

Baker continued, 'I didn't think he'd be so stupid as to dump them. But you know what happened next. You must have been so pleased when you caught him. I like Gaby. I guess you'll let him go now?'

'And the kidnapping?'

'I needed the McCain chip as leverage. Wahid called to tell me you were looking for me and had asked about my role in the firm. I wasn't sure if you had figured things out. But I thought it was now or never. I knew you were smart, Kamil.'

I felt only shame. The room fell silent.

'Anything else you wish to add?' said Tahir.

'No, I think that's all.'

'Then that wraps it up,' said Tahir. 'Now we need access to the information you uploaded before you destroyed the laptop.'

'I was wondering when you would come to that. Kamil was *very* helpful.'

Rogers swivelled to look at me, and I stared down at the table.

An unnerving and satisfied smile spread across David Baker's face. 'This is the part where I would like a lawyer.'

Chapter 40

Friday night.

Tahir sent me home before Rogers could upbraid me about not revealing that I had left my post in front of Fleishman's house and about my theft of the chip. I knew I would have to face the consequences, and that weighed on me, muting any triumph.

Anjoli and Maliha were at the flat, well into their second bottle of wine. Anjoli seemed to have few ill effects from her ordeal, although I suspected delayed shock would hit her over the next few days – these events had a way of worming into your psyche and coming out when you least expected. A prickle went down my spine when I saw them – the thought of the two women I had been closest to bonding over drinks didn't sit well. And my feelings about both of them remained unresolved. What had they discussed?

I took them through everything that had happened and how I had figured out the Zoom deception to crack the case. I'd hoped for exclamations of 'genius!' and 'brilliant!' but they just burst into a synchronised cackle and poured more wine. I went into the kitchen to get myself some water and take a few breaths.

When I returned, Maliha said, 'Don't be sore, jaa – erm yaar.'

I felt a stab. She'd been about to say Jaan – the term of endearment we'd used for each other when we had been together – my life, my love – and had instantly replaced it with 'friend'. Fair enough. I wasn't her life or her love anymore.

Anjoli said, 'Yeah, sorry we laughed.' Phew. It appeared she had missed Maliha's slip. 'We've been drinking since we got home, *my darling sweetheart.*'

Oh. She had noticed.

'Hey, do you remember that time in Kolkata when you screwed up that fraud case because you didn't realise the two signatures were different?' said Maliha.

This evening wasn't going the way I'd expected at all. I was still raw after Baker's confession and did not need this. I excused myself to take a long shower and by the time I came back down, the mood was a bit more subdued. I grabbed a glass, poured myself the rest of the wine, and sat in the armchair. If I was lucky, things would stay on a lower key.

'So, what happens to David now?' said Anjoli. 'I can't believe he was such a psychopath. He was so polite and charming – even when his gun was pointed straight at me. He kept reassuring me and saying everything would be fine.' She shivered. 'Shit. I was at *gunpoint.* It's only just hitting home. It all happened so fast. I could have *died.*'

She drained her wine. Maliha opened another bottle and refilled Anjoli's glass.

'He's confessed,' I said. 'So now Rogers speaks to the CPS, and they take it from here. He'll be in jail for life, I imagine.'

'You liked him, didn't you?' said Anjoli.

I thought back on my interactions with Baker. 'I suppose I did. He was a clever guy and was being helpful throughout. At least, I believed he was. And I felt sorry for him. Yael Klein had dumped him after all.'

'But underneath . . .'

'Yes.'

'What will they do to you now that they know you took that chip thing from the locker?' said Maliha.

'I don't know. Nothing good.'

'I'm sure you'll be fine. I mean, you caught the bad guy.'

'I hope so.'

'Well, if they fire you, you can always come back to TK,' said Anjoli. 'When life gives you lemons, make nimbu pani.'

Maliha laughed. I didn't.

'So now that this case is over, can I tell Polina what happened to her great aunt?' Anjoli said.

'Anjoli told me all about that, Kamil,' said Maliha. 'Amazing how she tracked those ancestors down. Sheer genius.'

Were they deliberately winding me up?

'She is a genius. I guess we can tell her. Maybe this weekend? Thank God I've got a couple of days off.' As soon as I said that I realised it might be longer, depending on how they disciplined me for nicking the RFID chip.

'Oh goodie, I can't wait to see her face. I must tell Dr Grayson as well – it was her DNA test that kicked it all off. I wonder if they'll let Polina have the bones.'

I stretched and yawned. I was wrecked.

'Okay, I better be off,' said Maliha. 'Was lovely to get to know you, Anjoli, although in awful circumstances. I hope we can spend some time together while I'm in London.'

My uneasiness from earlier resurfaced. What *had* Anjoli told Maliha? And vice versa. I wasn't sure which was worse.

'Well, *I* learned a new phrase,' said Anjoli. 'Kamil, why didn't you tell me you were trying a *love jihad* with me?'

'What?'

'Maliha told me when a Muslim man seduces a Hindu woman, it is a fiendish plot to convert her and create little Muslamic kiddies that will populate the planet with jihadis. Now that I know your master plan, I will ensure it fails, Mr Bond. Mwa ha ha ha.'

'I've hardly seduced you.'

'Correct. Because you are congenitally incapable of seduction.

359

But you *did* arrange dates with both of us this weekend. What was that? Your attempt to establish a harem?'

They both laughed again. I really did not like this.

'Listen, he was lucky to find even one person who was prepared to marry him – and he messed that up,' Maliha said. 'Okay, I'm going now. Let me know if Saturday is on, Kamil.'

'I will.'

After she left, I said to Anjoli, 'Are you sure you're okay?'

'Yes, for now. So, what's happening with you and Maliha?'

I felt myself go red.

'What do you mean?'

'Oh, come on, Kamil. You've been weird from the first day you got her text. You may as well tell me. *Are* you trying to rekindle things with her? At the same time as you've been declaring how much you want me?'

'I do want you! Maliha and I are just friends. Can't I have women friends?'

'You can have whatever you choose. But it looks to me that now you have your new job and you're earning a decent wage, you don't need me anymore. Especially since your beautiful lawyer fiancée is back on the scene. You can both make a go of it. Just do me the courtesy of telling me straight. It's the least you can do.'

'I don't know where you're getting all this from,' I muttered. 'I'm going to bed. And anyway, you kept saying you weren't interested.'

She pushed her face into mine. I could smell the wine on her breath. 'You are such a . . . *gaadha!*'

My lips twitched in a half-smile. Anjoli rarely broke into Bengali and her pronunciation of 'donkey' with a London accent was charmingly sexy.

That was the wrong reaction. She yelled, 'You find that funny? Didn't you see I *couldn't* go out with you when you were so dependent on me? *Working* for me and *living* with me. And you didn't even pay rent. How could I also become your lover? It would be much *too* much. Talk about co-dependency. But once you got your proper job . . .'

'You mean . . .'

'Jesus. For such a brilliant detective, you can't see what's right under your nose, can you? And anyway, what does Maliha have that I don't? Besides flawless skin, glossy hair and all her illusions? You're such a fucking idiot.'

'If it didn't take you two bottles of red to be able to talk about your feelings for me, we wouldn't be in this mess, would we?'

I regretted my words as soon as they left my lips, but she was already halfway up the stairs. I heard her door slam, and she didn't emerge for the rest of the evening.

She was absolutely right. I was a *gaadha*.

Chapter 41

Saturday morning.

After a fitful night, I sat at my desk in the station the next morning, reliving the events of the previous day as I waited for Tahir to come in. I'd have to try to make it up with Anjoli. If she really was interested now, then I had to let Maliha go and commit. She hadn't emerged from her room when I left for work, but I needed to sit down with her and persuade her of my feelings. Yes. I *could* make it work!

But any joy I felt at the prospect dissipated as I recalled the sly smile with which Baker had asked to see his lawyer. What was he cooking up? He must have something up his sleeve, or he wouldn't have cooperated with us. I had a growing fear it might be connected to my being, in his words, 'very helpful'. I'd certainly done enough to merit a severe dressing-down, if not something worse. And given my visa and residency in the UK were now tied to this job, that didn't bear thinking about. The chink of light I saw with Anjoli was getting overwhelmed by the storm clouds heading my way. I'd just have to batten down the hatches and make it through.

'Kamil! Have you gone deaf?'

Tahir stood in front of my desk and brought me back to the present. I started. 'Sorry, boss. Was a million miles away.'

'I've been calling for you.'

'What's up?' I gathered myself. 'Have CPS authorised charges?'

'We have a problem.'

'What?'

'SO15 came in this morning and took David Baker away. I think his lawyer is trying to do a deal regarding the stolen technology. Rogers wants to see us.'

Was Baker playing some sort of 'get out of jail free' card? Was I his ticket to freedom? And would that result in my being kicked out of the force? And the country?

With trepidation, I entered Rogers' office behind Tahir and saw Protheroe sitting there, which set my teeth on edge. 'I've briefed the sergeant,' Rogers said as we walked in. 'The Home Secretary wants to see me. She would like a complete report of where we are with the case.'

Protheroe avoided my eye. I'd be knighted before I'd get any kudos from him.

Rogers looked at me. 'DC Rahman. You stole the chip from the evidence locker and gave it to David Baker. You do know that is a criminal offence, and not just a sackable matter?'

'I know, sir,' I mumbled. 'I believed I had no choice, as a civilian was in danger. And we apprehended him.'

'The ends do NOT justify the means.'

'No, sir.'

'I have no alternative but to suspend you while we decide what course of action to pursue.'

Shit. Shit. Shit. Somewhere inside I'd expected this, but not accepted it. My heart felt like it had left my body. This couldn't be happening to me again. First Kolkata and now here. On my first damn case. It seemed that waitering was all I was bloody good for. But suspension was better than dismissal. There lay hope. Tahir gave me a sympathetic glance, while to my immense surprise Protheroe said, 'He didn't have much of a choice, guv. And he *did* crack the case. We should give him a break. He's a good cop.'

Rogers must have seen the agony on my face because his voice softened. 'Look, I understand, Kamil. Baker had your girl-friend, and that put you in an untenable situation. And I agree, you *have* done good work on finding that chip and collaring Baker for the murders. But we have to go through procedure and hold a proper enquiry, you know that.'

I gave him a nod, and a relieved 'Thank you, sir.' Rogers hadn't asked me to leave his office, so I stayed put as he said, 'David Baker says he has uploaded everything to the cloud and if the government wants it, they have to agree to his demands.'

'Which are?' said Tahir.

'His lawyer is preparing them. The Home Secretary would like a direct briefing from me this afternoon.'

'I don't see how he can avoid prosecution, sir,' I said, seeing Baker slipping from our grasp. 'He killed four people.'

'You think I don't know that, lad? But Priscilla Patrick only ever does what's in her own interest. And I wouldn't put it past her to let him go if she thinks the technology he has will further her political career. Becoming PM is all she cares about.'

'I wonder . . .' I worked out how to phrase an idea that had just formed in my mind. 'We may have a small bit of leverage?'

'Go on.'

'I am privy to some information and . . .'

'What is it?' said Protheroe.

I didn't trust Protheroe's new, friendly mien, which he was undoubtedly putting on to show Rogers that he looked out for his junior officers.

'It's very sensitive, sir,' I said. 'Perhaps we should keep the circle small?'

'What do you mean?'

'The Home Secretary might want to keep it confidential. DI Ismail knows, but perhaps I could speak to you in private?' Rogers looked irritated, then waved Protheroe and Tahir out of the room.

Tahir gave a slight smile, and Protheroe looked like he was sucking a lemon as he walked out. I might have just made an enemy for life. Fuck it, Protheroe would never be my best buddy. And my career was on the line.

'Well, as you know, sir, we found much older human remains near the first victim's body and . . .'

I told him the entire story of Anjoli's quixotic quest and how her doggedness had revealed the truth about Avram's death, ending with the revelation that his stolen daughter had been Priscilla Patrick's ancestor. '. . . maybe that's something she won't want to come out and we can use it to persuade her to do the right thing if she gets wobbly about Baker?'

'What wouldn't she want coming out?'

'That Peter Pennyfeather was *not* her revered great-grandfather but was a baby-stealing murderer. I've been reading her interviews. She's referred to him several times as one of the true English entrepreneurs who 'made Britain what we are today'. It won't help her career for this truth to come out. *And* the fact she has Jewish heritage, given her history of anti-Semitism. If she wants to be PM, she won't want any hint of hypocrisy to taint her bid.'

Rogers considered this. 'It's cling-film thin. But then she has made a career out of bashing immigrants to win the right-wing vote. And I *have* heard her talk about Pennyfeather. I suppose there's no harm in having an ace up our sleeve. If she's going off the reservation, we can try it. All right. Write me a confidential memo and I'll discuss it with her.'

'Yes, sir.' I turned to go, then said, 'Actually . . .'

'What?'

'I wonder if it might be helpful for me and Anjoli – the woman David kidnapped – to come and see the Home Secretary as well.'

His forehead wrinkled. 'Why?'

That was a good question. Why *had* I asked? My brain caught up with what my subconscious had been trying to tell me.

'Anjoli knows all the details and she might elicit some sympathy, since she was also the victim of David Baker's kidnapping. And it might be better coming from her than from a serving police officer? The Home Secretary won't have any power over her.'

And if it worked, having some leverage over the Home Secretary could help if they ever decided to deport me. I could see Rogers weighing up the pros and cons. It could give him deniability and allow him to put the blame on me if it backfired. Which was a risk I had to take. It didn't matter precisely which way I got fucked. I was getting used to it.

Finally, he said, 'It's irregular, but all right. We're supposed to meet her at 3 p.m. at her office in the House of Commons. I'll put both your names on the list.'

Did this mean I wasn't suspended? I decided not to push my luck and ask, so just thanked him, and exited smartly.

Chapter 42

Saturday afternoon.

'Maybe I should have brought some TK flyers and coupons to hand to MPs and these people,' said Anjoli as we waited outside the House of Commons for Rogers. 'Could be good for business. Look at this crowd. Guess the *Guardian* article really struck a chord.'

I looked at the placards that read NO FACIAL RECOGNITION, STOP BIG BROTHER, and END DIGITAL STRIP SEARCHES. A group of noisy protesters waved signs as they shouted for the Home Secretary to resign.

'What an OTT police presence,' she continued, pointing at around twenty-five police officers in yellow hi-vis vests. 'This is a peaceful protest, and they're being intimidated by the cops. You should have let me wear my T-shirt.' I'd had to dissuade her from wearing her Anjoli special: *Super Callous Fascist Racist Tories Are Atrocious*. 'But it is quite exciting, I must admit. Who'd have thought you'd be hobnobbing with the Home Secretary just a couple of weeks into your job? Even if she is evil. I might join the protesters after our meeting.'

I felt nauseous. We hadn't addressed her outburst the day before, and I had no idea what to do or say about it. But she seemed to have recovered, and I had to compartmentalise for now. 'Well, I'm about to be fired, so I should enjoy my moment in the sun.'

'You'll persuade her with your brilliance, and she'll promote you to DCI and Tahir will end up reporting to you. Wait and see.'

'Yeah, right. Anyway, it's all down to the work you put in to find Avram and Malka's murderer.'

Rogers arrived in his full dress uniform, making me feel underdressed in my off-the-peg suit. 'Good, you're here. Let's check in. It's quite a palaver.'

We went to the side gate and, after showing our ID, they ticked our names off a list. Then we were led into a Portakabin where we were checked off another list and taken through security. We were then shepherded to a third room, where they issued us with security passes on lanyards. Finally, we ascended the steps into a large, vaulted hall. Rogers walked ahead and Anjoli whispered, 'Take a picture of me!'

'I can't! Rogers will see. We're here on business, not as sightseers.'

'Oh, come on.' She thrust her phone into my hand. I took a couple of quick shots of her against the background of the ancient chamber.

A young woman walked up to Rogers, said, 'Our lady and mistress will see you now,' and we followed her down a narrow wood-panelled corridor lined with doors emblazoned with ministerial names, some of which I recognised and many I didn't. The woman stopped in front of a door with a sign saying 'The Right Hon. Priscilla Patrick' and we entered. There were two other women at a desk in the anteroom and our guide rapped on the door of the main office. 'They're here.'

The three of us trooped in after her into the Home Secretary's domain, which was tiny, even smaller than Rogers' office, which wasn't palatial by any means. I was surprised, having expected something a little grander.

'Thank you for coming all the way in to see me here instead

of at Marsham Street. We have an emergency Saturday sitting, and I have a vote soon,' Priscilla Patrick explained.

'That's fine, ma'am,' said Rogers. 'This is DC Rahman who helped find the killer and, er . . .'

'Anjoli Chatterjee,' said Anjoli.

The Home Secretary was a short woman, but what she lacked in the vertical she made up for in the horizontal. Dressed in a bright blue jacket, she looked curiously at Anjoli and me, shook our hands with a firm grip and sat back behind her desk, which was scattered with files and photos of her family. I gave her credit – she had genuine presence – you could feel the power in the room. It was exciting. I wondered if Anjoli felt it, too.

Patrick's assistant produced a pad to make notes as her boss gestured for us to sit. 'So, tell me about this David Baker. Have you found out where he uploaded the algorithm to?'

'Not yet, ma'am, we are still looking,' said Rogers.

'His lawyer has been on to us. He wants full immunity and £10 million in cryptocurrency if we want to get our hands on the Aishtar technology.'

That was worse than I'd thought.

'He *has* killed four people, ma'am, and kidnapped another,' said Rogers.

'I'm aware of that, Superintendent Rogers. But this technology is critical to the country, and we can't afford to have it fall into the hands of our enemies. We might save thousands of British lives if we have it, and that outweighs the death of four individuals, however regrettable that was. Do fill me in on the details. I'm interested.'

I looked at Anjoli, who was ready to interrupt, but I nudged her to keep quiet. I could tell she was disgusted, as was I, listening to this woman making it sound like the four deaths had been a mere inconvenience. I wished I could use Ari Levy's VR technology to bring her inside the room where I had seen his and Yael's bodies, drenched in their own blood. Then she'd see for herself how 'regrettable' it was.

Rogers talked her through what David Baker had done and how we had caught him. To his credit, he told her I had been the one to crack his alibi, and that earned me a chilly smile from Patrick. She was living up to her Prissy Priscilla soubriquet – a blow torch wouldn't melt this woman.

After Rogers had finished, Patrick said, 'Well, that is quite a story. Four Israelis dead and—'

I could sense Anjoli tensing next to me again, but Rogers interrupted, 'Mr Ram was a British citizen, ma'am.'

'Ah, yes, so he was.'

Not *truly* British, I could imagine her thinking.

She continued, 'And this Mr Baker is an American?'

'Yes, ma'am.'

She thought for a few moments, then said, 'Well, I don't know that I have much choice in the matter. Our security services tell me we must have that technology. It has already stopped three attacks we know of. We have the terrorists in custody.'

'Potential terrorists, I assume? Had they committed any crimes before they were arrested?' said Rogers.

The Home Secretary gave him a look that would have frozen the surface of the sun. 'The analysis provided a probability of 93.8 per cent. Regardless, we can pay Baker off and chuck him back to America, then he'll be their problem, not ours. I'll have to deal with the fallout in Israel, of course, but they need our support in Iran, so they'll fall in line.'

I was simultaneously shocked and unsurprised at her unapologetic cynicism. How much of her decision was linked to the benefit of the nation and how much to her mounting the next rung on the political ladder? Four people had died, but to this politician, all that mattered was a transaction to be brokered. It could be factored using basic, cold cost-benefit analysis, which allowed for no variables, no nuanced reasoning. No humanity.

'If that's what you wish, ma'am, then we will defer and let you handle it your way,' said Rogers. 'But this case has garnered a great deal of publicity and we'll have to come up with a story for the press. Especially as Mr Fleishman has already been released from custody.'

Clearing my throat, I found my voice and said, 'Also, ma'am, there is no guarantee David Baker won't sell on the tech after he releases it to you. The Americans will want it and there is a global market for it.'

She looked at me in surprise, as if I had broken some unwritten rule by speaking. 'Yes, I know that. My people tell me they can ensure he doesn't make a copy of what he has uploaded – he hasn't had access to it since you arrested him, so there won't be any existing copies. We'll get him to download it in a secure location, under observation by our techs, then erase whatever he uploaded.'

The thought of this ordinary-looking woman in front of me having the power to surveil the entire country was terrifying, but I said nothing. I was swimming in waters that were too deep for me.

'So, thank you again for coming in, Superintendent Rogers. I'll think about this and decide. If that is all . . .' said Patrick, standing up to indicate we should take the hint and leave.

Rogers got up.

Was this it? The murderer of four people would walk free, the UK would become the most extreme surveillance state in the world, and all we could do was meekly leave?

Just as we were about to exit, Rogers turned. 'My colleague here wanted to bring you up to speed on a related issue. I'll step out to use the facilities while he does, if I may.'

He had played his last card. I didn't mind that he didn't want to be there when we tried to pressure the Home Secretary. He was halfway up the greasy pole and there was no point in him stopping his ascent.

He ducked out of the room as Patrick looked at us, drumming her fingers on the back of her chair. 'I don't have much time. What is it?'

I nodded at Anjoli, and she went into what we had rehearsed on our way to Westminster. 'It's about your great-grandfather, Mrs Patrick.'

The Mrs Patrick was a nice touch. I was impressed she'd resisted going with Priscilla.

Surprise crossed Patrick's face. 'Peter Pennyfeather? What about him? And who are you, exactly?'

'I'm the woman David Baker kidnapped and terrorised at gunpoint. You may think of letting him go, but,' Anjoli looked her straight in the eye, 'I'm the victim who hasn't been able to sleep at night.'

I'd never felt prouder of her.

'I see,' said the Home Secretary. 'I am sorry about that, of course, but I'm not sure Superintendent Rogers should have brought you here, so if it's all right . . .'

'At the building site where the body of the first victim from Aishtar was found, a further three skeletons were unearthed and I'm *also* the person who found out who they were. And *that* is where Peter Pennyfeather comes in.'

'What are you talking about?'

'If you wouldn't mind listening for a minute, Home Secretary . . .' Patrick sat back down as Anjoli laid out the story. When she got to the part about Pennyfeather shooting Avram and Malka and stealing the baby, Patrick's face hardened and she shot a glance at her assistant, who was listening in fascination.

When Anjoli finished, Patrick said, 'That's the biggest load of rubbish I've heard in my life.'

'It's not rubbish. We have proof – documentation going back a hundred years. I'm 100 per cent certain if you do a DNA test, you'll find you have Ashkenazi Jewish heritage and are descended from Malka and Avram and not from Peter Pennyfeather. I'm afraid that man, who it turns out was not your great-grandfather, may have been an amazing entrepreneur, as you have said so often, but he was also a murderer and a child abductor. His fortune was made thanks to land he stole from a Jew. Think of the many, many Nazis who did that. In today's world, the past is very much present.'

In the silence that fell, we could hear the protestors shouting outside. 'Go! Go! The Home Secretary must go!'

Ignoring this, Patrick got up, walked around her desk, stood in front of Anjoli, and looked deep into her eyes. I could see Anjoli trembling almost imperceptibly. But she held her gaze as Priscilla said, 'Who else knows about this?'

'Just four people. The two of us, one of our other friends – Inspector Tahir Ismail – and Superintendent Rogers. But my plan is to tell Malka's descendants what we've found. That you're *their* relative. I think Sofia is your third cousin, by my calculations. Then, we'll take the story to the press – they'll leap on it. It has everything they love – murder, politics, reunited relatives.'

'Relatives? I have relatives?' Patrick whispered. 'Show me this proof.'

Anjoli showed her the printed dossier she had brought with her of Miriam's birth to Avram and Malka and Mary's baptism, as well as Malka's letters. 'There's no record of Mary being born to Peter Pennyfeather and his wife, and all the dates fit. Here are letters from Malka to her sister about how Pennyfeather wanted to buy their shop – we have the lot. You can keep these papers – I have copies, Priscilla.'

Oh good. Anjoli had now decided she was on first-name terms with the Home Secretary who could destroy my career with a flick of her pen.

Patrick looked at the documents and said, 'You can't prove any of this.'

'Not without you submitting to a DNA test. But there will be a lot of newspapers who would speculate. It's a good story. And the papers are not all your fans.'

The Home Secretary stared at Anjoli, then turned away and said, almost to herself, 'I remember my grandmother Mary, you know. I was ten when she died. She was a wonderful woman.' She pulled herself together, looked at me and something switched off in her eyes. I wasn't important to her anymore. 'All right, what do you want?'

'Well, ma'am,' I said. 'We don't want to cause you any trouble so we can keep this quiet. We can tell Sofia we found records of her ancestors, but we don't have to tell her what happened to them. We just don't think you should let David Baker go. He needs to pay for what he did.'

She went to her chair and picked up a colourful silk scarf that had been hanging on its back. As she arranged it around her neck, I could see the results of her previous cost-benefit analysis recalibrating in real time as she considered this new information. A family scandal (however dead her family were) involving a dark, murderous secret, her grandmother's questionable nativity, and the icing on the cake – the revelation of a cover-up of her Jewish heritage, after her years of statements stirring up jingoistic fervour in an already polarised and febrile nation. Even if it couldn't be proved, she had enough enemies in her party to bring about the death of her political career and her dreams of being Prime Minister. I remembered what Merrion had said. This was a scorpion, and we needed to be careful we would not get fatally stung if we got in her way.

'What about the technology?' she said. 'We need that. We need Aishtar. Since Snowden, there has been a lot of scrutiny about what our intelligence services do. It's useful to have a third party that . . .'

She stopped, as if annoyed with herself that she had said too much.

'Do you know Wahid Masri?' I asked. 'He is interim CEO of Aishtar. If the UK government buys the company and keeps it afloat, I'm pretty sure Aishtar will replicate the tech. Even without Ari Levy. They have the cream of the talent in the field working there. If David Baker is behind bars and you take away his access to the internet while he's inside, he won't be able to like a Facebook post, let alone sell the tech to a foreign government.'

She considered this, then gave an abrupt nod.

'My security services won't like it, but fine. I'll need you two and the others who know about it to sign a rock-solid NDA that this information about Peter Pennyfeather will never be made public. I am sorry about what you went through, Miss . . .'

'Chatterjee.'

'Oh yes. Miss Chatterjee. It wasn't personal. I have to do what's best for the country.'

Anjoli looked like she might demur, but I gave her hand a tight squeeze and she nodded.

I breathed out in relief as we walked out of the Home Secretary's office to find Rogers waiting in the corridor. He gave me a questioning look, and I said, 'She'll keep David Baker under lock and key. Anjoli did it!'

Rogers gave me a brief nod and said nothing. He just brushed some lint off his sleeve and walked on ahead of us through the ancient corridors that had seen and heard much worse over the centuries.

Chapter 43

Thursday. Five days later.

I t sounds like the start of a joke.

Three Muslims, two Jews and one Hindu are toasting the dead after attending a Jewish funeral.

But it wasn't funny.

Underneath the l'chaims and badhaai hos lurked sadness, tension and uncertainty.

Maybe that's what's needed to make a good joke.

Sofia Katz had arranged for the burial of the skeletons at Hoop Lane cemetery, next to where Rakesh Sharma had been cremated, in what seemed like another life. The only attendees were Sofia, Polina, Anjoli, Tahir, the imam and me. The imam had insisted on coming because we had found the bodies on his land, and he felt he owed it to them.

The remains were in a single simple wooden casket which we had lifted from the hearse and taken to an unadorned chapel, where the officiating Rabbi recited prayers. There was a recital of the Kaddish and Polina read a short poem by Heinrich Heine:

Our death is in the cool of night,
our life is in the pool of day.
The darkness glows, I'm drowning,
day's tired me with light.

After the recitation, the casket was taken to the grave where we shovelled soil onto it and it disappeared from our eyes, which were now more than a little damp. I looked at the simple gravestone Sofia had procured.

ברוך דיין האמת

AVRAM, MALKA AND LEAH PINSKY
BELOVED HUSBAND, WIFE AND DAUGHTER
Born 1800s – Died 1900s

'What does the Hebrew say?' I asked.

'Blessed the judge of truth,' said Sofia.

Avram, Malka and Leah's journey from beyond the Pale had ended under the earth of a North London cemetery, where they might find the peace of the cool night that had eluded them for over a hundred years.

As we walked out of the graveyard, I said to Sofia, 'How odd. The graves all have pebbles on them instead of flowers.'

Sofia smiled. 'It's a Jewish funeral custom. We are all equal in death and everyone can afford a stone.'

My throat closed up.

'Priscilla Patrick didn't show,' said Anjoli as Sofia and Polina left for our restaurant. She had sent the Home Secretary a message inviting her to the internment of her great-grandparents.

'You expected her to?'

'I thought she might have some small bit of humanity in her, but I forgot – she's a Tory. Oh!'

She pointed at a simple floral wreath that was leaning against the wall with a note: *Rest in Peace, Avram, Malka, Leah.* It was signed PP.

'Guess she didn't get the memo about the stones,' I said.

The Home Secretary had been true to her word and rejected David Baker's blackmail in favour of our own. We'd told Polina and Sofia we had found documentation about their ancestors but left out the details about Pennyfeather and Priscilla Patrick. I just hoped that Sofia didn't do her own research. Anjoli had kicked against this to begin with, but then accepted it as the lesser evil. It would have been a disgrace for Baker to go free.

'I feel quite powerful to have this hold over Priscilla. Now I can get her to chuck you out of the country when I get tired of you, Kamil – you're both my bitches now,' she'd declared two days ago while I was mooching around the flat.

'Who knows what my future holds if my suspension isn't lifted? Maybe leaving the country will be for the best.'

'Back in India with your *Jaan*?'

Oh god!

'There's only one person I love,' I blurted out.

'I know. The question is who?'

Her words slammed into me like a monsoon thundershower as she stared at me, unblinking, arms folded over her T-shirt – *And though she be but little don't fuck with her.*

Her version of 'the talk'.

I didn't have my dinner with either Maliha or Anjoli.

'Very similar customs to Islam,' the imam said to Sofia as we tucked into the dinner Anjoli had organised at Tandoori Knights after the funeral. 'We also say "Peace be upon him" for our prophets. We all have the same rituals but cannot get on. It is very sad. I have a joke. A reporter hears about this old Jewish man who has been praying at the wailing wall in Jerusalem twice a day for decades. She goes there one morning and there he is. After he finishes his prayers, she says, "Excuse me, sir, but how long have you been coming here to pray?" "For over fifty years," he says. "That is incredible," she says. "What do you pray for?" "I pray for peace between Christians, Jews, Muslims and Hindus. I pray for all of us to stop hating each other and I pray for our children to grow up being safe and being friends." "And how do you feel after doing this for fifty years?" "Like I'm talking to a bloody wall." '

The shock of hearing the imam utter a mild curse caused us to go silent for a second, then we burst into laughter. His eyes twinkled as he finished his lassi.

'Any news on when I might be back at work?' I said to Tahir.

'Sorry, no. They are still investigating. Don't worry, it will be fine – we wouldn't have cracked this case without you.'

Easy for him to say. There was an even chance I'd be let go permanently. Then what? Working with Anjoli in the restaurant was a non-starter given where we had reached. I had to get a job so I could move out. Would I even be able to get another job given my visa status?

Was I cut out for the Met? Could I live with the constant chipping away of Protheroe and his lot? Start at the bottom again, doing grunt work for years? There was no way Tahir would give me that acting sergeant job again, given I'd let him down twice.

He continued. 'Laurel and Hardy told me Wahid Masri is negotiating the sale of Aishtar to the UK government. They have David Baker locked up tighter than a mosquito's arse. He hasn't passed over the algorithm, but he'll never have access to the internet again and will be in prison for life. Did you see Merrion's article?'

'I did. Nelson Tang was liberally quoted in it this time. Merrion says that the government has lost the tech, so we are free of this surveillance, at least for the moment. How did he find out?'

'Not sure. Could have been planted by Priscilla Patrick's people. It'll suit her for voters to think the technology doesn't exist anymore. Merrion revealed Baker was the killer, playing up the angle that Ram wanted him off the board and he went crazy.'

I felt a fleeting pang of pity for David Baker. While he deserved all that he had got and more, when I saw Anjoli across the table,

I understood how losing a soulmate could drive one to madness. Not that I had lost her. I needed to build on what we had and take the imam's advice – one soulmate and one soulfriend. Maybe I had to move out and that would give me the start I needed.

The alcohol was making me maudlin, and a lump formed in my throat as I thought of the situation I was in. Sitting here, a couple of weeks ago, I had been on the edge of a new life and now ... I didn't trust myself to speak when Tahir asked if I needed my drink topping up, so just nodded, muttered, 'Bathroom,' and fled.

The imam was at the sink. He wiped his hands and said, 'Kamil, I wanted to speak to you for a minute.'

I didn't want to talk to anyone but cleared my throat and said with some difficulty, 'Yes, Sheikh?'

He looked at me with sharp eyes.

'Are you all right?'

'It's . . . been a tough few weeks.'

'You want to sit and talk? You are still struggling with your decision?'

His steady, compassionate gaze calmed me. I splashed water on my face. 'Maybe. Not right now. This is something I have to sort out on my own.'

He nodded. 'Inshallah. Your jihad will always continue. Come and see me at the mosque.'

'What did *you* want to talk to me about?'

He gazed at me, his eyes troubled.

'I have been hearing some disturbing things occurring in the Loxford Jamia Masjid and I thought you were the best person to discuss it with.'

His tone was calm, but there was a controlled tension underneath. I felt a prickle of unease. 'What things, Sheikh?'

His voice hardened. 'Anti-British . . . sentiment. I don't know exactly. I am looking into it but will tell you if it is anything serious.'

He had never asked *me* for advice before – normally I was the one going to him for counsel.

'Do you mean . . . terrorism?'

Someone entered the toilet, and the imam said, 'Come and meet me in the mosque.'

He walked into the restaurant as I stared at his back.

'It is sad we will never find out exactly how Avram and his family died,' Polina was saying when I returned to the table, feeling more composed. 'A murderer died without paying for his crimes. What a terrible thought.'

Anjoli saw me looking at her, bit her lip, then looked back down at her lamb and oat milk rezala.

'He will pay,' said the imam. 'He will spend eternity in Jahannam, repenting his sins.'

'I'm not sure we believe in that kind of afterlife, but I'll make an exception in his case,' said Polina as the restaurant bell tinkled and Maliha walked in.

I jumped up to greet her, Anjoli giving us a sideways glance. 'Hi, Maliha. Meet the gang. Come, sit and eat.'

'Ahh, it's nice and cool in here. It's so humid outside.' She sat next to me. 'Thanks for the invitation.'

There was an awkward silence.

'Let's drink to Kamil,' said Tahir. 'Massive props for cracking your first big case. Your good, old-fashioned police work did far more than any fancy-pants artificial intelligence could do – and hopefully that will remain the case or we'll *all* be out of a job.'

'To Kamil,' chorused the others.

'And Anjoli,' I said. 'Her perseverance in finding the identities of Polina's hundred-year-old relatives brought peace to them.'

'To Anjoli!'

'Aw, thanks,' she said. 'Maybe I'll start a detective agency above the restaurant. I can be the Lis Salander of the East End – the girl with the baingan tattoo. I'll call my agency ... Tan Knights! Instead of white knights, geddit! You can pass me your unsolvables, Tahir.'

'Tan Knights,' shouted everyone.

I raised my glass. A buzz of chatter filled the intimate pool of brightness that surrounded our table as the light sparkling off the wine glasses made diamonds on the walls and the clouds above the restaurant flashed white with sheet lightning. I was acutely aware of the warmth of Maliha's thigh next to mine in the booth. Maybe a page needed to be turned. The future might be uncertain, but when was it not? Let me enjoy this moment while it lasted.

There was a blast of thunder and the skies opened, the heat finally breaking as sheets of rain swept down Brick Lane and washed away the detritus of the day. The bell on the door sounded, and two tourists drifted into Tandoori Knights, seeking shelter from the storm.

Acknowledgements

The original inspiration for this book came from reading Israel Zangwill's *Children of the Ghetto – A Study of a Peculiar People*. This wonderful novel was written in 1892 and brought the East End of London to life in a warm, funny and moving way and I confess to having liberally borrowed from it for Ari's virtual-reality simulation. I followed this up with Hadley Freeman's *House of Glass*, which was also riveting. These stories of Jewish immigrants seemed so similar to what I had seen and read of the Bengali immigrants in the same area today that I had to figure out a way to bring them together. The *Times'* archives were also a great resource, and I transposed their description of the launch of Selfridges to Pennyfeather's Bazaar.

As always, thank you to the incredible team of editors and marketeers at Harvill Secker – Liz Foley, Katie Ellis-Brown, Anna Redman Aylward, Hayley Shepherd, Sophie Painter, Alex Russell, Mollie Stewart, Dredheza Maloku, Bill Massey and Kate Neilan. Their support and continued encouragement have been invaluable, as I have been tracing Kamil and Anjoli's journeys.

Many thanks also to Laetitia Rutherford, my agent at Watson Little, whose insights and gentle nudges helped me beef up the story and improved it no end; and to Dan Mogford, whose superb covers captured the ethos of Brick Lane brilliantly.

Thanks to Georgia Kaufmann, wonderful novelist, good friend and great cook, who read through my manuscript with great care and made invaluable recommendations, especially steering me right on Jewish names and ancestry. And to Hod Fleishman, who, with his customary good humour and kindness, corrected me when I got the Israeli sections of the book horribly wrong and gave me a (very) basic education in Yiddish and Hebrew.

Thank you to Dr Corinne Duhig, who teaches archaeology and Egyptology at Cambridge University, and runs the osteoarchaeology and funerary-archaeology consultancy Gone to Earth. She gave generously of her time to advise me on the treatment of ancient skeletons and DNA.

And thanks Kristina Young (whose fantasy book *In Search of Beira's Hammer* is a terrific read!) for educating me on wild goats algorithms and Tamara Ermoshkina for her great help with my website, ajaychowdhury.com. To Stuart Gibbon, whose *Crime Writer's Casebook* is a great resource for all budding crime novelists and to the many friends, bloggers, reviewers and well-wishers who kindly reviewed and gave me valuable feedback on *The Waiter* and *The Cook*.

And finally, my family. My wonderful mother, Indira, who always encouraged me to follow my passions, and to my sister Nandini, who kept me grounded and always pushed me to try harder. My daughters Layla, Eva and Tia have all been a little bemused by my change in career direction later in life but have given me help and feedback when I needed to write about things that I've grown too old to understand.

And, as always, my amazing wife, greatest supporter, incredibly valuable (and by no means uncritical) helpmate, Angelina. She took time out from writing her own novel to read every word more than once; google and correct inconsistencies and contradictions; provide great ideas; and gently, but firmly, remove some of my more terrible notions. These books wouldn't exist without you.

Credits

Vintage would like to thank everyone who worked on the
publication of *The Detective*

Agent
Laetitia Rutherford

Editor
Katie Ellis-Brown

Editorial
Sania Riaz
Elizabeth Foley
Kate Fogg

Copy-editor
Hayley Shepherd

Proofreader
Sally Sargeant

Managing Editorial
Leah Boulton
Sabeehah Saleq

Audio
Oliver Grant

Contracts
Laura Forker
Gemma Avery
Ceri Cooper
Rebecca Smith

Toby Clyde
Anne Porter

Design
Dan Mogford

Digital
Anna Baggaley
Claire Dolan

Finance
Ed Grande
Jerome Davies

Marketing
Sophie Painter
Helia Daryani

Production
Konrad Kirkham

Inventory
Georgia Sibbitt

Publicity
Anna Redman-Aylward

Sales
Nathaniel Breakwell

Malissa Mistry
Caitlin Knight
Rohan Hope
Christina Usher
Neil Green
Jessica Paul
Amanda Dean
Andy Taylor
David Atkinson
David Devaney
Helen Evans
Martin Myers
Phoebe Edwards
Richard Screech
Justin Ward-Turner
Amy Carruthers
Charlotte Owens

Operations
Sophie Ramage

Rights
Jane Kirby
Lucy Beresford-Knox
Rachael Sharples
Beth Wood
Maddie Stephenson
Lucie Deacon
Agnes Watters

Thank you to our group companies and our sales
teams around the world

Ajay Chowdhury was the winner of the inaugural Harvill Secker–Bloody Scotland crime writing award. He is a tech entrepreneur and theatre director who was born in India and now lives in London where he builds digital businesses, cooks experimental dishes for his wife and daughters, and writes through the night. His children's book, *Ayesha and the Firefish*, was published in 2016 and adapted into a musical.

The Waiter is the first in his adult crime series about Kamil Rahman, an ex-policeman from Kolkata who has moved to Brick Lane in London. It has been optioned by BBC Studios. The follow-up, *The Cook*, deals with the issue of homelessness and was published in May 2022 to critical acclaim. *The Detective* is the next instalment in the series.

ajaychowdhury.com
🐦 @ajaychow